Acclaim for Sibella Giorello

"Giorello's writing is poignant, concrete, and humorously descriptive yet sincere . . . adding to Giorello's reputation as a pro and a shining star."

—PUBLISHERS WEEKLY REVIEW OF THE STARS SHINE BRIGHT

"Giorello has won the Christy Award and received two Pulitzer Prize nominations. When you read this book, you'll see why."

—BOOKLIST STARRED REVIEW OF THE MOUNTAINS BOW DOWN

"*The Clouds Roll Away* is the work of a maturing novelist whose voice rings with authenticity, whose eccentric characters come vividly alive and whose storytelling skills are superior."

—RICHMOND TIMES-DISPATCH

"With great attention to detail, gritty descriptions and fast-paced action, Giorello's tale of suspense is a sure bet."

—PUBLISHERS WEEKLY REVIEW OF THE RIVERS RUN DRY

Also by Sibella Giorello:

The Rivers Run Dry

The Clouds Roll Away

The Mountains Bow Down

The Stars Shine Bright

A RALEIGH HARMON NOVEL

SIBELLA GIORELLO

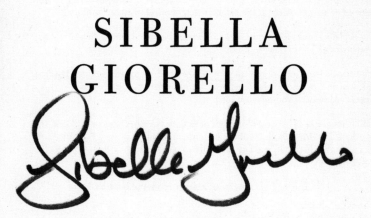

THOMAS NELSON
Since 1798

NASHVILLE   DALLAS   MEXICO CITY   RIO DE JANEIRO

Published in Nashville, Tennessee, by Thomas Nelson. Thomas Nelson is a registered trademark of Thomas Nelson, Inc.

Thomas Nelson, Inc., titles may be purchased in bulk for educational, business, fund-raising, or sales promotional use. For information, please e-mail SpecialMarkets@ThomasNelson.com.

Publisher's Note: This novel is a work of fiction. Names, characters, places, and incidents are either products of the author's imagination or used fictitiously. All characters are fictional, and any similarity to people living or dead is purely coincidental.

Library of Congress Cataloging-in-Publication Data

Giorello, Sibella.
    The stars shine bright : a Raleigh Harmon novel / Sibella Giorello.
        p. cm. — (A Raleigh Harmon novel ; bk. 5)
    ISBN 978-1-59554-536-7 (trade paper)
    1. United States. Federal Bureau of Investigation—Officials and employees—Fiction. 2. Women geologists—Fiction. 3. Horse racing—Fiction. 4. Forensic geology—Fiction. I. Title.
    PS3607.I465S73 2012
    813'.6—dc23   2012012626

Printed in the United States of America

12 13 14 15 16 17 QG 6 5 4 3 2 1

For my sons of thunder: Daniel and Nico

They sailed. They sailed. Then spake the mate:
"This mad sea shows his teeth to-night.
He curls his lip, he lies in wait,
With lifted teeth, as if to bite!
Brave Admiral, say but one good word:
What shall we do when hope is gone?"
The words leapt like a leaping sword:
"Sail on! sail on! sail on! and on!"

Then, pale and worn, he kept his deck,
And peered through darkness. Ah, that night
Of all dark nights! And then a speck—
A light! A light! A light! A light!
It grew, a starlit flag unfurled!
It grew to be Time's burst of dawn.
He gained a world; he gave that world
Its grandest lesson: "On! sail on!"

"Columbus" by Joaquin Miller

Chapter One

The glass skyscrapers towered over Puget Sound, like crystal-line prisons for office slaves. I stood at the corner of Third and Madison and watched the hurried workers, toting their Starbucks and battered briefcases, while down the hill, between the city's steep reflective walls, a basin of salt water sparkled under late-summer sunshine. Puget Sound looked dappled and calm, nothing like the busy people. Nothing like the emotions warring inside me. And nothing like the woman who walked beside me, gripping a strand of pink pearls.

"Don't do this," said Aunt Charlotte. Her pudgy fingers worried the silken beads. "Come work in my shop."

"It won't help."

"I'll pay you double minimum wage."

I waited for the crosswalk light to change. *Hurry up.* The breeze tunneled through the buildings, bearing scents of wet salt and city pavement and the close of summer. A city bus wheezed to a stop on Madison and belched diesel fumes before releasing more serfs. They lurched out, sighing like pneumatic doors.

I glanced at Aunt Charlotte.

She had switched the pearls to her other hand, presumably because her fingers were fatigued from all that rubbing. It had started early this morning, when she told me I needed some geological magic to save my job. I looked back at the light. It refused to change.

"I'm fine," I told her.

"I'll send you to all my rock shows," she said. "You're a geolo-gist—they'll love you."

I was a geologist, a forensic geologist, but I doubted the poor souls attending Aunt Charlotte's rock shows would love me. They were wannabe celebrities, pop musicians, New Agers all of them, believing Charlotte Harmon when she said malachite could enhance their visionary powers. That marble kept time with the earth's internal clock. That pearls provided clarity and wisdom.

My aunt was the most loyal of relatives, and she was a total kook.

The light changed, I stepped off the curb.

She hurried beside me. "You're afraid, I can feel it."

"No," I lied. "I just want my old job back."

"You're in denial. And who wouldn't be, with what you're facing?"

A sarcastic *Thank you* perched on the tip of my tongue. But we had now reached my own urban prison. Nine stories of pale steel, the building stood at the corner of Third and Spring with its cross-hatched architecture looking as unfriendly as graph paper.

"Take the pearls," she said.

"No, really—"

But she had already shoved the strand into my shoulder bag and was gathering me into her arms, squeezing tight. Plump and warm, loving and lost, Charlotte Harmon was one of the world's all-time great huggers. I breathed in the last of her patchouli scent.

Then I turned and walked away, without saying good-bye.

≈

At the guard's desk inside, I flashed the credentials that identified me as a Special Agent for the FBI, rode the elevator to the building's top floor, and headed straight for the receptionist who sat behind the largest console desk. She wore the blank mask of the dedicated assistant.

"Raleigh Harmon," I told her. "I have an appointment."

She pressed a button on her phone and spoke into the tiny headset receiver wrapped around her ear. Her controlled contralto was barely audible from two feet away, and the mask betrayed nothing as she listened to the response. Then she pushed the button again.

"They need a few more minutes," she said. "Please have a seat."

I nodded, as though agreeing. But I bypassed the leather club chairs and stood at the elongated windows that framed the view of Spring Street. Down below, pedestrians were bent at the waist, trying to climb the hill's forty-degree angle. They looked snapped in half, and I felt a pang tingling across my abdomen. Sympathy? Or maybe self-pity, if I were being honest.

I heard a door open behind me.

Don't look desperate.

The middle-aged man stepping out wore a white oxford shirt. Starched, but wrinkled around his waist, as though the meeting had gone on for hours. He nodded at the receptionist, but when he looked at me I couldn't read his eyes. The sunlight from the windows was flashing across his wire-rim glasses, turning the lenses opaque. He walked quickly to the elevator and pushed the down button. Twice, hard.

"Agent Harmon?" The receptionist's voice sounded almost tender. But maybe I was imagining that. "You may go in now."

The elevator dinged like the bell announcing the next round of a boxing match. The man in the wrinkled shirt stepped inside, then turned to face me. His mouth tightened as though he had tasted something bitter.

≈

The Special Agent in Charge of the Seattle field office had the best view in the building, naturally. But the chief had positioned his desk so that his back was to the window. When I walked in, he stood and placed a hand on his red tie. To his right, another man waited. He was leaning against a matching cherrywood console, his red suspenders flecked with small oily stains. Allen McLeod. Head of the Violent Crimes unit. My direct boss. Or so I hoped.

The SAC kept one hand on his tie, leaning over the desk to shake my hand. "Raleigh, good to see you again."

"Yes, sir."

The SAC had a spare and focused gaze, the expression of someone who realized anything could go wrong at any moment, and who was already working out various contingency plans.

I took the chair directly in front of his clean desk. The seat was warm.

"OPR was just here," he said. "They wanted to make sure I understood their concerns about you."

OPR was the Office of Professional Responsibility. The FBI's internal affairs unit. They had opened a file on me. In June. Right after I stepped off a cruise from Alaska.

"They're discussing your situation with the SAC in the Richmond office. Victoria Phaup?"

I nodded. Phaup was my boss in Richmond, Virginia.

"She's recommending a full suspension for at least six months."

No real surprise. Phaup had spent several years riding her broom over my career. We had disagreed from the start, and at one point she transferred me from Richmond to Seattle, a disciplinary transfer that first introduced me to the gentlemen in the room. And now I felt a prickle of sweat on my palms. And because I needed my job, I slid the receptionist's bland mask over my face.

"But," the SAC said, glancing at McLeod to his right, "Allen has been vigorously arguing against such stringent disciplinary action. He wants to keep you with us, Raleigh. And he insists a full suspension would force you to leave the Bureau altogether."

He waited for me to say something, and I stared at his blue shirt, waiting for the correct words to come. The shirt was starched, of course. The stainless appearance reminded me of an elegant table-cloth, the kind that made red wine bead up and roll away without a trace. He continued to wait for my response, and I decided my words would sound defensive, almost petulant. Seven weeks ago, the FBI had suspended me without pay. I had moved in with my aunt Charlotte and was struggling to pay for groceries and the gasoline needed to drive her old diesel Volvo to the state mental asylum that was holding my mother. My mother, who had lost her mind on the cruise to Alaska. My mother, who learned I was lying to her. My mother, whose paranoia now convinced her I was the enemy.

Somehow, I doubted the SAC would understand any of that. His honed appearance told me he didn't make mistakes. He followed the rules. And because I needed my job, I defaulted to my Southern upbringing.

"Yes, sir. I'm sure Ms. Phaup did recommend that."

"She also wants OPR's investigation extended. She's asking them to look at full termination." He waited for me to respond. "She sent OPR documents from your Richmond cases. All your cases, with field notes. She says there's a pattern of behavior here."

"No, sir." Something cold settled over my shoulders. "No pattern."

"See?" McLeod almost sneered. "Those OPR jackals. You know how much they love dirt. They won't leave any bone unturned."

The SAC tapped a finger on the desk, perhaps registering McLeod's malaprop. "Allen tells me you're the sole income for your family. Is that correct?"

"Yes, sir."

"Your father, he's passed on?"

"Correct." It was easier than saying, *He was murdered.*

"And your mother doesn't receive any other financial support?"

"Social security. As his widow." I paused, wondering how much he needed to know. And how much I should tell. "Most of the money goes to cover property taxes on her home in Richmond. And her medical care."

"I heard something about a nervous breakdown." He raised an eyebrow. "On the cruise ship?"

I gave a nod.

"About that ship," McLeod said, pushing himself off the console. "Don't forget what Raleigh managed to accomplish. How many agents could've closed that case—in four days? We had media calling coast to coast. The FBI put a movie star behind bars."

The SAC tapped the desk again. "You better hope the media never finds out *how* she solved that case."

Two days into the cruise, I realized a cold-blooded killer was traveling among us. Once we docked in Seattle, it would be almost impossible to track the case. But in my haste to find the killer, I "borrowed" several geologic specimens from a jewelry box. Without a warrant. Without clearance of any kind. I didn't follow the rules, and when the ship docked in Seattle, I had certainly pegged the murderer. But I had also opened the door for OPR.

"Raleigh, the FBI is like a family," said the SAC. "We have a code of honor. And when one family member breaks the code, it affects all of us."

"Yes, sir."

McLeod leaned forward, straining his suspenders. "Families also take care of each other. So let's cut to the UCA."

UCA. We might be a family, but the FBI was also a train with boxcars of acronyms chugging through our vocabulary. UCA stood for Undercover Assignment.

Please.

"OPR is arguing against you taking this case," the SAC said. "They want to finish their investigation before we even discuss reassigning you. Normally I would agree. But Allen has pointed out they've already taken up almost two months and still don't have a resolution. Additionally, he says the UCA only has two weeks remaining."

"Plus," McLeod said, "Raleigh's the only agent for it. She's got all the perpendiculars."

The SAC glared at him. "Perpendiculars?"

"We need somebody who has no connections here. Somebody that won't get recognized at the racetrack. Even better, she's from horse country. Virginia. You can hear it in her voice."

The SAC turned to me. His narrow features reminded me of an arrowhead. "Raleigh, do you know anything about horses?"

But McLeod jumped in again. "That's her cover. The newbie. She's supposed to be learning the ropes from that woman."

That woman was an eighty-four-year-old pistol named Eleanor Anderson. She began calling McLeod back in April, sometimes several times a day, insisting that races were being fixed at Emerald Meadows, Washington's largest thoroughbred racetrack. The pattern went like this: Her horses would win for several weeks and become odds-on favorites. Then suddenly they would start losing and come down with an inexplicable illness that defied diagnosis. Meanwhile, certain long shots would start winning—until they became favorites and started losing, repeating the pattern all over again.

Somebody was getting rich playing the long shots. Eleanor Anderson suspected the Mob.

But when McLeod told her the federal government wasn't about to pay an agent to hang around a racetrack all day, Eleanor wasn't deterred. She kept calling and eventually offered to cover the costs of an undercover operation—provided she approved of the agent. McLeod offered me the job when I stepped off the cruise ship. But the assignment was revoked: OPR launched its investigation.

And Eleanor kept calling.

"It's all ready to go." McLeod lifted a manila folder from the console. "The whiz kids backstopped her identity. Raleigh Harmon is now Raleigh David. Rich girl from Middleburg, Virginia. Parents died ten years ago in a car crash." He turned to me. "And per your request, your alias is also engaged. Your fiancé is back home in Virginia. Just like real life."

I nodded. *Please.*

But the SAC had the cold water ready. "I don't see how Raleigh can get enough information in two weeks."

"That's where Eleanor Anderson comes in. She's asked her niece, Raleigh David, to come learn the horse business. She wants an heir to inherit it when she dies." McLeod offered me the file. "Actually, Eleanor's words were 'if I die.'"

Keeping my head down, I read through the false information while McLeod relayed more details to the SAC. Eleanor was providing a condo in Tacoma. And a vehicle. I would keep my FBI-issued firearm concealed at all times. And there would be no contact with the Bureau, except through my case agent.

"Jack Stephanson," the SAC said. "That's your case agent."

I looked up. "Jack—?"

"OPR wants him on oversight. He reported the incident on the cruise ship. They trust him."

I felt sick. *Jack?*

McLeod misread the expression on my face. "Don't worry. I already explained that your relationship with Jack is plutonic."

My tongue was made of lead. "Can't Lucia Lutini be my case agent?"

"Lutini's not a full agent," the SAC said. "She's a CPA who works profiling."

"But," McLeod added, "Lutini offered to get your UCA wardrobe." He stole a glance at my blazer and slacks. "She says you need the help."

I looked down at the folder's contents. Two keys. The condo, I guessed. And the vehicle. The driver's license for Raleigh David had my picture, staring back at me.

McLeod reached behind his back again, then held out a cell phone.

"It's not programmed like your agent phone. Your name will show on anyone's caller ID. So be careful phoning your case agent."

Case agent. Jack Stephanson. *No. Please?*

"One more item," the SAC said. "And this is nonnegotiable."

I couldn't breathe.

"As you're probably aware, undercover agents are required to have periodic psychological exams. We've had too many agents struggle with their double identity. Furthermore, OPR has pointed out that with your mother's condition, you should undergo extra visits with a psychiatrist."

I felt a humming sensation. It filled my ears. High and strained, it sounded like electricity getting ready to blow. Somehow I knew OPR would be checking the shrink's notes.

"Don't look so concerned," McLeod said. "Jack found a convenient shrink. You won't have to go out of your way."

I closed the folder. I tried to smile. The men waited for me to say something.

Finally, the SAC said, "You do realize, if you found actual hard evidence of race fixing, it would benefit you in other areas."

"Yes, sir." Success on the UCA would dilute, or even negate, any ruling from OPR.

"But," he continued, "you only have two weeks. And given the circumstances, it's doubtful your forensic geology will help you." He gave a tight smile, barely conciliatory. "As they say in horse racing, good luck."

I didn't believe in luck. But I also didn't believe in shoving my foot in my mouth.

Clutching my new identity, I stood to shake the SAC's hand. Then I told him exactly what he wanted to hear.

"Thank you for this opportunity, sir. I won't let you down."

Chapter Two

Four days later, I was already doubting my pledge.

It was Monday evening. The weekend was spent dutifully following Eleanor Anderson around Emerald Meadows. From the barns to the betting office to the private dining room. Shaking hands, learning names, cataloging potential suspects. And now it dawned on me that two weeks, minus four days, wasn't enough time to build a case.

OPR would win.

"I'm spending the night," I said.

"No, you're not," Eleanor said loudly.

I glanced over. We were walking down an empty backstretch under a dusky sky. The stars were just winking into view, that gentle moment of evening. Eleanor, however, was anything but delicate. Trained as a thespian, she still had a dancer's light step. But her actress voice always projected to the cheap seats.

"Go home!" she bellowed. "Sleep!"

I lowered my voice, hoping it would give her a stage cue. "Time's running out."

"Time!" she called out, raising her chin. "Do you know there's a clock in every room? It goes tick-tock quieter than your heartbeat." She paused. "Who said that?"

"You did."

"Princess Kosmonopolis, act one. We staged *Sweet Bird of Youth* in Los Angeles. Sadly, the themes were lost on movie producers."

With ten days left, I had nothing to fight OPR with except lines from Tennessee Williams's plays. Lines that Eleanor dropped like philosophical bombs. In her younger days, she toured with an acting troupe devoted to the Southern playwright. During a 1959 performance of *Streetcar Named Desire* at Seattle's Moore Theatre, an industrialist named Harry Anderson took one look at the woman playing Blanche and swept her off the stage. They married, and Eleanor took up her husband's favorite hobby: horse racing. When Harry passed away in 1981, Eleanor did the unthinkable. Or what was unthinkable to everyone but her. She took over the horse racing business, and today the Hot Tin Barn was the most prosperous thoroughbred racing enterprise in the Northwest.

And still the playwright's words tumbled from her lipsticked mouth, with most of the lines intact.

"I'm paying the bills, Raleigh," she trumpeted. "And I will not have you bedding down with the animals."

We had crossed the backstretch now and stood beside a low-slung building that separated the horse barns from the general public. Above us, in the amethyst evening sky, Venus twinkled as though it enjoyed my misery. I reached for the door, holding it open, hoping Eleanor would continue her exit. But she didn't budge.

"And if you attempt such nonsense," she continued, "I will make sure—"

I held a finger to my lips. "Quiet, please."

She gazed down the backstretch, shaking her head. She wore oversized glasses with rhinestones embedded in the corners, glittering like more stars. She waited for a security guard to amble past the drug testing barn. He checked the lock, casually, then moved down the rest of the backstretch, whistling on his way. Tomorrow was Tuesday, the track's single day off. Most of the trainers and owners had left for the night and the bustling arena suddenly had an odd sort of silence. Like some mutually agreed-upon truce from the competition and money, but not the greed. The grooms remained in the barns, cleaning out the horse stalls, each worker with listening ears.

"Keep your voice down," I reminded her.

"And that's another thing," she said, in some behind-the-curtain whisper. "It looks suspicious if you stay in the barn all night."

"Not if I do it right."

"And how is that?"

"None of your business."

"You feel sorry for the horse because it's sick?"

One of Eleanor's prize fillies, Solo in Seattle, had suddenly come down with the mysterious ailment after winning for weeks. The horse's rise and fall fit the pattern perfectly: a favorite now struggling to place while long shots came from behind to win big money.

Eleanor wagged a finger at me. The gold ring she wore contained a garnet so large it looked like a deadly hematoma. "Do not fall in love with the horses, Raleigh. They're heartbreak. Every one of them. Pure heartbreak."

"You told me already."

"Then what about the suspicion?"

"I'm your niece. And it's just one night."

"You are a stubborn girl."

I leaned in close. "And you hired me to find out what's happening to these horses. I can't do that if I'm not here."

"My answer is still no. You look worn out. You cannot stay."

Biting my tongue, I held the door. She marched forward, passing under my arm. Her red ballet slippers made soft sashaying sounds down the hall. We passed the betting office. It was closed for the night. But a big brass scale waited for jockeys and saddles, its enormous round face encircled with numbers. It reminded me of a stopwatch. Time, running out. Time, sifting through my fingers. Time, I needed more to keep my job.

"Do you ever sleep?" Eleanor asked.

"Not really."

"I'm going to ask Doc Madison to give you a tranquilizer."

"The vet?"

"With your stubborn disposition, he wouldn't even need to dial down the dosage."

A security desk was situated by the exit leading to the private parking lot. No general public was allowed in this part of the track.

"Clement!" she called out.

The guard behind the desk jumped. He was reading a newspaper.

"Evening, Miz Anderson." He pushed aside the sports section. Headline: EMERALD FEVER. The media's nickname for the mysterious illness plaguing horses at the track.

"I want you to swear an oath, Clement!" Her voice rattled a small slider window above the guard's desk. "Are you ready?"

"Uh, sure." His watery eyes looked uncertain.

"My niece intends to spend the night with an ailing horse in my barn. You are not to allow her back into this building. Do you swear?"

He frowned. "You want me to . . . ?"

"Keep her out! I won't have her getting sentimental about the horses. If she defies my order, telephone me immediately. Especially if something untoward happens."

Great, I thought. *Way to keep things undercover.*

"You got it, Miz Anderson," he said. "Have a nice night."

"Night!" She raised her chin, signaling an approaching line. "Night was made for everything except what's nice."

The guard glanced at me, shaking his head. "Your aunt, she's got words for everything."

Eleanor signed us out for the night and I opened the door to the parking lot. She torpedoed for her battleship, a granite-gray Lincoln Town Car docked beside the building under an engraved brass plaque that designated the spot for E. ANDERSON. The other vehicles still here at this late hour were muddy trucks and wheezy Impalas, cars owned by the grooms who were mucking the stalls.

"Go home, Raleigh. Do you hear me?"

My only hope was that all this nagging made our relationship appear real, authentic. The bossy aunt. And I had to say, after four days her constant hectoring was already feeling habitual. A small part of me actually wondered if I enjoyed her steady stream of opinions about my life—sleep habits, food choices, why I should marry my fiancé in Virginia—because it reminded me of my mother. When she was well.

"You're not listening." She jangled her car keys, filling the dusky air with sleigh bells. "Take my advice."

"Yours, or Tennessee Williams's?"

"Don't get smart with me, young lady." She was already lifting her chin. "We all live in a house on fire, with no fire department to call. All we can do is stare out the window, trapped inside, and watch the house go down." She paused. "Who said that?"

"You did." I opened her car door.

"Chris, in *The Milk Train Doesn't Stop Here Anymore*."

"And it's supposed to make me feel better?"

"Of course not." She deposited herself on the front seat, delicate as a ballerina. "My point is, quit trying to save the world. It's on fire. And you're one girl with one bucket."

I closed the door, but the window came down.

She said, "I'm writing the checks, you know."

I leaned down, catching night air that clutched her jasmine perfume and pulled floral ribbons through the dark. "I'm fine."

"You've undoubtedly fed that line to people your entire life. Some people might even believe you. But I've heard every line ever written, so let me put this in plain terms. If I discover you stayed in that barn, I'll fire you."

The window glided up and the big car roared from the parking lot. I waited, watching it follow the wide curvature of road that connected to the interstate pointed south to Tacoma, where Eleanor would swing that battleship into the safe harbor of her historic Victorian. Even after the car was gone, I waited a moment longer, just in case she came back.

Then I walked to my car.

Or the car that I wished belonged to me.

An automotive thoroughbred, the Ghibli was part of Harry Anderson's vintage car collection. Maserati made only three thousand models of this particular version, and Harry bought one so that Eleanor could tool around Seattle looking like a movie star. The car had a full-width grill with pop-up headlights and a long bonnet that stretched back sail-like to the sharply angled windshield, its glass so smooth it seemed melted in place. The paint was an elegant white, almost ivory, and in the back two fuel tanks waited under the high rear end, begging for hundred-mile-an-hour speeds.

I dubbed it "the Ghost."

Turning the key, I listened to the feline engine growl with predatory glee. I cruised out of the parking lot, crossed the railroad tracks, and drove as far as the road leading to the interstate. Then I pulled a U-turn, which the Ghost took on a dime, and circled back to the parking lot, sliding between two jacked-up big-wheel trucks, in case Clement looked out the door.

I rummaged through my duffel bag until I found my Levi's, a T-shirt, and my brown Frye boots. The denim jacket on the floor in back covered two large bags of Lay's potato chips—in case Eleanor poked her nose in here. Sliding down the front seat's buttery leather, I ducked beneath the wood-grained dash and wiggled out of Raleigh David's linen trousers and silk blouse. I tossed her sandals in back. Girly things. Made by somebody named Ferragamo.

I let out a long sigh. My old duds felt like second skin. But something was still missing. I reached under the front seat, patting for the cold stippled steel.

My gun.

It was waiting for me. A girl's best friend.

Chapter Three

The Glock was shoved deep inside my left boot, and seriously pinching my calf. I limped across the parking lot, then crouched behind some bushes beside the betting office building. After Clement, the only other entrance to the backstretch was a small gatehouse. It divided two lanes used for horse trailers and delivery trucks. The security light over the green shack was bright enough that I could see the wooden arms were down, blocking the way. I could also see the guard inside. His hair was as white as his uniform and his head tilted forward, the neck crooked at a loose angle, suggesting sleep. I counted to eighty-four, in honor of Eleanor, who somehow believed my getting more sleep would reveal who was fixing the races, and on the count of eighty-five, I pushed through the bushes. The guard never looked up.

I walked slowly, trying to disguise the limp. There were four barns on the backstretch, each about forty yards long. A young groom was hosing down the pavement outside the first building, spraying away manure and hay and sawdust. Night had fully fallen and the lights inside glowed with a soft yellow hue, as if the sawdust on the floor was shaved gold. I nodded at the groom, acting like I belonged here, and continued down the wet pavement to the third barn. Hot Tin shared the barn with two other outfits—Abbondanza and Manchester stables. I was interested in Abbondanza because it was run by Salvatore Gagliardo, aka Sal Gag. Our Organized Crimes unit once tried to nail Mr. Gagliardo for running a bookie operation at the track. But the case went nowhere. Sal Gag had an ideal cover as a legitimate owner of thoroughbreds, and as I passed by the Abbondanza stalls, I saw his female groom watering the horses. Sort of. She was lifting a gallon bucket but swaying. Suddenly she placed one hand on the plank wall, steadying herself. She closed her eyes.

"Are you all right?" I asked.

She jumped. Her eyes were large and blue and scared.

"I don't need any help," she said, tugging at her shirt. It was pink. Bright pink. For reasons beyond my investigative skills, the barn's racing color was Barbie pink. She lifted the bucket again, tipping the water into the metal basin hanging beside the horse's stall. "I can do it."

I smiled, friendly and harmless, and tried not to limp as I walked down the sawdust path toward Hot Tin. The barns smelled of alfalfa and horse dander and worn dollar bills. Each barn was shaped like two Es facing each other. The long sides held horse stalls, connected by three lanes. I was walking down the middle lane when I heard a voice ask, "When did she run?"

"In the third," a man replied. "Came in last."

"Her stomach sounds bad."

"Don't worry about it."

"And there's too much fluid in her lungs," the second man added. "You shouldn't have run her; she needs rest."

"Are you lecturing me, boy?"

I recognized that voice. The sharp gravel of Bill Cooper. Head trainer for Hot Tin's horses.

"Nobody wants your advice," Cooper continued. "You just get her ready to run on Wednes—"

"That's impossible."

"Hit her with some Lasix. Or do you want me to call Doc Madison and tell him you don't know what you're doing?"

I heard the sound of footsteps behind me. The girl in the pink shirt waited at the end of the gallery, head tilted with curiosity. She had long pale blond hair that fell like bleached rain. I gave a friendly wave, then walked around the corner.

Bill Cooper stood at the edge of the stall. The top half of the Dutch door was open and I could see Solo in Seattle lying on the sawdust floor. The man kneeling beside her was the veterinarian's assistant, Brent Roth. Skinny and handsome in a scruffy sort of way, he had a permanent squint around his eyes that made him look thoughtful, and perpetually annoyed. But he was so young that his skin still had acne spreading across his cheeks and neck. It was half the reason Cooper called him "boy." That, and Cooper was a bully.

The trainer looked at me. His eyes were a cold gray-blue, like zinc. "What're you doing here?"

"Aunt Eleanor wanted me to check on the horse."

"Guess she wants you to learn something useful." He turned back to the assistant vet. "Get the Lasix."

But the younger man was now wearing a stethoscope, brushing the instrument's metal bell down the horse's side and pausing to listen. The animal's chestnut coat looked shiny, unctuous with sweat, and when Brent palpitated her hairless belly, she only gazed at the plank wall, her brown eyes glassy with illness.

"Lasix," I said into the silence. "What does that do?"

Brent glanced over his shoulder. "Opens the lungs."

"And it's safe?"

Neither man replied. I was almost getting used to that.

Like most places that revolved around money, Emerald Meadows was built on a libertine subculture. Every handshake made my radar quiver with questions. Gamblers and bookies and sharks. Narks and rats and foolish souls who plowed every ounce of faith into "luck." Many of them were hiding secrets. Most were hatching plans. And all of them treated newcomers with suspicion—even the supposed niece of Eleanor Anderson.

"What did I tell you?" Cooper said. "Get the Lasix. Now."

Brent Roth's eyes nearly closed with his squint. He yanked off the stethoscope. A flush of color came up his neck, enflaming the acne, as he dug through a black medical bag sitting on the ground.

"That's right," Cooper said. "Do what you're told."

I decided to try using Cooper's hostility to my advantage, since the assistant didn't like him either. Leaning over the bottom half of the Dutch door, I said, "She looks really sick. Are you sure this stuff's a good idea?"

"Butt out," Cooper said.

I saw the assistant turn his head, about to respond, when he was interrupted.

"You just don't care," she said.

The girl in the pink shirt stood three feet behind me, glaring at Cooper. But when she saw the horse, the disgust in her eyes shifted to sadness. Brent was wiping the horse's neck with an alcohol swab, then pressing his thumb down until a thick vein bulged. The jugular, I guessed. He stabbed it with a syringe and pushed the plunger. The horse didn't react. When he extracted the needle, he patted the spot gently, comforting her.

Cooper said, "Was that so hard?"

Brent still had his hand on the horse. Solo in Seattle turned her head, the fevered eyes gazing at him.

The girl's voice almost broke. "You're cruel, Bill Cooper."

"And you're outta line," he replied. "Especially after Cuppa Joe destroyed her morale."

When Solo in Seattle faltered in the third race today, a horse named Cuppa Joe flew past her to victory. He was the long shot. And he just so happened to belong to the Abbondanza barn. It was a big payday for Sal Gag.

"You should be ashamed." The girl's eyes were wet as she turned and walked back toward her stables.

Brent Roth sighed and began packing up his medical bag.

"Do you think it could be Emerald Fever?" I asked.

"What?" Cooper whirled. "You want to jinx my barn?"

"It's my aunt's barn," I said, keeping my eyes on the assistant vet. I was a bad liar. "And she wants blood tests."

"What?" Cooper repeated.

It wasn't quite what Eleanor said, but she did hire me to find out what was going on. And blood tests might reveal something.

Cooper said, "How come she didn't tell me?"

"You were busy," I lied. "But she thinks something's not right. Solo was winning. Now suddenly she's sick."

"Colic," Cooper said. "It's just colic."

But Brent Roth had already swabbed the neck again and was pressing down to find the vein. As he filled an empty syringe with crimson ribbons of blood, the horse blinked her large brown eyes. Brent patted her side and deposited the full syringe in a Ziploc bag inside his medical kit.

"That 50 ccs of Lasix should hold her," he said. "Doc Madison will come check her in the morning. But somebody should stay with her tonight. Just in case."

"Juan," Cooper said, referring to the barn's groom. "Juan will watch her."

Brent glanced at me, stepping out of the stall. I thought his squint looked skeptical. Cooper practically pushed him down the gallery, hustling him out. But he stopped when I didn't follow them.

"What're you doing?" he asked.

"I'll watch her. Until Juan can take over."

"Right." He rolled his eyes. "Because you know so much about horses."

He had a bandy-legged walk, and as he passed the third stall he rapped his knuckles on the plank wall.

"Hey, check on Solo when you get a chance!"

It was several minutes later when a man stepped from that stall. Cooper and Brent Roth were gone, and the man held a red bucket in one hand. The metal hasp was sunk deep into the flesh of his thick palm. His fingers were gray. As he closed the Dutch door's bottom half, the brown horse inside leaned forward and fluttered her lips. KichaKoo, a four-year-old filly. Juan Morales gave her whiskered chin a soft chuck.

Here's what I knew about him: Juan Morales came to the barn last year, when Eleanor hired Bill Cooper. He was taciturn and diligent, and his social security number belonged to a Native American from the Yakima Indian reservation who died seventeen years ago. Naturally, the bad trace bumped him up my list of suspects. I was also learning that grooms had the most access to the horses. Feeding, watering. Staying the night.

"Juan?" I walked toward him.

He was already stepping into the next stall, where a white horse tried to block his entrance.

"I want to stay with Solo tonight."

He pushed the horse aside. Her name was Checkmate. "Your aunt," he said, "she pay me to stay."

"I'll make sure you get paid for the night."

"El'nor, she no want you sweet on the horses."

"She doesn't need to know I'm here."

He glanced at me and set down the bucket inside the stall. The horse was rocking its head up and down, as if enthusiastically agreeing to something. A thin horse, she was shaped from neck to haunches like a silver blade. I waited while Juan reached inside the bucket and scooped out a handful of wet clay. It was gray and he worked the soil between his hands before leaning into the animal's side and clicking his tongue. The groom took her weight into his shoulders and back, and Checkmate raised her left leg, allowing him to massage the clay into her knobby knee.

"I would really like to stay."

"You know no-ting about horses."

"All she needs is someone to watch her. How hard is that?"

Still bent at the waist, he glanced up at me. His skin was the texture of raisins. And his dark eyes held a strange expression, like an old man who suspected any peaceful Sunday drive with his children might someday end at a retirement home. "Why?"

"I feel bad for her. She's suffering."

He returned to his work, massaging the mud into the leg. The horse looked like she was wearing dingy socks.

"I promise to be gone before Cooper comes back in the morning."

He said something in Spanish. The horse shook her mane.

"I'll pay you triple wages for the night."

He glanced up. "Tree-pull?"

"Guaranteed."

He straightened his back and dug two fingers into the front pocket of his jeans. The mud was such a fine clay that it had already started drying on the backs of his hands, flaking and falling like ash into the sawdust. He offered me a small brass key.

"What's this?" I leaned over the Dutch door to take it.

"Cold at night." He scooped another lump of clay from the bucket. "Get a blanket."

≈

I rushed up the gallery, feeling hope swirl around my heart. But as I passed the stalls, the horses nickered. Like they were in on my secret. I walked to the end of the barn, where the grooms lived in apartments. I keyed open Juan's door. His room wasn't much bigger than the horse stalls. No window. No bathroom. No closet. Just a thin cot pushed against the wall and a green blanket nubby from wear. Standing in the door, I glanced back at the stables, then closed the door.

By giving me the key, Juan had surrendered all his "expectations of privacy." It was a legal term that basically meant any objects in plain sight were fair game for law enforcement. But nothing could be touched or moved without his permission. And I wasn't tempted, not after making that mistake on the cruise ship.

A brown towel hung on a brass hook. The terrycloth looked rough as sandpaper. Below the towel, a pair of worn rubber sandals waited, probably for walking back and forth to the showers, which were in another building. A pile of dirty clothes slumped on the concrete floor, and a Spanish language newspaper lay next to a dented steel trunk at the foot of the bed. The trunk, unfortunately, was closed. I crouched down, checking under the bed. Inches from the metal frame, an aluminum pot sat on a hot plate and a scent rose from the simmering contents, earthy as tilled soil. Beans. Black beans, cooked down to the consistency of paste.

I stood up, looked around the room again, and saw the only thing resembling a spare blanket: a sleeping bag rolled up in the corner, with strands of hay protruding from the flannel like feathers in a cap. Picking up the bag, I headed back to the stables.

Juan had moved to the next stall and was working the clay into an equine warlord appropriately named SunTzu.

"Is this what you meant?" I lifted the sleeping bag.

He nodded, took his key back, and gave me a funny look. "You no tell?"

"As long as you don't tell Aunt Eleanor, I won't tell Cooper. And I'll make sure the triple time is in your next check."

He nodded but dropped his eyes, unable to hold my gaze. Was he ashamed of betraying Cooper? I wondered. Or was he calculating the resale, the amount Cooper would pay him to learn that I had stayed the night, against Eleanor's wishes.

Right now, I didn't care. I was in the barn for the night. Plenty of time to snoop while the grooms slept. But as I was heading for Solo's stall, I once again heard someone talking inside it.

"Don't worry," she said. "I'll make sure they take care of you."

I stood at the half-door, watching them. The chestnut horse was still on the sawdust, but now the girl from Abbondanza was nuzzling the animal's perspiring neck. Her long platinum hair blended with the mane like frosted extensions.

I opened the door.

"Oh!" She scrambled to her feet. "I'm sorry—I didn't—"

"I'm staying with her." I shifted the sleeping bag to my left hand and extended my right. "We haven't really met. I'm Raleigh David."

"Ashley." She shook my hand. Her fingers were child-sized but strong, the skin coarse. "Ashley Trenner."

I had so many questions for her, particularly about her employer, Salvatore Gagliardo. But she was nervously stuffing her small hands into the back pockets of her jeans and dragging the toe of her boot across the sawdust. I decided to hold my tongue. She seemed like the kind of girl who filled silences. I set down the sleeping bag.

"I just wanted, you know, to see how she was doing."

I nodded.

"I heard Brent say somebody should stay with her tonight. And, well, no offense . . ."

"For what?"

She dragged her boot again. "Juan."

"What about him?"

"He won't stay. Not all night. So I was gonna . . ." She stopped. "You think I'm spying on your barn."

"It is unusual that a groom from a competing barn wants to help."

"I'm not spying." Her voice rose, almost whiny. "Nobody gets it. I don't care about winning. I care about the horses. And I have to, the way some people treat them around here. It's inhuman."

I let the literal meaning pass. "I appreciate your concern, Ashley."

"Really?"

"Yes."

"Well, thanks. But don't tell Cooper I was here. He'll go ballistic."

I was about to say, "You have my word," when a thought wagged its finger at me. *Your word? You're living a total lie.*

"How about we make a deal," I said. "I won't tell anyone you were here and you won't tell anyone I stayed."

Her smile looked wan, like she agreed with the proposal but wished an agreement never had to be made. When she stepped out of the stall, the horse's glazed brown eyes followed her. A pang of guilt squeezed my heart. The horse would probably prefer her company tonight. But it was just one night. Ashley could stay tomorrow.

"Don't leave her." She gazed down at the sweating animal. "Promise, hope to die?"

"Promise," I said.

But I didn't hope to die.

Chapter Four

When my eyes opened, I didn't know what it was. Lying under the sleeping bag, with the ailing horse at my back, I could feel my heart beating too fast.

Then I heard it again. A train whistle. And with it, the dream rushed back.

I had been standing on a cliff overlooking the James River. My fiancé, DeMott Fielding, stood beside me, and an Episcopal priest was reciting marriage vows. When it came my turn to repeat the words, a crowd of women in floral dresses pushed forward. I opened my mouth, but all that came out was a howl, like the cry of a lonely wolf.

And now I could hear how it harmonized with the train's whistle.

I stared at the plank wall. No way could I ever tell my fiancé about that dream. Not unless I wanted another fight. Reaching back, I laid my hand on the horse, lying length-wise across the saw-dust. Her breathing was labored, loud, filling the small space with a chugging sound that made it seem like the locomotive was coming through the barn. Beneath my palm her ribs expanded with each inhalation. I could feel the ligaments between the bones, vibrating, wet, and ragged.

Not good.

I raised my arm, trying to read my watch. 2:33 a.m.

"Oh rats," I muttered.

Over the last two months, I hadn't managed more than an hour or two of sleep at one time. Each night my startle reflex threw me awake, tossing me from dreams where I dropped through thin air and plunged over waterfalls and tumbled off cliffs. Like the cliff where I howled my marriage vows. On the one night I needed to stay awake, I'd fallen asleep. And the bustle here started every morning at 4:00 a.m. My opportunity to investigate the barn was almost gone. And now the horse needed help.

Terrific.

I kicked my boots from the flannel bag. The horse shifted and I glanced over. Her chestnut coat was shiny, like wet ocher paint.

"Sorry," I said. "I'm going for help now."

The words burned at the back of my throat. Dry, hot. And the horse was drawing back her head. The deep brown eyes bulged. The whites were visible.

Fear.

"I'm sorry, I fell asleep."

I stood up and started for the door. But it was closed. Both top and bottom. I felt a sudden disorientation, like all that sleep had made me stupid. I wondered if I'd closed it before going to sleep. But I didn't. And I knew for a fact I didn't pull the bolt shut. I couldn't have locked the door from the outside.

The horse made a whimpering sound. When I looked over, her hooves were pawing the air. And greasy gray ribbons rose from the sawdust in the corner. Smoke.

Fire.

"Fire!"

The horse suddenly rocked back, shoving herself to a wobbly stand.

"Fire!"

I called again, but my voice was drowned out by the sudden scream of the smoke alarms. The horse staggered forward, blocking my path to the door. My eyes stung. I yanked off my jean jacket, holding it over my nose, and crouched in the sawdust. The flame was leaping inside the smoke, then dying, sparking and falling away like trick birthday candles. Flame retardant. On the sawdust. But no retardant was fireproof. Not on dried wood shavings.

The horse turned and curled back her lips. Her scream sounded human. Female. Terrified. And in the small confined space her body looked monumental.

"Fire—" I coughed. "With Solo!"

I could see red veins in the white crescents of her eyes. She staggered backward. Her back bashed into the wall.

Juan—where is Juan?

She stumbled forward and lifted her back leg, kicking the wall. Hitting it again and again until the wood splintered. I could smell her fear, oily and bitter beneath the smoke. Adrenaline fear. Killing fear. She kicked again, harder, and the wooden planks shuddered against my back. Powered by fright, she was growing stronger, not weaker. And now the other horses were kicking too. The sound echoed like rock crushers, pounding through the alarm's mechanical wail. I blinked at the sting in my eyes and watched her lungs. They were expanding like giant bellows and each breath sent out another high cry. She was punch-drunk with panic, staggering again. I crouched lower. Two steps to the right and she could pin me in the back corner. Nowhere to run. Nowhere to hide.

She could kill me.

The horse stamped her hooves into the sawdust, some frightened dance, gearing up for the next blow. I shoved my hand down into my boot. The Glock's barrel raked my skin. She turned her face to me. Her bulging eyes showed so much white she looked blind.

I lifted the gun.

She reared, raising her front legs. In the firelight I could see the metal shoes glinting, telegraphing the pain, the death she wouldn't even notice. I heard another scream.

Hers or mine, I didn't know.

But it was the last thing I remembered before squeezing the trigger.

Chapter Five

"Miss David?"

My mother was smiling. Her cheeks rosy, pink, and happy.

"Miss David?"

She nodded and sighed. *Oh, I miss David*, she said. *I miss him so much—*

"Hey, Miss David. You in there?"

I opened my eyes. For several seconds I stared at the face leaning into mine. The eyes were teal blue. And they matched his shirt. I stared at him until something ripped across my heart.

"Jack?"

"That's correct, Dr. Jackson." He lifted the plastic ID badge clipped to his hospital scrubs. *Mark Jackson, MD*, was printed below a picture of Special Agent Jack Stephanson. "Glad you recognized me, Miss David."

"How did—?"

He shined a penlight in my eyes. "Feeling better?"

I felt sick. And raised my hand to block the light. "That hurts."

But it was nothing compared to the pain searing down my right side. I gasped.

"Cracked ribs," he said with utter detachment. Like a real doctor. "Miss David, do you know where you are?"

I could only whisper. "Harborview."

"Correct, you are in Harborview Hospital. You were admitted at four o'clock this morning."

I reached for the tender spot on my right side. The skin felt hot, swollen. I looked at Jack, but he was watching the open door. Two nurses hurried past, their shoes squeaking down a hall of shiny white vinyl. He turned back to me. His eyes were aquamarine.

He dropped his voice to a whisper. "Thank you."

"What for?"

"For finding a way for us to play doctor."

"You're not—" I pushed myself up, ready to let him have it, when the pain sliced down my side again. I winced.

"That bad?" he asked.

"No." I forced back tears.

"It wouldn't hurt so much if you held still." He paused. "Not that you're capable of that."

"Wow. Some doctor you are." I tried to glare at him, but the pain kept blinking back the sting in my eyes. *Hold tight.* If the waterworks started, I didn't know if I could stop. Slowly, I tried two breaths and touched my ribs again, telling myself to pretend all the agony was physical. When the tears were back under control, I withdrew my hand. And gasped again.

"What's wrong?" he said.

I stared at my left hand. The ring finger. It was bare.

"Where's my—" But I stopped.

"Your what?"

Engagement ring.

But the hazy memory was coming back. Eleanor. Early this morning. She removed the ring, worried about theft. Despite the wave of relief, my heart kept pounding. Imagining what my fiancé would say if I lost his ring. One more fight.

"I can prescribe some pain meds," Jack said. "But I think what you need is a full-body massage."

"I need a real doctor."

"You don't think I can pass?"

"No."

But the terrible truth was, Jack did look like a doctor. Some good-looking, overconfident MDeity with an ego the size of Africa. And why not? The undisputed star of the Seattle Violent Crimes unit was cocky, savvy, and just over six feet. His body had the sculpted musculature of an anatomy chart, and his chiseled face framed bright eyes that could shift from green to blue and back again. I was forced to work with him twice, and both times I had to watch women launch themselves at him, flinging their dignity away because they'd found a Ken doll with a concealed gun permit.

Not that I cared. Our relationship, as our supervisor McLeod said, was "purely plutonic." Sometimes malaprops were spot-on. This guy was from another planet, some cold, dark part of the galaxy. And I wished he would go back.

"Something wrong with your phone?" I said.

"What?"

"You're taking a huge risk coming in here." Our contact since the UCA started had been by cell phone only. I kept the conversations punctual and courteous.

"I had to—I needed—Hey, I'm your case agent," he finally managed. "Don't you dare question me. And *you're* the one in trouble."

I gave him my best glare, but he was looking over at the door again. His name tag dangled from the scrubs. Around the FBI office, Jack was known as a compulsive ladies' man. I almost felt sorry for the nurses, imagining what *Dr. Jackson* had planned for them. He turned back suddenly and caught me staring at the badge. He grinned.

"Harvard Medical School."

"Big deal. Raleigh David's a millionaire."

"Okay, moneybags, tell me why you were in that horse stall."

"She was sick."

"Who?"

"The horse."

His eyes were turning green. "You know what the suits upstairs always worry about?"

"Paperwork."

"They get nervous about some thug seducing the beautiful agents when they go undercover. But wait until I write this up. Raleigh slept with a horse."

"Don't you have somewhere else to go, some malpractice you need to commit?"

"Management's nervous, Harmon."

I turned away, staring out the room's picture window. Harborview sat on Capitol Hill, otherwise known as Pill Hill for its many medical facilities. My aunt—my real aunt, Charlotte—lived less than a mile from here, with three mean cats and a collection of weird rocks. I could see the sun was shining in a burst of August's last days, but down the hill, the skyscrapers looked like ice that refused to melt.

"Hi there," Jack said.

A pretty woman stood at the door. She had short dark hair and was pushing a wheeled cart stacked with meal trays. But she stopped when her eyes locked on Jack. He walked toward her, asking her name. I hated to admit it, but loose cotton scrubs only made Jack's build look tighter.

"Becky?" he said.

She nodded. Speechless. Eyes the size of dinner plates.

"Becky, could you do me a favor? Come back in about fifteen minutes?" He lowered his voice. "I'm having some issues with this patient. Noncompliant, you know what I'm saying?"

She nodded once more, head moving up and down like a hormonal zombie. Jack patted her shoulder, then walked back to my bed. Becky's eyes combed down his back. Standing next to my bed, he picked up my left wrist and pressed his fingers into my skin, staring at his wristwatch.

"Your pulse is erratic," he said.

I glanced around him. Becky, returning to reality, was pushing her cart out the door, into the hallway. When she turned left, I whispered, "She's gone."

"Good." He didn't let go of my wrist. "Give me the 302."

I yanked my hand away and was rewarded with another round of stabs down my right side. But the pain was almost manageable now. Duller. Like lingering heartache. I kept my eyes on the door and gave Jack a careful description of last night. My whispers grew hoarse with the jackhammer rhythm of facts. The FD302 was a mandatory document, filed for every interview conducted by an agent. No speculations allowed. No emotions. No interpretations. Facts only, the tangible realities typed up for the bureaucracy.

"And where did you get the sleeping bag?" he asked.

"The groom. Juan Morales. He lives in the barn."

"I meant, *how* did you get it?"

"He gave me the key to his room."

"Did you happen to take anything else?"

"Yes. My pride. I learned my lesson on the cruise ship."

"Great. And here's another lesson. When you fire a weapon while undercover, it creates an avalanche of paperwork. And OPR gets involved. Again."

When I closed my eyes, the images kept playing in my mind. That horse. Blind with fear. Kicking. The scream, so human.

"Hello?"

I opened my eyes.

"Did you hear me? McLeod wants you to come in."

"Why?"

"He thinks the Mob pegged you."

"Tell him he's wrong."

"I don't know, this kind of thing is right up their alley. What about Sal Gagliardo?"

"He wasn't there last night."

"One of his capos?"

"No. And his groom even offered to stay with the horse. They don't suspect me."

"You know this for sure?"

"My gut tells me."

"Harmon, none of the suits have guts. That's a prerequisite for management. Evisceration."

"Then give them the cold logic." The words came out sharp, bitter. The anger bristled under my skin. The suits. The suits who directed my life from behind their safe desks, sitting in padded chairs, pushing paper through the system as if nobody was talking about life and death and justice.

"What logic?" Jack asked.

"One nanosecond of rational thought would tell them the Mob's not that dumb. Attempting to kill a federal agent? The FBI would descend on that racetrack—we'd make their lives miserable."

"So who lit that fire—the horse?"

My throat was raw from the smoke. I picked up a cup of water sitting beside my bed and drank it. The fluid went down like crushed glass.

"I don't know who did it," I said finally.

"They'll enjoy hearing that."

"*Yet*. I don't know who, yet."

"Any suspects?"

"Two people knew I was in that stall. One was Juan, Eleanor's groom." I reminded Jack he had a fake social security number. "And the groom for Sal Gagliardo's barn."

He almost laughed. "And you still think the Mob's not behind this?"

"Yes. Because that groom is horse-crazy. No way would she put that animal in any kind of danger." I looked up at him. "By the way, Eleanor won't tell me. Did the horse . . . ?"

More green seeped into his eyes.

"The horse shattered its leg trying to get out. The *Seattle Times* ran a story. They mentioned a barn worker who was lucky to be alive."

"I don't believe in luck."

"Reconsider. If that horse hadn't broken its leg, it would've kicked you to death."

I stared out the window again.

"Harmon, give me something solid to feed the suits. Otherwise they'll call off the UCA."

"Call it an opportunity. I saw an opportunity." The words tasted as metallic as blood. I had to justify a split-second decision in the field for people who deliberated in meetings. The same people who held my life in their hands. "That's the federal jargon, isn't it? An opportunity presented itself. The agent seized it. And—"

"And OPR is greasing their guillotine."

"I had to fire the gun. The door was locked."

He nodded and walked across the room. Beneath the wall-mounted television, a table was covered with floral bouquets.

"You're very popular, Miss David."

"I'm Eleanor Anderson's niece."

The biggest arrangement was a red-rose heart, mounted on an easel. It looked more suited for the winner's circle. Or a funeral. Jack took the small white envelope protruding from the crimson flowers, reading the note. "'From your friends at Emerald Meadows.'" He looked over at me. "The same *friends* who tried to incinerate you?"

"Maybe they were after the horse. Did you ever consider that?"

"No." He slid the card back into the flowers, then walked over to my bed. "Somebody disabled the sprinkler. Just the one above your stall. They wanted you dead."

"Or the horse."

"You keep saying. But theories won't get you reinstated."

"That's why I'm going to solve this case."

He laughed, crossing his arms over his chest. The biceps bulged. "You're a persistent woman."

I looked away.

"We still have to go over the firearm."

"The door was closed, I couldn't get around the horse, so I tried to shoot the bolt open."

"Right," he said. "Because any sane person would shoot the horse."

When I didn't reply, he said, "You are a great shot. According to the fire inspector, you blew the handle off. By the way, they're ruling this arson."

"Gee, really?"

"No need for the sarcasm, Miss David."

Miss David.

In the dream somebody was asking my mother if she missed her husband, David. My dad. Her face seemed as delicate as porcelain, the jasper eyes wounded and fragile. But her smile. Her smile was like the old days. I felt my throat burning again, only this time it was because I was six years old and telling myself, *Don't cry.*

"What are you thinking?" he said.

"I want to call Western State. See how she is."

"The line here's not secure. But your mom's fine."

"How do you know?"

"And speaking of Western State," he said, "you missed an appointment with Dr. Freud."

Dr. Freud, aka Nathan Norbert. The Bureau-assigned head shrinker. I stared at my hands and didn't reply.

"I don't like it either, Harmon."

I looked up. His voice sounded different. Soft. But not that keep-the-volume-down soft. It was . . . tender. I opened my mouth, about to say something, but Becky the orderly came wheeling into the room. She called out, making sure Jack noticed her. And I felt a strange sort of gratitude. Painful relief. Because in that last moment his voice reminded me of some slivers of time, when Jack came on the cruise ship and didn't seem like such a jerk. When he stepped up and revealed some depth. Real depth. I gazed down at my hands again.

No engagement ring. Nothing but a hospital gown. And a big bunch of lies.

I listened to them chatting and tried to ignore the goose bumps rising on my arms at the sound of his voice.

Chapter Six

The Northwest's winter, which pulled up its gray flannel blanket of clouds and slumbered through six months of steady drizzle, inoculated Seattle's population in several significant ways: people here rarely carried umbrellas, they refused to cancel outdoor events due to bad weather, and they seemed only mildly disappointed when the rain once again reared its head and poured during summer.

But since Raleigh David wasn't from Seattle, I carried a chic black umbrella. Just before 10:00 a.m. on Wednesday, I hurried through the morning rain and watched a practice run of thoroughbreds alongside the track's white rail. Thundering hooves shook the ground as I made my way to the grandstands, closed the umbrella, and climbed up the concrete stairs. The rain pattered on the metal roof overhead, sounding like fingers drumming impatiently for the first race. The regulars streamed from the public entrances, slipping into habitual seats. Men, mostly, they ranged from middle-aged to elderly and toted betting sheets and brown bags, their hooded eyes dull, almost dead. But a second glance revealed just how carefully cultivated that morbidity was, how each of them had erected a defensive wall to live with the inextinguishable spark of suspicion.

When I reached the top of the stairs, a track official in a green blazer smiled and made an extravagant gesture of tapping his watch before pulling open the door where a small sign warned Members Only Beyond This Point.

"You better hurry," he said. "She's up there waiting."

I sprinted the flight of stairs, glancing at my watch. But the engagement ring caught my eye. The peridot gems looked murky, a rheumy olivine, and clouds had gathered in the citrine stones, as if the morning sky had settled into the yellow quartz. I was still running up the stairs as I rubbed the stones on Raleigh David's fine slacks, feeling somewhere between foolish and guilty—foolish because I rubbed the ring while wishing like it was Aladdin's lamp; guilty because this seemed to be a sign about my decision not to tell my fiancé about the barn fire. The news would only upset him, waiting for me to come home to Virginia, waiting for us to get married and start a family. But the cruise to Alaska had upset those plans. A vacation of solitude and reflection had only strained our relationship further, and two months later we were relying on the U.S. mail. DeMott refused to use computers or cell phones, and I despised talking on the telephone. Once upon a time his old-fashioned attitudes struck me as quaint, ideal for a guy whose family had lived on the same vast estate of land since the 1700s. Now the quill-pen perspective annoyed me. So I rubbed and wished, praying for those once-upon-a-time feelings to come back.

After giving the ring one final swipe, I stepped into the track's private dining room. It was 10:01 a.m.

"You're late!" Eleanor bellowed.

The woman's schedule ticked like a bomb. Every day, at precisely 10:00 a.m., Eleanor ate breakfast in the members-only dining room. Coffee, black. Rye toast, dry. One poached egg, soft yet not fully cooked. A long rectangular space full of white-clothed tables, the dining room had picture windows perched high over the track's finish line. Sixty feet below, the horses zipped through needles of rain, finishing the final training runs. Somehow the wet weather made the dining room feel that much more exclusive.

As I took my seat at Eleanor's table, a waiter floated into view and asked for my order. His name was Raoul.

"I'll have a Denver omelet," I told him. "Hash browns. Bacon, sausage, toast. And the largest glass of Coca-Cola with no crushed ice. Thank you."

Eleanor said, "That food will kill you."

"So will life." I snapped open my napkin.

"With what you eat, you should be the size of a tree."

My first day out here she referenced the Hindenburg. Then a barn. Then a bus. I decided I was growing on her.

"Raoul," she told the waiter, who knew to hover after my order, "my niece will have rye toast and a poached egg. Please change the Coca-Cola to skim milk."

Raoul bowed and scurried away.

Eleanor picked up her coffee cup. The white rim was gilded with gold horseshoes. "How are you feeling?"

"Hungry."

"I was referring to your ribs."

"They hurt. Especially when I'm hungry."

"You should've stayed in bed."

I dropped my voice to a whisper. "And you were supposed to fire me, but that didn't happen."

She lifted her chin, telegraphing delivery. "When people have some slight disadvantage, they develop other things to make up for it, like charm. Who said that?"

"You did."

"Amanda, in *The Glass Menagerie*." She took another sip. "What's your plan for today?"

I shifted my gaze. Three tables behind Eleanor, Sal Gag sat hunched over the day's betting sheet. An unlit Havana rested in perpetuity between his sausage-like fingers, while the other hand pinched the handle of a demitasse. In his enormous hand, the tiny cup looked like it was stolen from a toddler's tea set.

"I think it's time to wager," I whispered. "What can you spare?"

"I'm insulted!"

Sal Gag looked up.

I smiled, stiff as a corpse, whispering again, "I didn't mean to insul—"

"If hanging around this place is going to ruin your Southern gentility," she trumpeted, "I'll send you back to those people who mangle the English language."

Please. I closed my eyes, praying. *Please let the Mob guy think "those people" are Southerners. Not Feds full of malaprops*. When I opened my eyes, Sal Gag seemed to be holding himself much too still. And Eleanor was lifting her chin again. I braced myself.

"You can be young without money but you can't be old without it. Who said that?"

I sighed.

"Maggie the Cat," she said. "Scene one. The critic in Toronto noted my purring."

Our dry toast arrived, doing its best imitation of cardboard, and I choked it down with the skim milk while Eleanor passed me her wallet under the tablecloth. I counted out $2,000, then excused myself.

"Don't do anything foolish," she said.

"Don't worry." I placed my napkin on my seat, an etiquette signal for Raoul, letting him know I would be back. "I'll be fine."

"My dear," Eleanor said, "I doubt that very, very much."

≈

From the grandstand's upper level, I watched the numbers flash on the light board in the track's inner circle. The first race's flickering odds were solidifying, but the numbers would keep shifting until the starting gate blew open at 11:00 a.m. I saw several names on the board that looked familiar, in particular SunTzu from Eleanor's barn. And Cuppa Joe, from Sal Gag's. The long shot that beat Solo in Seattle on Monday. But now SunTzu was marked for long odds, mostly because of the barn fire. Betting people were superstitious, and Solo's death was chalked up to Hot Tin's "curse" of "bad luck." Meanwhile, Cuppa Joe was the new favorite. If he lost, Sal Gag would make a bundle as a bookie. If he won, the bundle would also go to the bookie—as the horse's owner.

It was an ingenious setup, and from what the Bureau could fathom, Sal Gag was offering three percentage points more than the track. Betting on a winner with the bookie meant potentially more money. Of course, losing meant you owed him more, but gamblers always thought of themselves as lucky—that's why they kept gambling. But Sal Gag was smart enough to hire a numbers runner to handle his illegal operation.

The runner's name was Anthony Pilato. Otherwise known as Tony Not Tony.

On this wet morning, Tony Not Tony was standing on the second tier of the grandstands. A former jockey, he had narrow shoulders that drew forward and a tendency to walk on his toes, making him look like a mouse on its hind legs. The tassels of his oxblood loafers touched the floor, his navy slacks were pressed, and his silk shirt was the color of the silver rain. His small hands, veined with strength, held betting receipts in some attempt to appear legitimate.

"Thank you for the flowers," I said.

He looked over. "How are you feeling?"

"Much better, thank you." I made a mental note: *He never acknowledged sending flowers.* I wondered if he suspected my identity or if he habitually worried about surveillance wires.

"I heard the horse kicked you," he said. "Or maybe not. And something about arson, but is that possible?"

Eleanor had told me Tony got his nickname for hearing and yet not hearing things. Perfect for a Mob guy. But even if I was wearing a wire, our whiz kids would have a tough time picking up the voice. Rather than speaking, he aspirated his words. And here among the concrete floor and metal ceiling, with a crowd murmuring around us like a busy river, his words barely registered.

"Yes, arson," I said. "Somebody also closed the stall's door. And locked it."

"Frightening," he breathed.

I nodded. "But I know what would make me feel better. Making some money." I smiled. "Some serious money."

He glanced away. For several moments we stared over the seats. Down below the light board sparkled with illuminated greed, and the air smelled of hot dogs and morning beer and some kind of human-generated electricity.

"I enjoy wagering," I said in a low voice. "But Aunt Eleanor doesn't approve, so I'd rather you didn't say anything."

"Me?" The narrow shoulders came forward. "What would I know? I'm a simple jockey's agent."

Yes, that was the cover. Tony Not Tony worked as a jockey's agent, matching horses to riders and collecting a percentage of the winnings. Just like he collected a percentage on the bets that went through Sal Gag.

"Two grand," I said. "Cash on the spot."

"Cuppa Joe." The words floated from his mouth. "To win. He's a mudder."

"Mudder?"

"He likes to run in the mud. Doesn't mind the rain."

I reached into my purse. Tony Not Tony turned to face the track. His left hand dangled at his side. If the race-fixing pattern held, Cuppa Joe would lose. These guys would take home a bundle. I leaned toward him, as though speaking over the noise of the crowd, and surreptitiously laid twenty $100 bills in his open palm. Almost imperceptibly the money moved to his pocket.

"Ferragamos?" he said.

I stepped back. "Pardon?"

"Your sandals. Ferragamos?"

I looked down. The brown leather sandals were purchased for Raleigh David by Lucia Lutini, our profiler. But when I looked up, Tony Not Tony was smiling at me like we shared a family bond.

I smiled back. "How nice that someone recognizes true quality."

"What size?"

I hesitated, suddenly uncertain. "Nine . . ."

The smile stretched to the finish and revealed the former jockey's bridgework. "You know where my office is?"

I shook my head.

"Panel van," he breathed. "Backstretch parking lot. Meet me after the final race. We'll celebrate."

Chapter Seven

With sixteen minutes to post, the atmosphere felt like the moment between lightning and thunder. The moment when life seemed to balance on the brink, anticipating an uncontrollable force. Thrilling, almost frightening, it reminded me of the minutes in DeMott Fielding's pickup truck, when snow silently fell around us and he asked if I would ever consider marrying him. They were the moments when the very next thing will change everything, forever.

Running down to the bottom of the grandstands, I flipped open my umbrella and jogged along the white rail. The announcer's voice crackled above me on the loudspeakers.

"In lane one, we have that brisk brew from Abbondanza, Cuppa Joe. Monday's big winner. And in lane two, Loosey Goosey, a fine fresh filly from Manchester Barn." His voice sounded vaguely British, like a fake English accent. "In lane three, it's the mighty warrior known as SunTzu from the Hot Tin Barn."

I glanced across the oval. The eight horses were walking single file, heading for the starting gate. The jockeys hunched their shoulders against the soft rain.

"And in lane four, Bubba's Revenge . . ."

I glanced at my watch. Eleven minutes. Eleanor expected me back in the dining room by post time. I hurried down the backstretch and stepped around a clutch of smokers who stood outside the Quarterchute Café, faces as lined as topographic maps. Closing the umbrella and giving it a shake, I opened the door. And smelled heaven.

Fries. Cheeseburgers. Grease.

"Freddie," said a tiny woman behind the counter. "Love of my life, pay up." She turned to the man working the grill. "Raleigh's here."

On my first day out here, after Eleanor reordered my breakfast, I ran into this place like a beagle following a scent. By my second day, I had learned that Birdie Bidwell and her husband, Freddie, had opened the Quarterchute Café thirty-plus years ago, providing cheap food for the backstretch trainers, grooms, pony riders, and an assorted clutch of old gamblers whose wagers had won them small percentages of racehorses, just enough to qualify them as part-owners. The jockeys came in too, but only to drink water.

Birdie was a preternaturally tiny woman, almost childlike, with tourmaline-blue eyes and a round face. The cash register almost touched her chin. She held a Sharpie in one hand, carefully writing the day's word, which she hung daily on a birch tree beside the entrance. Spanish-to-English translations, for the track's many Hispanic workers. Today's sign read *Relaciones* = Relationships.

"Thanks for the flowers," I said.

"Honey." She capped the pen. "We were so worried about you we had to start a pool."

I took a jumbo cup from the soda dispenser. "What was the wager?" I hit the button for Coca-Cola. Breakfast of champion liars.

"The wager was 'Would Eleanor Anderson set foot inside the hospital?' That woman hates anything medical. But you know that."

I didn't, but I nodded.

"Then I remembered something," Birdie said. "When your uncle Harry got sick, that pneumonia killed him? Eleanor went to the hospital every single day. So I took long odds—and I won!"

"Congratulations."

"Ah, it was easy. Any idiot can see how much your aunt loves you."

I looked away, staring at the heat lamp on the counter. Underneath it, two foil packages waited, each labeled *Raleigh's BnE*. That acronym used to stand for breaking and entering. Now it was bacon and egg. I picked them up, feeling the warm, soft foil, and decided the worst part of being undercover was lying to the nice people.

"Thanks, Birdie."

"Those are on me."

"No, really—"

"Don't ruin my luck."

"Okay." I smiled. "Thank you."

But she had already turned to the television opposite the cash register. A man dressed like an English beefeater raised a trumpet and began playing the opening tune. The Café fell into a reverential silence, as if the Pledge of Allegiance was being recited. The television shifted views, showing the track, the grandstands, the people, and a final shot of the inboard lights. The odds were almost locked in. The last shot was of the starting gate. In their confined spaces, the jockeys looked both compact and loose, straddling the horses. The trumpeter stretched out his last notes, extending that moment between lightning and thunder.

I checked my watch and walked over to the gingham-covered tables. If I ate fast, I could still get back to Eleanor. There was an open seat next to the old guy everyone called the Polish Prince. He was circling names on the betting sheet, slashing through others.

He looked at my food. "That stuff will kill you."

"Aunt Eleanor already told me."

"She would."

He glanced up at the screen, waiting for the race to start, and I bowed my head to give silent grace, then unwrapped the first sandwich. One hundred percent pure American grease, God bless it. I took my first bite as the starting bell rang and looked up to see the gates bursting open and horses leaping out.

"What the—?" The Polish Prince stood up.

Five horses splashed down the muddy track. But the camera flashed back to the starting gate. Three horses hadn't left, but one was jumping out. A bay horse. A second—black as night—reared inside its small space, then leaped like it was clearing a hurdle.

But the third horse . . .

I stood up.

The Polish Prince looked at me, pointing at the television. "Hey, ain't that your aunt's horse?"

Despite the wide-open gate, SunTzu refused to move. The jockey was whipping his crop, over and over. But the horse stood like a statue. Standing in the saddle, the jockey whipped some more. The horse stumbled forward.

But suddenly the camera returned to the race. The announcer was calling the front runners. When it returned to the gate, SunTzu had taken several steps, ponderous as a Clydesdale. His head was drooping and the jockey stood again, yanking on the reins. But the horse was already coming down fast, crumpling like a marionette whose strings had been slashed. And in one horrifying second I realized the jockey was stuck. He was trying to get his foot out of the stirrup. The animal listed to one side, going down, taking the rider with him. And pinning him underneath.

I ran for the door.

Chapter Eight

It's Brenna Beauty running ahead of—of—of—" The announcer
stuttered through the race, and I ran down the backstretch, jumping over puddles. "In the back, far back, we have, uh, uh—"

A crowd was gathering at the white rail fence, streaming from the
grandstands, pointing across the infield to the starting gate. At the
front end of the backstretch, a security guard stood at the gate that led
to the oval. His green rain poncho was soaked and he held a walkie-
talkie to his ear. I lifted my owner's badge, panting.

"That horse." Every breath feeling like a knife in my ribs. "That
horse belongs to my aunt."

He shook his head and pointed the radio's antenna over my
shoulder.

I turned around. A white van careened down the backstretch,
heading straight for the gate.

"Nobody gets out there before the vet."

A dented fender hung from the van's grill like a drunken grin,
and despite the rain, its side panel door was wide open. Behind the
wheel, a man punched the horn, blasting people out of his way. Doc
Madison. The vet.

Just before the van reached the gate, the guard pulled back the
metal barrier. The van headed for the dirt oval.

And I jumped in front of it.

"Hey!" the guard yelled. "What're you doing?!"

Planting my Ferragamos, I stretched out both arms. The pain in
my side almost doubled me over. But I heard the brakes squeal. The
van skidded into a puddle. Whipped forward on its rollers, the side

door slammed shut with a bang. I stared at the old man behind the cracked windshield. He looked murderous. I ran forward and placed one hand on the hood, gritty with dirt.

"That's a Hot Tin horse out there," I hollered. "I need to go with you."

The vet bared yellow teeth.

Keeping one hand on the hood, I scooted to the passenger side and jumped into the seat. It was covered with newspapers, so dry they crackled when I sat down. The vet hit the gas before my door was closed and shot past the guard, still holding the gate open. I felt a bump as we left the pavement. The vet clunked the gearshift into low. Wet soil splatted the undercarriage like strafing gunfire.

"You ever get in the way again," the vet growled, "I'll euthanize you."

He was a large man, in his late sixties, with a full head of pale curly hair that looked like it might once have been red. His fleshy face carried a small nose and mouth and lucent blue eyes. A Celtic face. And right now, a face that looked one beat away from an aneurysm. The meaty hands gripping the steering wheel jerked back and forth as he plowed down the turf.

"Radio!"

"Pardon?"

He took one hand off the wheel and pointed at the floor, at my feet. "Give me the radio!"

I didn't see it but kicked through another mound of newspapers and greasy paper bags from fast food restaurants until my foot touched something hard. I picked up the black radio. He yanked it out of my hand and pressed his thumb into the side button.

"This is Doc Madison. I want blue screens! On the track—pronto!"

He threw the radio to the dashboard, where it slid down to the cracked windshield. With each crooked swipe of the wipers, I saw more people streaming out of the grandstands. They stood two- and three-deep along the rail, oblivious to the rain, while the track's security force tried to contain them.

Swerving to a fishtailed stop, the vet jumped out. We were fifteen yards from the starting gate and the bay horse that had jumped out first now pranced in agitated circles. Two men tried to grab her dangling reins—the jockey and a tall, lanky guy who moved like a goofy rodeo clown.

The vet headed straight for SunTzu.

Climbing out of the van, I tried to take a mental photograph of the scene. It had a simple horrifying focus. Like a drawing by a traumatized child. A man riding a horse. But everything was happening in a one-dimensional plane. On the ground, the jockey's torso rose perpendicular to the colossal horse, while his legs disappeared under the saddle.

"Radio!" the vet yelled.

I turned back automatically, grabbing it from where it was wedged between dash and cracked glass. The vet snatched it from my hand again and pressed the button.

"Brent! Where are you? Get over to the starting gate—pronto!"

His barrel chest was heaving, his large face florid, as he waited for a reply. When I finally heard the assistant vet's reply, his voice sounded calm. Studiously calm. Like he knew the vet needed steadying.

"I'm getting my—"

The old man cut him off. "I don't care what you're doing. We need an ambulance. I don't see the track's EMT out here. Something must've happened in the stands. Call 911—now!"

Brent replied, something about the equine ambulance on its way, but the vet shoved the radio at me. And I wasn't listening either because the jockey was staring at the rain, unblinking.

His riding helmet was still clasped to his head, the chin strap cinched for a race that never came. But his head was rattling from side to side with the spasms in his neck. His Moorish skin was turning a sickly yellow.

"Son." The vet moved toward him carefully, like somebody approaching a land mine. "Just hold still. Help is coming. *Ayuda*. Coming."

The rain pinged the man's dark eyes. But the jockey didn't blink.

"Son?"

The lanky man resembling a rodeo clown rushed toward the vet. His emerald-green vest with the track's gold emblem hung askew. "I don't know what happened," he said. "Everything looked normal. So I hit the buzzer. But the horses, the horses. They wouldn't—I couldn't—"

The vet pushed him aside and began waving his arms. Four green trucks tore down the turf from the backstretch. The vet pointed at the white rail and the trucks swerved toward the infield, coming to a stop. A dozen men wearing maintenance coveralls jumped out, then pulled long PVC pipes from the truck beds, carrying them to the rail and stabbing the spiked ends into the soil. Another pipe was attached, and when they drew it away, a blue curtain unfurled, at least twelve feet high. The grandstands disappeared from view.

Two men approached the vet, carrying a thick plank of plastic. It looked like a sled, with ropes on every side. The vet told them to place it in front of the horse. SunTzu's legs twitched, as though running the race in midair. His long face lay on the turf, a puddle forming under his nose. Every breath blew ripples over the muddy water.

"*Ayuda!*" the vet called out to the jockey trying to restrain the bay horse. "*Ayuda nessessito!*"

The jockey caught the leather straps and handed them to the man in the green vest. Then he ran to the vet.

"I need you to talk to him," the vet said. "Make him feel *bueno*."

The jockey kneeled beside the rider. He spoke soft words, but the pinned man didn't respond. With one hand, the jockey made the sign of the cross. "*Deo,*" he pleaded. "*Mi Deo.*"

The vet looked at me. "Go back to my van, open the hatch. Pull out the second drawer and bring it here."

"Bring what?"

"The drawer!"

I didn't understand but followed his orders, walking back to the battered vehicle. Sand and silt from the turf were filling the footbed of my sandals, and when I lifted the tailgate door, I saw a wooden bureau. It was secured to the wall with two-by-fours and its six drawers had handles made of rope. I yanked the second ligature. The drawer contained several dozen unmarked white boxes and wasn't heavy, but carrying it kicked another round of pain down my right side. I held my breath, and when I saw the jockey on the ground, I felt ashamed of complaining.

Doc Madison tore open four boxes and removed six glass vials, each marked with pharmaceutical labels. Stabbing the vials' rubber ends with needles, he filled two large syringes. As he was finishing the second, Brent Roth drove up in a truck and jumped out, running to the vet's side.

"I'm here," he said.

"My grandmother could've walked here faster," the vet said.

"I was busy with—"

The vet cut him off again. "Did you call for another ambulance?"

Brent nodded. His acne seemed to weep in the rain. "I just—"

"I don't care. Go hold the head." The vet placed one syringe in the chest pocket of his shirt. Turning to the jockey who kneeled beside the rider, he said, "Tell him just a few minutes more."

The jockey whispered in Spanish. The rider stared at the sky.

Brent dropped on his knees beside SunTzu. The horse was breathing faster now, that same locomotive panic I heard in Solo two nights ago. When Brent leaned forward, I felt a wave of nausea washing up my throat. He slid his hands down the animal's perspiring neck, wrapping his arms into an immobilizing hold that looked a lot like what FBI agents used on belligerent suspects. Only Brent's touch was tender, gentle. And the animal didn't protest. When the vet lifted the syringe, his assistant leaned even farther forward, shielding the horse so that it wouldn't see the needle.

"Son?" Doc Madison said, speaking to the pinned rider. "I'm going to get this horse off you now."

The jockey translated, and Brent turned his head, looking back at the man under SunTzu. He squinted at him, as if noticing him for the first time. Then he turned around, watching as the vet pressed his thumb hard into the animal's jugular and stabbed the engorged vein with the needle. SunTzu twitched.

"It's okay," Brent whispered. "Shh. It's okay."

The Spanish jockey kept up a low murmur. His words were rhythmic, incantatory. After a minute I realized he was praying.

"Where's that ambulance?" the vet hissed.

"I told you," Brent said. "It's coming."

Emptying both syringes into the horse, the vet stood. His chest was heaving again. He turned to face the maintenance crew. Behind them the wall of blue curtains covered fifty feet of white rail, removing the entire grandstand from view. The men stood in a silent half circle around us, and except for the horse's breathing and the jockey's low, murmured prayers, the world seemed too quiet, almost aquatic, as though the rippling blue curtains were an ocean, hemming us onto the sandy bottom beneath gray cumulous waves, while the animal rode on its side like a sea horse, floating to its destination. But the rain told me this was real. I could hear the drops tapping on the maintenance crew's green baseball caps, the water rolling off the brims as the men stared down at the immobilized rider, their own faces slack with fear.

"That horse will be unconscious in ten seconds," the vet told the crew. "I want two of you on each leg. When I give the word, pull the horse forward. Onto the board. Stop when I say stop."

SunTzu was out cold before the vet finished speaking. Grabbing the ankles, the men dragged the horse forward, the weight heavy and awkward as a dead body.

Now the rider was exposed. His short legs splayed, thin as stilts. The jodhpurs were no longer white but stained with dirt and sweat and the thin contents of the man's bladder.

"*Ayuda?*" the other jockey asked.

"It's coming," the vet said. "Tell him not to move. Anything, don't move anything."

His soft Spanish fluttered through the rain, intonations rising and falling like some bird of language. And finally the pinned man blinked.

"Brent," the vet growled. "Where the—"

He pointed down the track. "There it is."

The white ambulance raced toward us, fishtailing through the mud. The red light on top was spinning but the siren made no sound, silenced to keep the other horses from panicking. But the muted wail gave me that underwater feeling again, along with the futile hope that maybe none of this was really happening. Maybe it was a dream, soundless and horrifying.

I looked over at the jockeys.

The kneeling man wiped the rider's face, brushing away the rain that now mixed with tears.

Chapter Nine

Eleanor's gray battleship had come to a stop inches from the medical clinic's wooden siding. When the vet's dilapidated van pulled up, I could see the queen herself, standing apart from the crowd gathered by the door. Trainers, grooms, pony riders. But only one or two jockeys.

"Raleigh!" she called out as I climbed from the vet's van.

She stood under a bright red umbrella held by Bill Cooper, but as I walked over, the trainer's cold gray eyes stayed fixed on the equine ambulance pulling up behind the van. The crowd closed in as the ambulance backed into the garage door. The expressions on their faces were a parade of fear and hope. Nobody liked what had happened, but tragedy rarely doused fierce competitive natures.

The vet mumbled behind me, "My client is the horse." He said it twice, heading for the door, then glanced over at me. "Just remember that. I work for the horse."

Cooper lifted the umbrella's wooden handle, ready to pass me the baton. But the rhinestones started glinting in Eleanor's glasses. She shook her head.

"No, Bill. I want Raleigh to stay with SunTzu."

"You—what?"

"Raleigh's going to stay."

"She's bad luck." He stopped. "No offense to you."

"None taken. But Raleigh was on the track and saw everything."

"But she doesn't know one end of the horse from the other."

Eleanor pointed her finger at him. Her emerald ring looked as serious as a papal declaration, and when she wagged her finger, the stone sparked an electric green, as if fueled by the friction between them, the tension between servitude and independence. "Bill Cooper, you told me yourself that horse doesn't like men. You said that's why Juan was having trouble with him."

"But—Eleanor—I'm the *trainer*."

She raised her chin and I held my breath, preparing for the verbal bomb.

But the vet interrupted her, turning to look at us. "The horse doesn't like men?"

Cooper didn't reply.

"Bill!" Eleanor bellowed. "Speak!"

"Yeah, fine. SunTzu doesn't like men. He rides faster with a female jockey. But there's only two and they both ride for Manchester."

Doc Madison turned, surveying the crowd now gathered around the equine ambulance.

"Ashley," he called out.

The girl in the pink shirt looked up.

"Get over here," the vet said.

She stepped from the crowd, her pale hair dripping wet.

"Wait," Cooper said. His voice sounded incredulous. "Ashley? What is this—amateur hour?"

Eleanor said, "I believe Doc Madison has made an excellent choice. It's about time that girl's infatuation with horses was put to productive use."

"Ashley's a *groom*," Cooper said. "I'm a *trainer*."

"That's quite enough complaining for one bad morning," Eleanor replied.

When he looked at me, Cooper's eyes iced over. His face was tight with unspoken resentments. Ashley followed the vet into the clinic, and Cooper handed Eleanor the umbrella handle, pivoted, and walked away. The crowd parted, letting through the bandy-legged man and his bad temper.

"As for you," Eleanor said, turning to me. "Don't miss it."

"Miss what?"

"The moment." She raised her chin. "Life is all memory except for the one present moment that goes by you so quick you hardly catch it going."

I really didn't have time for this. But. "Blanche?" I guessed. "*Streetcar?*"

"Oh, for heaven's sake," she said. "It was Mrs. Goforth. Now—go forth!"

≈

The horse was flying through the clinic upside down.

Slung into a canvas blanket, legs encircled by padded cuffs, SunTzu was being carried across the open space by a series of heavy chains and pulleys. The contraption ran along the ceiling's steel I-beams, and the horse's path was controlled by Brent Roth. He stood against the far wall, depressing a series of levers that carefully maneuvered the passed-out horse to an enormous padded exam table.

Doc Madison was pulling on latex gloves and a rubber apron. Behind him Ashley stood, her bright pink shirt marred by dark lashes of rain.

"Look out," the vet said calmly. "I think he's waking up."

The horse's back touched the table. SunTzu's eyes fluttered.

"Ashley, start talking to him." The vet turned toward a stainless steel counter, pulling open a cabinet full of syringes.

The horse's eyes were rolling in their sockets. Ashley ran forward as the horse began rattling his chains. She placed her small chapped hands on his face, and when his lips pulled back, revealing long teeth, she pressed her face into his rippling neck muscles, whispering into his ear. The horse made a hollow sound, like wind blowing over an empty bottle. I glanced at the vet. He was holding a filled syringe, waiting, I supposed, for the horse to settle down. But I saw a bittersweet expression crossing his old face. Pity, appreciation. Bafflement. All of it tumbling together until he placed his thumb on the animal's glistening neck and pricked the bulging vein with the needle. But before the syringe was empty, the horse slumped back into its sling.

"Paddles!" The vet dropped the syringe to the floor.

Brent wheeled a cart across the bare concrete floor, pushing it toward the vet. Doc Madison yanked two paddles from its side. A high whine filled the clinic as he grabbed a plastic bottle below and squirted clear gel onto one of the paddles, rubbing them together. The sound of the defibrillating electricity seemed to harmonize with the girl, suddenly crying.

"Help him," she whispered. "Please help him."

Brent wheeled a second cart toward the table, with a machine shaped like a box. Several long, crimped tubes extended from its side. A warning label on its side read Flammable. Oxygen. As the assistant rushed past, I caught an acrid odor. Almost a stench.

The vet pressed the paddles into SunTzu's brown chest.

"Hit!"

A burst of unsynchronized electricity slammed into the horse, quivering his body. The vet waited, watching as Brent pried open the animal's long jaw and shoved a crimped plastic tube down its throat.

"Hit!"

Brent stepped back. Another shock wave pounded the animal. The chains rattled again, only the horse didn't wake up.

"Again!"

The ionized air smelled like summer thunderstorms. And with each hit, the horse's noble face seemed to grow longer. The black whiskers drooped toward the floor. The oxygen tube slipped to one side. Ashley backed up and reached for her own throat. Dirt was nestled in her fingernails and it spread across her chin as she covered her mouth. The vet gave one more hit. His own chest heaved again, but as he gazed at the horse, waiting, his old face collapsed into itself. Finally, he let go of the paddles, dropping them in a clatter of plastic and metal and defeat.

"No . . ." Ashley looked at the vet. "No. You can't . . . He can't be dead."

The vet continued to stare at the horse. His eyes had a distracted expression, like he was listening to his own thoughts, and when he stepped forward, he touched a gloved finger to SunTzu's chest. He tapped the spot.

Ashley said, "What's wrong?"

The vet touched the spot again. Right where the horse's brown coat formed a cowlick, the hair on either side meeting in the middle of his chest.

"Swabs," the vet said quietly. "Please."

Brent was also staring at the dead horse. On his pale skin the acne looked like measles.

"Brent!"

He jumped.

"Swabs!"

Stumbling for the counter, he pulled several cotton swabs from a tall jar and handed them to Doc Madison. The vet touched one to SunTzu's chest. When he pulled it away, the bleached cotton tip was pink.

"Is that . . . blood?" Ashley said. "He's bleeding? Why is he bleeding?"

The vet didn't answer.

"You did that," she said. "With those paddles. You hurt him!"

The vet shook his head and dabbed another swab, then dropped them both into a plastic bag, sealing the top.

Evidence, I thought. *He's gathering evidence.*

Ashley's voice quavered. "What happened to him?"

Keeping his back to her, standing at the counter, the vet wrote something on a small pad.

Ashley turned to Brent. "Tell me what happened!"

"Who knows." He shrugged. "Maybe he hit something. When he fell on the turf."

"He's *bleeding*."

"Get a grip on yourself," Brent said. "He's dead. You need to move on."

Her lips closed, but a keening sound was leaking through her mouth. I turned away, unwilling to watch all that agony and confusion distort her pretty face. Instead I stared at the horse. Stiff and immobile on the exam table, he looked perfect and dead, like the taxidermist had already come.

"I'll send the swabs to the lab." The vet waited for my eyes to move from the horse. "If Eleanor wants, I'll do X-rays."

X-rays. On a dead horse.

"Something looks suspicious to you?" I asked.

He glanced at the girl. She came forward again, grabbing the horse by its neck, burying her face in his mane. She cried into the bristly coat.

"Not SunTzu," she said. "Not SunTzu."

She repeated his name over and over again, until it sounded to me like she was saying, *Not you too, not you too . . .*

Chapter Ten

After Ashley bolted, sobbing, I left the clinic. I had taken a long, hard look at the wound on SunTzu's chest, and my years visiting crime scenes gave me some basic knowledge about blood evidence and injuries. The mark on the horse's chest looked like some kind of shallow puncture wound. But it was difficult to tell what sort of object had struck him because of the thick coat of hair.

I felt almost numb, walking across the backstretch toward the barns. Over the loudspeaker the announcer's voice sounded tinny. It ran rapid-fire without pauses. The races had resumed. The show must go on. But the rain had stopped, and the sun was peeking from behind the clouds, leaving misty tendrils in the humid air. The moist warmth was almost cloying, like summer air back home in Virginia.

And just like that, I felt homesick. Lonely. Alone.

I heard Eleanor before I'd even reached the corner of Hot Tin's barn. Bill Cooper's office door was open. I stood for a moment, listening, just out of view.

"You're wrong," she said.

"Eleanor, I get it. She's your niece. But she's not helping."

"She's learning."

"Learning how to mess us up? I don't want to give you an ultimatum, but at some point you're going to have to choose. Her or me."

There was a considerable silence. When I stepped into the doorway, Cooper had his dusty boots kicked up on a steel desk. The bulldog heels rested beside an open bottle of Jack Daniel's. Eleanor, to his right, perched on a worn loveseat, holding a shot glass like a teacup.

"We heard the news." She lifted her chin. "The grim reaper has put up his tent on our doorstep."

I nodded.

"Blanche." She threw back the whiskey in her glass and shivered. "Scene ten."

"Another way to say that, Eleanor, is we're cursed with bad luck." Cooper kicked his boots off the desk. "Bad, bad luck. And I won't stick around for much more."

He pushed past me in the doorway and strode down the gallery. The stabled horses watched him pass, swiveling their long heads, following his exit. I watched him too, but thought of another playwright. The one who said that a man doth protest too much. All the bluster from Cooper, all the finger-pointing at me. But the barn's trouble began long before I arrived at Emerald Meadows. Was he really blaming me—or shifting blame?

Eleanor said, "You have a question that hangs in the air."

I did. But I offered her a different one. "Do you want Doc Madison to take X-rays?"

"I want a full autopsy." She plunked the glass on the desk, stood up, then wavered a moment. Tipsy. "Did he suffer?"

"I thought you didn't care about the horses."

"You've misunderstood. I don't *want* to care. That is entirely different from not caring. Tell me what happened."

I described the events in the clinic, and the wound. "The vet seemed suspicious about the injury. He took samples. Without my asking."

"That old coot is a good vet."

"In all your years of racing, have you ever seen the starting gate malfunction like that?"

"Never. But it has tires, doesn't it?"

The starting gate did have wheels. It was rolled to different places on the track, depending on a race's length. "What do the tires have to do with anything?"

"Life has taught me a valuable lesson," she said. "If something has tires or testicles, it's going to cause trouble." She swayed again. "Take my elbow. I'm drunk."

We walked from Cooper's small office into the stables. The moist air was dusted with alfalfa.

I said, "Did you notice who won that first race?"

"The long shot. Cuppa Joe only placed."

He was the black horse, the one that jumped out as though clearing a hurdle. "Convenient results," I said. "The favorite didn't win."

"Especially good for a certain bookie. How much did you wager?"

"Two grand."

"I'll consider it tuition."

Juan carried water buckets toward the stalls. He glanced our way, paused, nodded at Eleanor, then lowered his eyes. He did not acknowledge me.

"They think you're bad luck," Eleanor said.

"I don't believe in luck."

"Why should you? For that matter, why should I?"

As we were crossing under the eaves, I saw his narrow shoulders coming toward us. Like a mouse sniffing for good cheese, Tony Not Tony tiptoed forward. He wore rubber slip-ons over his tasseled leather loafers. I decided he was coming to see if I wanted to place another bet. To make up for the 2K I blew on "the favorite."

"Eleanor," he breathed.

"What is it, Anthony?" She sounded irritable.

"I thought you should know, I heard something. But maybe not."

"Oh, for heaven's sake. Spit it out!"

"Mr. Yuck." Tony Not Tony smiled. "He would like to see you."

Chapter Eleven

A security guard stood outside an unmarked door inside the betting office building. He was tall and black with pale green eyes. When he saw Eleanor, he touched the brim of his cap.

"Sorry 'bout your horse, Mrs. Anderson."

"Thank you, Lou. Now could you please tell me where I might find that creature from the deep?"

Lou's mouth tightened, fighting a smile. He reached for the door, twisting the knob. "Here you go."

The room was square and bland, the walls white and empty. An oblong table was encircled by chairs, but nobody was sitting in them. Not Sal Gagliardo, who stood next to the one window. Not his trainer, a belligerent man named Jimmy Bello, who was muttering under his breath. And not the only other female who owned her own barn at Emerald Meadows, Claire Manchester.

They each faced the track's head of security, a man known as Mr. Yuck.

"Eleanor," he said, "how nice you could join us."

He extended his hand to me. It was wide, almost square, like the defibrillator paddles used on SunTzu. "We haven't met," he said. "Charles Babbitt."

We hadn't met, but I knew a bit about Mr. Babbitt. For more than fifteen years he had run the security at Emerald Meadows. His tenure raised a red flag with the FBI. For all we knew, he kept his job by looking the other way. Or even by staying tucked into Sal Gag's pocket.

Shaking the paddle, I decided either theory could be right. There was something definitely creepy about the guy.

"Raleigh David," I lied. "Nice to meet you."

"Pleasure," he said.

Placing his hands behind his back, he turned to the gathering.

"Three horses were clearly affected by the bad start this morning," he said. "I've called you here because each of you owns one of those horses. Cuppa Joe, Loosey Goosey, and SunTzu."

"Yo, Perry Madison," said Jimmy Bello, the trainer. "You want to fast-forward to some kinda point? I don't have all day."

The security chief swiveled his head. It was a large head, hemispheric and balding. The forehead's wide plane was punctuated by furrowed black brows that slanted over ever-narrowing eyes. The nose was flat, almost topographically insignificant, but the mouth was full and provided the most clues regarding his nickname. Moist as torn fruit, the red lips pulled down at the corners in an expression of permanent distaste, like a man ingesting poison. Charles Babbitt's face looked like the sticker that poison control centers placed on medicine bottles to warn children that the contents would make them very sick.

"Mr. Gagliardo."

Sal Gag gazed out the window, looking bored. The unlit cigar waggled between his fingers, and outside, jockeys were leading horses down the backstretch by their bridles, returning to the barns after the last race. The horses kept their heads down; the rain had returned.

"Mr. Gagliardo."

Sal Gag hoisted his heavy brows. "Yeah."

"There is one crucial difference here. Unlike the other two horses, your barn benefited from the bad start."

"What benefit? My horse didn't win."

Mr. Yuck turned toward the door. As if hearing a cue, the guard named Lou appeared. He had with him the nervous man from this morning, the one who reminded me of a rodeo clown.

"I believe you know Harrold Moser."

The guard escorted Harrold Moser to a chair; Harrold dropped into it. The guard stood behind him.

Mr. Yuck gave me a dour smile. "Harrold runs the start."

Harrold had long legs and they were bouncing on the balls of his feet. Mr. Yuck scooped two remote controls from the conference table and moved his thumbs over the buttons, closing the slatted blinds, darkening the room, and clicking on a flat-screen television that hung on the wall behind us.

"Harrold has offered to describe for us exactly what he saw," Mr. Yuck intoned. "I wanted all significant parties to be present for this information. Simultaneously. This place runs on rumors." He looked directly at Sal Gag and offered another dour smile. "And speculations."

But the bookie was staring at Harrold with a dark and unrelenting gaze. I suddenly wondered whether Mr. Yuck really was in the mobster's pocket.

"I already told you," Harrold said, much too loudly. "Everything looked normal."

"Everything?" asked Mr. Yuck.

"Okay, not everything." Harrold's legs beat a fast rhythm, and his sudden capitulation made me even more suspicious. Liars enjoyed throwing false crumbs down dead-end trails.

"Go on," said Mr. Yuck.

"One thing was Cuppa Joe."

"Please, tell us about it."

"He's a fighter, you know." Harrold continued to speak too loudly, as though he wanted to transmit the words to somebody in the next room. "That horse, he likes to mess with his competition. Last week he bit a filly in the next gate."

"*My* filly," said Claire Manchester. She was small and tan, almost elfin. "My best runner. She's traumatized. It was total male harassment."

"Yo, toots," said Jimmy Bellow. "Enough with the women's rights."

"Harrold." Mr. Yuck paced in front of the chair. "Did Cuppa Joe indulge in any harassments before this morning's race?"

"No. Not that I saw. But maybe the jockeys saw something."

"Not going with that one," said Bello. "No *hablo español*. And I ain't trusting no translations."

"So the horses were in the gate." Mr. Yuck's hands circled around his back again, his mouth drawing down at the corners. "Take us through the next moments."

"Okay, so, you know, I stare down the line from the cage."

I cleared my throat. "What's 'the cage'?"

Mr. Yuck turned professorial. "The cage is a three-foot box positioned perpendicular to the starting gates. It allows the starter, in this case Harrold, to look at the line of horses before the race begins."

I stared at Harrold. He wasn't the guy I'd pick for that job. Not only was he too tall for a three-foot cage, he had the nervous system of a caffeinated fruit fly. The long, skinny legs kept rattling up and down, thin as sabers, slicing the tension in the air.

"So, okay, I had my eyes on Cuppa Joe, you know, to see what he was gonna do. But all the horses seemed skittish. The rain. Horses, you know—you never know. But I just need one second. And there it was, everything fine. I heard the electric arm lock the back gates—"

I cleared my throat again. Their faces turned toward me.

"The back door is locked?" I asked.

Claire Manchester sighed. She wore a sleeveless shirt, her arms tightly muscled. "We don't have time for this."

Maybe it was a stupid question, but Raleigh David wouldn't know. And Raleigh Harmon needed to know.

"If you need some kind of tutorial," Claire said, "go get one. And while you're at it, find somebody to work that bad luck off you." She looked at Eleanor. "Sorry, Eleanor, but it's true."

Eleanor raised her chin. "All cruel people describe themselves as paragons of frankness."

Claire frowned, annoyed. "What's that supposed to mean?"

Eleanor squeezed my hand. "Mrs. Goforth again, scene two."

"Back to Harrold," said Mr. Yuck gloomily. "Please explain to Miss David how the gates work."

"It's just a word, *locked*. The gates aren't locked. I don't know why we say that. Because horses, you know, they can bolt. Freak out. They get all these weird signals, stuff that doesn't even make sense to us people. If you locked 'em in there, somebody'd get hurt."

Claire said, "Somebody did get hurt, moron."

"Oh, the mendacity," Eleanor said. "I need to sit down."

I helped her into a chair.

Harrold said, even louder, "Is anybody listening? I'm trying to tell you guys, everything looked okay. You know, with some tension. Because it's the first race. And the track's wet. But Cuppa Joe, he—"

Suddenly Harrold stopped.

"Ye-es?" intoned Mr. Yuck.

"I was gonna say, you know, Cuppa Joe was dying to run."

"Interesting choice of words. Do continue."

Harrold's eyes flitted around the faces in the room, searching for sympathy. But Sal Gag looked like he wanted to light his Havana so he could stick it in one of Harrold's nervous eyes. Jimmy Bello was sneering, and Claire Manchester began tapping soiled fingers on her cell phone, texting someone. Harrold looked at Eleanor. She wore the expression of an actress who feared the play was going to close after the first performance. And her chin was rising.

But Harrold got there first. "The horses, you know, were all in place. The back gate locked—closed. And I hit the button."

Mr. Yuck turned toward me, sensing another question. The dismal smile spread across his doughy face. "The button to which Harrold is referring opens each gate simultaneously. All at once," he added, as if the word was beyond my comprehension. "That button also freezes the totalizator."

"Totalizator?" I asked.

"Hey, Kojak." Bello again. "It's the tote board. Nobody calls it the Totalizator."

"Thank you, Mr. Bello. But I prefer real names." His ominous tone implied he knew his own nickname. "That same button also triggers the bell that can be heard at any public location on track property."

The bell. Harrold's loud voice. I suddenly realized the man was going deaf. If he sat next to that bell, he heard it five times a day, six days a week.

"But when all the horses didn't take off," Harrold said, "I thought maybe the doors got stuck. I leaned over the line, trying to see the gates." He stretched his neck out over his jiggling legs, demonstrating for us. "And then I saw, you know . . ."

"No, we don't know." Mr. Yuck aimed the second remote at the television. "But this is what you saw."

An image of the starting gate flashed on the screen. It showed the empty gates from a side view. Mr. Yuck clicked through stilled video images, showing the horses entering the gate, one by one. Jockeys adjusted grips and helmets, or made the sign of the cross over their bright silks. And the horses' faces—brown and bay, black and chestnut—were as beautiful as marble busts. The gates blew open.

In slow motion, the animals' long heads seemed to stretch out. The front legs kicked forward. Shiny coats shimmered over rippling muscles.

Cuppa Joe hesitated. Loosey Goosey didn't move. And SunTzu . . .

Eleanor placed the back of her hand across her forehead. "I can't bear to watch this again."

I glanced at the people in the room. Watching the images, Sal Gag's face seemed as implacable as stone. Jimmy Bello scowled. But Claire Manchester's dark blue eyes were shifting between the two Italian men. Her shrewd expression suggested she sensed a traitor.

When I glanced back at the television, Cuppa Joe was proving his competitive streak. Though he didn't leave the gate for several frames, when he finally took off he leaped like a standing long jumper, and that first stride drew a moment of silence in the room. It was sheer appreciation for a curvet of power, the absolute might of a horse that could cover fifteen feet from a stationary position. Clinging to his back in Abbondanza's bright pink silks, the jockey looked like a tropical fish holding on to a black leviathan.

Mr. Yuck nodded. "That horse seems suspiciously healthy, Mr. Gagliardo."

"Everything's suspicious to you." Sal Gag tugged back his cuff-linked shirtsleeve, exposing a gold Rolex, and checked the time. "How long you plan to string this out?"

Mr. Yuck hit the remote again. "Let us examine those horses left behind."

The images shifted to normal speed. Cuppa Joe was tearing up the muddy track. But when the picture returned to the starting gate, the jockey riding Loosey Goosey had already jumped from his saddle. His face looked familiar—the rider who translated for the vet this morning—and in the next gate SunTzu was pitching forward, dragging the jockey down. Watching it again, I felt the futile pain of seeing a car crash in slow motion. And I didn't want to see the jockey's face again, that look of shock, that realization of defeat in his soul. Lowering my gaze, I stared at the bottom of the screen. The groomed turf had the soothing appearance of a mandala, all the soil combed into fine rows still untouched by the horse. I could even see the drops of rain, clinging to the grains of sand.

"Harrold," said Mr. Yuck, "how much money did you put on Cuppa Joe?"

The silence that fell on the room felt like the moment just before a bomb detonates.

"How much?" Mr. Yuck repeated.

"I didn't place a bet." Harrold wiped his forehead. "That would be illegal."

"Yes. It would. How much?"

"My sister placed the bet."

Mr. Yuck gave his sick smile. "Fifty dollars on Cuppa Joe, wasn't it? Not to win, even though the horse was the favorite. But fifty dollars to place. Did you know something, Harrold?"

Harrold looked at his jiggling legs, staring at them as if they belonged to another man.

Claire Manchester almost spit. "I knew it. Abbondanza's as crooked as cat poo."

"Poo?" said Jimmy Bello. "What is this, kindergarten?"

But Mr. Yuck had turned his gloomy gaze on Sal Gag. "When Harrold placed that bet on Cuppa Joe—"

Harrold jumped in. "My sister—"

"Doesn't matter." Mr. Yuck hit the remote, backing up the film to the first tragic images. Then he zoomed in on the three gates. "The track's rules specifically state that Emerald Meadows employees are prohibited from betting on races in which they are working. Tell me, Harrold, what did you plan to do with your two hundred dollars?"

Sal Gag made a guttural sound, deep in his throat. "Two hundred bucks? You hauled me in here for a measly two hundred bucks?"

Mr. Yuck had placed a paddle hand on Harrold's shoulder and squeezed. Harrold winced.

"While Harrold broke the rules to make some money," Mr. Yuck said, "I am certain that you, Mr. Gagliardo, and you, Mr. Bello, and perhaps even you, Miss Manchester, have profited even more handsomely. The only person who lost in this instance was Eleanor."

"Mendacity," she said as her chin came up. "Mendacity's the system we live in. Liquor is one way out and death's the other." She sighed. "Brick said that, in act two."

But I was the only person who heard her. The other three erupted with a round of protests: Sal Gag saying it wasn't his problem that Harrold bet on the race, Bello tossing out insults, and Claire accusing them both of equine abuse. Mr. Yuck gave a dour retort, but his exact words passed me by because I was looking at the image on the television. Specifically, the turf soil. It looked like mud rubbed across the screen with a dark line bisecting the brown area. I stepped closer. It looked like some kind of shadow. Maybe. But it was raining then. No sun. When I turned around, Jimmy Bello was leaning into Mr. Yuck. And the security chief wore a weird smile, like that involuntary rictus gripping a person's mouth right before they vomit.

I waved my hand. "Excuse me." The next words required effort. "Gentlemen. I have another question. Did anyone look at the turf?"

"Yeah, it's mud," Bello said. "And if your horse is a pansy, that's your problem. Cuppa Joe's a mudder. So shoot me."

Tempted, I turned to Mr. Yuck. "Could you reverse the film, back to where the doors open?"

"Gates," he corrected, putting me in my place.

"Yes, the gates." I pretended to be embarrassed. "And would it be possible to zoom in on SunTzu's gate?"

He clicked and clicked until SunTzu's beautiful face pierced my heart. The horse looked confident in the gate, completely unaware that the next seconds would finish him.

"Please keep zooming in. On the turf."

The soil grew into a vague brown smudge with large silver freckles, and the dark line was clearly visible now, though slightly out of focus. I pointed to it. "At first I thought it was a shadow. But we all know there was no sun this morning."

Harrold wiped his forehead again.

Mr. Yuck pressed the remote button. The shadowed line changed to a series of bursting blurs, each shaped like a funnel and each erupting from the ground. Pyroclastic blasts. They lasted two frames, then disappeared. I glanced at Mr. Yuck. The corners of his mouth were coming down, like some overfed trout caught in an ever-tightening lure. He reversed the film again, zooming in and out. We saw SunTzu balk. Loosey Goosey buck, causing the jockey to jump. And Cuppa Joe, who waited, then leaped like a coiled spring.

"How incredibly well timed," said Mr. Yuck. "Makes one wonder if the horse knew to expect something."

"Gimme a break," said Jimmy Bello. But his voice had lost its confident bluster.

Mr. Yuck turned to the guard named Lou, who had remained silent behind us. So silent I almost forgot about him.

"Lieutenant, get the vehicles ready," Mr. Yuck said. "We're all going to take a ride."

Chapter Twelve

The afternoon rain fell like graphite shavings, dull and gray. I gazed out the windshield of the track's official Suburban, which was carrying us to the turf. All of us except Eleanor and Sal Gag. They both had declined to see the starting gate for themselves. Mr. Yuck didn't argue with them, since he had a representative from each barn. I sat on the second-row seat with Jimmy Bellow, separated by Claire Manchester, who chatted on her cell phone.

"No comment," she said.

A *Seattle Times* reporter was calling each barn, putting together a piece about the morning's bad start. He tried Eleanor first. She gave him Big Daddy's extended soliloquy about mendacity from *Cat on a Hot Tin Roof.* I figured Sal Gag and Jimmy Bello wouldn't talk to the media. But Claire Manchester took the call inside the car. As I listened to her answers, my stomach growled. My only food today was dry toast, skim milk, and a bite of one BnE in the Quarterchute. But I almost lost my appetite listening to Claire's answers. Whatever the question, she always came back to herself—how she felt, how things were when she was a jockey, how frightening it was for her to see Loosey Goosey bucking in the gate.

"And they're doing some investigation," she added. "I'm going to look at the gate right now."

I turned in my seat. Harrold sat behind us on the third-row seat, by himself. The expression in his eyes reminded me of so many suspects. So scared that a guilty conscience was going into overdrive.

"No comment," Claire said. "But I think they suspect somebody messed around with the starting gate. Not my barn. Another barn."

There was a pause. I assumed the reporter was asking, *Which barn?*

"No comment. But it's not my barn. And it's not Hot Tin."

"Hey, Norma Rae," said Jimmy Bello. "All you're doing is feeding blood to the sharks."

Our driver slowed down. The starting gate was thirty yards ahead. Claire suddenly snapped her phone shut, without saying good-bye.

Standing in the rain, Mr. Yuck waited for us. He was wearing a green fedora now and the color clashed with his pasty skin. Raising his cheerless voice to the rain, he said, "I don't want any complaints later. Or any rumors. You're all witnesses to whatever we find."

He wasn't being nice; he was being smart. A breeding ground for paranoia, Emerald Meadows' owners didn't trust management, and the management suspected the barns of illegal activity that could get the track's license revoked by the state. All that distrust made under-cover work difficult, but now I felt a sudden gratefulness. Without that chronic ill will, Raleigh David would never get this close to the crime scene. And once again, something like hope floated around my heart. Hard evidence. It would help me push back against OPR.

"Lieutenant Campbell." Mr. Yuck nodded at the security officer Eleanor called "Lou." "I am considering you another witness. Does anyone object?"

"Yo." Jimmy Bello held out both hands, palms open to the rain. "Notice something? It's raining. Crank up the show."

Mr. Yuck turned and walked to the starting gate. He had a churning stride, the short steps digging deep into the soil. The start-ing gate had been rolled back to its position for the first race, at the three-quarter mile mark. The small tires had carved channels into the turf, filling with rainwater, and hoof marks pocked the surface. Staring at the soil, I felt a desperate desire to collect samples. It was a mixture of sandy quartz and fine clay. Under a microscope I was cer-tain a portion of the sand grains would have angular shapes. It was called sharp sand, or builder's sand, used in concrete and gardening projects to aerate the soil. Somewhere out there, an expert waited to explain the exact proportions necessary for running horses, and where these soils came from. But as Raleigh David, I could only stare at the hoof-shaped puddles and feel grateful that the track was so well groomed before the first race. Otherwise I might've missed the shadow. It was the most elementary lead in forensic geology: always check the topography for unnatural changes in a soil's profile.

"Well, well, well." Mr. Yuck bent down, digging his paddle hands into the soil. "What do we have here?"

I wanted to scream, *Stop! Put on gloves—you're contaminating evidence!*

He pulled at the object buried in the soil. A black tube came up, running like a buried cable. I bit my cheek so hard I tasted blood. *Please! Call the state lab!*

He yanked again. The black tube ran across the turf to the infield's white rail.

Bello said, "The horses tripped over that?"

"You moron," Claire said. "None of the horses tripped."

Harrold was dancing again. "I never saw it. I swear, I was in the cage. How would I see that?"

Suddenly they turned to me. It was apparently my turn to say something.

"Doesn't security watch over the turf?" I asked.

Mr. Yuck glanced at the lieutenant, who looked at the track official who had driven the Suburban. He was management, I guessed. A pink and stocky man, he drew himself up, sending the accumulated rainwater sluicing off his emerald-green hat.

"Of course we watch the track," he said.

Claire crossed her arms. "Twenty-four seven?" She still wore the sleeveless shirt, oblivious to the weather, and the drops of rain beaded on her tanned, oiled skin like it was hide. "You can account for every single minute, what goes on out here?"

"Well . . ."

"Uh-huh," she said. "Who's out here at night?"

"Night?"

Bello said, "Yeah, night. You know, when the sun don't shine?"

The official looked indignant. "We can't see the track at night. It's pitch black out here."

"Is that some kinda joke?" Bello said.

Mr. Yuck stepped forward. "Lights cost money."

"So what are we paying fees for?" Claire Manchester pointed her cell phone at him. "A couple thousand every month—for what? Stressed-out horses and some kind of virus that's ruining my barn. Now somebody's burying lines that—"

"Hey." Bello turned to me. "You saw it first."

I tried to look dumb. "Pardon?"

"On the video." He scowled. "You were looking for it."

In the humid air, I smelled fresh scapegoat. And Bello looked ravenous for someone to blame.

"And," he said, "you were in the barn when it caught fire."

Claire picked up the scent. "She was also in the clinic when SunTzu died. Two dead horses in one week, and she happens to be connected to both. I don't like coincidences."

I didn't either. Standing there, reeking of scapegoat, I felt my brain trying to slap into hard reality, into something void of emotions. What came back was physics. The situation was some horrible example of the first law of thermodynamics, where energy changes from one form to another but can't be destroyed. Right now, my only hope was to go with the current. I sighed.

"You caught me," I said. "I'm a coward. I couldn't watch that jockey get crushed again, so I was looking at the turf. When I saw that dark line, it looked weird."

Bello looked over at Claire.

She shook her head. "Still too convenient. I heard she asked to stay in the stall with Solo. And she rode out here with the vet this morning."

"You're forgetting something," I said. "Both of those horses belonged to my aunt."

"I didn't forget that," she said. "I was just wondering what other disaster you have planned for the last week of the season."

When I looked at Mr. Yuck, he wore a sour yet pleased expression that said his favorite dish was being served up. And it wasn't fresh scapegoat. It was the perfect target.

"Y'all are way off base." I sounded baffled, and it was genuine. Here I was, finally telling the truth—that I looked away out of cowardice—and I was being accused of lying. By these people. These secretive people. The irony made my head hurt. "Here are the facts. I stayed with Solo because she was sick. I was in the clinic because Doc Madison wanted women in there with SunTzu, and because Aunt Eleanor ordered me to go."

The summer rain felt cloying, suffocating. I waited for somebody to reply and counted the drops as they hit my head—four, five, six. And my brain said my next best shot was to try the second law of thermodynamics. Entropy. Chaos. Diversion.

"This is ridiculous." I reached into my bag, pulling out my cell phone. "I'm calling Aunt Eleanor."

"Please do." Mr. Yuck's ill smile was growing. "And I'll call the police. Nobody leaves until they give their statement. Especially you, Miss David."

Chapter Thirteen

At 4:00 p.m., after a day that felt seventy-two hours long, I followed Eleanor's car south on Interstate 5. She was woozy from the day's drama and her two shots of whiskey with Cooper, and wanted to make sure the battleship returned to port. I didn't mind being her escort. The Ghost made every trip feel like a vacation, especially after my two Bureau-assigned heaps, one of which was a K-car with vinyl bench seats. The other car was purple and stunk of perp vomit. With Italian butter-leather caressing my back, I gazed out the smooth wash of windshield. The temperamental summer rain was taking another break and the spent clouds splintered sunlight. Mount Rainier's peaks looked as gilded as crowns of ice. I could've stared at that view forever, but my rearview mirror held an even more interesting picture.

A black Cadillac left Emerald Meadows when we did. Its darker-than-normal tinted windows led me to assume it was a private limo. But it should have passed us by now because Eleanor was motoring down the freeway at forty miles an hour, peering through her steering wheel and singing along with the golden oldies on her tape deck. Irate motorists kept giving her colorful hand signals, conveying their sentiments about her speed, or lack of. But the black Caddy hung back six or seven cars. When she took the exit for Tacoma's North Slope neighborhood, it did the same, then dropped back a little farther at J Street, when Eleanor swung the Lincoln into the curving driveway of her old Victorian. One bejeweled hand came out the window, waving good-bye to her escort. I waited at the curb until she was inside the house. When I pulled back into the street, the Cadillac was a block behind me.

"All right," I told the growling engine. "Let's roll."

Stepping on the gas, I shifted into second almost immediately. Just before Division Street, the car begged for third. We made a sharp cut left and flew back uphill to the North Slope. Obeying my commands with the walnut steering wheel, the tires stuck to the pavement like unrequited love. When we plunged down the hill again, I opened up the engine and zipped down Dock Street to the 1700 block and into the parking lot for Thea's Landing.

The Caddy was nowhere in sight.

"Well done." I patted the burled wood dashboard and gathered my belongings. For the first time in days, weeks, I was smiling, feeling so good I started to plan my next meal. Unfortunately, there wasn't anything to eat in the condo, and as I was crossing the parking lot to my building, I was debating whether to go shopping or eat out. But something caught my eye. I turned, looking at the street.

The Cadillac passed slowly. The late-afternoon sun made the black paint sparkle like crushed anthracite. And the driver was hidden behind the dark glass.

I felt a sudden temptation. *Fire up the Ghost, chase him down.*

But the thought was doused by the image of OPR, and my boss in Richmond, warming their hands over my incinerating career.

Let it go. I keyed open the lobby door. *For now.*

Thea's Landing was a sleek and modern complex, named for the matriarch who founded the largest fleet of tugboats in the Northwest, Thea Foss, a Tacoma pioneer who passed away in 1927. The brand-new building sat on the waterfront, and the lobby still smelled of gypsum board and the volatile compounds leaking from the walls' inoffensive beige paint. I keyed open the brushed nickel mailbox labeled *#202, Raleigh David* and walked up two flights. The biggest envelope in the pile of mostly junk mail had the return address of Three Springs, Vesuvius, Virginia. The David family's estate. Supposed estate. I was coming down the hall to my door, turning over the envelope to check the tamper-proof seal, when I saw two brown bags sitting outside my door. I walked up to them carefully, looking over my shoulder.

They were full of groceries.

Eleanor, I decided. Probably a delivery of rye bread and lettuce.

Carrying the bags inside, I set them on the polished granite countertops that gleamed from lack of use. My two-bedroom corner unit had a balcony that overlooked a small harbor. The place was so far beyond my budget it was laughable. But Eleanor hadn't batted one false eyelash. Like the Ghibli sports car, she insisted her niece would have only the best. She and Harry never had children, and I sometimes wondered if she was making up for that by spoiling me.

Picking up the envelope again, I inspected the back flap. If there had been any tampering, the nearly invisible tape would have come off in annoyingly small pieces. But the seal was intact, and inside I found two smaller envelopes, both addressed to me.

The real me. Raleigh Harmon.

The first note was from Aunt Charlotte, telling me that my mom was "okay." My eyes burned reading her big exuberant handwriting. Such sweet deceived words. Deceived by me. She had sent the note to the Seattle field office, believing my assignment took me far away. Yet I was less than an hour from her house on Capitol Hill. I hated lying. Especially to the people I loved.

The second note was sent "care of Charlotte Harmon." The ecru stationery was embossed with a silver scalloped edging and had the fine calligraphy used for important occasions. When I flipped it over, the envelope showed its own tamper-resistant seal: melted red wax stamped with the letter W. It stood for Weyanoke. My fiancé's estate in Virginia. A real honest-to-goodness estate. Three thousand acres along the James River, Weyanoke had been in the Fielding family since the 1700s and DeMott planned to live every day on that land. I was supposed to join him there right after we married on the cliff above the river. We would build a home on five acres, not far from his family's three-story Georgian mansion that was almost four hundred years old. The place was storybook beautiful, secure on the National Register of Historic Places, and no way could I see myself living there.

I stared at the calligraphy. It looked like an announcement.

He wouldn't . . . No. He wouldn't set a wedding date without asking me. Would he?

I tore open the envelope. And let out a sigh. The invitation was for a baby shower. His sister MacKenna was expecting a baby. MacKenna Fielding Morgan. The sister who hated me. I glanced at the details and found a small handwritten note inside.

Raleigh,

DeMott says I shouldn't bother sending you this invitation. He says you're working on something top secret and can't come. But I thought you would like to know what's going on here at Weyanoke. The family is very excited for the impending arrival of another generation!

And DeMott misses you, terribly. Please come home soon.

With love, Jillian

Jillian. His older sister. Who actually liked me.

I shredded the notes for security reasons, then unpacked the groceries while listening to the messages on Raleigh David's answering machine. The first came from a campaign worker, begging me to vote for some congressman who promised to "clean up Washington, DC." The campaign worker, I decided, was probably also dumb enough to believe in luck.

I pulled the first item from the bag. Hamburger buns. The second message began as I removed a jar of Kraft mayonnaise and a golden brick of Tillamook cheese. In the background, an earnest environmentalist tried to scare me about global warming, carbon emissions, and how coal plants would bring an end to the human race. Just for that, I left the refrigerator door wide open. Then I opened the freezer and left that open too. The second grocery bag contained frozen French fries. And one box of hamburger patties. And a note.

Bake at 425 degrees. Dip in mayo.

P.S. Shrink at 8:00 p.m.

Jack

The environmentalist signed off, and in the ensuing silence every spotless surface glared back at me. I slammed both doors and checked my watch.

It was three hours later on the East Coast. And at Weyanoke they dressed for dinner. Summer guests were constant, parading through the grand dining room. Richmond's corporate lawyers and investment bankers. All those First Families of Virginia. Maybe DeMott would want to come to the phone. I stared at my landline. The FBI had a wire tap on it, to monitor taps from other sources. But hey, Raleigh David was engaged. She could call her fiancé. Right?

The housekeeper answered. She asked me to wait while she went to find "Mr. DeMott." Holding my breath, I stared out the patio door. The early evening sunshine sparkled on the water and I thought of the crystal chandeliers that would be glittering above the mahogany table that seated twenty-six comfortably.

"Raleigh?"

Oh, his voice. My heart flew.

"Raleigh, is that you?" DeMott's voice was bred by the Old Dominion. My name in his mouth sounded like a song.

"Yes, it's me."

"I can't believe it—you're on the phone!" He laughed.

I couldn't believe it either. What joy in his voice. He missed me, he really missed me. The real me.

"Wait—" he said. "What's wrong? Raleigh, are you all right?"

I held back the sigh. All that joy, once again clobbered by his mallet of worry.

"Everything's fine," I said, but added, "Aunt Eleanor had a hard day." Just to remind him. He knew the bare minimum about my assignment and my assumed identity. "But otherwise we're doing fine."

"Are you sure? You sound upset."

I took a deep breath and wished the sudden pain in my ribs could evict the terrible thoughts in my mind. DeMott's fear, his anxiety, they annoyed me so much. What happened to calm DeMott, peaceful DeMott? He disappeared almost immediately after he put this ring on my finger. The even-keeled guy I'd known since grade school was replaced by a man of worry, full of *what-ifs* and *shoulds*.

"I got the invitation to the baby shower." I checked my watch. If the call was longer than what was needed to order a pizza, the case agent would check the conversation. That meant Jack. Listening to this. "Congratulations," I said. "That's great news."

"Oh. You're calling about Mac's shower?"

"Yes."

"It is wonderful, isn't it? Pretty soon we can start our family. The babies will be cousins."

In the significant pause that followed, the stainless steel stove glared at me, clean and accusing. No fingerprints. No smudges. No home-cooked meals. Not one trace of human life in this place. The appliances seemed to wonder why I wasn't leaping at the chance to marry DeMott and join that esteemed line of Fieldings. Life at Weyanoke. On the historic register.

"DeMott, I can't talk long. I have to—"

"So that's it," he said. "You just called to say congratulations?"

"I'm really busy, I should—"

"Should what?"

There was one very big *should* in all this: I should never have called.

He said, "You haven't even asked how I'm doing. Or Madame."

My mother's dog, Madame. DeMott had offered to keep her while my mom and I took that cruise to Alaska. Ten days going on two-plus months. And counting.

"So how's Madame?"

"She's on antidepressants," he said.

"Pardon?"

"Something called Clomicalm. The vet prescribed it. He says she's suffering from separation anxiety."

"Madame?" The small and willful dog was so self-sufficient I sometimes wondered if she was a human trapped inside a dog suit. "Madame's never been depressed. Ever."

"Really? She quit eating."

"What are you feeding her?"

"The most expensive dog food I could find."

"Well, there's the problem, DeMott. Just give her a Big Mac."

"Raleigh, she won't go outside either. I thought it was the summer heat. But even at night I have to carry her out in my arms."

I glanced at my watch. *How long does it take to order a pizza?* Two minutes, thirty-five seconds. *Not that long.*

"I'm sorry, DeMott. What can I do?"

"Come home."

I stared out the sliding glass door. Two kayakers were floating past, their paddles windmilling like double-edge swords. "Aunt Eleanor needs me here right now."

"There are other people who need you too."

"I can't leave." The first kayaker lifted his paddle to point at something in the water. "Not yet."

"Then how much longer?"

A sea otter. It was rolling through the water, then floating on its back.

"Raleigh, how much longer?"

"I don't know."

The otter held a fish between its paws. The silver scales were flashing in the sunlight.

He said, "I'll bring her out there."

"What?"

"Madame. I'll bring her out there. She needs you."

Whatever the feeling was, it shot across my chest, circled my lungs, and began choking out my air. I couldn't speak.

"Raleigh, she's so thin. And her eyes, they're . . ."

"Okay, all right. Send her out. What, air freight?"

"Are you serious?" He sounded indignant. "I'm not going to toss her on a plane. Alone? Not in the condition she's in. She could die."

I loved this guy. Really, I did. "You're right. I'm sorry. I wasn't thinking."

"I'll bring her. But I won't stay." He paused. "Unless you want me to."

I was trying to decide which thing scared me more. DeMott coming out here, or Madame suddenly needing a home when my mom was in an insane asylum and I was working day and night. And my real aunt kept a house full of vicious cats, and I couldn't go see her anyway. But just like that, another concern popped up. I looked at my watch. How was I going to explain this call to Jack? To OPR? And if this phone was tapped by somebody else, did they just figure out Raleigh David might not be who she said she was? And all that wondering stretched out, creating a weighted silence that finally snapped.

"Fine," he said. "I won't stay."

"DeMott—"

"You're welcome."

He hung up.

Chapter Fourteen

Out of sheer spite, I refused to eat any of the groceries from Jack. And out of resentment, I yanked off my Raleigh David clothes and changed into my own Levi's, T-shirt, and Teva tennis shoes. Then I stomped downstairs and flew the Ghost down Dock Street, checking the mirrors every third second.

But the black Caddy wasn't there. Which made me wonder about any taps on my landline. Did the driver leave to report on the conversation? And who would he report it to? My first guess was Sal Gag. That Caddy looked like a complete Mob taxi.

Near Wright Park, I found a convenience store with a sign proclaiming "Gas. Beer. Food." If my mother were with me, she would read those words in the opposite order and tell me they made better sense that way—gas came after food and beer—and then she would've turned the words into an acrostic until she found some hidden message, some horrible warning about people trying to hurt her, about spies watching her every move. In the paranoid Olympics, my mother could win the gold medal.

Inside the convenience store, I saw a little girl running down the aisles, singing to herself. The air smelled of cumin and onions, mangoes and curry, but I saw only breaded chicken wings and glistening hot dogs under heat lamps on the counter. Farther back, an Indian woman wearing a sari stood at a grill stirring several pots. She was jabbering with an elderly woman who also wore a sari. The only man, also Indian, stood silent at the cash register. His name tag read *Raj*.

"Do you have cheeseburgers?" I asked.

"Oh yes. I make very good cheeseburgers. Very, very good." His accent was thick, that Indian tongue that somehow made every word sound both lyrical and staccato. "I will load that thing to the very bun. It is delicious."

"Fries?"

"Many fries."

"Perfect. Thank you. I'll take one cheeseburger, loaded, and a double order of fries."

I walked past the refrigerated cases and down a hall, searching for the restroom. It was next to an old pay phone. When I stepped inside, turning to close the door, the little girl was right behind me. Her two black pigtails stuck out above each ear. I locked the door, opened my cell phone, and saw a small dual shadow under the door. The girl's feet.

Jack answered on the second ring. He said, "No need to thank me."

I was still thinking about DeMott's last words—*"You're welcome"*—and suddenly wondered if Jack had listened to that phone call. "Pardon?" I said.

"The food. No need to thank me."

"Fine, look, I need you—"

"I know."

"Excuse me?"

"You need me, Harmon. And the sooner you figure that out, the sooner you can start living your life."

I was tempted to flush the phone down the toilet.

"Listen, you—" I held back the word *jerk*. "The track just found some suspicious material under the starting gate. They called in the Auburn police department, and the cops sent everything to the state lab. I need you—"

"Again."

I gritted my teeth. "To call the state lab. See if Tom O'Brien's working in the forensics lab. If he's not, get his home number."

Tom O'Brien was a lab technician who worked on my last case in Seattle. He was my only chance for access to this new evidence. But I didn't want to call him directly, because I didn't want my number showing up on any records. If the case ever got to court, some defense attorney could suggest to the jury that I influenced the technician. Those technicalities sometimes freed even the guiltiest. "Tell O'Brien I'll meet him at the lab."

"Harmon, you can't go to the lab."

"The track closes in six days."

"So wait six days."

"Right. So I can read OPR's report. Sitting there, like a dead duck?"

"You know, when I was buying those groceries, I got to talking to the checkout girl. She didn't believe all that food was for one girl. And that you were skinny. She also didn't believe me when I said you dipped your fries in mayonnaise."

"Jack. Call O'Brien."

"Did you learn nothing on that cruise ship?"

"I learned plenty, like how much I need my job. Tell O'Brien my visit is anonymous. No sign-in, no ID badge."

He muttered something—I thought I heard the word *stubborn*—but finally he said, "If I do this, then you have to give me a full debrief. I'll need to file it tomorrow morning."

"Fine."

"Tonight. Seven o'clock."

"Fine."

"In the cemetery."

"Fine."

I closed the phone, washed my hands, and opened the door. The little girl's pigtails bounced as she jumped back. Disarmingly cute, because the truth was her dark eyes looked as sharp as a Calcutta street vendor.

"Who were you talking to?" she asked.

"Myself."

"Why?"

"I'm crazy."

She followed me through the store. I grabbed a can of Coke from the refrigerator case and picked up my meal at the front counter. The cheese was dripping off the burger in gooey yellow stalactites. The fries were crispy, golden, greasy, glorious.

"Do you have any extra mayonnaise?" I asked.

Raj put the mayo in a small paper cup. I carried the food to a narrow counter near the front window. Outside, people were tapping numerical codes into the automated gas pumps. But there was no black Caddy in sight. I sat down, closed my eyes, and thanked God. For everything. For promises. For all these difficult things that I knew would somehow work together for good because of love. DeMott's worry. Madame's depression. The crime scene tragedy. And this paper plate of American food, made by foreign hands—

"Are you really crazy?"

The girl climbed onto the stool beside me.

I picked up a fry. "No, not really."

Her face was solemn. She watched me dip the fry in the mayonnaise. I pushed the plate toward her. "Check it out."

She dipped it delicately, then bit. The pigtails bounced with a strong nod of agreement. We ate in silence while her father, then her mother, then the older woman in the sari, presumably her grandmother, told her to leave me alone. I didn't really want her to go away, and the girl seemed to sense it. In a calm voice she told them that they were wrong and that I happened to like her. When we had almost polished off the fries, my cell phone rang, filling the store with a Muzak rendition of "Camptown Races."

Jack's joke. He had programmed my ringtone to play the corny racing song. The girl dipped another fry. "If you open the phone," she said, "we wouldn't have to listen to that music."

Chapter Fifteen

My favorite radio station—770 AM "The Truth"—was reminding its listeners that the Mariners were playing tonight at Safeco Field. Traffic heading into Seattle would move about as fast as a walk to first base.

Cutting over to Route 99, I let the Ghost soar across the city's industrial section beside the Deschutes River. We slipped by the shipping cranes and the rusted boxcars on the railroad tracks until just south of Boeing Field, where I turned down a side street and parked outside a laundry warehouse. Steam was rising from the building's aluminum stack, the gray tendrils floating up to the clouds like prodigal mist. But I stayed in the car for several minutes, pretending to answer my cell phone while gazing in the rearview mirrors. Still no black Caddy. And no other car seemed to be following either. But to be safe, I walked into the laundry building. The parched air smelled of ground cornstarch, and an Asian man answered the desk bell. He looked like every ounce of moisture had evaporated from his skin. When I asked him for an estimate on dry cleaning horse silks, I felt ill as he did several calculations and offered me a price.

"Thank you," I said, feeling even worse with my next fib. "I'll be in touch."

I stepped back outside. A row of white panel trucks were backed up to the loading dock, and across the street a propeller repair shop was closed for the night. The junkyard next to it looked almost abandoned. Hopscotching over a series of kettle lakes created by the earlier rain, I ran to the next building. It was one of those square boxes built in the 1970s, back when bronzed steel seemed hip.

But at five thirty on a Thursday night, the Washington State Crime Lab was so quiet that the sound of the front door opening startled the girl sitting at the front desk. Her hazel eyes widened, as if to say the witching hour didn't usually begin until Friday.

"Here to see Tom O'Brien," I said.

She set down a paperback novel and picked up the telephone on her desk. The book's cover showed a knife with dripping blood, bleeding into the title and the author's name, and moments later a steel door opened down the hall. Tom O'Brien held a visitor's badge and checked a mark on the receptionist's log.

"She's with me, Sandie."

But the receptionist was reading again. She only nodded.

I waited until the stairwell's steel door had slammed behind us. It had a loud tumbler lock, the definitive noise of prison cells. "Sorry to keep you so late," I said. "But it's urgent."

"I accept your apology." He took the stairs by twos. "But it's really no problem. My wife and I have season tickets for the Mariners. I can work late and leave the car here. No parking fees, no driving in traffic."

"Your secret's safe with me."

"Thanks." He was tall with big feet and hands. Since I'd seen him last year, his black hair had turned white at the temples. "Last thing this place needs is more bad publicity."

The local media was continually hammering the understaffed lab for its slow turnarounds on DNA evidence. They had also convinced the state legislature to freeze funding until the pace picked up, which was a complete catch-22 because a leaner budget meant the lab couldn't hire new technicians. But the battle was nothing new. During my five years in the FBI's mineralogy lab, I learned that two of the worst bedfellows were justice and politics. While justice focused on the truth, politics manipulated the truth for its own gain. Throw in the media, which only reported the truth that fit their pre-conceived ideas, and it was little wonder that the fallen world was speeding toward hell in a handbasket. The political games were part of what pushed me out of the lab. But the biggest reason was that after my dad was murdered, I couldn't sit at a microscope anymore. I needed to do more.

The main exam room was stretched out down the length of the building. The dozen workstations were divided by high counters that were further elevated by thick books that focused on everything from blood evidence to pharmacology to skin cells. The lower counters held centrifuges and high-resolution microscopes and plastic caddies full of glass pipettes, along with that steady workhorse, the Bunsen burner. At the far end of the lab, a young guy sat in front of a large computer monitor, and behind him, the tinted windows framed a section of Interstate 5. The northbound traffic into the city was at a standstill.

"Did you have a chance to look at the stuff from the track?" I asked.

"Just a little. After that agent called and said you were coming in."

"What's your first impression?"

"Agricultural." He offered me a small cardboard box, like a Kleenex box, only it contained latex gloves. "But I could be wrong," he added.

It was probably my favorite remark from a scientist: *I could be wrong*.

He waited for me to snap on the gloves. "The black tube doesn't look like something that sells general retail," he said, "so we'll try to track it through wholesalers. Farm mercantiles. Ag-supply companies, those places."

"Be sure to check any place linked to horses."

"I'll make a note."

The black plastic tubing that Mr. Yuck had pulled up now lay on an exam table. It had been cut into sections and placed inside clear evidence bags the size of pillow cases. With my gloved hands, I picked up one bag, trying to get a close look at the tube. Dense but pliable plastic. And brown tape was wound around it, the earthy color ideal camouflage in the track's turf. But the tape didn't cover the funnel cones that rose from the round surface like miniature volcanoes.

I glanced at Tom. He was waiting for me to say something.

I chose my words carefully, thinking of attorneys. And OPR.

"The first people who picked this up weren't wearing gloves. So fingerprints and DNA analysis might be a bit of a mess."

"You saw them collecting it?"

"Most of it." I didn't tell him about SunTzu's fall or his subsequent death, because that information could influence his investigation. He could always read something in the newspaper, but then he would be making his own connections. I described the evidence collection because Mr. Yuck's tearing it out of the soil would be pertinent to his forensics. While I spoke, I tapped my index finger on the bag, feeling the funnel cones. Each one was about 3 millimeters wide. When I picked up a second bag, the tape completely covered the tubing, including the funnel cones.

"Did they happen to mark where these sections were on the track?"

Tom picked up a clipboard and lifted the paperwork, scanning it. "Not that I can see. No sketches, no measurements."

"I'd like you to check the open cones for any chemical residues. Or remnants of an object. Friction marks, striations."

"Projectile?"

"Not sure. You'll want to see the video, showing the first race. Did they send that?"

"No."

I didn't blame the Auburn cops. Few local police departments were trained to collect forensic evidence. Again, a funding issue. Again, justice and politics.

But Tom walked to the phone on the wall and tapped four numbers, asking for a sergeant by name and for a video copy of the first race. He also recommended the Auburn police return to the track with a metal detector. "Run it over the soil where you guys collected this tube." He cupped his hand over the receiver. "Anything else?"

"Tell them to hurry," I said. "The grooming equipment goes back out there tomorrow at 4:00 a.m. The horses start running at five."

As he gave the instructions, I picked up the bag again. To my naked eye, the tape's cotton threading reminded me of what the grooms wound over the horses' forelegs. I'd seen Juan wrap it over his clay poultices too. And before the races, to protect the delicate leg bones from the metal horseshoes. The tape usually matched a barn's color. But I couldn't recall seeing any barn with brown silks.

Tom hung up.

I said, "Tell me what you think about the tape."

He glanced at his watch. "I was hoping to get the threads-per-inch count done tonight. Tomorrow I'll start testing the adhesion. Unfortunately, this stuff doesn't look like a specialty tape."

Meaning: the forensics trail had many paths. A tape's thread count and the composition of its threads—cotton, polyester, nylon, and blends of everything, in varying degrees—helped track down the manufacturer. Even more helpful was a microanalysis of the adhesion's chemical compounds, further narrowing down the manufacturer. But this tape looked almost generic, which meant a number of companies could have made it and distributed it to every hardware store in America. It would be hard to prove where it came from unless we hit the holy grail and found the exact roll used. Matching the end tears was almost as good as DNA. And any jury could grasp such an elementary concept.

But when I lifted another bag, squinting, I saw the tape's ends were cut clean. Sliced, not torn.

"Rats," I said. "How about looking for fingerprints in the adhesion? Tests for saliva residue?"

"I wrote it down. But I don't see the tape as the big hurdle." He pulled on fresh gloves and reached over the large bags for a smaller one. Three objects were inside, each shaped like a masonry brick. They were brown, covered with the same tape, and when Tom turned the bag over, to show me a section where the tape had been pulled away, I saw a band of copper. And the word *Duracell*.

"Whoever built this is no idiot," he said. "It's nine-volt batteries, bundled together, and all different brands. The collection report says these were attached to the tubing. It's some kind of power source." He handed me the bag. "I did a quick calculation by square inch and area. Thirty-four batteries in each brick. About a hundred total."

I turned the bag. The dried soil rolled across the plastic, sounding like some kind of mocking hiss. "Nine-volt batteries won't narrow things down."

"Right. Panasonic, Energizer, Duracell."

Forensically speaking, lithium nine-volt batteries were almost untraceable. They were sold in almost every store, from gas stations to groceries to warehouses like Sam's Club. I felt my hope diminishing, staring at the careful architecture. The batteries were stacked as straight as Legos, each side aligned perfectly before being taped together. Somebody created one giant battery, and it was a patient experiment for evil purposes.

"They're almost compulsively constructed," I said. "A perfectionist?"

Tom was writing something on the clipboard, checking his watch again. "What's your time frame for this?"

I tried not to sigh, setting down the bag. "Can you expedite this?"

"Reason?"

"The thoroughbred racing season ends in six days."

"I can try." He gave a conciliatory smile. "I already put in the DNA request. I'll start arguing with them first thing in the morning."

I nodded, but felt the whole case galloping away. The forensics could stretch out for months. And OPR wouldn't wait. Not for something that could help me explain myself.

Tom was eyeing me. "You look like you could use some cheering up. Want to come to the game? With the way the Mariners are playing, there should be plenty of tickets available. A summer night at Safeco Field? There's nothing else like it."

"Thanks." I tried to smile. "I've already got plans."

"Hot date, huh?"

Now the sigh came, and it was heavy.

"No," I said, "it's more like a long, cold shower."

Chapter Sixteen

The sinking sun pushed copper swords through gunmetal clouds, and the Ghost glowed down the highway. To my right, across Puget Sound, a mountain range that earned its name, Olympic, stood like a geologic chorus, the bright glaciers singing with the light's close of day. I was born a Virginian and I loved that state, but the Old Dominion's natural charms were the kind that worked into the heart over time, over many seasons. Washington's landscape, like Alaska's, was blunt-force gorgeousness. The views stole human breath. And made me wonder if I'd ever look at the Blue Ridge Mountains the same way again.

But when I pulled into Fort Steilacoom State Park, I felt almost forlorn. It was just past 7:00 p.m., and the softball fields were empty and puddled. The park's rust-painted exhibition barns waited for something to happen. At a split-rail fence, I turned down a gravel service road. It was lined with green hedges, and a graveyard was laid out to my right. Up ahead a muscular man was leaning on the fence rail, stretching his quad muscles. He wore black nylon running shorts and a black singlet. The Jeep parked behind him was also black, but I decided the picture still wasn't complete. Climbing out of the car, I placed an imaginary black hat on my nemesis, Special Agent Jack Stephanson.

"You had me worried for a minute," he said. "Thought you wouldn't show up."

"I can always change my mind."

"And the shrink can always notify OPR. And OPR can always recommend immediate dismissal."

I stepped over the fence's low rails, moving into the cemetery. The ground was spongy, more moss than grass.

"Harmon," he said, following me. "Just take it one appointment at a time."

I kneeled down and picked a pinecone off a flat headstone. Eroded and gray, the eight-inch rectangle of cheap granite was sinking into the moss. The FBI approved this cemetery for our face-to-face debriefs because it appeared safe. We were twenty-five miles from the track, and a high hedge shielded us from the road. At six-three, Jack could stretch, peering over the hedge, but the sad fact was nobody ever came to visit these graves. Directly across the road was the largest psychiatric hospital west of the Mississippi. Western State opened in 1871 and started burying dead patients in this plot of land soon after. The graves were marked with numbers. No names. There were hundreds of them. My mother was now a patient in that hospital. And the FBI, in its brutal benevolence, had decided the most "convenient" way for me to get my shrink appointments while undercover was for me to see the same psychiatrist who was treating my mother.

"He gives me the creeps," I said.

"He's a head shrinker," Jack said. "I'd worry if you liked him."

"I know he's sending his notes to OPR."

"Probably." Jack was silent for a long moment. "Don't worry about the undercover repercussions. If she changes her mind, I'll figure out a way to deal with it."

It would have been easy to act like I didn't know what he meant. But pretense only delayed the inevitable. "Thanks. But she's still refusing."

My mother, according to the shrink's clinical diagnosis, was a paranoid schizophrenic. Growing up, I just thought she was eccentric. Strange and wonderful, and the South was full of people like that. But the shrink was telling me my family was "in denial" and had too many "defense mechanisms." In our minds, all we knew was love and God. Yes, she sometimes got ideas about people following her, or somebody trying to poison our water or steal our mail. Bad days, certainly. But they were always bookended by great days. And David

Harmon. My dad devoted himself to making his wife feel loved and secure. When they married, I was five years old; he adopted me and my sister, Helen. He was the only dad I ever knew, and he was the greatest father on earth. But the plaster started to crack when he was murdered. My mother and I limped along under the falling debris until this summer, until the cruise from hell. Somebody told her my secret; somebody thought she should know that her daughter worked for the FBI. I had kept that from her, trying to protect her fragile mind. But when she learned that I worked for the people who wire-tapped and monitored people and kept files on suspicious citizens—and that I'd lied to her about it—her mind couldn't handle it. In the ship's chapel, praying to a God who seemed very far away, my mother suffered a full psychotic break. She refused to see me now.

I stood and walked across the mossy grass, snapping off the pinecone's brown claws. The graves were in no particular order. No. 1178 was next to No. 1209, which was next to No. 554.

Jack said, "Give me the rundown. For the 302."

Facts only. I described the death of SunTzu and how Mr. Yuck discovered the black tubing. I told him about the battery-operated contraption that was now in the lab, and as I spoke, I tried to ignore a persistent little thought camping in the back of my mind. Given this same situation, DeMott would've pressed me to talk about my feelings concerning my mom. He'd ask too many questions and then get upset when I had no answers. And if I changed the subject, he'd accuse me of shutting him out. Which meant I could feel guilty on top of already feeling sad.

"Wait a minute," Jack said. "You're saying some kind of poisoned dart shot out of that tube? And it hit the horse?"

"I don't know. That's why I wanted to get into the lab. Whoever set up that tubing mechanism is smart. Really smart. The problem is, between the DNA backlog and the generic nature of the physical evidence, the evil genius might get away with it."

On the other side of the hedge, a car splashed through a puddle. I kneeled down again, gazing at No. 329. Jack stretched and looked over the top of the bushes.

"Stay down," he said. "Can't tell."

Weather and time had eroded the headstone. A lacework of pale green lichen was growing into the engraved numbers, as if trying to obliterate the person again. No name in life, no number in death. I scratched at the fungus, ripping it off the granite. After several moments, I realized Jack was still standing there. I looked up, but his gaze had shifted. He was staring across the cemetery's hummocky field toward some spindly pines that looked equally abandoned. I knew this expression on his face. When his eyes turned aquamarine. I waited, feeling something like a moth flutter inside my chest. I tried to kill it.

"It doesn't fit," he said.

"What doesn't?"

"This gizmo you're talking about. Fixing races is one thing. But you're describing murder. Premeditated murder. Maybe even chemical warfare."

"It fits," I said. "Somebody lit a fire to kill a horse."

He turned, staring at me now. "Maybe you were just collateral damage?"

"That's what I told you, remember? In the hospital?"

But he wasn't listening. His eyes were still focused on some inward idea. "We should ask Lutini to do a profile."

Lucia Lutini. I stared at the gravestone. Lutini was the person I wanted to be my case agent. *Let it go.*

"One more detail," I said. "Sal Gagliardo's horse was slightly affected by the bad start. Cuppa Joe. He balked before he ran. He was the favorite. But only placed."

"Fits the pattern."

"Giddyup."

"And his horse wasn't seriously injured?"

"No. Neither was the second horse. Just Eleanor's."

"Gagliardo's horse being part of this is a great cover," Jack said. "Makes it look like he didn't have motive."

"Right. And the guy who runs the start bet on that horse. What if he looked the other way while it was being set up?" I thought back to Harrold's nervousness and the way Sal Gag stared at him. Maybe it meant something. Maybe not: Harrold was high-strung, and Sal Gagliardo didn't look at anyone with much warmth.

"Time?" Jack asked.

I checked my watch. Freud in ten minutes. I stood, feeling dizzy walking back to the Ghost. Jack stepped over the fence ahead of me and opened the car door.

"This thing suits you," he said. "You realize that?"

I sat down, and he closed the door. But the window was open and the air suddenly smelled of pine and earth. I gazed at the ground, searching for conifers. But I knew that wasn't it. Jack. He had a deep green scent. Woodsy and warm. Sun on evergreens.

"You okay?" he asked.

"I was just thinking about how much money I would've won if the horse had come through."

"Harmon, it's Monopoly money."

I turned the key. The Ghost gave an impressive growl. But Jack didn't step back. Instead he leaned down into the window. "Do me a favor?" he said.

I felt a cynical smile tugging at my mouth. *I should've known.* "Do you a favor because you delivered some food I never asked for?"

"No," he said calmly. "I told you, Harmon. You don't owe me."

The heat flushed up my throat, burning into my cheeks. My comment sounded rude, out of line. "Okay, then what?"

"Don't hand him any ammo."

"Who?"

"The shrink," he said. "Don't let that guy have one bit of your true self. Understand?"

Chapter Seventeen

Every time I walked into Western State Hospital I felt another layer of duality falling over my life. Outside, summer burst with color and vitality. But this place was darker than the deepest cave. The gothic architecture divided sunshine into tiny rays, a light too fractured to penetrate the diamond-shaped window panes and too cold to warm the pervasive atmosphere of trouble. Making my way down the second-floor hallway toward an arched doorway, I could hear laughter on the floor above. But it had no humor. Cheerless and remote, it sounded like mirth raised like a weapon, trying to deflect a wicked opponent.

I looked at my watch. Three seconds before 8:00 p.m. I knocked on his door.

Dr. Nathan Norbert might have seemed at home at the track, standing among the jockeys. He was about two inches over five feet, wearing creased blue jeans and a monogrammed button-down shirt, tucked in. We'd already had two visits during my first weekend at the track, and I'd never seen him without a colorful tie that looked like some conversation starter. Or Rorschach test. Today a bunch of pandas were cavorting on the blue silk—*dancing? fighting? copulating?* His brown hair sprouted from a tightly lined forehead, and rimless glasses almost concealed the expression in his eyes. His clipped beard tried to disguise a lantern jaw. And failed.

"Ah, Raleigh," he said. "I was beginning to wonder."

If only, I thought, walking into his office. *If only you were the type who wondered.* But Dr. Nathan Norbert was a clinical critic. He diagnosed, contained, cataloged. When I had told him how much my parents loved each other, he gave me a new word for it: "codependent."

I sat on the long brown couch that reminded me of a coffin while Freud lowered himself to his big chair that was placed to the side. He positioned the notepad on his knee and wrote something across the top of the page. Maybe noting that I showed up. Or that there was a scowl on my face. But I couldn't see the words because Freud kept his leg elevated, just so, tipping the pad away from my prying eyes.

"How are you?" he asked.

My palms were sweating. And I couldn't wipe them off because this was enemy territory. One vulnerable gesture, the predator would pounce.

"I'm fine." I smiled. "You?"

"You missed our last appointment."

"Short visit to the hospital."

He stroked the beard. For Freud, the gesture was the equivalent of yelling, *What?*

He said, "You didn't call to tell me."

"I couldn't."

He adjusted his position. The chair was one of those back-saving numbers, with heavily padded leather. The chair for people who sat around all day sticking their fingers in other people's business.

He said, "I did receive a message from your case agent. Something about an injury."

"Just a few bruised ribs."

He waited.

"Sort of painful."

Waiting, waiting.

"I'm a little sore," I added, hoping to score points for vulnerability. "And I would rather be resting, but I didn't want to miss another visit."

He wrote something on the pad and I slid my palms over my jeans, pretending to adjust the sleeves of my jean jacket. When he turned his head, watching my movement, I smiled and glanced around his office, pretending to admire the place. The old wooden moldings were almost black with age, and the bookshelves swallowed most of the wall space. One window faced Steilacoom Boulevard. The diamond-paned glass was embedded with chicken wire. Iron bars over that, soldered together. No jumping allowed.

"Aside from the minor injury, how are things going?"

"Fine."

"No problems?"

I searched for the right words. Silence only encouraged him. "My mom's dog is coming to live with me."

His eyes showed almost genuine interest. I congratulated myself and kept talking. He wrote another note. Wrote and wrote. Then I stopped.

He looked up. "You say your fiancé will be bringing the dog. How do you feel about that?"

"Fine."

He waited.

"I mean, excited. I'm excited to see DeMott. I miss him."

"You miss DeMott," he repeated as the pen scratched across the paper. "In what way do you miss him?"

"He's my fiancé."

He looked up. "You haven't answered my question."

Uh-oh.

I glanced at the doctor's hands. The left hand. No ring. And here we were at eight o'clock on a Thursday night. At a mental asylum.

I said, "Are you married?"

He hesitated. "No, I am not married."

"Have you ever been engaged?"

There was another pleasurable moment of silence. He scooted back into his chair. "No, I have not been engaged."

"Well, let me tell you, it's the greatest thing. Just knowing that somebody wants to spend the rest of their life with you. Nothing compares to that."

"Nothing compares?"

"No."

"And you're not concerned that your fiancé's appearance might compromise your identity?"

"You mean my undercover status?"

"Do you feel that you have another identity, Raleigh?"

Oh boy. Jack's words echoed in my mind. *"No ammo."*

"DeMott won't blow my cover." I lifted my hand, flashing the engagement ring. "Raleigh David is engaged. And her fiancé is a wealthy guy who lives in Virginia. That pretty much describes DeMott. And he's a horse guy. So everything fits."

"Everything fits?"

"Yes."

"How long will he be here?"

"We haven't discussed that."

"I see."

The pen scratched the paper. The sound made my teeth itch.

He said, "You invited him, or he decided to come?"

"He's bringing my mom's dog."

Freud looked up. "The animal, the one named Madame?"

"Yes."

"Your mother talks about that dog. Frequently. It seems she misses it a great deal."

This was the most intimate information he'd ever divulged to me about her. But it put me on the defensive somehow. Was he taunting me with how much he knew and wouldn't divulge? Was he retaliating for my marriage comment? I could see a mild expression on his face and decided Freud was just petty enough for this. As he might diagnose it—the guy had some serious passive-aggressive tendencies because the heavy inference hung in the dimmed light. *My mother talked about her dog; she missed her dog. But she didn't miss her daughter.* Because I lied to her. Because I called the men in white who took her away.

No ammo.

I straightened in my chair. "I'm glad she talks about Madame."

"You're glad?"

"Yes. She loves her dog."

"Animals are not allowed in the building."

"That's pretty stupid."

"Stupid?" His eyebrows rose.

"I mean silly."

"Silly?"

"Unnecessary." I smiled, tightly. "It seems like a visit with her own pet would be helpful."

He was writing again. I considered telling him that Madame was depressed. Maybe the dog could come in for an appointment.

He said, "I concede the dog might improve her mood. Perhaps something can be arranged. A therapeutic visit. To elevate your mother's mental outlook."

"What is her mental outlook right now?"

"Raleigh." He laid the pen on the pad, the fountain tip like a miniature sword. "We've been over this."

"These drugs you're giving her, what are they supposed to do?"

"We have privacy laws. Even with involuntary commitments. You know that, which means you're asking because—"

"Because I have a right to know what you're doing to my mother."

He picked up the pen. "You sound angry."

I bit my tongue. And prayed. *Seal my mouth. Tight.*

It took several moments of silence, but finally he said, "She shows signs of improvement."

"Is that the clinical way of telling me she's not trying to kill herself?"

"She's interacting with the other patients. And she seems very fond of one orderly. When this particular orderly makes a request, your mother complies. That's a significant step. It's a sign of attachment. And the orderly is a young female, no less."

I felt an irrational stab of envy. "Can I see her?"

He didn't write anything.

"Please?"

"Raleigh—"

"Okay, I get it." It wasn't something I wanted to hear, but the words hurt less when I said them myself. "She's improving but she still doesn't want to see me."

He moved the pen, adjusting it on the page without picking it up. This wasn't even worth writing about: she didn't want to see me. I could feel my lungs holding back a long scream.

"Raleigh, do you ever feel that your life is all or nothing?"

Right now, nothing. "Pardon?"

"I'm curious about your perspective on life. Oftentimes, when a parent 'checks out,' the abandonment produces in the child an all-or-nothing mentality. They can develop into a person who is unable to handle gray areas. Nuances. That poses significant challenges later in life."

"Is that so?" *Thanks, you just called me a simpleton.*

But I was smart enough to see what he was doing. He wanted to provoke a heated response. And maybe OPR asked him to do it. No, not maybe.

Definitely.

I counted to seventy-five and listened to my breathing, steady and strong.

Finally, he said, "Was there anything else you'd like to discuss?"

I shook my head.

"All right, then," he said. "I'll see you on Saturday."

Chapter Eighteen

I kept the Ghost restrained to second gear, motoring away from Western State at thirty miles per hour. I navigated back roads, skirting the Puget Sound waterfront that faced Fox Island, then cut across Tacoma's North End neighborhood, all the while resisting the urge to stop at Eleanor's house. Drop in. Find somebody who was happy to see me. Or somebody just to see me.

But I didn't trust myself.

There was an edge, just past my feet, so close that one more step might bring the long, descending cry. And never-ending tears. That precipice where self-pity beckoned.

You're an orphan.

One parent dead, murdered. The other had left for another world, a land so remote nobody issued passports.

And your lies sent her there.

When I reached Thea's Landing, my condo looked precisely the same. No mess. No family. No life. Staving off the weeps, I walked to the refrigerator and threw a frozen burger into the microwave, sliced the Tillamook cheese, and toasted a bun, slathering the bread with mayonnaise. Freud would diagnose this moment "emotional eating." And I wouldn't disagree, but I could guarantee we disagreed on the outcome. A cheeseburger made me feel better. And there was nothing wrong with that. In fact, after polishing off the first, I was trying to decide if a second one would taste even better, but the phone rang. I glanced at the clock on the microwave. Almost 10:00 p.m. The caller was probably a telemarketer. Or DeMott. Or Jack.

And I didn't feel like talking to any of them.

But the voice that trumpeted through the answering machine sounded like human reveille.

Eleanor.

"Raleigh! If you are not home—you should be!"

I picked up. "Hi, I'm here."

"No time for chitchat," she said. "The arson investigator is coming to the barn tomorrow."

"All right."

"Don't be ridiculous! He wants us there at six in the morning!"

"Okay."

"*Okay?* I'll have you know, the last time I opened an eyelid before 8:00 a.m., it was to vote for Eisenhower."

"I'll take care of it. You don't have to be there."

"Let me warn you, the man did not sound friendly."

"He's not selling Amway."

"Are you being smart?"

"Yes, ma'am."

"Well, don't attempt it with this gentleman. He's one of *those* people."

"Which people?"

"I haven't told you—the two kinds of people in this world?"

I tapped my finger on the plate, picking up the crumbs, laying them on my tongue. The playwright was coming, I could feel it. "Tennessee?"

"Are you listening?"

"Promise."

"The great difference between people in this world is not between rich and poor or good and evil. It's between the people who've had love and those who haven't, the people who just look at love with envy. Sick envy."

The words scraped up my throat. "Who said that?"

"Chance Wayne. Act one of *Sweet Bird of Youth*. My first husband uttered those lines during the show in Kalamazoo, and from that moment on, I knew we were doomed. But that's another story."

I nodded, then realized she couldn't see me. "I'll meet the arson inspector at the barn. Thanks for the warning."

She wished me sweet dreams and hung up.

In the otherwise empty sink, I rinsed my dish. The stainless metal had a flat gray light and it seemed to accuse me. I turned away, drying my hands on a spotless towel and refusing to look at my reflection in the microwave's glass door. I walked through the quiet untouched rooms, preparing myself for bed and refusing to admit the feeling that was pressing down on my heart. But it was there.

Eleanor's description of the arson investigator might just as easily be applied to me.

≈

Friday morning, I wore high-styled armor. The brass buttons on my Chanel jacket looked like military bars. The ironed creases in my silk-blend trousers stood out like battle greaves. And dark sunglasses visored my eyes. Big sunglasses. The waterworks had arrived with last night's bedside prayers. My eyes were still puffy.

The backstretch was nearly empty as most of the horses were out running on the track or being prepared for it. There was a faint blanket of dew glistening on the sawdust, and I lifted the sunglasses to get a full glimpse of Mount Rainier. In the morning light, the glaciers had the pink and purple hues of fresh bruises. But I dropped my shades when I saw him. It wasn't hard to pick him out. In the closed circuit of the backstretch, strangers stood out like neon signs. Strangers like me. But when I came up beside him, I realized Eleanor was right.

"You must be the arson inspector," I said.

Instead of answering, he cataloged my appearance. His eyes were dark gray—a color like smoke, I decided—and his hair was also gray but closer to the hues of fog. The hair grew from the top of his head, the roots lifting straight up before the strands fell to the sides into an ash heap of a hairstyle. A brushy mustache covered his upper lip and inevitably reminded me of a chimney sweep's broom.

I extended my hand. "Raleigh David."

"Walter Wertzer." Rather than shake my hand, he opened a notebook and took out his business card, offering it to me.

I read it carefully. The name and title were in large print. Too large. "Nice to meet you," I lied.

"I already talked to your trainer, Bill Cooper."

"Bill's the one to talk to." I placed the card in my Coach bag.

"Funny. He said I should talk to you."

I smiled but the bad feeling crept across my neck, like the whisper of a noose. "Bill's just being generous. He knows much more about the barns, the horses, everything. I'm still learning."

"You do that often?"

"Pardon?"

"Sleep in a stall. With a horse."

"No. In fact, never."

"So why that night?" He clicked his pen, flipping to a fresh page in the notebook.

I stared at the empty page. My life was overpopulated by note-takers. "I stayed in the stall because the horse was sick. And the vet, or rather the assistant vet, wanted somebody to stay with her. I was available."

He wrote in the notebook, head down. I stared at the smoky haystack radiating from his scalp and realized two problems. One, Cooper should've already told him why I was in the stall that night. And two, Wertzer was writing down my statement without any concern for how the transcription made me feel. He didn't care. Which meant the trainer was setting me up, and the investigator didn't intend to play nice.

He looked up. "Trainer says he asked the groom to stay with the horse. But you went behind his back."

The trap was laid. And the facts were in Cooper's favor. Backed into the corner, I knew my only defense was total offense. Summoning an attitude of condescending wealth, I pulled myself to full height and thought of the way DeMott's sister MacKenna treated their hired help.

"We do keep underlings around the barn," I said, "and Bill Cooper is one of them. But that night our groom seemed unusually tired. I offered to help. Does that surprise you, Mr. Wertzer, that I care about our employees?"

He reached into his jacket and rummaged in the side pocket, wincing slightly as he pulled out a small device. "I'm going to record your statement. You mind?"

I shook my head.

He hit Record and a cold swallow went down my throat.

Holding the machine near his gray mustache, he spoke into it with great care. "Statement from Raleigh David." He gave the date, time, and place.

And I realized a third problem. In addition to envying love, this guy hated the rich.

"Let's start at the beginning." The broomy mustache bumped up and down as he winced again. "You went into the stall to stay with the horse because . . ."

I started to repeat the statement. Word for word.

"Yeah, fine," Wertzer said, cutting me off. "And when did you realize the place was on fire?"

"When—do you mean what time?"

"Yeah. What time."

"I'm not sure." I couldn't explain why, but something told me that knowing the exact time would only bolster Cooper's case against me. "I do remember waking up to a train whistle. Maybe you should check the schedules."

"Maybe I should." He waved the recorder. "Let's go in the barn."

The recorder was in his right hand, the notebook in his left with the pen secured between two fingers. He grunted slightly as we walked across the sawdust to the burned-out stall. I glanced around for Cooper. Or Juan. But it was only horses, sticking their heads out of the stalls, eager for distraction. KichaKoo blew her lips, fluttering her opinion of the whole thing.

"The gun," he said suddenly. "You got a license?"

"Yes."

Raleigh David had a concealed gun permit, courtesy of the FBI's whiz kids. But Wertzer had to know that since the weapon was fired and the police didn't confiscate it. And I knew this guy must have combed all that paperwork. Standing beside the burnt stall, where the air smelled of soot and water-soaked wood, I felt the bad feeling creeping down my neck. Wertzer's mustache twitched under his nose as he sniffed the air, tilting his head to catch an exact odor. He reminded me of a ragged hunting hound on the fox's trail.

He said, "You don't look like the type to carry."

Go on offense. Don't give in. "Are you all right?"

"Huh. Why do you ask?"

"You keep wincing. Is something wrong?"

His gray eyes compressed into slate. "I've got a hernia."

"Sorry to hear that."

"Back to the gun," he said. "You carry it because . . . ?"

"It's a private matter."

"Not anymore."

"Pardon?"

"Miss David, this is an arson investigation. And you managed to get yourself right in the middle of the whole thing."

"Are you implying I'm somehow responsible for the fire?"

He narrowed his eyes. "Why do you say that?"

"Something about your tone."

"My tone."

"Yes. You're making it sound like I lit the fire."

"Did you?"

"Mr. Wertzer, do I look suicidal?"

He lifted his pen, poking at the stall's charred wood. "I checked you out, Miss David."

"I'm sure you did."

He pushed the pen deeper. The blackened wood snapped. He caught the shard with his notebook, leaving a charcoal smudge on the white paper.

"You're not a groom," he said. "And you're not a trainer. And you're not really an owner. You just suddenly show up at Emerald Meadows, right after the place gets remodeled and all the smoke detectors are replaced. And suddenly, there's a fire. In the exact stall where you decide to sleep. Where the sprinklers have been cut off. And somehow, you've got a gun, loaded, to shoot your way out."

"What's your point, Mr. Wertzer?"

"Like I said. You don't seem the type to carry. Especially a Glock."

"It's for protection."

"From what, barn cats?"

Juan stepped out of Stella Luna's stall. He seemed to studiously avoid looking our way, but the black horse tugged against the lead. Her sculpted muscles flickered as she turned her white-blazed face, looking directly at me. She nickered. Juan tugged on the bridle, pulling her forward again.

"What's the gun for?" Wertzer asked.

I raised my chin, doing my best impression of Eleanor Anderson's niece. "If you must know, I was once attacked."

"When was that?" He was writing now.

"The attack?"

"Yeah."

"Several years ago."

"Where?"

"Back home."

"Which is?"

"I thought you looked into me, Mr. Wertzer."

"Virginia. This happened in Virginia?"

"Yes. I was in college."

"What college?"

"Ho—" I almost said Holyoke, as in Mount Holyoke College. "Hollins."

"How do you spell that? H-a-w-"

"No." I sighed, glanced at my wristwatch, and spelled the name of the women's college in Roanoke, Virginia, that was Raleigh David's alma mater. She graduated magna cum laude in art history, versus my magna in geology at Mount Holyoke. "Mr. Wertzer, is this going to take much longer?"

"You need to be somewhere?"

"I lead a busy life."

"Really," he said. "From what I heard all you do is hang around the track, sometimes throwing money away."

My smile felt as cold as the glaciers on Mount Rainier.

He pressed his thumb into the recorder's Stop button. "Next time carve out an hour."

Next time?

"Oh." He pretended to be surprised. "I didn't mention it?"

"No, you didn't."

"I need you to take a lie detector test." He deposited the recorder into his pocket. "Unless you got a problem with that."

"On the contrary. I look forward to it."

"Me too."

"Have a nice day, Mr. Wertzer."

Pulse pounding, I walked down the gallery. The horses were bobbing their long heads up and down, agreeing with me that the guy was one of *those* people. When I reached the end of the barn—still no sign of Cooper—I stepped under the eaves. The morning sun felt like a warm hand on my back, but it couldn't remove the chill sinking into my gut. I passed the shower building, the testing barn, and continued all the way to the gate that led to the turf, making sure the barn was far behind me. Then I turned around.

No sign of Wertzer.

The track was groomed and the big John Deeres were resting beside the maintenance hut. I looked at my watch. Just past 6:30 a.m. But the turf was empty. Right now the first and second training runs were usually ending, and the horses would be walked back to the barns. Whatever the delay this morning, I wasn't about to question opportunity. Lifting my sunglasses to see the numbers on my phone, I called Jack. He picked up on the first ring.

He said, "I was just thinking of you."

"Interesting. I just met a highly annoying person who reminded me of yo—"

"Not me," he said. "Couldn't be me. And why are you whispering?"

"I need you to backstop another detail for Raleigh David." I told him about the arson investigator. "Have the whiz kids write up an assault report from the campus police at Hollins College. Link that doc to a local hospital, adding a sealed medical report. And make a note that the attacker was never found, so the case couldn't proceed any further. But make it look like Raleigh David was pretty shaken up."

"Okay, got it. Why campus police?"

"Hollins is small, a private college. With students coming back from summer break, this guy might have trouble reaching anybody in campus police right now, especially someone who would remember what happened more than ten years ago. Oh, and tell the whiz kids the attack happened in January," I added. "Guy wore a ski mask. She never got a good look at him, you know what to say."

"I got it," he said. "Stop worrying."

"You haven't met the arson inspector."

"That bad?"

"He has a hernia. I think it's from throwing people into the wood chipper. Feet first."

"Just what you need."

"Right. And he's figured out something doesn't add up with Raleigh David. The problem is, he came to the wrong conclusion."

"Wait a minute—you're a *suspect*?"

I gazed at the oval track. The groomed soil looked as patient and ordered as a furrowed field ready for planting. No horses had run yet. Friday morning. Last week of races. *It shouldn't be this quiet right now . . .*

"Harmon—"

"I gotta go. Call me if there's a problem with the backstop."

I closed the phone and crossed the empty backstretch to Quarterchute. Once again, the Café's perfume made my knees go weak. Bacon and onions and fried potatoes, luxuriating in peppered oil. And my breakfast sandwiches were waiting under the heat lamp.

Only something felt wrong in here too.

The old guys leaned forward around the gingham tables, huddled in conspiracy. Yet none held a betting sheet. Nobody was smacking the racing form, calling the winner and telling the next guy he was full of it. No, they clutched Styrofoam coffee cups and whispered. When the Polish Prince looked over at me, he twisted the toothpick parked between his lips.

I nodded hello. He didn't acknowledge it.

At the soda bar, I pulled a jumbo cup from the dispenser and filled it with cubed ice and Coca-Cola. On the other side of the room, the jockeys had formed another huddle next to the betting window. The chin straps that dangled from their helmets were shaking with disagreements. I moved down to the cash register. Birdie was writing today's word. The black marker's thick wool tip squeaked on the cardboard.

La Verdad, she wrote.

"You're early," she said.

"So how come I feel late, like something's going on without me?"

"Nice try." She wrote the translation for *La Verdad*: The Truth.

I decided it was God's idea of a joke. Once again, I was telling the truth, but nobody believed me.

"Birdie, I really don't know what's going on."

"Come on. The barn inspection?"

I shook my head. "I don't even know what a barn inspection is."

She capped the pen and punched a key on the register, catching the cash drawer before it hit her chest. "You didn't call it in?"

"No, ma'am."

"You didn't come this early to see Mr. Yuck on the war path?"

I shook my head and handed her my money. "Aunt Eleanor asked me to come talk to the arson investigator."

She straightened the bills, carefully aligning George Washington so that all his profiles faced the same direction before going into the drawer.

"Birdie, I really didn't know. What happened?"

"Yuck closed down the training runs this morning. The jockeys"—she chucked her chin toward the huddle in back—"they ran in here, scared that he's gonna do random drug tests. And the geezers"—she nodded at the old guys—"they're about to start a pool on who Yuck takes out first." She closed the cash drawer. "My advice is you take that sandwich to go. Your aunt's barn was near the top of Yuck's list."

Chapter Nineteen

Bill Cooper stood outside Stella Luna's stall with his cowboy boots splayed in the sawdust. As I came up behind him, I heard his cell phone ring. He snatched it from his belt clip like a gunslinger in a shootout.

"He's still here," he said. "Probably another five minutes."

He closed the phone, then turned. As if sensing my presence.

"Hi," I said.

"What're you, spying on me?"

"You're standing in the middle of the barn."

The expression in his pale eyes sent a shiver down my spine. Turning his face to the side, he spit a black stream of tobacco juice into the sawdust. "I know your game."

"Really?" I said. "Because I don't know what's going on."

"Play dumb. Go ahead. Nobody's buying it."

Juan came out of KichaKoo's stall, leading the horse. He was followed by Mr. Yuck, who held a BlackBerry in his pudgy palm, tapping the screen with one finger. A delicate tap, like a guest at a cocktail party choosing the tiniest hors d'oeuvre.

Cooper headed toward him. "Did you comb the sawdust, you pathetic excuse of a—"

"Your groom's hot plate," Mr. Yuck said, not looking up, "it won't be returned."

"You'll starve my groom so you can pretend you're actually doing something around here. It's pathetic. How do you sleep at night?"

"Like a baby on whiskey." Mr. Yuck gave a dolorous smile. "And considering that fire, you should be thanking me for confiscating the hot plate."

The lieutenant who had guarded the conference room door yesterday was striding toward us, holding a sheaf of white paper and waving it like a surrender flag. Only surrender wasn't on Mr. Yuck's face. Removing one sheet from the stack, he handed the page to Cooper. Then smiled, bitterly. I moved to the side, reading over Cooper's shoulder.

FORMAL COMPLAINT was typed across the top. It mentioned "contraband," which I assumed was the hot plate, and offered numbered steps for appeal and remediation. Cooper clutched the paper in both hands, but suddenly the words disappeared under a spatter of tobacco juice.

Cooper held out the paper to Mr. Yuck. "Here you go."

The security chief gave a smile as dark and acidic as the trainer's spit. "Have a nice day, Mr. Cooper."

He pivoted and walked toward the gallery that connected the next stable, his small feet churning through the sawdust. Lieutenant Campbell hurried after him. But Cooper stood rooted to the spot. Crumpling the paper, he threw it to the ground. His hands were opening and closing, the rough fingers flexing as if preparing to take a swing. I stepped back and Juan turned away, leading KichaKoo to the hot walker. The groom kept his eyes down, but something about his stooped posture made me wonder. How did I convince him to let me stay with Solo in Seattle that night? Money. Just money. I glanced at Cooper. How much did the trainer have to pay, to cover anything covered up?

So many guilty consciences, I thought, *so little time.*

And then, as if punctuating my thought, a scream shot to the barn rafters. High-pitched and horrified, it sent Cooper running down the gallery toward the sound. I took off after him, but my girly shoes were slipping on the sawdust. He turned down the same path where Mr. Yuck had gone, but he was a good fifteen yards ahead of me. But I saw a flash of pink.

Ashley Trenner was struggling to hold on to the black beast named Cuppa Joe. The horse was stamping its hooves, bucking around a tight circle, as the girl clung to the bridle and jumped out of his way. And that wasn't even the real problem.

Two men staggered over the sawdust, locked in battle. Jimmy

Bello's elbows were raised high, with his hands wrapped around the thick neck of Mr. Yuck. He drove the security chief into the plank wall. They hit with a thud that sounded like a clap of thunder. Cuppa Joe gave a high whinny.

"Stop!" Ashley cried. "Stop—you're scaring the horses!"

But Bello only pressed down harder. Mr. Yuck's face was changing colors, the droopy eyes bulging. When his lieutenant raced forward, I heard that distinctive rip of Velcro, the nylon hooks ripping apart. He held a small black can in his hands and I shut my eyes. I didn't open them again until Bello started howling.

He was no longer choking Mr. Yuck but clawing at his own face, stumbling across the gallery, blind from the Mace. His left foot kicked a metal bucket, tripping him. When he fell to the ground, nobody moved to help him up.

The lieutenant looked at Mr. Yuck. "Are you all right?"

The bitter eyes were watering. He coughed, once, and reached down to pick up his BlackBerry that had fallen into the sawdust.

Bello cried, "I'm blind!"

Mr. Yuck took a wide path around the trainer and marched into an empty stall. The lieutenant stayed, keeping the Mace can's red nozzle pointed at Bello. His other hand lifted a radio from his belt.

"Problem at Abbondanza," he said into the receiver.

The reply came quick: "Now what?"

"Trainer. What else."

Bello lifted one hand from his face. The eyelid was swelling shut, but he looked up at the lieutenant and flexed his middle finger.

The lieutenant spoke into his radio again. "Bring Mike and Keith. With the restraints."

"10-4!"

Mr. Yuck stepped out of the stall. His dour smile looked almost beatific as he lifted a small bag. The brown paper was crumpled and covered with sawdust. "No wonder Mr. Bello didn't want me to go in there," he said. "I just found buried treasure."

The lieutenant clicked the radio once more. "Bring a property box. With a lock."

Mr. Yuck shook the bag, sending the sawdust falling to the ground like snow. "Yes, my Christmas in August."

Bello kept shifting his face, trying to see, but the left eye was almost completely closed and the right eye was so bloodshot no white remained. His mouth, however, managed a hard sneer. "You know what you are, Yuck?"

"Yes, lucky." He lifted the bag as if toasting a good friend. "I believe we have snake venom. How wonderful."

Bello said, "It ain't mine."

"Of course not. The horse went out and bought it." He turned to the lieutenant. "Shut it down."

Bello tried to push himself up. "What—? You can't shut us down!"

Mr. Yuck ignored him. "And call the state police. We're reporting this contraband. I want every one of these horses gone. ASAP."

"I'll sue you!" Bello cried. "I'll sue this whole place!"

"Certainly, Mr. Bello." The sour smile crept across the doughy face. "But you'll need to wait your turn. I'll be suing you first. For assault. And I have witnesses."

The trainer wiped at his eyes. He seemed to want to scowl but the tears kept ruining it. He only looked distraught. "You got no search warrant. You can't do this without a search warrant."

"Read your contract." Mr. Yuck passed the bag to the lieutenant. "The track reserves the right to inspect any barns for any suspicion of illegal activity. No search warrant necessary. Your little bag of treasure means you are closed for the season. Perhaps for good."

Bello sank back into the sawdust. But a moment later, he glanced up again, as though remembering something. The bloodshot eye roamed until it found Ashley. She held one small hand to Cuppa Joe, brushing down the ripples of tension in his black neck. He flared his nostrils and his ears flicked back and forth, then suddenly froze. A split second later, I heard a high whine, like an insect, and an electric golf cart zipped up to the barn.

Three security officers jumped out. The lieutenant kept the Mace poised while the three men grabbed Bello and dragged him forward. When the trainer fought back, I closed my eyes again. All those FBI training exercises meant I had an almost instinctive response when it came to Mace. When Bello cried out again, I opened my eyes. His dragging feet carved a trail through the sawdust. Mr. Yuck and his lieutenant turned in the other direction, heading for the next barn. The security chief tap-tap-tapped on his BlackBerry.

Ashley buried her face in the animal's coat. He looked as shiny as spilled oil, flanks quivering as Bill Cooper took a step closer. The trainer's cold eyes held a strange expression. A light, but the kind of light refracted through an icicle.

"Ashley?" he said.

She lifted her face. Her cheeks were scalloped with color, the skin mottled with rushing blood. "Cuppa Joe woke up sick." Her mouth quivered. "He's not himself. I'm not leaving him, even if they shut down this barn."

Cooper nodded, using his tongue to shift the plug of tobacco in his cheek. Then he spit. "We got a stable open."

But she didn't look at him. She gazed down the line of horses, leaning over their Dutch doors like town gossips.

He said, "SunTzu's stable is empty. You want it?"

"I don't know."

"You don't know? You need a job, don't you?"

She nodded.

"And I need some help." He glared at me. "Real help. Somebody who knows what they're doing. Stella Luna's running today. KichaKoo is in the sixth. Go on. Go help Juan."

Her hand stayed on the big black horse.

Cooper said, "He can come, I just told you."

"Like, now?"

"What, you think Yuck's gonna change his mind? Okay. Go ahead, stay. But I live in reality. And right now reality says your barn is officially toast."

She stole another glance at the horses. I didn't believe in telepathy, but her adoration for those animals felt tangible, like something filling the air. Tears welling in her eyes, she dropped her head and led Cuppa Joe by his bridle. They walked down the connecting gallery to Hot Tin, looking like a small pink girl with her gigantic black balloon.

"And you," Cooper said, whirling on me. "I'm so onto you. Where did you hide while Yuck tore up our barn?"

"Pardon?"

"*Pardon.*" He spat. "You go talking to that fire dude—then as Yuck shows up for inspection, you're gone. Poof. Like magic. What, afraid we'll figure out what you're up to?"

He was close enough that I could see the ragged scar on his nose. And a bump. Broken nose. Healed wrong.

"I went to get breakfast," I said. "Birdie told me he was going through the barns. I came back and happened to—"

"Yeah." He laughed, cold. "Like you just *happened* to spend the night with Solo. And just *happened* to see that tube in the dirt."

"What's your point?"

"Keep outta my way. I don't care if you are Eleanor's niece. I'm running this barn. Not you."

I stayed where I was, watching his bandy-legged walk back to Hot Tin. There was no point in following. And there was no point in explaining myself. Whatever I said would only dig a deeper hole.

And after this morning, I could already see China.

Chapter Twenty

The faint scent of Mace lingered in the air, that peculiar spicy aroma that came from its source—the outer layer of nutmeg seeds. But the barn was so quiet I could hear the horses breathing, their rhythms as uncertain as the feeling that wound through my heart. All my life, I'd managed to muscle through trouble, always fighting. And winning. But lately I was realizing that my problems were getting bigger and my self-sufficiency smaller. I needed help. Real help. And standing among the snorting animals, when I closed my eyes to pray, my mind felt fuzzy from last night's crying jag. From this morning's blitzkrieg by an arson inspector and Hurricane Yuck. There was nobody to talk to about it, except an invisible element that was more real than what I could see or touch. It was the one who rescued me, who redeemed me, who saw each loose end, every question, all my worries—and knew every answer. I would never be able to explain it in rational terms, but when I was at my worst, that was when I clearly saw Jesus. The greatest inverse relationship in the universe: when I was weak, He was strong.

But He wasn't a piñata. He was a mystery. And for all my pleading, the dots still refused to connect. When I opened my eyes, the horses were staring at me. And my stomach was growling. My breakfast sandwiches were inside my Coach bag. The foil was still warm. Unfortunately, the food had also warmed up the can of Coca-Cola I stashed in there, for emergencies, in spite of a long lecture from my wardrobe buyer Lucia Lutini. I turned my body to shield the expensive leather and popped the can's aluminum tab.

One of the horses smacked his lips. He was cinnamon colored, and his long tongue swabbed over his whiskers. Then he smacked again, stretching out for the can.

"No way," I told him. "Y'all are in enough trouble already."

"Who's in trouble?"

I jumped.

Ashley Trenner came around the corner. Her head was once again tilted with curiosity, draping the long platinum hair. "Who are you talking to?"

I lifted the Coke sheepishly. "I think that horse wanted some."

"Oh, Henry." She laughed and walked over to him. "This guy is Henry the Ate. All he thinks about is food."

She reached out to pet him. The horse flicked her hands away, lunging for her neck. He knocked her off balance, but she only laughed. Gathering her hair with one hand, she presented the golden strands like a sheaf of wheat. Henry drew back his whiskery lips and started chewing.

Apparently my thoughts were written on my face.

"I know, crazy, huh?" she said. "It's my strawberry shampoo. Drives him crazy."

After Henry had finished grazing on her hair, Ashley wiped his saliva on her jeans. She gave him a pat on the nose, then picked up the bucket that Bello had tripped over. Henry eyed her hungrily as she filled the bucket at a spigot. She poured cold water into the deep hanging basins beside each stall. And she made a point of touching each horse. Brushing necks, scratching softly, murmuring words. I stood back, eating my breakfast and enjoying that vicarious pleasure that comes from seeing someone enjoy their work. Doing what they felt born to do. She was breathing hard but moving efficiently, now pulling hay from rectangular bales stacked against the wall, stuffing it into small nets. The horses gazed at her adoringly, like children watching for a favorite teacher. Except Henry. Having finished his water, he torqued his brown neck, snuck his nose under the empty metal basin, and flung it. The tin clattered across the barn floor.

Ashley turned, smiling. "Oh, Henry. You are such a handful."

Grabbing the nets, she carried the hay down the gallery. But just like that first night, when I saw her struggling to make the hooks, she seemed surprised that her jumps didn't make the hooks. She was breathing harder, her face flushed with effort. And I noticed a small potbelly that didn't go with the rest of her lean physique.

I said, "You want me to help?"

She startled and turned suddenly. Transported by work and love, she had forgotten about me. But it was even more than that. She seemed woozy and put a hand on the wall to steady herself. I rushed over. Her pupils were dilating, black ink seeping into the blue ocean.

I took the nets from her hands. "Are you all right?"

"I just . . . need to sit down." She sagged against the wall. Henry turned, licking his lips, but Ashley was out of his reach. I watched her carefully. She looked tired, weary, but otherwise all right. I took the nets and began hooking them beside the stalls. They didn't weigh much, but the alfalfa scent of the hay was as green and cruciferous as broccoli. One of the horses, dark brown with a white spot on his forehead, nodded, as if thanking me before he bit at the net, pulling out the stiff stalks and chewing.

"I hate being this short," Ashley said. "And I'm getting fat."

"You look plenty healthy." I hooked another net and wondered if she was one of those girls who tortured themselves to be skinny. I hoped not.

She reached over, picking up Henry's basin. She walked over to the spigot, filled the water bucket, and gave Henry another full drink. She brushed his nose. "You can finally get rid of your thirst, Henry. That's the good news. You can drink all the water you want."

I hooked another net. "He couldn't before?"

She shook her head. "Ever run on a full stomach?"

"Not if I can help it."

"Exactly." She looked over her shoulder, down the gallery, waiting a moment. Then: "But Jimmy used to do mean stuff to them too. Like restrict their water for days, then let them drink until their stomachs were almost bursting. Right before a race."

I phrased my next question carefully. "Wouldn't that slow them down?"

She nodded.

Only two nets remained. I moved slowly. One subtle way to fix a race was to water-log a horse. No drugs, no evidence. Just a lot of urine. "Ashley, can I ask you something? What was in that brown bag?"

"The bag?" She reached up to her face, picking at a small red sore.

"Mr. Yuck said something about snake venom."

She glanced over her shoulder again.

"I'm just curious," I added. "All this stuff is so new to me. Aunt Eleanor wants me to learn everything."

Her voice came at a whisper, but heated and urgent. "Stop asking questions."

"I won't tell anybody."

"No, you won't. And while you're asking me, take my advice. Don't ask Bill anything. Especially about his mud."

"Bill—Cooper?"

"You didn't ask him, did you?"

I shook my head.

"Good. Because he'll go ballistic."

"What's the problem with the mud?"

"Are you listening?" She rolled her eyes. *"Don't ask."*

"Okay, got it." I nodded. "Thanks for the tip."

"You're welcome. Now I have to get back. I told Bill I needed to use the bathroom. I wanted to make sure my horses were okay, after what just happened."

It took willpower not to press her further. But I couldn't risk alienating someone who knew so much. And who was now working for Cooper. Hooking the last net, I followed her pink shirt down the short gallery to Hot Tin. Juan was leading Stella Luna, saddled, and Cooper waited at the other end of the gallery. Tony Not Tony stood beside him. They were arguing, their voices loud.

"Try five percent," said Tony. "At that price, you're stealing from me."

Ashley picked up the rake outside Stella's stall and stepped inside.

"Four percent," Cooper said.

"Four?!"

I pretended to watch Ashley rake the sawdust. She was catching the clotted bits of wood with the tool's metal teeth. But her head turned, as though listening to the negotiations.

"Nobody rides for four percent," said Tony. "He's got to split that. Which means I'll get two percent."

"Better than zero," Cooper said. "If you don't like it, go whine to Yuck. He shut down that barn, not me. I got my own bills to pay. Like that stinkin' vet. If I didn't know better . . ."

Ashley stopped. She looked up. Our eyes caught.

"What?" Tony said. "You heard something?"

"Doc Madison."

"What about him?"

"You haven't noticed?" Cooper said. "The only guy making money this season is the vet. Seems a little weird, don't you think?"

Chapter Twenty-One

The vet's office was in the back half of the medical clinic. The door was open, but probably because it couldn't close. Mounds of paper covered the floor, making the small space look like a stationary model of his dented pharmacy on wheels. A pigsty. The vet himself was sitting behind a desk smothered with more paper, and a plastic plate perched on one of the plateaus, proffering a half-eaten ham sandwich.

"Got a second?" I asked.

He looked up from something he was reading, then picked up the sandwich and took a bite, talking around the food. "You're just the person I wanted to see."

I used my foot to move the piles, enough to close the door.

"Yeah, go ahead," he said. "Make a mess, why don't you?"

I managed to close the door, barely, then lunged over stalagmites. They seemed built from mail-order catalogs. The room's one chair was covered with newspapers that crinkled dryly when I sat down. The vet glared at me. Next to him, thumbtacked into the unpainted gypsum wallboard, note cards held handwritten reminders. They all started with the same words: *Don't Forget!* Car keys, glasses, prescriptions . . . I shifted in the chair, hoping the paper's yellow color came from oxidation. I was learning that horse people had a certain scatological "earthiness." Just in case, I stood and moved the newspaper to the floor.

"Just shove that stuff on the floor." He chewed his food.

I sat down again. "You said your client is the horse. I heard you say it yesterday, with SunTzu."

"Yeah. And I have a limit for people. Three questions. That's my limit."

"Okay. Here's my first question. Snake venom. What's it used for?"

"Why do you want to know?"

"Mr. Yuck just found some in Sal Gagliardo's barn."

"Snake venom's an illegal stimulant." He took another bite. "Makes horses run faster. And it's almost impossible to detect in tests. Next question."

"Where does the mud come from?"

"What?"

"The mud. The grooms rub it into the horses' legs. Where's it come from?"

"Distributors." He gestured toward the floor. "I have plenty of catalogs. Feel free. But if you're asking about your trainer, Cooper doesn't buy from anybody. That's probably your next question. I'm counting it too."

"Where does he get it?"

"That's three. He won't say. It's a secret. I could tell you, but you have to tell me your secret first."

"I don't have a secret."

"Horse poop you don't." He finished the sandwich and brushed the crumbs from the front of his shirt onto the desk. "Why the questions about the mud?"

"I was told not to ask Cooper about it. In the same way nobody's supposed to ask Jimmy Bello about his brown bag of snake venom. That seems suspicious. I'm just looking out for Aunt Eleanor."

"Cooper digs the stuff up." He slapped his hand across the desk, searching for something.

"He told you that he digs it up?"

"That's four questions." His hand found a pair of reading glasses. "But I'm feeling merciful today, so I'll tell you. Trainers have to stay in touch with me. Even when they go out of town. Cooper takes off every six weeks or so. He's usually gone two days, then comes back with buckets of mud and that evil temper." He twirled the glasses by the stem. "Pretty good deduction on my part. Maybe I should've been a private eye. What do you think?"

With my foot, I pushed another pile away, pretending the mess bothered me more than it did. "Does anybody check his mud?"

"That's five questions." He put on the glasses but started slapping the mess again. "But since you're Eleanor's *niece*—"

He stopped on the last word, letting the inflection on the last word hang in the air. He stared at me, waiting. But somebody knocked on the door.

He yelled, "Open it!"

The door opened slowly, inches at a time, until Brent Roth could poke his head into the room. The assistant vet stared at the floor, as if expecting to hit something with the back of the door. Then he looked over at me, squinting. He nodded. I could see the acne spreading down his long neck.

He looked over at the vet, squinting again. "Manchester's got a gelding with an infected hoof."

"Another one?"

"Claire wants you to look at it."

"You got antibiotics."

Brent didn't reply.

"Oh. She threw you out." Doc Madison looked at me. "That woman's a real *pistol*."

Another inflection. And another pause, waiting for me to reply. I didn't.

Brent filled the silence.

"She says she's trying to get you on the radio."

"It's in the car."

"She wants to know when you're coming."

"She runs every man like he's a horse. Tell her I'll be there in a minute."

Brent nodded and closed the door.

"I can't wait for that kid to finish vet school. I can finally leave. Fifty years is a long time out here."

"Brent's still in school?"

"What is that, six questions? Yeah. He's still in school. Couple credits short. But I worked my way through college, and if you ask me, it makes a better vet. But you can't ask me because you're past my limit. But I'll tell you anyway. It's hard to find a guy like that these days, somebody who wants to work. And doesn't complain. These kids coming out of vet school, they all want big salaries, fancy offices. You know what I did for my first job out here? I was the pee catcher. You know what that is?"

"I'm okay not knowing."

"It was before we had these high-tech testing barns. We got urine samples from the horses—in a Dixie cup. I had to hold the cup under the horse. And then wait. You think kids these days would do that? No. They're all too good for real work."

"Speaking of testing."

"You're over the limit."

"And horses are dying."

He lowered his head, glaring at me over the reading glasses.

"Do all the horses get tested for drugs?"

"No. When a horse wins, it goes to the testing barn. First, second, third. They all go. Sometimes another horse gets picked at random. But not often." He tossed his glasses on the desk. "And if you want to know the truth, it's all a game. Horse barns smell like manure but they're actually shark tanks. And by the time the track develops a test, the trainers already have a new drug."

"And the girl, she must look the other way."

"Nice try. That's still a question. What girl?"

"Ashley." I described the events from this morning, when Mr. Yuck found Bello's brown bag, and how Ashley later told me Bello was also waterlogging the horses. "She knew what Bello was doing. And as soon as Yuck shut down Abbondanza, Cooper offered her a job. But we already have a groom."

"So what? Every trainer wants her."

"Because she looks the other way."

"I'm losing count." He shook his head. "Trainers all want Ashley because she's got a way with horses. When it comes to thoroughbreds, that's saying something. They're high-strung athletes. And if that girl had one lick of sense, she'd try to make some real money with her gift. But all she cares about is helping the horses." He found a paper napkin on the desk and wiped his mouth, tossing it back on the desk.

"Jimmy Bello, now he's another story. The way he sees things, horses are race cars. Machines. You just add fuel—legal or otherwise—and let 'em rip. If they run fast, great. If they don't, get rid of them."

"Get rid of them—how?"

The vet stared. His blue eyes were an old pale color but the expression was anything but weary. "I got a secret," he said finally. "You know what it is?"

"You never throw anything out?"

"That is true. I'm a collector." He pushed at a pile. The stack shifted, slipping like a tectonic fault. He pulled out a catalog, lifting it high so I could see the cover. A firearms catalog. He stared at me over the top.

"One of the things I collect is guns." He licked a finger and began turning the pages. They sounded like scythes, slicing the air. "To answer your next question, no, I don't like to hunt. I don't enjoy shooting animals. People, that might be another matter."

I felt a sudden heat spreading across my back and circling in front to my stomach. "But in my forty-plus years collecting guns, I never met a woman who carried a Glock. Most of them can't handle the recoil."

I looked at my watch. "I should really get back to the barn."

"Except for law enforcement. They carry Glocks." He looked at the catalog, reading from the pages. "Glock, nine millimeter. Lays flat. Fits nicely into a holster or under a belt. Tremendous firepower. Compact design. A favorite with law enforcement."

He looked up just as my left hand covered my right thumb. The callus, created by the Glock's recoil.

"Are you a cop?"

I could feel sweat beading on my back.

He said, "Then private eye."

When I didn't respond, he pulled off the reading glasses and pointed them at me. "My client's the horse, that's a fact. I see stuff out here that I don't like. But that's racing. High-stakes thorough-bred horse racing. It ain't pretty on the backstretch. But most folks out here are good people. They pour their hearts into these animals. People like your *aunt*."

I decided not to blink.

"Whoever you are, if you're looking to bust somebody for hurting horses, fine. I'm with you. But if you're some animal-rights kook trying to shut down this place, hear me now." He shook the glasses at me. "I'll run you out of here so fast your head will spin."

His gaze was too intense. I couldn't hold it. I stared at his desk. The plate. The piles. A magnifying glass, flecked with dust. Shoelaces still in their packaging. Box of latex gloves. Empty coffee cup on its side. When I looked up again, his small mouth had tightened.

I pointed at the box of gloves. "Can you spare some?"

His eyes never left my face. Reaching out with one hand, he slapped around until he caught the box. He threw it at me.

I caught it, pulled out several pairs of gloves, and stuffed them into my purse.

He said, "You're not going to tell me."

I placed the box on his desk. "There's nothing to tell."

"You're lying. Don't forget I'm the one who let you in here when SunTzu got hurt."

I nodded and stood and walked to the door. When I turned around, his mouth had tightened even more. Frustrated. He knew something. But he knew it wasn't the whole picture.

I said, "You did let me in to see SunTzu. So I guess I do owe you the truth."

His eyes brightened. He smiled.

I lifted my hand, brandishing my calloused thumb. "The recoil on that Glock is terrible."

He bared his teeth, grabbed the box of gloves, and flung it at me. But I had jumped out of the room. The box hit the back of the door, and I was running down the hallway when he started yelling.

The old vet told me my name was as good as mud.

≈

And mud was key.

Back at the barn, Cooper seemed to be gone, presumably at the track watching Tony Not Tony's jockey ride Stella Luna. Over by the hot walker, Juan was talking to another Hispanic groom. And Ashley was in Cuppa Joe's stall, cooing like a pigeon.

"I'm here," she told him. "I won't let them take you."

Juan came back to the barn and barked something at her in rapid Spanish. I couldn't understand his words but Ashley nodded. She gave the horse a kiss and followed Juan down to Checkmate's stall. He handed her several brushes, watched her work for a moment, then continued down to the end of the gallery. He turned right. Toward his room.

Quietly, I opened the Dutch door to Cuppa Joe's stall.

"Hi there," I whispered.

The black horse faced forward, with his rear end pointed toward the back corner. He gave me a noncommittal look.

"I'll just be a second," I said.

The red bucket of mud sat in the far corner. I slid down the plank wall, pushing images from my mind. This horse was even bigger than Solo. And even though Ashley said he woke up feeling sick, he looked way too healthy to me. With his teeth, he yanked hay from the net hung by the door. A noisy eater, he chomped and snorted and ate some more. His rear end was two feet from my face when I leaned over the bucket. A sheet of clear plastic covered the mud. I decided Juan put the bucket here after SunTzu died. Probably thought the stall would stay empty for the last week of the season. And the space was in the middle of the stable, which would save him steps, instead of lugging the heavy bucket from one end to the other.

I used a latex glove from Doc Madison and scooped out a handful of mud. Then I smoothed the surface inside the bucket, leaving no trace. I wrapped the damp ball of clay with two more gloves and placed it inside my purse.

Cuppa Joe turned toward me. His mouth was twisting over the food, teeth clacking inside.

"Thank you," I said. "I appreciate your cooperation."

He turned back to the hay and lifted his tail, releasing a powerful cloud of gas.

Chapter Twenty-Two

Seattle's morning traffic was usually a deadlock, but it broke as the Ghost flew north on Interstate 405. And there were no black Cadillacs following me. I settled into the soft leather seat for an all-time favorite drive: Seattle to Spokane.

Interstate 90 cut across Washington State in nearly a straight line. The highway's most obvious thrill was its mountain pass, where the Cascade Range gathered sheered blue-granite peaks that stabbed the sky like battle swords. Running north to south, the mountain range separated the west's evergreen forests and the east's desert plains. Most drivers considered it an anticlimax when the road dropped out of the mountains to the eastern flatlands. The mountains moved to the rearview mirror and the road leveled onto a basalt platform so bare and abandoned that it looked lunar. At that point, travelers cranked up the radio.

But as a geologist, I leaned forward. This deceptively bland desert was a battleground in the great war that still rages today. This particular skirmish began in the late 1920s, when an idiosyncratic geologist named J. Harlan Bretz walked across eastern Washington. Bretz wanted to document the area's mineralogy and topography because the land looked unlike anything else in the United States. Though it looked flat, Bretz discovered the dense basalt actually rolled gently toward the west. He also found deep canyons that appeared suddenly, with plumb-straight sides and level bottoms. Like bathtubs hundreds of feet deep. Bretz named the area "the great scablands" and called the sudden depressions "coulees." But most puzzling was the loose soil gathered in the middle of the coulee floors. The rocks didn't match the surrounding geology, not for hundreds of miles.

There's a pervasive theory in geology called uniformitarianism. It's a long word for a basic idea: the landscapes seen today were
formed by continuous forces exerted over millions of years. Geologists
claimed that eastern Washington's flatlands were the result of slow
and steady erosion over eons of time. But Bretz, who had a PhD in
geology, claimed the evidence said otherwise. This strange geology,
he wrote, could only result from massive flooding. In fact, one flood.

"A flood of biblical proportions," Bretz wrote.

Maybe it was the word *biblical*, but the science journals started
banning Bretz's academic papers. His peers mocked him in print.
Vilified his geology. Conspired to discredit every bit of his geology. For
the next thirty years "Bretz's flood" was treated like amateur science.

Yet Bretz never wavered.

The Great Depression came. World War II began. And ended.
The 1950s ushered in unprecedented prosperity, along with developments in science and methods of documentation, such as aerial
photography. The pictures of eastern Washington taken from airplanes showed solid rock that rolled, undulating like beach sand when
a wave suddenly pulled from shore, rippling the surface. Geologists
took soil samples inside the coulees and discovered the minerals came
from western Montana, hundreds of miles away. To figure out how
it got there, engineers devised computer models based on the facts.

And the facts showed anything but uniformitarianism.

Scientists concluded the following: During the last Ice Age, a gla-
cier suddenly melted. The ice cap was so large it smothered most of
Montana. Miles and miles of frozen water. And it melted in less than
twenty-four hours. A sudden ocean, the water swept toward the west,
crashing through present-day Idaho and scouring miles of eastern
Washington. The hydraulic force was so powerful it stripped away
every bit of vegetation, then began cutting through solid rock like a
buzz saw, slicing through hundreds of feet of volcanic basalt. On the
water's surface, boulders bigger than houses bobbed and tumbled,
washing all the way to present-day Portland, which would have been
submerged under as much as four hundred feet of fresh water.

Not millions of years. Not even years.

The flood happened in one day. Perhaps even hours.

At age ninety-six, J. Harlan Bretz shuffled into Washington, DC, to receive geology's highest honor, the Penrose Medal. Bretz's "flood of biblical proportions" was now scientific fact, geologically proven.

And I couldn't help giving thanks for Bretz every time I saw eastern Washington's otherworldly topography. A scientist who thought for himself. A geologist who knew that some of Earth's best puzzles surpassed human comprehension. I was still feeling buoyed by the man's bravery as the Ghost floated past Eastern Washington University. On the edge of campus, I parked beside a small State Patrol building and carried my muddy purse inside. Washington had two crime labs—the one in Seattle that I visited last night, and this outpost beside Idaho's rugged border that specialized in rural crimes. Poaching, mining intrigues, wildlife. And this lab was led by a forensic geologist named Peter Rosser.

He was talking on the phone when I walked into the lab. His clothing seemed coated with a fine layer of dust. The Western shirt with pearl snap buttons, the jeans and snakeskin boots, all of it looked like his investigations were settling on him in sedimentary layers. But as I waited for him to finish the conversation, I felt a familiar itch. I knew how to run every test for this clay, but I couldn't risk doing them. Not unless I wanted the evidence tossed out of court later because the same agent who collected the evidence also did the forensics. Conflict of interest. And Rossser had skills that rivaled geologists in the FBI's lab.

"Yes, indeedy," he said into the phone while gesturing to me. He was opening and closing his big paw of a hand, like a kid greedy for a present. "I'm gonna ride to the edge of town."

I took the mud ball from my Coach bag and dropped it into his palm.

"Tumbleweeds?" He peeled away the glove's deflated fingers. "I'm mighty partial to tumbleweeds. Means fewer people."

He pinched off a piece of clay and put it in his mouth.

"Psst," I whispered, "that stuff might be poisonous."

He ran his tongue along his lip, making sure he didn't leave any clay on his mouth, then finished up the phone call.

He hung up and turned to me. "That's some mighty fine clay."

He meant grain size. *Fine* covered grains measuring about .002 millimeters. *Mighty* was Rosser's Western vernacular.

"And possibly deadly," I said.

"I can taste kaolinite." He smacked his lips. "Least I won't get the runs."

An aluminum silicate mineral, kaolinite was used in everything from kitty litter to clay pigeons. It was also the definitive ingredient in the antidiarrheal medicine Kaopectate.

Rosser, still smacking his lips, gathered some chain-of-command forms and began filling in the blanks—what arrived, with whom, when.

"What d'you need from this, Raleigh?"

"Basic mineralogy first. Particularly anything that poses a health threat. Then provenance."

Provenance was location, the geological location of a specific mineral. Geology had some distinct advantages among the forensic sciences. The biggest might be that while most investigators were searching for the needle in the haystack, geology could actually shrink the haystack. Provenance was particularly helpful when a soil was highly unusual. It worked like a fingerprint, distinct and telling.

"Hate to say this," Rosser drawled, "but you caught me at a bad time."

He pointed his pen at the lab's outer wall. Stacks of cardboard boxes rose to the ceiling, their brown sides marked with terms such as IGNEOUS, FELSIC, and FOLIATED METAMORPHICS.

"I'm getting outta Dodge," he said.

"Pardon?"

"Ridin' into the sunset. Pointed at the prairie."

"You and Dale Evans?"

He grinned. "It's the lucky cowboy who gets a gal like Dale. But I'm ridin' solo. Opening my own lab."

"How come?"

"How come?" He scratched the pen into his black hair, pretending to look baffled. "Those Feds make you drink a lot of Kool-Aid?"

"I'm just wondering. What's the advantage?"

"Raleigh, if I gotta explain that to you, then I'm wasting breath." He carried the clay across the room to a stainless steel counter, placing the lump on a glass cutting board. "But you ever figure out why I'm doing this, gimme a holler. I need another forensic geologist."

He sliced the clay with a sterile scalpel. Each section was about one-sixteenth of an inch wide. He placed them in separate Petri dishes set under a heat lamp but dropped another slice into a glass beaker. Adding ten ounces of distilled water, he capped the container and shook it—hard—then placed it on the counter. The water was brackish, the grains so fine they could remain suspended for days.

"You know the source of this stuff?" he asked.

"Yes." We both knew I could only divulge so much for legal reasons, and to avoid swaying his investigation. "The clay's not being used for manufacturing purposes. And it's probably dug up by hand, perhaps with a shovel."

"Exposed at the surface?"

"I don't know."

Rosser pinched what clay remained on the glass cutting board. Once again, he put it in his mouth. "It's the consistency of toothpaste."

"Only it's not toothpaste. And it might be poisonous."

As he worked the soil around in his mouth, his eyes were focused on a middle distance between us. I could see light in his dark eyes and thought of what Newton once said, how his scientific work made him feel like a boy standing on the seashore, staring out at the undiscovered truth. "The great ocean," Newton called it.

Under the heat lamp, the dried clay had turned a pearly white color. Rosser dusted the grains on a glass slide and placed them under the stereoscope. A simple device, almost elementary, the stereoscope had two magnifying lenses that worked separately to give a three-dimensional view of the specimen.

"No maggots." Rosser stared into the lenses. "Don't see any excrement either."

"You didn't want to check that before eating it?"

"That's no fun." He looked up from the lenses. "But then, you probably forgot how to have fun. Working for the government does that to a person."

He coated another glass slide with petroleum jelly and sprinkled more dried clay over the surface. That slide went under the polarizing light microscope. PLMs were used to find subatomic structures. Beams of white light struck the magnified grains at precise angles, and the refractions revealed a mineral's "invisible" architecture. When I taught elementary geology—otherwise known as Rocks for Jocks—during my senior year at Mount Holyoke College, I used to explain the PLM to students who hated science by having them read their textbooks through a clear calcite crystal. With a cubic atomic structure—shaped like a sugar cube—calcite produced a double refraction of white light, which showed up as doubled letters on the page. Once a geologist had a mineral's atomic structure, he was that much closer to pinpointing its identity.

"I thought you rode back to Virginny." Rosser gazed through the PLM's lens, turning the knob that adjusted the optical axis. "Couldn't stay away from Seattle, huh?"

"Something like that."

During my disciplinary transfer last year—banished to the Northwest by my boss in Richmond—Rosser had run some soil exams for my missing person case. Not only did he nail the mineralogy, but he got provenance down to a pinpoint. It was quite a feat: Washington State had almost forty-three million acres.

He looked up from the scope. "Seattle grows on people. Always check for moss behind your ears."

I smiled.

He went back to the lens. "Still like working for the FBI?"

"It's okay."

"Mmm."

He looked up again, but I had already turned away, staring at the computer monitor attached to the PLM. It showed the same view as the microscope, where the grains, magnified by hundreds, appeared as random objects tumbling across a clear floor made luminous from the petroleum jelly. I saw linear pieces, oblongs, which looked to me like random bits of hay. Maybe hair from the horses. But some cubic shapes were pronounced. Their sharp edges glowed in a way that reminded me of Richmond's streetlights on summer evenings, when humidity produced auras around the lamps.

"Haloes," I said.

"You got it. First guess?"

"Zircons."

"What I was thinking too."

I leaned into the monitor, trying to get a closer look. I'd seen zircon with haloes, but nothing as powerful as this. The crystals beamed like flashlights, and I knew only one source could produce that much energy.

I said, "Those are radiation haloes."

But Rosser had already picked up a dry slice of clay, toting it across the lab, ducking his head under the ropes that hung from the exposed steel I-beams. Nooses and slipknots, forensic samples of restraint and torture and death. I followed him to the Scanning Electron Microscope. It was shaped like a large metal box and produced a near-constant din of squeaks and whirs, like a clock about to break a cog. Rosser tapped a carbon plug into the dried clay and slid it into the SEM's side opening.

"See if we get a direct hit," he said.

A metal filament inside the SEM produced electrons, similar to what happens in a lightbulb. But the SEM had magnets that focused the electrons into a single beam. When aimed directly at an object, the beam could draw an object's shape and structure, down to the finest details. SEMs were essential to crash evidence forensics, detecting structural flaws that may have existed before impact—weaknesses in airplane wings, faulty headlights. It was used on excavated pieces of the *Titanic* and revealed how the cold water caused the ship's hull to become brittle and more vulnerable to impact with ice. Although it worked best on cleaned samples, I didn't have time to wait for the grains to settle from the brackish water. Rosser, sensing my urgency, hadn't even asked if I wanted to wait.

"Thanks," I said.

He nodded and clicked the mouse that switched the monitor from a 3-D display of shapes to bar graphs. We knew these minerals were cubic; we needed to know what they were, exactly. Several "unknowns" were already appearing on the screen. Hay, I figured. Dust, barn particles. But kaolinite appeared. Then zircons, identified as zirconium by the SEM.

"I'm two for two," Rosser said.

"Quit gloating."

"There's your radiation." Rosser pointed at the screen. Thorium and uranium were the next minerals identified.

I glanced back at the beaker on the counter. A thin dark line of sediment was beginning to form across the glass bottom. Heavy metals dropping out first. Thorium, uranium. While I waited for the SEM, Rosser walked back across the lab. Turning left at the ropes, he opened the bottom drawer of a file cabinet and removed several boxes that were wrapped in a lead apron.

"Washington's got a passel of radioactive deposits." He carried the metal containers to the stainless counter. "I keep samples for comparison purposes."

"Wrapped in lead blankets."

"I look stupid to you?" he asked.

"You ate that clay."

As if to say *touché*, the SEM pinged. The scan was complete and the bar graph looked like a rigid rainbow, each color representing another element. The "unknowns" were there, but with high levels of aluminum and silica. The kaolinite, I decided, the aluminum silicate minerals. I read down the rest of the list.

"Selenium," I called out to Rosser. "In high concentrations, right behind aluminum and silica."

"Check the periodic table."

"Come on, just tell me."

"I'll give you a hint. Arsenic's neighbor."

Arsenic was number 33 on the periodic table. "Thirty-two or thirty-four?"

"Four," he called out. "And sometimes as poisonous as its neighbor."

"Good thing you ate two servings." I walked over to a bookcase across from the SEM and used both hands to pull out the monstrous *Kerr's Optical Mineralogy*. The definitive source, *Kerr's* described more than five hundred different minerals. The tome was my personal manual when I worked in the FBI's mineralogy lab, and the pages of clear photographs felt as familiar as a family album.

Selenium's periodic table symbol was Se, and *Kerr's* described it as a grayish-purple semimetal. Selenium often formed poorly shaped crystals but sometimes appeared as tiny acicular—hair-like—structures. The mineral was used in glassmaking, paint pigments, and photovoltaics. When I suddenly heard a series of distinctive rolling clicks, I looked up from the book.

Rosser was waving the small instrument over the clay. The closer it came to the soil, the louder and quicker the clicks. *Click-click-clickclickclickclick*. Radiation detector.

I said, "The clay is used for therapeutic purposes."

"Where—death row?"

I went back to *Kerr's*. The notes mentioned selenium's toxicity but without much detail. I walked over to another computer, set aside from the exam equipment. Rosser told me the lab's security code and I logged onto the Internet. After several Google queries, I had some basic information. Selenium was necessary for good health, but in high concentrations the mineral was toxic. In humans, symptoms of selenium poisoning included weak and/or rapid pulse, labored breathing, bloating, abdominal pain, and dilated pupils. In animals, the symptoms were about the same, and included a stiff gait. North and South Dakota had soils that carried naturally heavy concentrations of selenium, and in that area pastured animals were known to accidentally poison themselves by eating too many field-grown grains. However, it was difficult for farmers to catch the toxicity early because symptoms were vague—stomach problems, difficulty breathing, disorientation . . . symptoms that sounded eerily similar to "Emerald Fever."

I turned to Rosser. He was placing the radioactive materials back inside the metal boxes, covering them with the lead apron.

"Any chance you get provenance," I said, "before you ride off into the sunset?"

"It's that serious?"

I stared at the screen. Most people recovered from selenium poisoning, the article said. There was an antidote, which was easy to administer.

But animals were another matter. Particularly horses. There was no antidote. Every incident of selenium poisoning was fatal.

"Yes," I said. "It's that serious."

Chapter Twenty-Three

The Ghost demanded speed, ripping across that flood-scoured bedrock all the way back to Seattle. Traveling this fast, this effortlessly, was a total thrill. Maybe close to what it felt like to ride a thoroughbred down the track, surpassing human limitation, melding with the wind.

I downshifted over Snoqualmie Pass and floated across the Cascades into evergreens that unfurled as rich as emeralds. When I-90 came to an end in the city, I followed the curve of road toward the saltwater basin cupping pieces of the Pacific Ocean. I parked in an alley off South Jackson, thanked the car for a truly marvelous ride, and walked over to an unmarked metal door. Lucia Lutini was waiting.

The official profiler for the Seattle field office was long-limbed with olive skin. In winter she wore cashmere and merino wools; in summer the finest linens. Tonight her skirt looked spun from sun-bleached Tuscan fibers.

"Fair warning," she said as I walked through the door. "My sister showed up."

We passed a dishwashing station with an industrial sink and nozzle that snaked from the ceiling. In the kitchen, her father, Donato, stood at a blackened grill. He was short, powerfully built, and wore a white chef's jacket. A young woman stood next to him, stout with curly black hair. I drew a deep breath, smelling sautéed garlic. Simmering tomato sauce. Pork browned, seasoned with soft green sage and fennel. My mouth watered.

"I no wanna say it again!" Donato yelled. His Italian-immigrant

English swooped like vines, every syllable swinging to the next. "You make-a me say it again!"

The young woman had olive-toned skin like Lucia, but she was even prettier. "Papa," she said, "you can stop. I get it."

"You no get it! You got a head like a rock. I'm a-telling you, no oregano in the sauce!"

"I just said it could use a little."

"Thirty-seven years!" His arms shot up. "I run this place thirty-seven years. You see me askin' you for a recipe?"

Lucia grabbed my sleeve, tugging. I followed her along the outer wall, past the work island and pot rack. My eyelids were almost fluttering with the scent of meat falling off its bone.

"You might want to try adding some oregano," the woman said.

"Merone!" His fingers gathered on his thumbs, his wrists circling the air. "You wanna know why you got no husband? Because you no listen!"

Lucia opened the door to the janitor's closet and pushed me inside, closing the door behind us. She leaned her back against it and sighed. But the argument pushed through the door.

"Your sister, she knows how to listen."

"Lucia? She's an old maid."

"But she no want to ruin my red sauce."

"Ruin it? All right. That's it. Where's the oregano?"

I heard a Vesuvius-like eruption of Italian from Donato, punctuated by banging pots and yelling from the young woman. Lucia's eyes were closed. I watched her clavicle rising and falling with each breath, the delicate bones as symmetrical as a bridge span.

"Is this a bad time?" I asked.

She opened her eyes. They were sloe eyes, large and brown.

"No," she said. "Papa will be glad to see you. The problem is Giuliana. My sister. She's unemployed. Again. But now she's decided Papa needs her help. Believe me, that kind of help will send him to an early grave."

Donato's restaurant was a literal hole in the wall. No tables, no chairs. But the line for lunch circled the block Monday through

Friday. The window closed for the weekends, and Friday nights the Lutini family gathered here for a meal. Lucia had extended an open invitation after she chose Raleigh David's wardrobe piece by piece from Nordstrom's flagship store a few blocks north of here.

She turned over an empty bucket, offering me a seat. But I remained standing after the long drive.

"I heard about the fire," she said, sitting on the bucket. The contrast only made her look more elegant. "I'm glad you survived, of course. But I worried. The smoke must have ruined your clothes."

"I was wearing my own jeans and boots."

She pointed at my purse. "So what is that?"

I looked down at the bag. "Nothing."

She leaned forward and swiped her finger over the gold Coach emblem. "That's . . . dirt."

"Mud, actually."

"Raleigh, the handbag is not a backpack."

"I'll clean it. Saddle soap—I hear it works on anything."

She sighed. "It was too much to hope for."

"What was?"

"I was hoping Raleigh David would rub off on you. But I should know better. People don't change from the outside. Proceed."

"What do you remember about Bill Cooper, the trainer?"

"Forty-eight. Married once. Divorced. Sporadic child support. Employed by Eleanor Anderson for, what, a year?"

"Little over."

The woman was a computer. Which was why I came here tonight. Well, one reason. She listened carefully as I described the buried tube, the battery bricks, and the state lab's forensics. "Cooper uses clay poultices to soothe the horses' aching muscles. But I just found out it has at least three poisonous substances. Selenium, uranium, and thorium. And Cooper won't tell anyone where he gets the mud."

"You think he's poisoning the horses on purpose?"

"I can't prove his intentions right now. But the minerals wouldn't show up in any blood tests. Not unless the tester knew to look for them specifically."

"Clever," she said. "Very clever."

"Tell me what you're thinking."

She dangled a leather sandal from her foot, thinking a moment before speaking. "Eleanor pays him for wins, I'm sure. A percentage of the purse is fairly standard for good trainers. So if he's poisoning the horses, that means somebody is paying him more to lose. Do any funding sources come to mind?"

This morning, when Mr. Yuck inspected the barns, Cooper was warning someone on his cell phone. *"Five minutes,"* he said. Yuck's next stop was Abbondanza. "Sal Gagliardo, maybe. The bookie. But Sal Gag's horse was involved in the starting gate fiasco."

"You're committing an error in logic. Don't assume the mud and this tubular mechanism are related." She bobbed the sandal on the end of her foot. "Unless . . ."

I waited. The woman could read motive like a spreadsheet.

"It was raining that day. Am I correct?"

"Yes."

"What if the substance sprayed from the tube dissolved in water? Or blended with the turf?"

"Like the clay." I thought of the soil suspended inside the beaker of water. "And if a horse was already suffering from mineral poisoning, one small projectile of uranium or thorium—"

"Carried quickly by the adrenaline, which would be coursing through the animal's circulatory system prior to a race—"

"And then shock," I said. "Shock would send more adrenaline into the bloodstream." I told her how SunTzu's heart gave out in the medical clinic, and how the vet tried to resuscitate him.

"One problem." She reached down, tugging the sandal back on her painted toes. "This Bill Cooper sounded rather crass on paper. Is he clever enough to carry out this hypothetical scenario?"

"From what I saw this morning, he's ruthless and devious." I described the way Cooper plucked Ashley from the ruins of Abbondanza. "He convinced her it was for her benefit. The whole thing happened quickly, but it was as if Cooper already had a plan."

Lucia smiled. It was the sly and quiet smile of Mona Lisa, with the gravitas of understanding the criminal mind. "You would like me to do a deeper background check?"

"Could you, please?"

"If you apologize for ruining that beautiful handbag."

"I'm sorry."

She reached for the shelves behind her. They held gallon cans of olive oil and a pencil that dangled from a string. Tearing paper from what appeared to be a shopping list, she wrote something quickly. "You will want another favor."

"Not right now."

"Are you sure?" She smiled again, but another expression was playing in her sloe eyes. Like a cat who had cornered a mouse and was playing with it. "Wouldn't you like me to steal your photo from Jack's desk?"

My photo. *Jack's desk.* "Excuse me?"

"Oh, that's right. I forgot. You're not in the office these days."

"You never forget anything."

"That is true." The corners of her mouth lifted again. "I was being disingenuous."

"Or worse."

"I presume this picture was taken on that cruise to Alaska. I can see mountains in the background." She folded the scrap of paper. "But perhaps you two went on another trip?"

"Lucia, nothing's going on. You know that."

"Of course."

Yet she continued to smile. And I felt heat coming up my throat. I said, "Get it over with. Tell me."

"Well, it's interesting from a profiling standpoint."

"From a profiling standpoint, Jack's insane. We know that."

"Ah, but this particular photograph has an intriguing quality."

My face felt hot, like it was the color of Donato's tomato sauce. And I couldn't seem to make it stop. *When did Jack take a picture of me?*

"You remember his desk," Lucia said. "That display of girlfriends, each of questionable reputation?"

Jack's photo harem was a running joke inside the Violent Crimes unit. Nobody knew if the women were his dates or his suspects.

"They're gone," she said. "Every one. Now there is only a picture of you."

I lifted my left hand, brandishing my ring finger. "Engaged. Remember?"

"Oh, but of course." She stood and opened the door. Smiling. "Shall we eat?"

Her sister, Giuliana, was standing at the stove. She lifted a ladle from a sauce pan and sipped. "Oregano," she said. "I was right."

Donato wasn't there to hear her. Standing by the alley door, he greeted the crowd of family streaming inside. I saw Lucia's elderly uncle, his withered posture curling him like a violin scroll. And two couples with seven children between them, all under the age of ten. Donato followed them back into the kitchen. When he saw me, he exclaimed, gave me a hug, and introduced me to everyone. Lucia's friend Raleigh. That was all. Just Raleigh. The uncle grunted and took the only seat in the house, a kitchen stool with a kick-step, while everyone else stood around the big island, talking loudly beneath a copper cloud of cooking pots, their voices saying nothing important but each word delivered with great emphasis, bouncing off the metal above us. Our meal was dished out on the same paper plates that the customers got, while Donato and Giuliana relaunched their argument. The children ran to the service window to play res-taurant—girls served food; boys pretended to eat—except for one plump boy also called Donato. He stood beside his grandfather at the stove, listening to the old man ladle out cooking advice.

"First a-thing," Donato said. "You no listen to the women, *capiche?*"

I lifted my paper plate. The roasted tomato sauce had a silken texture. It bathed a glistening brown sausage bedded on a crusty roll with sautéed peppers and onions. I closed my eyes to give thanks and listened to the music of the people around me. My first bite sent garlic waltzing across my tongue, pirouetting with the sage, while the slow-roasted pork and beef stepped forward, luxuriating on my palate until fennel took its final bow.

I almost gasped, giving thanks again.

Donato served me a second sandwich. My paper plate and napkin looked like a crime scene. Lucia remained pristine, without a speck of red sauce anywhere on her linen clothing. And all the while, the happy cacophony continued. Mothers yelled at the kids, husbands yelled at the wives for yelling at the kids, and the kids yelled back that it was all unfair. I drew a deep breath and continued eating.

"Ey, Raleigh." Donato's face seemed to glow with joy. "You like-a my food?"

I could only nod.

And later that night, as I sat outside on the condo porch, I was still trying to find the words. In the sky above, the Summer Triangle was blinking into view–Altair, Deneb, Vega—and my eyes felt tired, almost gritty from so much driving. But when Polaris peeked out, I recalled a summer night long ago, when a thunderstorm knocked out Richmond's electrical power. My dad never wasted opportunity. He led me outside for the blackout so we could name the stars. Dippers—Ursa Major, Ursa Minor—and Orion with his belt and sword. And this same Summer Triangle that was also known as the Swan, Lyre, and Eagle. It was a good memory, but I started to feel cold and went back inside. I walked through the sleek and empty rooms that belonged to a woman who didn't exist, and climbed into her fresh, anonymous bed in a room where an air conditioner sucked dry every trace of warmth. And for hours I tossed and turned. Too many thoughts were flitting through my mind, and finally I rolled over and turned on the bedside lamp. The red leather book waited. But tonight I could only flutter the pages, too tired to choose, and wishing that whatever wisdom I needed would simply appear and mend the ache inside my heart. The pain. It went far beyond the usual hurt. Past the grief of missing my dad. My mom's condition. The situation with DeMott. And yet I couldn't name it until Proverbs rustled into view. Suddenly I recalled all the good food and bickering inside that kitchen, all the echoes of children at play and heated arguments. My heart ached because open rebukes were better than hidden loves. Because wounds from a friend were more faithful than the profuse kisses of an enemy. Because this night had glimmered with the tight entropy, the skimming blows, the eruptions that came from long-simmering resentments.

The needles born for our souls.

It was family.

And I had none.

Chapter Twenty-Four

Saturday morning I woke early. While the coffee brewed, I picked through Raleigh David's junk mail and listened to the messages on her answering machine, a litany of political pleas and lies recorded yesterday. By the fifth call, from a candidate who could only lift his stature by vilifying his opponent, I reached over to hit Stop.

But the sixth message began, "It's me."

I stared at the machine.

"Delta Airlines says Madame can stay under my seat, in a cage," DeMott said. "Here's our flight number."

I grabbed a pen and scrawled the number across a political flyer.

"The flight's scheduled to arrive at one in the afternoon, but since we're changing planes in Atlanta, thunderstorms might delay the flight. Be sure to check the arrival time before you drive to the airport."

I moved my jaw back and forth. Maybe it was the way he said it. Like he didn't expect me to think of this myself. Lecturing me. Again.

He said, "We'll see you tomorrow."

"Tomorrow?"

"It's sudden, I know," he said, as if hearing my reply. "But Madame won't survive like this much longer. And Mac's baby is due next week. I want to be here for that."

There was a long pause. My feet felt riveted to the kitchen floor.

"Probably best if I call your cell phone when we land. Then you won't have to park. You can pick us up at the arrivals." He paused again. "I can't wait to see you, Raleigh."

He hung up. I hit Play again. One thought was looping through my mind. *DeMott, in Seattle*. I felt sweat breaking out under my arms. *Today. DeMott in Seattle. Today.* But on the second listen my panic turned to fury. *He couldn't give me some notice?* I hit Stop before he finished talking and scrolled through the call log. His message was recorded yesterday. Friday. At 6:00 a.m. When I was meeting with the arson investigator. Gone all day, and last night too tired to check the messages. A sensation like a piercing arrow hit my heart. He had given me notice. And like those politicians, I was vilifying him to elevate myself.

As I was pulling the plank from my eye, I saw another message was on the machine. My finger was poised over the delete button, expecting another politician, but it wasn't.

"Miss David, this is Walter Wertzer with the Pierce County Fire Department. I'm calling Friday afternoon."

Oh boy.

"Since you seemed eager to take it, I scheduled your polygraph."

The lie detector test.

"I know you horse people work on Saturdays"—his tone was somehow snide—"so I'll expect you at the Auburn station off Black Diamond Road. Tomorrow morning. Eight o'clock."

I whirled toward the microwave. The red numbers were red as fire. 7:09 a.m.

≈

Hair dripping wet, I ran into the food-beer-gas deli. Behind the counter, the Indian family was gathered for a breakfast that smelled of mangoes and cumin. The man named Raj took my order. And the little girl with pigtails dashed under the counter and followed me to the refrigerator case where I removed a liter of Coca-Cola and took it to the counter where the condiments were kept. Ripping open salt packets, I poured the white crystals on a napkin.

The girl was just tall enough to peer over the counter. She said, "Can I do some?"

I nodded.

She took a handful of packets and tore them in half, grinning mischievously. When my burger was ready, I lifted the burger's bun and asked the girl to pour the salt on it. She asked no questions. Forming a funnel with the napkin, she poured several thousand milligrams of sodium chloride on what was already a salty meal. She even shook the napkin, making sure no salt was left behind.

"Thank you," I said.

"Let's do another one."

"Next time."

"Really?"

"No. But I'll buy you a donut."

"Okay."

I paid for the soda, burger, and donut and added another dollar for the salt. Carrying everything to the Ghost, I drove around back of the store and searched for the black Cadillac. I didn't see it. Parked next to an abandoned air pump, I bowed my head and begged for help. A shallow prayer, but I asked for help to choke down the world's worst hamburger.

I chewed slowly despite the bitter flavor, letting the salt seep into my taste buds and bypass my stomach so the sodium got an expedited delivery into my bloodstream. About halfway through the meal, I could feel the veins rising on the backs of my hands. My fingers swelling. And this was how lying worked, I decided. At first I lied because it seemed like it would make things better for my mother. But things got worse. They always did with a lie. When I took another bite, the salt stung my lips. I was now a professional liar. Paid to live undercover. Officially ordered to lie. But no way was the truth coming out during a lie detector test. I checked the mirrors again. Still no black Caddy. Opening my phone I tapped out the numbers, my fingers so bloated that the engagement ring hurt.

Jack didn't bother with hello. He said, "It's like the Bat signal."

"Pardon?"

"I was thinking of you again, and you called. It's like sending up the Bat signal."

When I didn't reply, he said, "How's it going?"

He was probably the only person in my life who didn't immediately ask, "What's wrong?" DeMott asked every time I called. And
my sister, Helen, who considered the FBI equivalent to the KGB.
Then again, so did our mother.

"I'm on my way to a lie detector test."

"That seems extreme."

"What?"

"You can just admit you're in love with me. No need to take a test."

"Jack, this isn't a joke. The arson guy called. I've got thirty minutes to get to the station and take the test."

"Hold him off. I'll call the lawyers. We'll throw him off track
somehow."

"No," I said. "It'll only make him more suspicious." And lawyers,
with my OPR file growing, seemed like a very bad idea.

"You have a plan?"

"Salt."

He hesitated. "It doesn't always work."

Polygraph tests weren't admissible in court, but law enforcement
agencies used them to decide whether or not to pursue a suspect
because the tests indicated evasiveness and nervousness by tracking
blood pressure and heart rate changes. When asked certain questions,
people panicked. I was hoping to ingest enough salt that my blood
pressure would skyrocket no matter what was asked, confusing the
polygraph's readout.

"There's another trick," he said.

"Anything."

"Squeeze your butt."

No words came to mind.

"Harmon, are you there?"

"I'm here."

"Did you hear me?"

"I heard you."

"If you tighten the anal sphincter, it raises your blood pressure.
But you have to be careful."

"Really."

"Yeah, the guys giving these tests know every trick. I heard some chairs have sensors now. But you could put some thumbtacks in your shoes. Pain raises blood pressure."

"Pain. Then I could just think about you."

"Not a bad idea," he said cheerfully. "Any kind of excitement works. You could think about hiking in the mountains. It's sunset. Nobody else is around. Except me, and I don't have my shirt on. I turn to you and say—"

"I shouldn't have called you."

"No, I turn to you and say, 'Harmon, you are the most—'"

"Okay, fine. I got it." I stared at the salt. It looked like a layer of crystallized cheese on the burger. I blamed it for the sudden flush creeping into my face. "I'll be fine."

"I know you will. Just use that brain of yours. Send up the Bat signal when it's over. I'll be waiting."

Chapter Twenty-Five

I wasn't originally from the Northwest, but my background in geology told me Black Diamond Road was named for coal mined from the surrounding hills. On that missing person case here last year, I learned that so many "black diamonds" had been mined from the area's banded layers that during the 1920s a man could enter a tunnel's south end and walk north seven miles before he saw daylight. As I pulled up to the fire station, I tried to think about arcane geology. It helped distract my mind. Breathing was becoming difficult, my pulse clanged against my wrists. And when I stepped out of the Ghost, the station's fire alarm shrieked. My heart beat like a war drum as two chrome-and-red engines screeched from the garage doors.

When the engines were gone, I walked to the entrance. In the glass door, the reflection showed a woman dressed in navy blue slacks with a quartz-white silk blouse. Cool as a sociopath, she wore two-inch heels that lifted her to five foot eleven. But when I glanced down, I saw that my toes were poking over the sandals' footbed, swollen from salt. Lovely sandals. Black leather. Chosen by Lucia for Raleigh David. Sandals made by Pravda.

No, wait. Prada.

I drew a shaking hand over my still-damp hair, pulled into a sleek ponytail.

Raleigh David, I told myself. *You are wealthy, imperious.*

But apparently not that impressive. The woman behind the front desk was on the phone. She barely looked at me.

"No soliciting," she said, returning to her conversation. "I know, can you believe it? People are such idiots."

I glanced around the station. The architecture was Northwest government-lodge. Lots of wood, exposed steel beams, concrete slab floor. But it looked purged, as if everyone left on the last siren call. I glanced at the receptionist. Dark roots bisected her blond hair. When I opened my mouth, my lips stuck to my teeth. I licked them, feeling a tongue rough as a cat's.

"Excuse me," I managed to say.

She didn't raise her head. "I told you. No sales."

"I have an appointment."

"Hang on," she told the person on the phone, then looked at me. She seemed to be trying not to roll her eyes. "What do you need?"

I was tempted to give a literal answer. Just to annoy her further. *Love*, I would say. *I need love. And a place to call home. Family.*

Instead: "I'm here to see Walter Wertzer."

She slapped an intercom box. "Mr. Wertzer, you there?"

"Affirmative," he answered.

Affirmative. Not "yeah." Not even "yes." Affirmative.

Uh-oh.

"Name?" She kept the phone to her ear. "Hey, what's your name?"

"Raleigh David," I lied.

≈

It was affirmative all right: Walter Wertzer's office gave me the willies.

His desk was an inch-thick slab of pale green glass and no paper rested on it. No fingerprints marred the shiny surface. And even the phone wasn't allowed to sit there. It was placed on a shelf between two galvanized tin caddies marked To Do and Done. No paper in either.

"Thank you for coming, Miss David."

"My pleasure," I lied.

He turned to another man in the room, wincing slightly. When his back was to me, I tugged at my blouse. The silk was sticking to my sweating armpits.

He said, "This is Mr. Roberts."

Mr. Roberts stood beside a table in the corner of Wertzer's office. His white beard looked like something from the Old Testament. What was visible of his face seemed about as happy as Moses coming down the mountain to discover the grumblers were worshiping a gold bovine. Mr. Roberts tried to smile. And I tried to smile back.

"Mr. Roberts will be administering your test."

The machine sat on the table. An electronic arm was attached to it, the pen resting on the graph paper.

Polygraph paper.

"Please," Moses said. "Have a seat."

The chair was padded on the arms and seat and was positioned to face a wall, putting the machine behind my back. The padding felt suspiciously thick. Butt sensors.

Wertzer stepped in front of me. "Just so you know how this works. Mr. Roberts is going to administer the test. He'll ask you some of the same questions I did." He shifted his lips. Some kind of simulated smile under the gray mustache. "Are you nervous, Miss David?"

"A little." The pulse in my ears sounded like ocean waves. "Is that a problem?"

Now he smiled. Really smiled. Nervous was good. Nervous meant he was right about Raleigh David; she had something to hide. "No, no," he said, "that's not a problem. But maybe you'd like some practice before we start. Would that help?"

I opened my eyes wide. "Is that allowed?"

But I knew what he was doing. By "practicing" the questions with me, Wertzer could later claim any emotional response from me wasn't due to surprise. Only deception.

"Here's a question Mr. Roberts will ask: What is your name?"

"Raleigh David," I lied.

"Your age?"

"Thirty-one." That was the truth.

"Is Eleanor Anderson your aunt?"

"Yes," I lied.

"See? Nothing to worry about."

My pulse beat ten thousand milligrams per second as Moses

strapped the heart monitor around my upper ribs and instructed me
to place my palms on the chair's arms. He secured my wrists with
nylon straps, which told me the padded arms did indeed have sensors.

"I'll be right back," Wertzer said.

No, he wouldn't. He didn't want to be in the room during the
test. That way, I couldn't claim his presence influenced my answers.

While Moses did something behind my back, I glanced around.
No two-way mirrors. Maybe a hidden camera somewhere. I took a
long, slow breath, counting four beats in and four beats out. The way
we were taught at Quantico. I wanted to bring my blood pressure
down for the start of the test and fixed my eyes on a poster across
from me. It showed a mountain lake. Still water. The sun setting
behind encircling hills. An inspirational message ran along the bottom. I squinted.

Opportunity, it said. *Today's plans are tomorrow's opportunity.*

Wertzer, I decided.

"Are you ready to begin?" Moses asked.

"Yes." I exhaled slowly but didn't breathe in again.

"Is your name Raleigh David?"

A control question. A softball. The answer shouldn't have any
emotional response. Moses would use my body's reaction to this
question to compare all "truthful" responses. But without air in my
lungs, my pulse started hammering at my temples. I let it go up.
"Yes," I lied. "My name is Raleigh David."

He hesitated. Then: "Do you live at Thea's Landing?"

"Yes." Pulse still pounding.

"You are thirty-one years old. Is that statement true?"

"Yes, that's true."

There was another pause, longer than the first. He wasn't getting
the correct responses to the control questions. So he asked more.
Color of my eyes—brown. Day of the week—Saturday. And when he
paused again, I stared at the silly *Opportunity* poster, breathing slowly.
I felt my heartbeat dropping and stared at the placid surface of the
mountain lake. The curveball question was coming, I could feel it.
And I wanted my pulse all the way down for it.

"Have you ever lied to someone you love?"

Curveball.

"Yes." The truth.

More silence.

I stared at the water, imagining a cool evening swim. Lake water slipping over my skin and—

"Today is Monday," he said. "Is that statement true?"

"No, today is not Monday."

I sensed his next question creeping up, trying to trick me. None of my reactions were going according to plan. Determined to stay calm, I kept my eyes on *Opportunity*, gazing at the soft coral light of sunset. It spread wings over the mountains and Jack's words jumped into my mind—*"It's sunset. Nobody else is around. Except me, and I don't have my shirt on. I turn to you and say—"*

"Did you set fire to the barn?"

"No."

But my heart wasn't cooperating. Cartwheeling, flipping, it was doing everything I didn't want it to. That answer needed to be the calmest of all—not nervous, freaking out. I closed my eyes and took another slow breath, wondering if a salt-induced stroke was coming. The room smelled dry and cool but I could also detect fear. And last night's garlic and onions, seeping through my pores.

"Do you know who set fire to the barn?"

I tried to exhale slowly, but Jack refused to get out of my head. When I opened my eyes, the poster suddenly looked like Smith Mountain Lake. In Virginia.

Virginia.

DeMott.

Coming today!

Moses said, "I'm going to repeat that question. Do you know who set fire to the barn?"

"No."

"Do you own a cat?"

What? "No."

"Did you ride a bicycle here today?"

"No."

There was a pause.

A long, long pause.

"You may relax now, Miss David." He walked around from behind and unbuckled the heart monitor, removing the wrist straps. "Feel free to get up and stretch. I'll be back in a minute."

He walked to the door. I heard it open and close, but I remained seated, facing that blasted *Opportunity*. The hidden camera, I decided, was somewhere in those dark mountains. Wertzer was watching, waiting to see if I stood up and checked the polygraph's readout. Or whether I dropped my face into my sweating hands. Or danced a jig.

I sat still, listening to the accusation inside my head.

Liar.

When the door opened again, Walter Wertzer strode inside and stood in front of my chair. He placed his hands on his hips, winced, and blocked my view of *Opportunity*.

"The test came back DI," he said.

Deception Indicated.

I tilted my head. "What does that mean?"

"It means you're not telling the truth."

My jaw dropped, shocked. *Shocked, I tell you!* "I did not light that fire."

"Miss David, do you have any idea what the punishment is for arson?"

I wanted to say, *Federal or state?* Instead I lied. "I have no idea. But if this test came back—what did you say, DUI?"

"DI."

Moses added, "Inconclusive." He stood at Wertzer's side, stroking his beard.

"Your machine must be broken," I said.

"The machine's fine," Wertzer said.

"But I didn't set that fire."

"You're lying, Miss David."

My mouth was dry. I was thirsty, so very thirsty. But dry mouth helped if you were trying to sound like a dignified Virginian. The

Old Dominion's finest speech emerged from a stiff jaw and a tight tongue, and an attitude that said all Yankees were evil.

"Mr. Wertzer, I came in here this morning to answer your questions. All of your questions. I don't see what more I could possibly do to convince you."

"Your firearm," he said.

"Pardon?"

He plucked at his lower lip. Plucking and plucking, like a man repeatedly striking a match, hoping it will ignite. "Your weapon. I want to have it tested."

"For what?"

"Ballistics."

Baloney.

He almost smiled. "Is that a problem?"

"Yes, it is. As I told you, I keep that gun for personal protection."

Now the smile came, full enough to lift the brushy gray mustache. "A woman of your means," he said, "I'm sure you can afford a replacement while I run a few tests."

"And how long will those tests take?" I asked.

"Not long," he said. "Not long at all."

Chapter Twenty-Six

I was guzzling Coca-Cola when it slithered into view. The black paint sparkled on the hood like crushed coal had floated out of the hills. I drove slowly through the valleys of Auburn, and the black Cadillac stayed just far enough behind that I couldn't see the person driving. Except his pale hand. It dangled over the steering wheel and the morning sun caught his ring. Gold. Pinkie ring, I was betting. Mob jewelry.

When I whipped into the private entrance for Emerald Meadows, I jumped out of the car, hoping to get a look at the driver. But the Caddy was pulling a U-turn. He was so far away the rear license plate was a blur.

Crabby from salt bloat and layers of big fat lies, I grabbed my purse from the Ghost and stomped toward the track's private entrance. Eleanor's battleship was parked under the brass plaque, its front bumper almost kissing the building. I checked my watch. I wasn't in the mood for dry toast or Tennessee Williams. But before I could get away, a voice came singing across the parking lot. I turned to see a red conversion van. The back doors had flown open, bouncing on their hinges while music floated into the air, ting-a-ling-a-linging.

Dean Martin.

And Claire Manchester.

She jumped from the parked van, her black hair loose and following her head like a swarm of angry bees. Dean Martin was describing a gay tarantella.

"Hurry up," she said. "I don't have all day. Lucy's running in the first."

Tony Not Tony emerged slowly, elegantly, one gnarled hand hoisting a hanger draped with clear plastic. His diminutive size made him look like a lawn jockey delivering dry cleaning. Offering Claire the hanger, he took a bow.

She ripped the plastic off. The short-sleeved shirt underneath was a deep blue color, like sodalite minerals. Yanking it from the hanger, she scrunched the shirt into a ball and headed for the door, where I stood. Dean Martin kept insisting a cloud was beneath her feet.

"Nice shirt," I said.

Her sharp eyes flicked from side to side. "It's—it's for my son."

She pushed past me, barked at the guard behind the desk, and didn't bother signing in. She left a trailing scent, a mixture of expensive perfume and horse manure.

"Raleigh!"

Tony Not Tony waved. Right now all I wanted was a giant glass of water and the chance to tell Eleanor about the poisonous mud. But two days had passed since I promised Tony I would meet him at the van. That was Thursday, right before SunTzu took the fatal fall. When I walked toward him, his narrow shoulders pulled forward.

"I thought you were avoiding me, but maybe not. Ready for your shoes?" He pointed into the van. Dean Martin, that great astrophysicist, was insisting stars could drool.

I stepped inside.

Two steel poles ran from the back doors to the front cab. The poles were crammed with hangers, each draped with thin protective plastic or zipped into designer suit bags.

"Women's wear," he said, "is forward to the right."

I stooped and walked forward. Red shag covered the floor. It matched the van's exterior. As I passed the plastic bags they whispered, a susurrus that recalled deep memories of my father's closet. Hide-and-seek with my sister. I would sneak far in back, crouching under the comfort of his pressed shirts and dark suits. But there was one crucial difference: my dad's clothes didn't fall off a truck.

I sat on the bench built over the wheel well. Tony kneeled at a column of white shoe boxes. "Nine, not ten," he said. "Ah, yes, here they are. These have Raleigh David written all over them."

The two-inch pumps were olivine suede, an elegant green incapable of offense. A small silver buckle was embossed with the initials D&G.

"Very nice," I said. "How much?"

"For you, thirty dollars."

They were either knockoffs or hot as automatic rifles. "Perfect," I said. "I'll take them."

"Excellent choice. Anything else you'd like?"

I nodded.

He nodded back. "I heard something about Loosey Goosey. Or maybe not. But in the first race, it could be nineteen-to-one."

"A thousand dollars," I said. "To win."

Loosey Goosey belonged to Claire Manchester—that was the horse she called "Lucy." The horse that went through the disastrous start with SunTzu and was now considered an underdog. It made me wonder about Claire Manchester's visit to Tony. Was that why she seemed nervous when I mentioned the shirt? Because if the pattern held, the long shot Loosey Goosey would come out ahead in that first race. The win would pay sixteen-to-one for the great unwashed in the stands. But Sal Gag's insiders would get three more points.

Tony's gnarled jockey hands were warming each other, expecting another good bet. "Was there something else?" he asked.

I stared down at Raleigh David's shoes. The suede matched the peridot in my engagement ring. A sign, I decided. Because DeMott was arriving—I glanced at my watch—*in three hours.* I pressed back a bolt of panic and tried to smile.

"My fiancé is coming to town," I said.

The shoulders came forward. "Your fiancé."

"Yes. He's flying in from Virginia."

I decided the best strategy was to release the seeds of gossip, letting the news sprout so that Raleigh David's story would seem to match reality. Cover on top of cover. With the Cadillac following me, it was necessary. They were watching my every move.

"Marvelous news," Tony said. "When does he arrive?"

"This afternoon. But I haven't had a chance to buy him a present. Maybe you have a suggestion?"

"Certainly, certainly. The fall sport coats just came in. What's his size?"

DeMott's size. I should know that. *What a rotten fiancée.*

"Forty-two," I guessed.

"Menswear, right this way."

Ducking my head under the van's ceiling, I followed Tony to the other side of the van. Dean Martin was still singing, saying love had found me, just in time, it found me.

"He must be worried," Tony said.

"Pardon?"

"Your fiancé. About what happened. The fire?"

"Right. Yes. Very worried."

"Terrible, just terrible." He slid his hands between zippered suit bags and removed two sport coats. Compared to Tony, size 42 looked extremely large.

"I don't have many regular customers at the track who can wear this size," he said. "So my stock is a little thin." He lifted the dark brown jacket in his right hand. "Ralph Lauren. Tweed. Ideal for fall and the early winter months." He lifted the other jacket. "Hugo Boss. Cotton-linen blend. Adequate for autumn. But the color isn't for everyone. Retail, these run about four-fifty each. But for you? One-twenty. Two hundred for the pair."

I made a note to contact the Bureau and find out where these clothes were coming from. "That's very generous."

"Well," he said, smiling, revealing all his bridgework. "You could return the favor. Put in a good word with Cooper. Ask him to use my jockeys."

If Tony Not Tony thought I had any influence over Bill Cooper, he was wrong. But I wasn't about to tell him.

"Done," I lied. "And I'll take the linen."

He folded the money into a clip shaped like a golden horseshoe. When I climbed out, he handed me the jacket and bowed, just like he had with Claire.

"Perhaps he can wear it here," he said.

"Pardon?"

"Your fiancé. You are bringing him to the track, aren't you?"

Now I'd stepped in it.

"Of course."

"Excellent. But you must have a million things to do before he gets here. Don't let me keep you."

Walking toward the Ghost, I wanted to kick myself with my new shoes. I hung the jacket in the car, then looked back at Tony Not Tony.

On his tiptoes, he hurried for the track entrance, his tasseled loafers flapping on the ground with the seeds of fresh gossip.

Chapter Twenty-Seven

Eleanor was waiting outside the Quarterchute Café, staking out my next move, which was water and one BnE sandwich. But it wasn't going to happen, I could tell. She was pacing between the Café and a small brown building that was propped up on concrete blocks, as if waiting to get hauled somewhere else.

"Where have you been?" she demanded.

But she didn't wait for my reply. Grabbing my arm, she steered me toward the brown building. A chain-link fence ran across the back, keeping out the green tractors parked by the maintenance hut. I made a mental note to find whoever groomed the track that morning when SunTzu died. Find out how they missed that tube.

"You look terrible," Eleanor trumpeted.

"I've been—"

"I told Birdie to cut you off. No more greasy food, young lady. It's catching up to you."

Arguing with her seemed futile, especially since the salt had turned my spit to the consistency of paste. I managed to whisper, "Is there somewhere we can talk, in private?"

"Whatever it is, it can wait. Father MacIntyre is expecting us." The rhinestones on the hem of her trousers were throwing prismatic light back at the sun, daring it to compete. "These services are not optional. Now come along!"

This wasn't my morning.

Inside the building, the single small room had an iron cross hanging opposite the door. The plywood floor smelled of chemicals. Folding chairs were set up in two halves, with an open middle aisle that Eleanor dragged me down. The Hispanic jockeys waited silently in the chairs, some wearing racing silks. But all of them clutched rosaries, rubbing their thumbs over the beads in a way that reminded me of people scratching Lotto tickets. Birdie sat in one corner, at an organ that looked too big. When she saw Eleanor, she stood to reach the foot pedals. She began playing a hymn I couldn't name. Bill Cooper was seated by the wall, next to Juan. The groom's head was down, fingers on the rosary, but Cooper's icy glare shot straight through me, sending a shiver down my spine and helping me recall the hymn's name. "What Wondrous Love Is This?"

At the front of the room, two empty chairs waited, directly facing the iron cross. Eleanor took one and patted the other. I sat down and felt something gnawing at my conscience. Something wasn't right, but before I could figure out what, an old priest came shuffling through the door. He wore a white robe, its hemline embroidered with gold thread that had turned the color of brass. His hands gripped a thurible, swinging the incense burner by its chain, casting puffs of smoke across his path to the front. The warm air began to smell of ash and honey. And I could feel the cold on my back from Cooper's stare.

Eleanor swatted my thigh. Her head was bowed but she still managed to give me the eye. "Turn around."

Keeping my back to this many people—this many suspicious people—ran counter to my FBI training. But I obeyed and listened to the tired old priest conduct the mass. It was mostly in Spanish, with some Latin thrown in, but his tone of voice was so flat the words felt like lukewarm water.

"Are you listening?" Eleanor hissed.

I nodded. Time had introduced the priest's earlobes to his fragile shoulders, which looked weighed down by the embroidered robe. His hooded eyes were a smudged gray, and I tried to concentrate on specific words. Deo. Gloria. Dominus. But my mind kept circling back to poisonous mud, a black Caddy, and DeMott arriving—I peeked at my watch, my pulse jumping—two and a half hours. The priest sighed and began a sermon. He talked about SunTzu and the jockey who might never walk again, and suddenly the room grew very quiet. So quiet I could hear the roof beams creaking under the sun's heat.

"Each day could be our last," the priest said, in a bored tone that implied he might check out right now, move on to something interesting. He gave a final blessing on the riders, and the horses, and the barns, then closed with two words: "Good luck."

The men rushed from the room. The first race started in eighteen minutes.

But Eleanor stayed in her chair.

"Father," she said in her projecting voice, "we could use extra prayers."

His toothsome smile was equine. "What would you like me to ask of your heavenly Father, Eleanor?"

"Ask Him to watch over my niece."

The priest's smile told me this tiny temporary church, this odd building for religious services held on Saturdays, only survived because of Eleanor's cash.

"As you wish." The priest's cloudy eyes shifted to me. "I will say the novena for His providential gaze to fall upon her."

"Thank you," she said.

He nodded, like a man checking off an obligation, then asked about her horses. By name. By the third question, I was wondering whether betting on horses was considered a carnal or a venal sin. But then I decided lying was probably worse than wagering, even if the betting was done by a priest. Plank firmly in my eye, I stared out the window. Some of the plain-clothed jockeys had gathered with Juan. In the bright sun, the groom's tan skin looked like rotten putty. The poisons must be seeping into his body, since he applied the clay with his bare hands. I shifted in my seat, looking for Cooper, but he wasn't out there.

"I'll visit the barn," the priest was saying, "right after I take care of Mr. Gagliardo."

"Didn't you hear?" Eleanor said. "Abbondanza is closed."

"Yes, I heard. Mr. Gagliardo wants me to come sprinkle holy water. He believes his horses are cursed."

I watched the priest, searching for irony. There was none.

"Remember the novena for my niece," she said.

He nodded. Carrying his incense burner, he shuffled to the door. The white robe floated around his feet like a hovercraft. I looked over at Eleanor. Her eyes were closed. Hands clasped. Praying.

I waited, keeping an eye on the entrance. When she opened her eyes, I whispered, "Cooper's mud is poisoning your horses."

"I beg your pardon!"

"Keep it down, please. The mud contains high levels of a mineral called selenium. It's poisonous and might even explain this so-called Emerald Fever."

"You're mistaken. That mud's our winning secret. Bill told me himself."

Her last words hung in the air, mingling with the priest's incense.

"Selenium poisoning is fatal in animals, always. And there's no antidote." I described the symptoms—stomachaches, breathing problems, stiff joints—everything that matched Emerald Fever. By the time I got to the radioactive elements, Eleanor was twisting an enormous ring on her left hand. A clear stone, five carats. Diamond.

"If you don't believe me," I said, "the mud was checked by a forensic geologist."

"That's where you disappeared to?"

"I was also busy flunking a lie detector test. The fire inspector thinks I'm the prime suspect."

"But that's absurd—you almost died in that fire!"

I glanced at the door. Nobody was nearby. "He knows something doesn't line up."

"Oh, the mendacity! The stench of mendacity."

"Big Daddy," I said. "*Cat on a Hot Tin Roof.*"

She sighed. "There might be hope for you yet."

"You'll need to get Juan to a doctor. There's an antidote for humans with selenium poisoning. But please—please—be careful how you reveal this information. If Cooper finds out I had the mud tested, he'll shut me out completely."

She closed her eyes again, then gave a long, quivering sigh.

"Sorry," I said. "And there's one more thing."

She didn't open her eyes. "There always is."

"My fiancé arrives in less than two hours."

Her eyes opened. "The gentleman named DeMott? He's coming here?"

"He's bringing my mom's dog."

"What a sweet and pathetic excuse to see you. He can stay at my house."

"I have an extra bedroom."

"You can keep the dog. But the man stays with me."

I almost laughed. "Were you always like this?"

"Yes. And you should be taking notes. All my life I've had to listen to nitwits and dolts tell me I was too bold. 'Eleanor, women don't do that. Eleanor, be quiet.' But I knew what their comments meant. 'Eleanor, don't rock the boat; the rest of us are coasting along nicely doing absolutely nothing constructive.'"

She grabbed my hand, squeezing so hard the engagement ring dug into my bloated fingers. "I was fortunate to have husbands who loved me just the way God loves me. Do you understand?"

I nodded. My throat had closed. And it wasn't the salt's fault.

"Good." She let go. "You don't care for that priest, do you?"

"He's . . . okay."

"You mean he's fine for a bunch of superstitious horse people. I can't blame you for that. We didn't get the purest man of the cloth. But then again, none of us are pure. The service is the best I can do right now. My barn is required to attend mass, including any jockey who wants to ride my horses. I want to make sure they don't forget."

"Forget what?"

"Their audience."

"In the grandstands."

"You can't possibly be that dense," she said. "I'm referring to the audience of one. The One who knows what we're like on the inside." She stood, and the rhinestones glittered from her glasses to the hem of her trousers. "Now, if you'll excuse me, I have a boat to rock," she said. "Perhaps next time you can come get wet."

Chapter Twenty-Eight

When I walked into the Quarterchute, the old guys were gathered around the tables, looking like withered cavemen nourishing a dying fire. Birdie and her husband worked behind the counter, preparing for the lunch rush, and she'd clearly ignored Eleanor's order to cut me off. My BnE sandwiches sat under the heat lamp, waiting there so long the foil was almost too hot to touch. I filled a jumbo cup with ice water, guzzled it on the spot, and refilled with Coca-Cola. Since nobody was at the cash register, I laid my money on the keys and stepped outside.

The Saturday crowd was packing the grandstands. I stayed by the white rail, eating and watching the light board tick through its greedy numbers. In my five years as an FBI agent, I'd probably had more adrenaline rushes than a cliff jumper, but horse racing had just as much exhilaration. When the gates blew open for the first race, no horse faltered. They pounded the turf for the first turn and a thrill ran down my arms, raising goose bumps. The sheer majestic paradox: animals weighing fifteen hundred pounds, running so fast they seemed to float. They passed the rail where I stood, and the sound of their thundering hooves shook the air, tapping against my chest. They were so close I could see the jockeys, perched on a half-inch bar of metal, their leg muscles straining beneath the white jodhpurs. I leaned forward to watch the final stretch. KichaKoo was chasing Loosey Goosey, her beautiful brown neck stretched so far forward she looked like she was biting the air. But a third horse suddenly pulled ahead. It was copper-colored and despite a lopsided gait, it caught the leaders in the last twenty lengths. Loosey Goosey's jockey turned his head twice, surprised. I glanced at the light board.

Mr. Tea. Another long shot.

My wager for Loosey Goosey was gone. I lifted my hand, shielding the sun to watch the horses loping down the backstretch, cooling down. Loosey Goosey's jockey patted her neck, consoling her, and I wondered if he was one of Tony's jockeys. Was that why Claire Manchester was in the van? Did the jockey agree to hold back the horse? But the animal's stride did look thick, almost leaden. I searched for KichaKoo. She was yanking her head over her shoulder, as if giving the jockey a piece of her mind. Her fade in the final stretch might've been from simple fatigue, with the mud's selenium affecting her system. Or because this jockey was another of Tony's crew, holding her back as well.

I crumpled the foil from my sandwich. An ebullient Mr. Tea was prancing his way to the winner's circle, throwing back his head and shaking his golden mane. The jockey tipped forward in his saddle and spoke into the horse's pricked ears.

Walking down the backstretch, I passed Birdie's handwritten sign on the birch tree. Today's translation was *La Ayuda* = Help. A convoy of horse trailers was parked outside the third barn. Men were leading Sal Gag's horses into the containers. The horse's hooves knocked on the metal ramps, hollow and somber, while the mobster-bookie watched with a grim expression. His dark eyes kept shifting toward Ashley. She was once again trying to control Cuppa Joe.

"C'mon, baby," she pleaded.

His black coat glistened over flank muscles coiled with fear. The whites of his eyes were visible, like Solo's the night of the fire. An animal verging on panic. But Ashley stepped in front and pulled on his bridle, trying to lead him up the ramp. The horse balked and pulled back, dragging her down. She scrambled to her feet.

Sal Gagliardo watched them. His dark eyebrows had quirked upward in a questioning expression that also looked sad. I chalked it up to the scared animal. That kind of fear could pierce even the meanest heart. When the mobster glanced at me, running his eyes from my head to my new shoes, I smiled. Ever-helpful Raleigh David.

"Anything I can do?"

"You got your own problems," he said.

I waited a moment, trying to hold the smile. "Pardon?"

"I heard something's wrong with your mud."

Way to go, Eleanor. She wasn't one for the subtle approach. But I tried to sound surprised. "What about our mud?"

"Yuck just confiscated it. Came over, asked if we used any of it."

"Really?"

"Hey, Ashley." He waved the unlit cigar. "Be careful, would ya?"

Cuppa Joe had lowered his head, like a ram about to charge, but Ashley refused to get out of his way. Whispering under her breath, she parried his thrusts like a fencer. A violent dance, hypnotic to watch.

She said, "I won't let them hurt you. You know I won't."

Sal Gag sighed. *"Strunze."*

He shoved the cigar in his mouth and walked toward Ashley, stopping short of the horse. Cuppa Joe raised his head and gazed down his nose at his owner.

Ashley said, "There are too many trailers. He doesn't want to leave."

"Really. You coulda fooled me."

"He told me he doesn't like trailers."

"He *told* you? What're you, the Psychic Hotline?"

She grabbed the sleeve of his dark suit. "Please don't make him get in there. He's not ready. Please, please?"

I'd never seen lard melt, but it probably looked a lot like this. Sal Gag's beefy shoulders slumped and the big head fell forward until his chin nearly touched his black shirt with its silver tie. "Ashley, honey."

I heard no sarcasm. No edge in his gravelly voice.

He spoke tenderly, as if talking to a weak child. "The horse don't got a choice. Yuck closed us down. He's got to go."

"One more day." Her fingers squeezed into his arm. "Just one more day, two at the most. Let him calm down. He knows something we don't."

"He knows you're gonna treat him like a baby!"

He said it with disgust. She stared at him, blue eyes watering, chin quivering.

"Aw, no." He made a low guttural sound. "Don't do that to me."

Her first sob came as a gasp.

"Ashley, don't cry." He was pleading now. "You know I can't take it when you cry."

But she cried. She cried like a little girl lost at the mall.

He threw his hands into the air. "All right! We'll try tomorrow. Satisfied?"

She hugged the horse first, grabbing his black neck. Cuppa Joe looked like he knew he'd won the standoff. He blew air into her pale hair, no longer balking. Then Ashley turned to the mobster, throwing her arms around his neck too.

"Cuppa Joe says thank you."

Sal Gag patted her back, awkwardly, with the cigar braced between his fingers. "Nothing else, you can call the Psychic Hotline, ask 'em for a job."

She pulled back. Her eyes were wet but she was smiling. A perfect smile, teeth as straight as a Colgate commercial.

"I love you, Uncle Sal."

He waved the cigar. "Get outta here."

And my one thought was: *Uncle Sal?*

Chapter Twenty-Nine

B ut there wasn't time to figure out the family bond between Ashley and Sal Gag: I had a plane to meet.

Heading south on I-5, I pulled into Sea-Tac Airport's "cell phone parking lot." It was a concrete pad that faced some freight terminals, and I found a spot between a silver BMW convertible and a dark green Suburban. In the SUV, children were jumping on the backseat while a pretty blond woman behind the wheel talked on her phone. The solitary man in the Beemer stared straight ahead, stiff as a crash-test dummy.

Turning off the engine, I leaned into my rearview mirror and pretended to put on lip gloss, while making sure there was no black Cadillac following me. But suddenly my mother stared back at me, the memory of how she always checked her lipstick in a compact mirror when we picked up my dad. She wanted to look perfect. The first time she did it was in the Richmond airport. I was seven years old, and until then my idea of long-distance travel had revolved around the Greyhound bus station. Each December we boarded a musty motor coach in Richmond and rode for hours to a remote part of North Carolina to visit my grandmother. The trips always felt long and sad, partly because my grandmother wasn't a kind person, and partly because of the bus itself. The cloth seats smelled like other people's beds, and when we arrived at the North Carolina station, nobody was ever there to greet us. On the trip my mother kept her Bible open while my sister, Helen, sketched pictures. I stared out the filmed window, taking in the winter's bleak and deciduous landscape.

But when my mom married David Harmon, our lives changed

completely. For one thing, we never rode the bus again. Instead, we went to the airport. And my mom started checking her makeup. The first time he left it was for some kind of judges' meeting in Boston. He was gone three days, and I remember thinking that his time was spent walking around Boston in his black robe, carrying his gavel. On the fourth day, my mother drove us to Byrd Airport. We stood with a crowd of strangers, everyone staring at a door marked with one letter and one number.

When the door finally opened, the crowd pressed forward. The plane's passengers streamed out single file, most of them looking slightly lost. They searched the crowd for familiar faces, until somebody would rush forward, calling out their name. Then hugs. Back slaps. Tears of joy.

My dad was among the last passengers out of the plane. When my mother saw him, she ran forward as though pulled by magnets, and he dropped his briefcase, right there, catching her in his arms and planting a luxurious kiss on her painted lips. When I came up beside them, I heard him humming. A husband harmonizing with his wife. Tuning in to her particular melody.

It was nothing like the Greyhound station.

My sister, Helen, said waiting at the airport gate was "tedious"— a pretentious word for a ten-year-old, foreshadowing of the woman to come—but I leaped at every chance to go. I couldn't have articulated it then, but there was something about standing with all those people. Everyone breathless with anticipation. So very eager to see someone they loved come through that door. And then the person arriving from long distance, through the narrow gate, and hearing their name called out. Coming home. Tears of joy. Celebration.

Only later did I realize what it was: a hint of heaven.

But nobody waited at the gate these days. Not since nineteen Muslims followed Muhammad's dictates to the letter and murdered more than three thousand "infidels," flying our own airplanes into our own skyscrapers. The religious fascists robbed families of spouses, parents, grandparents, children, generations to come. And they turned our airports into charmless bus stations.

No more heaven, and too much earth.

But that was always part of evil's strategy. Take away the reminders. Help us forget. Remove every indication that a homecoming waited on the other side, that people were pressing forward and we should be straining to hear the ultimate prize—our name called out upon arrival. Homecoming. Tears of joy. Celebration.

Evil wanted us to forget that.

And so I waited in the drearily named "cell phone parking lot" and tried to decide how DeMott could call me when he didn't carry a cell phone. He'd have to find a pay phone after landing, and the complication sent a niggling annoyance into my neck. To avoid thinking about how much his arcane lifestyle bothered me, I applied another coat of lip gloss. And when my phone rang, I was still holding the gloss and my index finger was sticky, so I slid my pinkie across the screen.

I said, "Your timing is perfect."

"That's because I'm perfect."

I cringed. *Jack.*

He asked, "How was the lie detector test?"

I glanced over at the Beemer. The driver held a cell phone to his ear, his elbow bent like a mannequin. Over on the right, the Suburban's kids were pounding on the windows and the woman behind the steering wheel had laid her face in her hands.

"Hang on a sec." I climbed out of the Ghost and walked across the lot, to where it overlooked the air freight terminals. A dozen brown UPS trucks lined up outside a corrugated steel building while cargo planes painted the same brown color waited on the other side, ready for takeoff. I turned a slow circle, scanning the parking lot. No black Caddy.

"Harmon?"

"The polygraph was ruled inconclusive."

"Thank me later."

"For what?"

"Those exciting thoughts. I know that's what did it."

I hated lying. I really hated it. But no way this side of heaven would Jack Stephanson hear that he crossed my mind while I stared at that sunset-in-the-mountains poster. Especially when my fiancé was arriving in—I glanced at my watch—six minutes. My heart valves seemed to clutch at each other. I took a deep breath, trying to relax.

"The test came back Deception Indicated. The arson investigator is now convinced I had something to do with that fire. You want me to thank you for that?"

"Speaking of deception," he said, "Dr. Freud called. He says you tried to skip today's appointment. He wanted OPR to know."

A jet came roaring down the runway. I covered my open ear and watched the thing lift off the tarmac. The tail wing had an Eskimo on it, Alaska Airlines.

"Harmon?"

I could barely hear him over the noise. "What?"

"Where are you?"

I watched the small wheels folding into the plane's underbelly, while another plane came in for a landing on the next strip. The reverse thrust roar rattled the air, raising the hair on my arms.

"Harmon." He paused. "Are you at the airport?"

Technically, no.

Technically, I was in the cell phone parking lot *next* to the airport. And the truly pathetic thing was that my life had become so twisted that I kept finding new ways to justify every lie. This time I decided to shut up, hoping sins of omission weren't as serious as sins of commission.

"Are you all right?" Jack asked.

"I'm fine."

"You sound stressed."

I wondered whether I should tell him about the black Cadillac. But what good would that do? It would only add to the things OPR could use against me; they would probably allege it was my fault somebody was tailing the Ghost. "Really. I'm fine."

"No, you're not," he said. "But I can cheer you up."

I closed my eyes. The irony was, I liked Jerk Jack better. It took more effort to dislike Genuine Jack, the guy who kept peeking from behind the Stephanson facade, pretending to care. That Jack showed up on the cruise ship, a lot. But I wasn't about to get suckered. It was like making friends with a scorpion. Eventually it was going to sting you.

"I had a little chat with McLeod yesterday," he was saying. "Seems his wife hauled him to a wine-tasting event. Right there, it's funny. McLeod, surrounded by Seattle wine snobs. But it gets better. He told me he liked one of the wines. A chardonnay. Because it had a flagrant bouquet."

I bit my lip, refusing to give him the satisfaction of laughing. "I need you to call the state lab. See if O'Brien has any updates on the forensics."

"Done," he said. "McLeod also told me the wine expert was a huge suppository of information."

I bit down harder. "Ask if they found any clay inside that tube."

"Got it. And you will be going to your appointment."

"With Freud?"

"Harmon, you already missed one. The hospital stay was a legitimate excuse. But he says you wouldn't give a reason why you were canceling tonight. I told him you'd be there."

I sighed. He was right. Skipping another appointment would heap more misery on me. "Fine. I'll go. But not tonight. Tell him three o'clock."

"Okay. Good. But don't let him see you this stressed out."

He hung up.

Much as I hated to admit it, McLeod's malaprops had cheered me up. It reminded me that the suits in charge of my life were human. But after watching airplanes come and go for another fifteen minutes, the good vibe did its own takeoff. Finally, I called Delta and learned that DeMott's flight from Atlanta was delayed, dropping my mood even further because he had suggested that I check for delays before driving to the airport. And I didn't. And I knew if he were here right now, we would start arguing about it.

I closed my eyes and sent up prayers that wove between the jets' sonic roar. Desperate for help. Vulnerable. I confessed everything, honestly. And when my cell phone rang again, my fingertips felt tingly, numb, falling asleep from the tight clasp of my hands.

"Hello?"

"I'm here," DeMott said.

Chapter Thirty

DeMott stood at the curb, looking like he'd landed on Mars. His white oxford shirt was buttoned high and his seersucker jacket was flung over his right shoulder, a finger hooked into the rippled collar. He watched the Seattle types sweeping past in ripped jeans, grungy shirts, and hair that looked liked it hadn't been combed in years.

I stopped at the curb, slid the gearshift into neutral, and pulled the emergency brake. When I ran around the long white bonnet, he opened his arms, caught me when I jumped, and spun me around. The memories soared through my mind, running at the speed of smell. This scent of DeMott. Clean laundry, warm skin. Southern sun. And his laughter, it always rumbled inside his chest before coming out to play.

"Oh, Raleigh, I've missed you so much." He set me down and stepped back. "But you sure look . . . different."

I lifted a finger to my lips. "We can talk later."

A familiar expression washed over his face, but I was already kneeling on the ground. Inside the plastic dog crate, Madame's wagging tail pounded at the sides, beating with the rhythm of my heart.

"Hello, you perfect dog!" I pinched the metal handle and opened the door. The small black dog fired like a cannonball into my arms. I buried my face in her soft fur, but when my hand felt the washboard ribs, my eyes stung. Burning with love and sadness and another memory flashing through my mind. A recent memory. That girl groom, Ashley Trenner, as she nuzzled Cuppa Joe. She loved that horse the way I loved this dog. Lifting my face to DeMott, I saw him smiling.

The blue eyes sparkled, that birefringent blue that split light and made fire. Gemstone eyes. Some kind of knife scored across my chest.

"Hey!" An airport security guard barreled toward us. "This is a no-parking zone! Move that car!"

"Yes, sir," DeMott said.

"And that dog's supposed to be on a leash!"

"Yes, sir," DeMott repeated.

"'Sir'?" The officer narrowed his eyes. "You making fun of me?"

I picked up Madame. "DeMott, get in the car."

"No, sir. I'm sorry, did I say something wrong?"

I was climbing behind the Ghost's wheel, holding the dog in my lap. But DeMott stayed, thanking the security guard. But the man only looked more baffled. I rolled down the window. "DeMott, throw everything in back."

Standing on my lap, Madame leaned out, sniffing the air. While DeMott loaded her small crate and his duffel bag in back, her tail beat against my side, renewing the pain in my ribs. The most wonderful ache. DeMott climbed in and I pulled away from the curb.

"This is your car?" He ran a hand over the walnut dash, marveling.

"Cool, huh? It's a Maserati Ghibli."

"It looks like something James Bond would drive."

I laughed and glanced in the side mirror to merge with the traffic. And suddenly all my joy flew out the window. The black Cadillac was four cars back, coming down the middle lane. *Maybe it's a limo*, I thought. *Hotel pickup.*

"It sort of reminds me of your mom's car," DeMott was saying. "Vintage, elegant. By the way, I ran it yesterday."

I merged to the left, watching the mirror. "Ran what?"

"Your mom's car. You asked me to run it, for the engine?"

"Oh, right, thanks." My mother drove a 1966 Mercedes sedan. It had the original push-button dashboard and red leather seats. It stayed in the garage under my carriage house apartment, and I had worried it would suffer in our absence. "Thanks for remembering."

"Of course. I wouldn't forget."

The Cadillac kept coming. Now three cars behind us, it wasn't

184 | the stars shine bright

making a pickup at the curb. I moved toward International Boulevard South and stayed on that path until the last possible moment. When I suddenly changed lanes, the Caddy was six cars back, the windshield glinting in the sunlight. It changed lanes with us.

DeMott said, "I'm sure you don't miss the K-car."

My Richmond supervisor made sure my Bureau vehicle was the ugliest bucket of bolts ever to roll out of Detroit. A white K-car with vinyl seats and no air-conditioning. The same supervisor, I was thinking, who sent all my casework and field notes to OPR, hoping to get me fired.

"Raleigh?"

"Yes?"

"You miss me?"

We were heading north on International Boulevard. I stopped at the red light and glanced over. His wavy brown hair was combed back. His forehead was freckled with summer. He had a classic face with almost no visible flaws. A face that could only be produced by a gene pool in which a swimmer could trace its ancestry back seven generations. I let my eyes wander over the familiar features. His easy smile. The right incisor, with the tiniest of chips, a small imperfection my tongue always found when we kissed.

"I really missed you, DeMott. And you're right about Madame, she's too thin."

He smiled. "You're welcome."

Behind me a car honked. The light had turned green and when I stepped on the gas, Madame did a little tap dance on my thighs. DeMott reached over, touching my hair. I was taking stabbing glances—the road ahead, the Caddy behind, DeMott at my side—trying to keep all three in focus. DeMott's fire-filled eyes roamed over my clothing, pausing on the Calvin Klein shirt that Madame was quickly turning into black angora.

"You look great," he said. "Different, but great."

I heard the edge in his voice.

"And you look like DeMott." I smiled. "In other words, perfect."

"Did you pick out those clothes?"

We stopped at another light. I glanced in the mirror. The Caddy was sticking close enough to make it through the intersections with us. Leaning over, I pulled a small key from my purse and pointed it at the glove box. DeMott unlocked the small walnut door. And the light turned green.

I knew Tony Not Tony would tell Sal Gag that my fiancé was flying into town. And I figured they would send the tail, perhaps to see if my story actually lined up. But since I hadn't said what time DeMott was arriving, I suddenly wondered. Was it that stiff guy in the Beemer—did he call the Caddy? Or was I right to think they'd stuck a tracking device on the Ghost? It was simple enough to do, taking just a few seconds these days to slap onto the undercarriage. But just in case the tracking device had listening capabilities, I had jotted down some notes before heading to the airport. And placed them in the locked glove box. DeMott was reading my instructions, reaching into my Coach bag. He took out my wallet and opened it, staring at the clear plastic pocket that held Raleigh David's driver's license.

I switched lanes again, playing cat-and-mouse all the way to Southcenter Mall. I slowed down, letting the light up ahead turn yellow, then stopped. The Ghost was first in line for the light change. The Caddy was three cars back and the tinted glass so dark all I could see was that gold ring on his hands. I looked over at DeMott.

He was still staring at the driver's license. A lock of his hair fell forward, hanging like a comma over his eyes. Madame did another quick tap dance on my thighs. I looked at the mirror again. Then the light turned green.

I hit the gas pedal like somebody killing a bug. The Ghost obliged by shooting across the intersection, demanding second gear, then third as we raced for the freeway on-ramp to I-5. In my rearview mirror, I could see the Caddy trying to pass a yellow taxicab. He swerved around, zooming down the left shoulder, while the cabdriver leaned on his horn. But I was already in fourth, merging into the fast lane before breezing diagonally, covering three lanes in seconds. DeMott turned around in his seat, rummaging through his carry-on bag, as I passed four cars in the next seven seconds so that we could make the exit for Pacific Highway South. The Caddy was trying to merge into the right lane.

DeMott said, "That hasn't changed."

"Pardon?"

"Your appetite. Isn't that why you're driving like a maniac, because you're hungry?"

"*Starving.*" I downshifted and took the exit. At the bottom of the ramp, the stoplight was green, but I braked, downshifting again. The Ghost wailed its protest.

"Please, no McDonald's," DeMott said. "I've already had airplane food today. Pick something else."

The Caddy came down the ramp. He was going too fast, and I was holding up traffic. When he braked, his front end dropped from the sudden friction. I glanced up at the light again. It turned yellow. I hit the gas.

"Raleigh—!"

The burst of speed threw DeMott back. As we zipped under the light, Madame barked. I took the Pacific Coast Highway at forty miles an hour.

"You can stop with the theatrics," DeMott said. "I'm impressed with the car. Okay? Now slow down!"

Behind us at the intersection, the Caddy drove down the shoulder, moving around the line of cars stopped at the red light. But he couldn't cross the intersection with all the traffic going back and forth. I downshifted, heading toward a blind curve, and finally he disappeared from my mirror.

And up ahead—hallelujah!—the king.

"Burger King?" DeMott said. "You've got to be kidding."

I took the turn into the parking lot so quickly Madame slid off my lap. DeMott caught her, threw me a harsh look, and I barely noticed. The Ghost blasted right past the plastic menu display, past the microphone used for ordering, and—

"What the—?" DeMott said.

—stopped at the ordering window. A wall of yew bushes blocked the drive-through from the road so nobody driving past would see us.

When the pickup window slid open, a teenager leaned out. His hair was so greasy he could've been a lifeguard in the deep fryer.

"You're, like, way over?" He pointed back, toward the ordering station. "You gotta, like, drive around again."

"No."

"What?"

"No," I said. "I'll take one Whopper, no condiments. One cup of ice water. No straw."

Madame crawled back into my lap, sniffing the air. She wagged.

"One BK special," I continued. "Extra-large fries. And your biggest chocolate shake."

The teenager frowned but started tapping some flat keys on a register. When I glanced over at DeMott, he was scooting forward to get his wallet from his pocket. No Virginia gentleman allowed a woman to pay. Ever. I took a deep breath of the greasy air. How I missed his chivalry. Especially in a land where militant feminists had trained men not to open doors.

"DeMott, what would you like?"

"Real food." He handed me some money. "I'll wait."

I held the bills out to the teenager. "And one fish sandwich."

"Seafood," DeMott muttered. "Borderline healthy."

But the fish sandwich wasn't for me. It was for delay. I wanted the Caddy to get down the road before I pulled out again, so I also ordered another chocolate shake and a chicken sandwich with special instructions on the condiments. After the teen counted out my change, frowning as though performing high-level calculus despite a computer that told him exactly how much to give back, I turned to give it to DeMott. He had opened my wallet again, staring at my license.

The teenager said, "It's gonna be awhile? You can park, like, until it's ready?"

"No."

This time he nodded, as if expecting me to say that. He closed the plastic window.

DeMott picked up the notebook, rereading my instructions that reminded him Eleanor was my aunt; if anyone asked, my name was

Raleigh David; and any conversations in the car beyond idle chit-chat should be written down, just to be safe. He rummaged in his overnight bag again, pulling out a pen. Fountain tip. Made of burled wood. Like something Jefferson used to write the Declaration of Independence. So very DeMott.

He flipped to a blank page in the notebook and wrote:

Raleigh David?

He offered me the pen. But I reached into the glove box, where I'd stashed a cheap Bic.

Raleigh David is my undercover name. It had to be a name I wouldn't forget. Like my real name.

YOU picked the last name David?

Yes. For my dad. David.

You couldn't pick Fielding?

I looked up. His blue eyes burned like gas flames.

"David" reminds me of my dad. It's like he's with me.

The plastic window slid open. "You want straws, like, for the shakes?"

"Yes."

I looked at DeMott. He was staring out the side window. In the next parking lot some guys stood by a dirty gray van with a ladder on its roof. Their clothes were spattered with paint. They smoked cigarettes and laughed, and when the ordering window slid open again, I turned and handed the drink tray and food bags to DeMott, because he would be careful not to get anything on the car. Then I drove forward slowly and parked behind the yew bushes. Madame got out with me, but DeMott stayed in the car. Tail wagging, the dog lapped from the water cup, splashing as much as she drank, then wolfed down a Whopper. I'd have her fattened up in no time. When I looked into the car, hoping to show DeMott, his head was resting on the seat back. Eyes closed. *Tired*, I thought. *That's all it is; he's just tired.* Madame and I shared the fries, but I carried the rest of the food into the restaurant. The same teenager from the window walked over to the counter.

"Is, like, something wrong?"

"No, nothing's wrong. But we didn't touch this other food. Could you offer it to the next person who comes in?"

He glanced at a guy standing at the fry station. Then back at me. More confused than ever. "You mean, like, for free?"

"Yes. For free."

When I climbed back into the car, DeMott reached over, taking my hand.

"I'm sorry."

"No, I'm sorry. This is a lot to think about. And you must be really tired."

He nodded, giving a weak smile. "With the baby coming, Mac's had everyone running around. Just like before her wedding, only worse."

"I can only imagine."

"Guess what she's naming him?"

I turned the key. "It's a boy?"

"Yes. Fielding DeMott Morgan."

And the words came right back. *"You couldn't pick Fielding?"*

"That sounds just right for them." I inched the Ghost past the yew bushes and gazed down the highway both ways. No Caddy. I pulled out of the parking lot and reversed directions, heading north to catch I-5 south. Madame leaned out my window, contented and full, but DeMott's fountain pen was scratching the paper again. I looked over. He held up the page so I could read the words.

Can I see your mom while I'm here?

Once again that knife scored across my heart, completing the X that marked the spot.

He held the notebook so I could write with one hand on the wheel.

I'm headed down there right now.

He wrote beneath that:

I thought she didn't want to see you.

She doesn't. I have a shrink appt. At the asylum.

Her shrink?

Mine.

??!!

Mandatory. All undercover agents have to.

What??

Undercover agents sometimes forget what's real.

What about you?

I smiled and shook my head.

But you look so different. New clothes. Cool car.

Just for cover.

And you don't look unhappy anymore.

I shifted my eyes, gazing in the rearview mirror. I knew the Caddy wasn't there, but the sudden pain in my heart wouldn't let me look in DeMott's eyes. Changing lanes, I took the on-ramp to the interstate. The Ghost glided for several minutes before I realized our silence was too long. It might seem suspicious to anyone listening. I cleared my throat. "You're going to stay at Aunt Eleanor's house. She's our chaperone."

"I can't wait to see her," he said. But he was writing:

And your real aunt, Charlotte? Visit?

I shook my head.

Too risky. Another time. Promise.

How much longer, Raleigh?

The track closes in four days.

And then . . . ?

Take Mom home. To Virginia.

That's what you want?

I nodded.
"Really?" he asked, out loud.
I nodded again. That was what I wanted. For her.
But as we drove down the highway and Mount Rainier filled the sky, our silence extended again. It was easy to say what I wanted for my mother. But figuring out what I wanted for myself was a bigger problem.
Except the truth.
I really did want the truth.

Chapter Thirty-One

I signed my fake name on the official visitors' log at Western State Hospital. It was a quarter to three and the air already smelled of dinner. Institutional dinner. That prickly odor of salted green beans and oily yellow chicken, all of it reeking of vitamins and reconstituted illness. The receptionist at the front desk was a square-faced girl whose eyes were set too close together. She seemed less than pleased to see us. She pointed her pen at DeMott.

"Is he here to see Dr. Norbert too?"

"No."

DeMott gave me a look, letting me know my tone was harsh. Bad manners always bothered him.

I tried again. "No, ma'am. But he might be visiting a patient later."

"He's just going to waltz onto the ward—is that what you think?"

"No." I stretched the word out, hoping to neutralize her sarcasm. "Dr. Norbert has to approve it first. And the patient has to agree to see him."

She tapped the pen on a sign above the visitors' log. "You'd better find out quick. See what that says for Saturday?"

"Yes, visiting hours are over at three o'clock." I tapped my watch, the same way she tapped the sign. "So he's still got fifteen minutes."

DeMott stepped forward, breaking up the fight. "Thank you, miss. We appreciate your help."

He turned and walked across the foyer, taking a seat by the stairwell door. The receptionist's expression seemed baffled, like that of the airport security guy. Out here, DeMott's Southern gentility sounded like a foreign language. For all they knew he was kidding, pulling their leg. Except he wasn't. DeMott's etiquette was pure distilled Old Dominion—the Virginian who could face a guillotine and still call the executioner "sir."

I tried to smile at her. "Do you allow dogs in the lobby?"

"Seeing eye dogs?"

"Ordinary dogs." Not that Madame was ordinary. "Pets. That belong to the patients."

"What do you think?"

She really didn't want to know.

Closing my lips over my tattered Southern manners, I walked over to where DeMott was sitting. The foyer's floor was covered with small white hexagonal tiles. The twelve-foot ceiling seemed even higher because of the dark wall panels. The Gothic architecture reminded me of some of Richmond's downtown buildings, built in the late 1800s after the War of Northern Aggression. But the effect was ruined by the plastic chairs placed beside a wood-laminate table, where pamphlets fanned across the surface.

I said, "I'll be back as soon as possible."

He picked up a pamphlet. The cover read *Signs of Clinical Depression*. He asked, "How long does it usually take?"

"It's hard to say. He stretches it out or cuts it short, depending on his mood."

"You see him often?"

His forehead was tightening, the skin rippling. I knew this expression. It meant my answers weren't clear enough. I was being evasive, again. And DeMott was worried. Again.

"You know," I said, "this would be a lot easier if you'd carry a cell phone."

"And if people used them only for emergencies, I might. But I refuse to spend my days with a phone stuck to my ear."

"But if you had a phone, I could call you from upstairs. Let you know what he says about the visit."

"Why can't you walk back here and tell me in person?"

"I can't." That wasn't really true—I just didn't want to walk back. Which meant I told another lie. *Wonderful.*

"Call her." He nodded at the receptionist. "She can give me the message."

"I guess you didn't catch her drift. The desk closes at three. What if I'm not done by three?"

"Which brings us to my original point. The old-fashioned method still works. Come tell me in person."

Less than two hours together and already the bickering had started. It felt sadly familiar, known and uncomfortable, like a river current that started miles back and continually forced us to swim against it. Once upon a time, his manor life at Weyanoke charmed me. It seemed romantic, especially compared to the FBI's barking acronyms, triplicate legal files, and electronic databanks. But eight months after our engagement, I was learning something crucial about relationships: the same quality that charmed in the beginning became annoying later.

Reaching into my purse, I handed him my cell phone and car keys. "If you don't hear from me by three, take Madame for a walk. The grounds are actually nice. For an insane asylum."

"You shouldn't call it that."

"DeMott, I'm so far beyond euphemisms." I turned to the receptionist, waiting for her to unlock the stairwell. When the door buzzed, I swung it open.

A woman sprang out.

She must've been crouched below the small window in the door, planning her escape, because she pushed me away and headed straight for the main exit. The receptionist immediately slapped her hand on the wall, and I heard locks snapping in the front door.

The woman shook the door handle. "Let me go! Do you hear me? I'm getting out of here."

"You're not going anywhere." The receptionist picked up the phone. "You don't have a pass."

"But I want to leave." The woman waddled over to the desk. She was short and fat and her hair looked like oiled gray strings. "You can't keep me here."

I was still wondering what to do, holding the stairwell door, when she turned and smiled at DeMott. Her yellow teeth looked like torn celery stalks.

She said, "What're you doing here?"

"I'm waiting," DeMott said.

"Well, I'm going to town. Come with me. We can drink three beers."

"Three?"

"Yes. Three."

The receptionist hung up the phone. "Margaret, you're not going anywhere. You don't have a pass."

"I'm riding the bus."

"You need money to ride a bus."

"No, I don't." She turned to DeMott. "My boyfriend is the bus driver."

Too polite to stare at this creature, and too gentlemanly for sudden action, DeMott was glancing around the foyer, looking shaken. But another door suddenly opened, beside the receptionist's desk, and two men stepped out. One was a stocky man with red hair. The other was a large black man wearing a gold cross necklace. Both wore white uniforms. And both smiled at Margaret.

"You are not taking me," Margaret said.

I looked at DeMott. "I shouldn't be more than an hour."

"That seems long," he said.

"You have no idea," I said.

≈

The long, narrow hallway on the second floor felt like a tunnel, with Dr. Norbert's office waiting at the end. In the small room full of books, he had drawn the slatted blinds against the afternoon sunlight. One small lamp illuminated the space and made the furniture fall into ambient grays and blacks, so that every object looked both vague and significant, like he was expanding the Rorschach tests.

"I'm curious about why you wanted to cancel our appointment," he said, closing the door behind me. "And then eager to move it up to three o'clock."

He pointed at the brown couch, anxious for me to sit. Maybe because when I was standing I towered over him.

But I didn't sit, and I stayed by the door. "My mom's dog is in my car." I searched for the exact term he'd used during our last visit. "You said a visit might be therapeutic."

He stroked the clipped beard. "Does this dog bite?"

"If you kick her."

His smile came thin and strained, an expression I might diagnose as passive-aggressive. He walked over to his desk and picked up the phone, dialing a three-digit number and asking if a meeting room was available on ward three. "I'll need it in about thirty minutes," he said. "Bring the patient Nadine Harmon. And the orderly she likes. Is she available?"

I glanced around the room. Books were usually a good sign. But something about the tightly aligned spines in the darkened room told me otherwise. This was a neat and narrow library, the kind that contained only the books that agreed with Freud's perspective, a library that had relinquished its true purpose of opening hearts and minds. Even in the dim light I could see the word *clinical* on several dozen covers.

"That sounds acceptable. One moment." He placed his small hand over the receiver. "How do you propose to get the dog onto the ward without her seeing you?"

"I have somebody bringing her."

He hesitated, then finished speaking to the person on the phone. When he hung up, he pointed to the couch again. "Have a seat, Raleigh."

"May I use your phone first?"

"My phone?"

I nodded.

"You don't have a cell phone?"

"Not with me, at the moment." I smiled but felt the chill of his question. This little tidbit of information would probably join his notes for OPR. *Didn't have cell phone with her.* "I need to make a call. About Madame."

"The dog."

"Yes."

He lifted the receiver and offered it to me. "Press nine to leave the system."

If only, I thought. If only I could press a number and leave this entire system. As I called my own phone, I read the letters placed under his desk's protective glass. Several looked official, marked with the state seal of George Washington's image. I wanted to read the contents, but Freud stood by my shoulder, and my phone was ringing too many times. I started counting. Five, six rings. And still DeMott didn't answer. I ground my teeth. He probably didn't know how to slide his finger over the screen. When the seventh ring started, I began composing a voice-mail message, something for Freud to overhear. But DeMott suddenly picked up.

And I couldn't resist. "You have to slide your finger over the screen."

"Yes," he said. "I figured that out when your friend called."

"My friend?"

"Jack."

Which was worse, I didn't know: DeMott talking to Jack, on my cell phone, or little Sigmund Freud carefully watching me right now.

Before I could decide, DeMott said, "That's him, isn't it?" His voice came fast and heated. "Your *colleague?* The guy who just *happened* to show up on the cruise to Alaska."

I wanted to vomit, right there on Freud's official letters. But if there was ever a time not to show fear, this was it.

"Great news," I said cheerfully. "Dr. Norbert says Madame can come in. But since I can't be seen, you'll need to—"

He hung up.

No problem figuring *that* out, I thought bitterly. I wanted to slam the phone down. Instead I continued talking, refusing to give the shrink any more rope. "—bring her in. I'll meet you after the visit."

And, because my life was a total fraud, I pretended to listen.

"Pardon?" I said. "Right. Sounds good. About thirty minutes."

When I hung up, my hands felt detached from my arms. Woodenly, I walked over to the brown couch and sat down.

Dr. Norbert sank deep into his padded chair and took out his notebook, tilting it just so. "Who was that?"

"My fiancé. He flew out here with Madame. Today."

The doctor gave a long, slow nod, savoring the moment.

Our four visits had taught me to wait out his silences. But my nerves got the best of me. "I told you he was coming."

"Yes. You did. But you only mentioned the dog was here. Not your fiancé."

"Just because the front desk closes"—I lifted my arm, making an extravagant gesture with my wristwatch—"in about two minutes. I wanted to make sure the dog could get in."

"Your fiancé is downstairs waiting?"

"Yes."

"Why doesn't he join our session?"

"That seems dangerous."

"Dangerous?"

"Risky. Since I'm undercover."

"You picked him up at the airport?"

I nodded.

"And drove him here. And you are requesting a visitor's pass. All of which poses much more risk to your undercover status than a visit to my office." He tilted his head, feigning curiosity. It was the gesture of a man who enjoyed setting traps but didn't have the courage to admit it. "Why wouldn't you want DeMott to join us?"

I stared at him. This little man. Surrounded by a sea of certifiable lunatics. And who chose to pick apart his only patient who wasn't locked up. Right there, every nerve inside of me turned to steel.

"Well, Doctor, my first concern is for my mother. She needs to see her dog. I wasn't thinking about myself. Or my fiancé. Or you, frankly. I was thinking about her and the dog."

"The dog, yes. I know more about her than I do about you." He tilted his head again. The round spectacles glinted like quartz in the lamplight. "Tell me how you felt seeing DeMott."

"What do you want to know?"

"You were happy to see him?"

"Of course."

"Not anxious, nervous?"

"No."

"Not even undercover?"

"I told you, Raleigh David is engaged. DeMott only makes my cover look more real."

"But Raleigh David isn't engaged. Raleigh David doesn't exist. The woman engaged to DeMott is Raleigh Harmon."

I pressed my palms together. "I thought you were referring to the case. How it would appear. To anyone watching."

"Do you think you're being watched, Raleigh?"

My mother was a schizophrenic. Paranoid schizophrenic. If I told Freud that a black Cadillac was following me, how would he react? I suddenly saw those men from the lobby, coming through the door in their white uniforms. What a giddy note Freud could write to OPR.

"Nobody's watching me."

"Does DeMott support your work?"

"Yes."

"He doesn't mind you working undercover?"

"No." I decided to stop counting my lies. "He doesn't mind."

"And how does he feel about you living here, in Washington?"

"He wants to know when I'm coming home. Naturally."

"Naturally. And by home, you mean Virginia?"

I nodded.

"What did you tell him about going home?"

"I said it depended on my mom. I told him she can't travel until she's well." I closed my lips and deployed my official FBI smile. "I think she'll be very happy to see Madame."

"What about DeMott—would she enjoy seeing him?"

I kept smiling. "There's only one way to find out."

—

Ward Three was one floor above his dimmed office. Dr. Norbert stood at the two-way tinted mirror that was embedded with chicken wire. He kept glancing between the view inside the meeting room and me.

"Your mother's agreed to attend group therapy," he said. "They meet in there." He rocked back on his heels, checking my expression. "She even contributed to some artwork."

The artwork was finger paintings. Paintbrushes were probably too dangerous, potential weapons. Taped to the gray walls, the pictures exploded with primary colors, saturated and disturbing. Plastic chairs with no sharp edges had been placed in a circle, but DeMott pulled two out and sat directly across from my mother. She held Madame in her arms like a baby and the dog wagged its tail. My eyes felt hot, stinging. That durable burn from damming up tears. I didn't want to take my eyes off my mother, but there was a third person in the room. The orderly. The one she liked.

Felicia Kunkel.

"The orderly," I said to Freud, keeping my voice casual, "she works on the ward?"

"She's something of an aide. Minimally trained in medical matters."

I placed a hand on the wall, swallowing to control my voice. "How long has she worked here?"

"Not very long. But the staff say your mother immediately took to her."

Little wonder. My mother already knew Felicia. But my brain was struggling to make sense of her presence here. Last year I'd spent a memorable night babysitting Felicia for Jack, before she testified in federal court. When she later met my mother, they became fast friends. But watching these three people and the dog, I felt scared. Out of control. Something was going on and I couldn't quantify it and Freud's gaze was on me. I felt like I'd stepped into a bad dream at the halfway point.

"Feeling all right?" he asked.

"Fine."

He turned back to the mirror. "It's interesting. Your mother's paranoia almost disappears with the girl. She'll even take her medicine."

"That's good."

"Good, yes," he echoed. "But odd."

I didn't want to ask. But I needed to know. "How is that odd?"

"This young woman doesn't resemble you. Not in the least."

Felicia had the figure of an overripe pear, and her white skin was pocked from sores acquired through her former drug addictions. Leaning against the wall, she looked bored and bit her nails in a nonchalant manner, spitting the pieces to the floor.

"Perhaps there's some connection to your sister," he said.

My sister, Helen, looked nothing like Felicia either. Lithe and intellectual, Helen was beautiful in a contrived Bohemian way. But the doctor's probe had hit something. On the inside, Felicia and Helen were nearly twins. Both insecure and self-loathing, they each fell for controlling men who were themselves weak. Women without any center or foundation. The lost types that often gravitated toward my mother. Hurt people. Who needed to know love, and that such things as redemption and salvation existed. Those people were drawn to her, because she was acquainted with pain.

"There's some resemblance to my sister," I said.

"I thought so." He turned, fully facing me. "How does it feel, seeing your mother after all this time?"

Her porcelain skin was shiny and bloated, like rising bread dough. Every time she looked down at the dog curled in her lap, I saw the wide stripe of gray hair, stretching down her scalp, dividing her black curls that hung on either side, tangled and loose as abandoned nests. She wore a pink calico shirt, nothing like her normal wardrobe of extravagant clothing, but I wondered if she even saw the thing. Her eyes had a dull glaze.

"She looks good," I lied.

"Good," he repeated. "But something bothers you?"

"No."

"No?"

I gritted my teeth. Yes, something bothered me—his incessant tactic of repeating my last word. But I kept my eyes on the dog. Madame's tail swished drowsily. Her small black face lay on my mother's arm, gazing up at the still-lovely neck of Nadine Shaw Harmon. Whenever my mother looked down, the wagging accelerated.

I turned to Freud, fastening the official smile to my face. "I'm just glad she's improving."

"Improving, yes. And enjoying your fiancé. Perhaps he could come again."

DeMott sat with his back to the mirror. I could see the solid shoulders, the hair on his forearms where he'd rolled up his shirt-sleeves, as though work needed to be done. He was telling her a story, some elaborate tale with gestures. I watched the lean tensile muscles in his arms, the honest strength of a good man. When she smiled at him, it felt like a punch to my gut.

"DeMott leaves tomorrow," I said.

"Tomorrow? Rather a quick visit, considering you're engaged."

"His family needs him. But Madame will be staying. She could come back."

"The dog. Perhaps. But notice how your mother is listening to him."

Her jasper eyes already seemed clearer, more focused, and a light pink color was brushing her cheeks. From where we stood, DeMott's voice was just a soft rumble. But it sent tingles down my back, reminding me of all those times I laid my head on his chest, listening to the low thunder of his voice, the beat of his heart steady as a clock.

I didn't dare look at Freud. "Can the dog stay?"

"Stay—here? Absolutely not. But perhaps it can come for another visit."

"She."

"She?"

"Madame is not an it," I said.

He turned to the glass, watching them again. And I was grateful. The war inside my heart felt close to spilling out, a mess of raging emotions that would bloody this sterile hallway and provide Freud with years of material. I hadn't seen my mother in months, but it was even longer since I'd seen her smile like this. She stopped looking at me that way long ago. Because of my lies. Because deep inside she knew what I was telling her didn't make sense.

A good daughter would now be happy to see the joy on her face.

But self-pity was a wicked little snake and it came slithering forward on the realization that DeMott had cruised in here so easily. And Felicia, half-bored Felicia, picking at her hangnails. And here I was hidden on the other side of a fake mirror with a fake identity and a little doctor who faked his concern.

"Are you sure nothing's bothering you, Raleigh?"

"I'm just glad to see her."

Not a complete lie. I was glad. And some *thing* didn't bother me; many things bothered me. DeMott's visit was already bubbling over with our simmering conflicts and resentments, and yet here was my beloved, my fiancé, visiting an asylum—*asking* to come—and talking to my drugged-up mother behind security doors and safety glass, chatting away as if nothing was wrong. DeMott Fielding. He knew chivalry. Profound thoughtfulness. Respect for my mother, even amid these horrid circumstances. He was wonderful, heroic, and I couldn't figure out why that made me feel so sad.

"Raleigh?"

Sad. That's what I felt. Not just the self-pity. It was the realization: maybe, just maybe, I loved DeMott for the way he dealt with my crazy mother.

"Raleigh?"

But that wasn't love. Not romantic love. Not the love DeMott felt for me.

"Raleigh, their time is almost up."

I nodded, vaguely.

"We need to leave before she sees you," he said.

Gratitude and sadness. That's what I felt. And it made me wonder. What about love?

Chapter Thirty-Two

Sunday at dawn, the Ghost was the only car in the Point Defiance parking lot. The air smelled of cedar and cloistered dew.

I looked at Madame. "Stay close."

We ran over the woodland trails, our steps almost silent on the soft forest floor. Overhead a canopy of evergreen boughs blocked the gray light, making the world feel secluded and beautiful. Madame ran beside me, pulling hard for the first miles. When we reached a rose garden, the trail was carpeted with blush-colored petals. Every step perfumed the air, and the fragrance lured something from my mind. Twain's words about forgiveness—it was the flower shedding its fragrance on the heel that crushes it.

When we reached the beach, I couldn't tell if I was panting or crying. Madame splashed into the cold water, tail high and happy, but I turned away, walking toward a sandstone cliff. The brown and taupe layers rose above the water, as evenly spaced as pages in a book. Kneeling in the rocky soil, I listened to the water lapping at the shore and smelled the briny chloral odor of the kelp that high tide left behind. I closed my eyes. Last night, after leaving Western State, DeMott and I ate dinner with Eleanor. The two of them charmed each other. Of course. Eleanor with Southern words purloined from the playwright, and DeMott entertaining her with tales of Weyanoke. For the most part I remained quiet because my mind kept flashing with images of my mother. The once-proud and ladylike Nadine Shaw Harmon looked like any other mental patient. Lost, lonely. Loaded with pharmaceuticals. And Felicia Kunkel, watching over her. All through dinner I resisted the urge to pick up the phone and call Aunt Charlotte. Surely she was behind

Felicia's new job. When we took the cruise to Alaska, Aunt Charlotte had hired her to house-sit her place on Capitol Hill. But I couldn't call, not while undercover. And when dinner ended, DeMott and I sat on Eleanor's porch, talking for a while. We studiously avoided the topic of my mother. And DeMott's internal clock was three hours ahead. I left at nine, heading straight for bed.

But I barely slept. All my dreams circled the asylum. Freud showed up calling me a liar, liar, liar. My mother appeared dressed in a clown costume. She stood next to DeMott who wore a tux and tapped his watch and told me we were late. Every time I woke up, I couldn't breathe.

Now I pressed my knees into the coarse sand and asked for help. No. That wasn't right. I begged. I begged for wisdom from the same God who created my mother in all her perfect imperfection. Who placed DeMott in my life. Who promised that if I asked in His name, it would be done. I asked for the answer: If I wasn't the fiancée DeMott deserved, did that mean I wouldn't be the wife he needed? Or would things settle down with time, when I moved back to Virginia, went to live at Weyanoke, and . . . something wet touched my hand. I opened my eyes. Madame pushed her nose beneath my clasped fingers. Her fur was soaked with salt water. And she was happy. Ready to run again.

"All right," I said. "Let's go."

We finished five miles and I drove back to Thea's Landing, smuggling her warm body into the building under my windbreaker. Something about the condo's sleek atmosphere and modern attitude told me dogs weren't welcomed. And right now I didn't have time to renegotiate a lease that would end when Raleigh David disappeared, in about a week. Upstairs, I fed the dog, then showered and dressed myself in the nice clothes that didn't belong to me. Just before leaving, I took a pillow off my bed and carried it into the living room, placing it inside Madame's dog crate.

"Please," I said.

She looked at me as if I'd offered a final meal before the electric chair.

"Just for today. I promise to come home as soon as possible."

She tiptoed into the box, her head hanging low between her shoulders. When I locked the wire door, I felt like a complete creep.

≈

Eleanor demanded we eat breakfast with her, right after she gave DeMott a tour of the Hot Tin barn. It was just past 9:00 a.m. when I found them touring the stables like old friends. She had paired fire-engine red ballet slippers with a midnight blue pantsuit—rhinestones on the pockets—while DeMott was dressed for the Kentucky Derby. Chinos, another white oxford, the blue seersucker jacket, and a deep blue tie that graciously matched Eleanor's outfit. She kept both hands wrapped around his arm.

I was coming up from behind, about to call out, when I saw DeMott stop at Stella Luna's stable. Eleanor, sensing something, let go of his arm. He moved toward the horse, and Stella responded by craning her neck to the side, as if reading him the way children and animals and prophets search people for signs of dishonesty. Slowly he lifted his hand, and after a moment the horse pressed her face into his palm. She closed her eyes, and my stomach tingled. DeMott's many gifts included a gentle touch. That cultured strength. Somebody once tried to apply the cliché to him—about still waters running deep—but that wasn't it. DeMott was deep water capable of holding perfectly still.

Until my cell phone erupted. That awful version of "Camptown Races" doo-dahed through the barn. All three of them turned to look at me. DeMott, Eleanor, Stella. But only DeMott's eyes were full of pain.

"Sorry," I said, rummaging through the bag. *Please, God, don't let this be Jack. Please.* "Hello?"

"You ordered roasted pork on a ciabatta roll?"

Lucia Lutini.

I felt relieved and almost laughed. But DeMott's hand was slipping from the horse, and Eleanor rushed to his side, once more wrapping her ringed fingers around his arm. I gave a signal, indicating the call would just take a moment, but Eleanor was already lifting her chin, delivering choice words to his wounded Southern sensibility.

"Hang on a second," I told Lucia, walking out from under the barn eaves.

The horses were coming back from training runs and had been hooked to the hot walkers. They circled the sawdust with prancing strides, long legs sashaying like supermodels. I headed toward the big tractors sitting idle beside the maintenance hut.

"Go ahead."

"Mr. Cooper got himself kicked out of Saratoga."

"What for?"

"*What* was never proven, but the *accusation* was sufficient. You may have noticed, the racetracks don't believe in innocence beyond a shadow of a doubt. They operate on the presumption of guilt."

"Without search warrants."

"Correct. Suspicion alone is probable cause. And in the case of Mr. Cooper, he was suspected of throwing his races."

"Wouldn't that destroy a trainer's career?"

"A trainer, perhaps. But Bill Cooper was a jockey."

I lifted my hand, pretending to shield the sun from my eyes. I tried to imagine Cooper as a jockey. He was short. Probably five-two without those cowboy boots. His torso had been colonized by middle age, but now that expression in his cold eyes made more sense. Cooper was a high-performance athlete, ruthlessly competitive. He wanted to win at any cost. Maybe even death. "How'd he throw races?"

"He was suspected of pulling back on the reins." Lucia, the profiler, offered a quick biography. Cooper was a working-class kid who got a job as a pony rider at Saratoga, the prestigious track in upstate New York. Hardworking, strong, and competitive, Cooper rose up the ranks to become a jockey. "He made his first mount at sixteen. By seventeen he was making good money. But by nineteen he apparently switched to losing. Care to guess why?"

The simplest answer was always money. But after watching Cooper deal with Eleanor, my instincts told me there was another element. Our records showed Cooper was divorced, chronically late with child support, and upside down on his mortgage. But that wasn't what scratched at my mind. It was his simmering servitude. The resentment that seemed to radiate from his tight neck.

"Money," I said. "But money he's forced to make."

"Very good. He began losing because he owed somebody. I'll give you a hint. They are men who reside in various Manhattan boroughs and whose last names contain far too many vowels."

"The Mob?"

"Correct. Organized crime."

I turned, looking down the median between the barns. Grooms removing the thoroughbreds from the hot walkers and adding others. Ashley was among them, leading KichaKoo to an empty station. The horse nodded its brown head up and down as though agreeing with something the girl said. But Ashley wasn't speaking. She looked bedraggled; the blond hair looked flat as a melted yellow crayon.

"Do we have any hard evidence to support Cooper's connection to the Mob?" I asked.

"Yes. But it's not what you're thinking of."

"Pardon?"

"Despite my background as a CPA, I consider signed napkins from my father's restaurant official. Should any of this information prove incorrect, my sources have enjoyed their last sandwich at Donato's."

"Your dad would cut them off."

"*Abassolutamente.*"

"How did Cooper get here, from Saratoga?"

"Unfortunately, my sources couldn't answer that question. But we can assume he paid off the debt. Or he is still paying."

"We can assume that?"

"He's still alive, Raleigh."

Point taken.

"However," she continued, "I did find out when he arrived at Emerald Meadows. Five years ago, as a trainer. He worked for that famous female jockey, the one who still makes the papers—"

"Claire Manchester?"

"Yes. Eleanor Anderson hired him away from that barn."

I thanked her and hung up, then spent several moments gazing at Mount Rainier and trolling the information through my mind, committing it to memory. But something moved over to my right. By the maintenance hut. I saw a dark-haired man. Young. Shaking his head back and forth, flinging a ponytail across his shoulders. He paused to puff on a cigarette.

I moved over to the tractors. The front tires so big the tops were level with my head. The nubby treads held bits of turf soil. When I pinched the sediment, sliding it between my fingers, I could feel the combination of sand, silken clay, and a creamy loam that came from the finest silts. And the fineness of those grains bothered me. How did the tractor driver fail to notice that buried tube?

When I came around the other side of the machine, the pony-tailed smoker was blowing his nose and staring at the tissue.

"Hi," I said.

"Yeah, hi." He threw his cigarette into an empty oil drum that sat by the door. "Help you?"

A contrail of gray smoke rose from the oil drum. It smelled like sweat socks and moss, a stench that explained his expression. Half annoyed, half scared. He had just thrown away a joint.

"I'm looking for the track's groomer."

"Which one?"

"Whoever worked Thursday." I smiled. "My aunt's horse was in the first race. SunTzu."

"You must be Raleigh."

I felt a burst of adrenaline, caught off guard. "Have we met?"

"No."

"How did you know who I was?"

"SunTzu, he belonged to Eleanor Anderson. And everybody's been talking about her niece being in the barn fire. You said the horse belonged to your aunt. I can put it together."

He leaned back against the building. Mr. Casual. His eyelids were swollen, like sandbags holding back the murky color of his brown eyes, and he couldn't hold my gaze. He watched the smoke rising from the oil drum. The music playing inside the maintenance hut sounded tinny, bouncing against the corrugated metal sides.

"And you are . . . ?"

"Gordon."

"Were you driving the tractor that morning?"

"Yeah." He blew his nose again and once more stared at the Kleenex. It was stained with blood.

"Are you all right?"

"Hey, no biggie." He shoved the tissue into his back pocket.

"Thursday morning, did you notice anything amiss?"

"Amiss?"

"Different, out of order, not right." I wasn't sure how many synonyms his pot brain required. "Did you feel any weird bumps in the turf?"

"There's always bumps. That's why we groom it."

"Right."

"But we're not pressing down real hard. Pack the turf and it's rough on the horses. They can break an ankle. Like that." He snapped his fingers, indicating sudden fracture. "And you don't want it too loose either, 'specially when it's dry. Horses start running and it's a dust storm. Or it rains and you've got a mud bowl."

"It rained that day."

"Yeah. But we only got some puddles. Because I did a good job grooming. And I didn't see anything weird." He squinted, puffy eyes almost closing. "Wait. Is somebody blaming me for what happened to the horse?"

"No."

"'Cause I heard they already hauled Harrold off for questioning. The starter? I heard he might go to jail." He wrinkled his nose and reached into his pocket again. After giving the Kleenex another blow, he once again stared at the blood that came out.

"Gordon?"

He looked up.

"Are you in charge of grooming?"

"No, my dad is. Gordon. Senior. I'm junior."

"Is he here?"

"No. My mom's sick. He gets here at three in the morning. Then he goes home at eight to get her to the doctor."

"I'm sorry."

"Something about her blood. It's not working right." He shrugged. But it was the gesture of a kid who got slugged and insisted it didn't hurt.

"Maybe I can call your dad."

"He's pretty busy, running her back and forth to Fred Hutch."

"Where?"

"Fred Hutchinson. The cancer place, in Seattle? He doesn't want to leave her alone."

"He sounds like a good man. Thanks for your help, Gordon."

"That's it?" He looked surprised, then annoyed. He lost a joint—for this?

I smiled and lifted my fist for a bump good-bye. As I was walking away, I heard a sudden burst of metal music. Then it disappeared. When I turned around, Gordon was no longer standing by the back door. Circling back with a frown that said I'd forgotten to ask something, I walked up to the oil drum. The music was louder now, and clearer, rocking through the corrugated steel. Mick Jagger was pleased to meet me, hoped he guessed my name. I leaned over the oil drum. No burning joint remained. Gordon must have grabbed it. But there was some trash in there. Soda cans, foil wrappers that looked like they came from the Quarterchute. And some bloody Kleenexes.

Holding my breath, I pinched a white corner, carefully lifting it from the drum and thanking Gordon for his DNA sample.

Chapter Thirty-Three

I was hurrying back to the barn, ready to apologize to DeMott for running off, but I never got the chance.

Sal Gag stood next to my fiancé and asked, "How many horses?"

"Twelve." DeMott stepped aside, giving Ashley room to walk Cuppa Joe from his temporary stall to the hot walker. She still looked glum.

"A dozen ponies is a good start." The bookie watched Ashley. "Got plans for more?"

"My sister does. She's the equestrian. She bought her first horses from Rokeby."

Sal Gag's eyebrows shot up. "You mean, Sea Hero—that Rokeby?"

"Her husband grew up just down the road from the farm."

It sounded so quaint—"down the road." But Rokeby Farm belonged to billionaire Paul Mellon, whose thoroughbred Sea Hero took the Triple Crown. And the man DeMott was referring to, his sister MacKenna's husband, was a dubious achiever named Stuart Morgan. I had strong reservations about Stuart, but they paled in comparison to Sal Gag, perched at the top of my suspect list. And now I was worried about what DeMott had revealed, what information might have slipped out. And where did Eleanor go?

"Hi," I said.

DeMott turned around. "There you are." He put his arm around my shoulder. "Mr. Gagliardo was just telling me how rough it's been for you."

And this is what a heart attack feels like.

He said, "No wonder Eleanor kept changing the subject last night."

"Speaking of Eleanor," I said, smiling like a wooden puppet, "where is she?"

"She demanded her breakfast."

"Your aunt," Sal Gag said, shaking his head. "Ten sharp."

DeMott squeezed my shoulder. "I told her I wanted to wait for you. But she said something about everyone being sentenced to solitary confinement inside their own skin. Whatever that means."

My hands felt hot, clammy. I glanced at my watch. By the time we reached the private dining room, Eleanor would be finishing her dry toast. "I know where we can get a great bacon-and-egg sandwich."

"Let me guess. Burger King?"

"No, not Burger King."

"I'm not eating at McDonald's."

I glanced at Sal Gag. He watched us with a shark-like smile. But DeMott wasn't getting it.

He said, "Raleigh takes in more grease than Jiffy Lube. But I can't handle that food."

"You kids are welcome to eat with me." He was still smiling when he said it. "I got a private table."

"Oh no," I said, "we—"

"We would love to," DeMott said, giving my shoulder a good hard squeeze, letting me know my manners were failing again. "We would enjoy that very much. Thank you."

≈

Eleanor was sipping from her gold-rimmed coffee cup in the members-only dining room.

"You're late!" she bellowed.

"Don't berate me." I leaned down, whispering, "I'm already being punished enough. DeMott accepted another invitation."

Her white-haired head made a slow swivel, like a turtle, until she was facing the table reserved for Sal Gagliardo. The large man set his unlit cigar on the white china, while DeMott took the seat across from him. When she turned back to me, just as slowly, her voice was surprisingly quiet. "I might bear some fraction of responsibility."

"How big a fraction?"

"I was trying to help."

"You didn't."

"I thought if DeMott knew how hard you were working, and how hard it was for you to get to know people at the track—"

"That would help, how?"

"He seemed so upset; you don't call him enough. I explained that you're working day and night. But really, Raleigh, you need to call him more often."

"Don't start."

"Then be glad he wants to help."

"Whose side are you on?"

"Probably his." She sighed. "I have such a terrible weakness for handsome men."

Sal Gagliardo was waving his paw-like hand, urging me to join the table. I threw Eleanor one parting glance worthy of her own abilities to wither, then walked over to the men with a fake smile on my face. Ever the gentleman, DeMott stood and held out my chair. Sal Gag remained seated while the waiter poured coffee for us and brought espresso for the bookie. When I picked up my white cup, holding it with both hands, I gazed out the window. The men fell into another competitive banter about horses and money. I listened vaguely but was too busy sending up silent prayers and fist-shaking worthy of the Psalms. Outside the wind blew disc-shaped clouds across the face of Mount Rainier. Lenticular clouds, a sign that rain was coming. I placed my lips on the cup's gilded rim. *Please. Do not let this blow up in our faces.*

"We get these stop-and-start summers," the mobster was telling DeMott. "One day it's eighty-two degrees. Bee-you-tee-ful. Next day, clouds and rain. The ponies, they don't know what to run. Mud. Dust. Who knows? It's been a tough season."

DeMott nodded. "How did you get involved in horse racing?"

I choked on my coffee.

Sal Gag looked at me. "You all right?"

I nodded, eyes watering. DeMott patted my back, then looked back at the mobster.

"You must have quite a few stories to tell."

"How's that?"

DeMott gestured to the sign beside the table: Reserved for Salvatore Gagliardo. "You're a fixture."

"Yeah, I got stories," he said. "Me and this place, we go way back. I started out small but hired the right people. Close. Like family." He glanced at Eleanor. She was staring at the wall, chin raised, lips moving. "Like what Eleanor's doing with Raleigh. Only I heard Raleigh don't know nothing about ponies."

"That is certainly true." DeMott took my hand. He held it on top of the table, and I wondered if he could feel the sweat on my palm, my pulse hammering like a blacksmith. "Horses aren't Raleigh's passion. But we'll have a barn on our property, once we're married."

"Married." Sal Gag pinched the handle of his demitasse. "When's the big day?"

"Soon," DeMott said.

He looked surprised. "You don't got a date?"

I jumped in. "Aunt Eleanor needed me here right now. So we put the wedding on hold. Just until things settle down for her."

His dark gaze shifted to DeMott. "Nice-looking girl *and* she waits for her wedding to help out family? That's some girl. Don't let nobody steal her."

DeMott's hand tightened. "Excuse me?"

Sal Gag held the cup midair, ready to sip. "What?"

"What did you say?"

"I said something?"

"Yes." DeMott smiled. Politely. "You said somebody might steal her."

I tried to pull my hand back. "No, DeMott, he—"

"I believe your exact words were, 'Don't let nobody steal her.' Is there something I should know?"

Sal Gag placed his little cup in the white saucer. Carefully. "I was just saying, Raleigh seems like a good catch."

"She is a good catch," DeMott said. "But who else is fishing?"

"DeMott." My voice sounded odd, probably because my heart was beating in my throat. "It's just a saying."

He suddenly released my hand. It slumped into my lap, the fingers numb. I turned to stare directly into his blue eyes, hoping to reach him telepathically. *Stop. This. Now.* But the fire inside was burning like internal combustion, the blue flames too hot to be extinguished by any words. I tightened my smile.

"You must be tired from that long flight."

"Planes," grumbled Sal Gag. "*Madonn'*, don't get me started. The lines. The X-rays. I'm gonna buy one of those Winnebagos. No more airports and no more . . ."

But DeMott wasn't listening. He was glaring at me as though Sal Gag didn't exist. For the first time in my life, I could say he was being rude. And my face hurt from smiling, looking back and forth from DeMott to the mobster who was continuing his diatribe about airports.

DeMott looked at me. "I just don't understand. Is that it?"

Sal Gag paused.

"No," I said. "I just don't think—"

"You don't think I know *jack.*"

The waiter appeared. "Are we ready to order?"

The silence hung over the table for several moments. Sal Gag opened his big hands, indicating I should order first. My voice still didn't sound right, but I asked for a deluxe Denver omelet, hash browns, toast with jam, an English muffin, a side order of bacon, and a Coca-Cola, no crushed ice.

"Where you putting all that," Sal Gag said, "in your purse?"

The waiter turned to DeMott. "And for you, sir?"

"Thanks, but I just lost my appetite."

Oh, terrific.

He handed the waiter his menu.

I glanced across the table. Sal Gag's dark eyes were on DeMott. A clever man, sizing things up. I folded my starched napkin and placed it on the white tablecloth, all very ladylike and Southern and Raleigh

Davidish. But inside I was wondering whether God had finally tired of my pathetic pleas for help.

"Now that you mention it," I said, "I'm not feeling a hundred percent either. We better take a rain check."

Sal Gag lifted the espresso cup to his lips. The dark eyes stared over the delicate rim and shifted between DeMott and me. But they came back to me. To stay.

I smiled. "I'm sure you understand."

"Oh, sure," he said. "I understand."

As we were leaving, I saw a new expression in his eyes.

Not just mischief. Not just malice.

It was mendacity.

Pure mendacity.

Chapter Thirty-Four

DeMott barreled down the sidewalk, hands shoved into the front pockets of his chinos. His shoulders were hunched with anger, and I tried to catch up, running across the parking lot. But the stupid girly shoes were slowing me down.

"DeMott!"

He didn't stop until I yelled a third time. Even then, he didn't turn around. I walked down the sidewalk. The wind was in my face and the road was choked with cars, all heading the opposite direction. The first race started in less than fifteen minutes and greed was pulling everyone to the entrance. And DeMott was glowering, refusing to look at me.

I tried to control my temper. "Do you have any idea what you just did?"

"Work," he said.

"Pardon."

"Work."

"What about it?"

"Raleigh, I'm here two days. And you can't stop working."

"*I* didn't ask to sit with that guy—*you* accepted his invitation."

"Because I know you want to be working. I was trying to help."

The wind was pulsing from the north, rustling leaves in the maples planted along the sidewalk. I glanced at the traffic, feeling both embarrassed and oddly grateful for this public spat. How could anyone think this relationship was fake when we went at it like this, for all to see? But it was one of those times I was losing for winning.

"DeMott, I have to work. I need my job."

"Marry me and you'll never work another day of your life."

I held back my sigh. It came too easy, too cruel. He was leaving this afternoon, and I might not see him again for a long time. *Calm down.* "What just happened in there," I said, "that wasn't like you."

"You mean standing up for myself?" His tone was hostile again.

"No. Being rude."

"You're right." He nodded. "That wasn't like me. That was like you."

The gusting wind shook the leaves. "I can't believe you just said that."

"I can't believe you didn't tell me about the fire."

The trees were too loud, the sound filling my ears. And something cold was settling into my stomach. I felt myself pulling away, turning from him. When I looked at the cars, I suddenly remembered the black Cadillac. Was it in this traffic jam? Watching us?

"You have nothing to say?" DeMott swept his arms out. "Oh. Wait. Don't tell me. You're worried the trees are bugged."

"DeMott, that man in there, you don't understa—"

But he was striding down the sidewalk again, walking away. I felt a strong temptation. Let him go. Because he'd have to turn around, eventually. He had nowhere to go. And when he cooled off . . . No. When he cooled off, all of this would be waiting for us. And now Sal Gagliardo was involved too. With gossip. Track gossip. What would be their reaction, when they learned I didn't tell my fiancé about the fire?

I ran to catch up to him. He stood beside the railroad tracks, where that train had whistled that night to wake me. DeMott's mood seemed as hard as the iron rails.

"Sal Gagliardo is a bookie."

He looked over at me.

"And not just any bookie. He's the prime suspect for race fixing. The track closed his barn after his trainer was caught drugging the horses."

"Fine. But what about the fire?"

I hesitated. The full story would only make things worse. But I didn't want to lie to him. "Nobody knows who set the fire."

"You mean it could be that guy? Who we were about to have breakfast with?" He shook his head. "Raleigh, doesn't that strike you as odd?"

"Sure it's odd. But that's my job."

"And you won't even introduce me to your real aunt."

"I can't."

"You could if you wanted."

"You're right. If I wanted to put you both in harm's way."

"But you'd let me eat with a guy who looks like he chews on hubcaps."

I glanced down the road. Nobody was following us. Not even a black Cadillac. The traffic was winding its way toward the main entrance and the sidewalk lay empty, a pale, flat ribbon. But the wind kept rustling the maples, fluffing the leaves into green pom-poms that cheered on our fight.

"DeMott, I was trying to decline Sal Gag's invitation, but you interrupted me. Then you overreacted to a simple comment—"

"This is all *my* fault?"

I stared down at my shoes. My Dolce & Gabbanas. Counterfeit shoes that belonged to an imaginary woman who would never trounce down a sidewalk having a public spat with her fiancé. A woman who didn't hold two identities separate but equal. I looked up. DeMott was here. In Seattle. Close enough to touch. And yet he looked like a complete stranger. As if all the years we'd known each other never existed and my mother hadn't asked me all through high school and college, *"How's that DeMott Fielding?"*

He waited for me to say something.

"DeMott," I said, "what happened to us?"

His shoulders slumped. He let out a long sigh. "Come home."

"What?"

"Come back to Virginia."

"What about my mom?"

"I'll fly you out here. Every week. I'll come with you. Whatever you need."

"The FBI won't let me leave town every week."

He smirked. "Here we go again. Work."

"Yes, work. My family doesn't have a lot of money."

"But I'm offering to take care of you, Raleigh. You don't have to work."

I bit back the words. *I'd have to work at getting your family to accept me.*

He sighed. "At least give me a solid date. When will you come home?"

"When my mom can go with me."

"Raleigh, your mother can't even hold a conversation right now."

"She's getting better."

"Did the doctor tell you that?"

No. Dr. Norbert would never say that. Through his little round spectacles, Freud saw a chronic maze, the hopeless and never-ending trudge of the humanist. But I knew different, and I believed. She would get better. And deep down I knew DeMott believed it too, because I saw a flicker of forgiveness in his eyes. We stared at each other and he stepped forward, wrapping his arms around me. I tried to take in his scent but the wind stole it. I looked up into his great and classic face to see that blue burning bright in his eyes. When his lips parted, I closed my eyes and waited for his kiss.

It never came.

That horrible tune sang from my purse. I opened my eyes. His expression had gone flat, almost dull.

"You better answer that," he said.

I heard the challenge in his voice. If I didn't answer, I would prove his suspicions were right. Reaching into my bag, I ended "Camptown Races."

Not Jack. Please.

"Hello?"

"Where are you?" Eleanor bellowed.

"I'm outside. With DeMott."

"Get back here. Immediately!"

"What's wrong?"

"Right now!"

"Tell me what's wrong."

"You are insufferable! What's wrong? I'll tell you what's wrong. Somebody just kidnapped Cuppa Joe."

"Sal Gag's horse?"

Chapter Thirty-Five

We ran for the entrance to the backstretch and the young maples cheered. DeMott took the lead and yanked open the door, holding it for me.

But a security guard blocked my path.

"No admittance," he said.

His name was Larry. This morning I'd signed the log for him, but now he threw darting glances over his shoulder and acted like he'd never seen me before. I pulled out my owner's ID tag and brandished it like a priest raising a crucifix to a vampire.

"I'm Eleanor Anderson's niece. Remember?"

"Nobody goes in or out. That's an order."

"When?"

"When—" His mouth parted, uncertain. "What?"

"When were you told nobody could go in or out?"

"Why?"

Because the timing would tell me more about the kidnapping. Sealing the entrances and exits meant Mr. Yuck believed Cuppa Joe could still be on the premises, or the people who were responsible for his disappearance. But looking at the hapless Larry, I thought of a third option: a security guard messed up.

I lifted my ID again. "I know about the horse, Larry. My aunt just called me. She needs me in the barn."

He shook his head. The dyed brown hair was fading to a color like rust. "I can't let you in."

"Then you can tell Eleanor." I grabbed my cell phone and started dialing a number. Any number. Eleanor left her phone in her car, for emergencies. "I'm sure she'll want to recommend you for a promotion."

"Now wait a minute." He looked scared. "Maybe you can go back, but he doesn't have a badge." He pointed at DeMott. "He's got to stay here."

"No, he's coming with me. And if you were paying attention, you'd remember him from this morning. He came in with Aunt Eleanor. Now step aside."

Larry grabbed the visitors' log. He shoved it at DeMott. A last-ditch effort at credibility. DeMott signed, but Larry then asked to see his driver's license. I saw where this was going.

"DeMott, meet me up ahead." I jogged down the hall.

A crowd was gathered outside the betting office. A man wearing an official track polo shirt stood on the large scale used for weighing jockeys and saddles. His quick movements bounced the long black needle, shifting it between 160 and 170 pounds.

"We need everyone to keep their eyes open," he said. "If you don't know Cuppa Joe, he's a black four-year-old, no color marks on him."

"You gotta be kidding me," somebody said.

I tracked the voice to the posse of old men. The Polish Prince was waving his betting sheet.

"Horse his size," he said, "where's he gonna hide—in the bathroom?"

There was a round of laughter. But the track official didn't crack a smile. The needle shook again.

"This is a very serious matter, Mr. Timadaiski."

But the posse was already ignoring him. A bald guy next to the prince was holding up three fingers while another crustacean held up five and triggered a series of hand gestures from the other old guys. Betting pool. I decided it was counterproductive to ask those guys what happened. They feasted on speculation. I needed facts. Scanning the crowd, I saw Tony Not Tony balanced on his toes like a veteran eavesdropper. A group of Hispanic jockeys in front of him were whispering. This was the problem with gossip and crime: It had a firecracker quality. One explosive bang of false information that ruined people's ability to hear the truth later.

But I decided right now, even gossip would help.

I moved over to Tony and dropped my voice to a whisper. "What happened?"

He ran his eyes down my clothes, pausing at my shoes. "I heard you left the dining room. Quickly. With your *fiancé.*"

The spat with DeMott was already old news. But I was more disturbed by the way Tony said the word *fiancé.* He made it sound dubious. Like the whole thing was a sham. Suddenly I realized how our fight looked to Sal Gag. Melodramatic. Some ploy to get out of breakfast. Or even a diversion for Cuppa Joe's kidnapping. The irony hit me again. The truth brought more disbelief than my lies.

I glanced over the jockeys' heads and saw DeMott coming down the hall. His face had the same disturbed expression I'd seen last night, after we left the asylum. A man stuck somewhere he never wanted to be. I pressed through the crowd toward him.

"It would be easier if you waited here," I said.

"Raleigh, you owe that guard an apology."

"For his incompetence?"

"If you acted like that in Richmond—"

"Don't lecture me, DeMott."

He glanced around the crowd, refusing to look at me. He was taking in the toothpick-sucking old guys. The starved jockeys with their sunken eye sockets. The betting office personnel who resembled used-car salesmen. All the backstretch regulars who were nursing their predatory instincts. I tried to hold my own judgment of him.

"Go to the private dining room," I said. "Tell them you're with Eleanor. I'll meet you there after I—"

"Work." He glared at me. "You have work to do."

I opened my mouth to say something, but reconsidered. This crowd had ears like satellite dishes. Turning to leave, I felt a pain in my heart. Like he'd kicked it. But suddenly he grabbed my hand. I turned around.

"Sorry." He squeezed it. "Really. Just be careful. Okay?"

I nodded.

And he let go.

≈

The thoroughbreds paraded down the backstretch to the first race, resplendent in their bright silks. But the prerace jitters were palpable in the air, along with something else. The jockeys' dark faces had ratcheted down with the same clamped expression I saw after SunTzu fell on his rider. Scared jockeys. Who couldn't afford to be scared. And the thoroughbreds must've picked up on the emotion, because more than the usual number of pony riders were accompanying them to the track. Appaloosas and quarter horses, they clopped beside the high-strung racers like stout chaperones escorting beauty contestants to the stage.

I glanced down the line. There were no Hot Tin horses, and I got impatient. Dashing across to the lane, I tried to make a run for the barns. But my sudden movement startled a dark brown filly wearing orange silks. The horse reared and neighed, and triggered a chain reaction. The horses began jumping out of the procession line. The pony riders galloped around the confusion, a deafening thunder of *clippety-clop clippety-clop*. It was followed by barrages of Spanish, unleashed from the jockeys, directed at me.

"*Estupida!*"

"*Idiota!*"

I pressed my back against a stone building that blocked my path to the barns. The jockeys passed in front of me and threw dirty looks. I kept my eyes down, listening to the announcer's voice crackle over the loudspeaker. Gusts of wind brushed away half the words, and the other half were drowned out by a hissing sound. It took me a moment to realize where it was coming from. I glanced up and saw steam curling from the building's raised roof. The showers.

And then another sound. Louder. Clearer. Distinct.

A woman, crying.

I glanced at my watch. *What a morning.* Nine minutes had passed since Eleanor called, and I could only imagine how much evidence had already been destroyed. Frustrated, I looked down the line. Four more horses still needed to pass, and the next horse was shifting sideways, deflecting some invisible blow. The pony rider had quickened around its rear, and he came between the horse and me, so close I could smell the animal's loamy breath. I pressed myself back again, feeling every vertebrae touch the stone wall.

The pony rider looked down from his saddle. A teenager with red hair and freckles, he misread my distress.

"She's fine," he said. "Barbie's just bawling her eyes out again."

The procession continued to pass, but the sobbing never ceased. *Barbie.*

I checked my watch. Two horses remained, and thirteen minutes had passed since Eleanor's call. It would take me another four or five minutes to reach the barn, and by then the entire backstretch would've beat me there. I knew who the rider meant when he said *Barbie.* One more minute didn't seem that crucial. I stepped into the shower building.

Four faucet heads—two on each wall—were twisted to spray the fully dressed girl bent over the central drain, vomiting. Her long blond hair no longer looked platinum, or even pale yellow. Saturated with water, it looked almost orange.

"Ashley, are you okay?"

She clutched her stomach. "Go away."

Her heaves were dry and convulsive, the kind of retching that triggered my own gag reflex. The stench wasn't helping. The steam smelled poisonously sweet, like apple juice being stirred with her stomach's hydrochloric acid.

I stared at the floor. "Do you need some help?"

She didn't answer.

I looked up. Her fingers trembled, wiping her mouth.

"Is this about Cuppa Joe?" I asked.

She lifted her face. "Cuppa Joe?"

I watched her expression. "Somebody took him. He was kidnapped—"

She leaned against the wall, then slid down the ceramic tiles to the floor. Her eyes were glassy. Broken blood vessels made her cheeks look bruised.

"Do you need a doctor?"

She looked at me, desperation in her eyes. "I'm pregnant."

Before I could catch myself, I glanced at her shirt. The soaked cotton stuck to her like a second skin, outlining her stomach's small pouch. I wasn't sure what to say. *Congratulations. Condolences?* The silence stretched out.

"Don't worry about me," she said bitterly. "I'm just peachy."

Condolences.

But before I reached the door, she called out.

"Wait."

She worked her fingers into the front pocket of her wet jeans, grunting because the fabric was so wet and tight. "I need some dry clothes. Can you get them?"

She held out a key. Brass. Just like Juan's.

"It might be awhile," I said.

She nodded, but the look in her eyes said she knew nobody would ever hurry for her.

⁓

"What took you so long?" Eleanor shouted.

"There's a circus in town." I walked around the back bumper of her Lincoln, parked six inches from the barn. A golf cart was parked beside it, and I presumed Mr. Yuck had driven it because the security chief was presiding over the two men hollering at each other: Bill Cooper and Sal Gag.

Eleanor grabbed my arm to balance herself over the sawdust floor.

"One day!" Sal Gag stabbed the air with his unlit cigar. "I leave a pony here one day. And you lose him!"

Cooper paced back and forth outside KichaKoo's stable. The horse was craning her neck like a tennis judge, watching both men. In the stall next to her, Stella Luna drummed a hoof against the wall, a steady catatonic rhythm. Spooked.

"You told me somebody was coming for that horse," Cooper said.

"Yeah," Sal Gag said, "but you see me here when it happened?"

"He was *supposed* to get picked up."

"By me!" The mobster stabbed the stogie at Mr. Yuck. "And I wouldn't leave no note!"

The security chief held a piece of paper in his hands but his face told me nothing. It had its usual sour countenance. I gave Eleanor a nudge.

"Charles," she said, "show Raleigh the note."

Mr. Yuck held out the note, and I felt Cooper's icy eyes on me. But I didn't touch it, certain there were already too many finger-prints. From what I could see, the words were cut from magazines and glued to the page. It was almost comically simple, except for its cruelty. It read: *You have 48 hours. Then we start killing.*

"Death." Eleanor raised her chin. "Death has set up its tent at our door."

There was a polite silence, but Eleanor never got the chance to tell us who said that because two police officers were approaching. Their hands rested on their gun belts. The older cop had a wrestler's fire-hydrant neck and an expression in his eyes of practiced boredom. The look of a veteran cop. He immediately zeroed in on Sal Gag.

He said, "We got a call about a missing horse?"

"Not missing, stolen," Sal Gag said. "Because somebody screwed up."

"Now hold on." Cooper waved his hands, as though wiping away the accusation. "We were doing this guy a favor by keeping the horse. And it was temporary. Like a day. So when two guys showed up with a trailer, saying they were here to pick up the horse, what were we supposed to say—no?"

"Yeah!" said Sal Gag.

"You *told* us the trailer was coming."

"When Ashley said he was ready."

The next silence felt as itchy as the sawdust.

Finally, Mr. Yuck said, "Who?"

"The groom, Ashley. Ashley Trevor."

"Trenner," Sal Gag corrected him.

"Whatever," Cooper said.

Mr. Yuck looked around, the odd smile playing on his lips. He looked like a toad preparing to snap his tongue at a fly. "And where is this groom, this Ashley person? Hmm?"

Nobody answered.

I said, "She's in the shower."

Cooper narrowed his eyes. "Why's she takin' a shower?"

"She's throwing up."

"Oh great," Cooper said.

Sal Gag leaned toward him. "She shoulda been watching my horse. You're workin' her too hard."

"You got that right. She was supposed to watch that horse. Not Juan."

As though answering to his name, the groom stepped out of KichaKoo's stall. And I now understood why the horse had been leaning forward earlier. Her back legs were taped, matching the green silks that draped over her muscular shoulders.

"Yo." Sal Gag pointed at Juan. "Get over here."

"Oh, courage." Eleanor lifted her face toward the rafters. "Could you not dwell in the frightened heart of me?"

The police officers stared at her.

"*Night of the Iguana*," she told them. "Nonno's last poem."

The younger of the two cops turned his head sideways, as if Eleanor might be carrying a weapon. Juan still had not moved and his face looked as remote as mesa rock. When Cooper said something to him in Spanish, the groom came closer and handed the trainer the horse's reins. KichaKoo didn't like it. She bit Cooper's shoulder.

"Hey!" Cooper pushed the horse's face away.

I gave a small gasp.

"It's nothing," he said. "She does that."

But it wasn't the bite that startled me. It was Cooper's shirt. Unless I was mistaken, it looked like the same one Claire Manchester bought from Tony Not Tony. My mind began reeling with questions. Was Cooper conspiring with Claire Manchester? Why? I watched

230 I the stars shine bright

him walk the horse down the gallery, remembering what Lucia said. Cooper was Manchester's trainer, until Eleanor hired him away. At the end of the gallery, Tony Not Tony waited with a jockey dressed in green silks and white jodhpurs.

"You were here," Mr. Yuck began his inquisition of Juan. "When the horse was taken, you were here?"

"*Si,*" Juan said. "Trailer come. Take horse."

"Trailer." Sal Gag waved the cigar. "The trailer drove itself?"

Juan shook his head. "*Dos* men. *Desaseado.*"

"Speak American," Sal Gag said. "*Capiche?*"

But the young cop was lifting his hand, signaling a truce between Latin cultures. "He's saying two men. And they were dirty." He turned to Juan, asking a question in Spanish.

"*Si, si.*" Juan ran his rough hands through his hair. "*Muy desaseado.*"

The cop asked another question. Juan replied in Spanish, and the cop turned to his older partner. "He says they both had dreadlocks."

"Hippies?" Sal Gag's eyes seemed to bulge. "You're telling me hippies stole my horse?"

Mr. Yuck made a phlegmatic sound, clearing his throat. "Did he notice anything about the trailer, such as a license number?"

The young cop asked several more questions, but the only answer I understood was "blanco."

"White trailer," the officer said. "Two windows. One window on each side."

Sal Gag jammed the cigar between his teeth, biting down and muttering. "When I had the chance, I shoulda shoved that pony in the trailer."

"License plate?" Mr. Yuck asked.

The younger cop asked. Juan replied by tracing the air with his finger, spelling while he spoke.

"Doe-bell-u," he said, spelling W. "And aye."

The cop clarified. "W-A?"

Juan nodded.

"*Jibone.*" Sal Gag tore the cigar from his mouth. "Every plate's got W-A. We're in Washington!"

But Juan shook his head, saying something more to the cop.

"He says it's not the state letters," the cop said. "There's also an E and a K. But the rest of the plate was covered with dirt."

"*Si.*" Juan nodded.

"I see," Sal Gag said. "I see something smells fishy."

The older cop stared at the mobster, dragging his tongue across the inside of his cheek. "What's the horse look like?"

"Black as coffee," Sal Gag said. "His name's Cuppa Joe. Get it?"

"Any reward?"

Eleanor stepped forward. "Fifty thousand dollars!"

"El'nor." Sal Gag placed a hand on his chest. "That's very generous."

"It's not for you," she said. "It's for that poor animal."

She had let go of my arm, stepping forward to offer her reward. And now I took a small step back, inching toward the open section where trailers pulled up. The weight of the vehicles had tamped down the sawdust, which was further compacted by horses and people walking over it. But the scrim of new treads ran like rickrack over the surface. It was the kind of evidence most local police weren't trained to handle, and I was in too much of a hurry to try to segue them into it. While the older cop asked more questions about the reward, I reached into my pocket and let Ashley's key fall from my fingers. Then I kicked it into the sawdust.

"Oh rats," I muttered.

The men turned and Eleanor glared. I had interrupted her speech.

"Sorry." I tried to look sheepish. "Ashley wanted me to get her clothes. I dropped her key."

They were already focused on Eleanor again when I lifted a steel rake from the stable wall.

"Anybody got a picture of the horse?" asked the older cop.

Sal Gag foisted the cigar at Mr. Yuck. "Do something useful. For once."

Mr. Yuck asked the officers to follow him. He didn't invite Sal Gag, but the bookie went anyway. I drew the rake's teeth through the sawdust. Cooper was coming down the gallery. The brass key rose, swimming to the surface like a fishing lure. Eleanor watched me push the key back down into the sawdust.

The actress was a pro.

"Bill," she said, turning to Cooper. "May I speak to you, in private?"

"Now?" Cooper watched the three men leave. "It's not a good time."

She took his elbow. "Five minutes. Your office, shall we?"

Juan followed them as far as Stella's stable. The horse was still kicking the wall and the groom opened her Dutch door, stepped inside. I heard his voice singing, in Spanish. The song drifted out as I pinched some of the clay scattered over the open area. I saw some small pebbles. Porphyrous, like pumice. I carried them across the hall to the storage shelves, where the Saran Wrap waited. No longer needed in the stalls, since the mud had been confiscated. I tore two sheets. I placed the geology in one, then reached into my purse and took out Gordon's bloody Kleenex. I wrapped it and shoved it back into my purse.

Eleanor's stage voice projected around the corner. "I'm very pleased with how you've handled yourself, Bill. And I do believe we will find Cuppa Joe."

Cooper looked at me. The cold arctic eyes matched the color of his shirt.

"Raleigh," Eleanor said, "did you find the key?"

I reached down, plucking it from the sawdust. Cooper squinted at me.

"How sick is she?" he asked.

"Very," I said. "And she needs some clothes."

Eleanor let go of Cooper's elbow. "Let me help you."

She took my arm and I could feel the trainer's eyes on my back. I didn't speak until we reached the end of the gallery.

"Everything okay?"

"Such an encompassing generality," she said.

Ashley's room was easy to find. The door was pink. Barbie pink. And inside, the walls were the same color. A musty and sodden odor permeated the small room. The cot was neatly made, but the white pillowcase looked stained with sweat. A paper plate on the floor held a stalagmite of saltine crackers, right next to a plastic bucket for retching.

"They say it's good to see how the other half lives," Eleanor said, "but I disagree."

Her clothing was neatly folded into milk crates. I collected jeans, another pink T-shirt, and was going through a third bin to find socks, underwear, and a bra when Eleanor sighed.

"It's pathetic," she said. "Like the equine version of *Teen Beat*."

I turned, holding the clothes in my arms. Eleanor was looking at some pictures on the wall. Horses. With their names above the photos. War Admiral. Secretariat. Seattle Slough. And a dozen bumper stickers with militant slogans about animal rights.

"Most people's lives are trails of debris," Eleanor said.

But I barely heard her words about *Suddenly Last Summer*. I was reading the wall calendar above Ashley's bed. Some promotional thing from a feed store, it had red Xs over the days. I tugged loose the page tacked to the wall to see July, and saw every day was Xed out too. But for June it was only the last week.

"She's about eight weeks along," I said.

"Pregnant?" Eleanor sounded shocked.

I nodded.

"But Ashley doesn't even like human beings." She reached up, fiddling with her necklace. "I hate to sound perverted, but is it scientifically possible a horse is involved?"

"No."

"But that girl has worked here for years and there's never been so much as a whiff of romance. It's always been horses, horses, horses."

I searched for a towel.

"I'll bet it's a jockey." Eleanor shook her head. "Do you smell that?"

"Yes. Stale vomit." I found a clean towel, folded in a cardboard box.

"Not that," Eleanor said. "Bleach." She leaned over the bed, sniffing. "The sire of her child probably has fleas."

I decided Ashley might need shoes too and found two pairs in

the far corner. But they were different sizes. Women's 7. And men's
12. The soles were caked with mud. I lifted the men's pair. "Have you
ever seen a jockey wear shoes this big?"

"My next guess would be a rodeo clown."

The mud caked on the bottoms had dried to a pale color, almost
white. It looked like the mud I'd taken to the lab. And the mud I just
collected from the open area in the barn. I thought of Rosser, tasting
the soil for kaolinite, but I wasn't so brave. I wondered who the shoes
belonged to. Cooper's feet weren't that big. Nor Juan's.

Uncle Sal?

I looked at Eleanor. "May I have your lipstick case?"

"You may have the shirt off my back, but the resulting view
would kill a man."

She removed a small red leather case from the pocket of her pantsuit. One of those ladies-of-a-certain-age, Eleanor considered lipstick
a biological necessity. I took out the filamented brass canister inside
the case, handed it back to her, then kneeled on the floor. I gently
tapped the big shoes until the mud cracked. I placed an ounce or two
inside the lipstick case.

"That's a Chanel case," she said. "Not that you care."

"I'll buy you a new one."

"I doubt it. But I don't mind."

"Thanks."

"You're welcome. It's like Jim said in *The Glass Menagerie.* Other
people are as common as weeds. But you are blue roses."

Chapter Thirty-Six

Eleanor drove her battleship to the private dining room, to keep DeMott company. I took Ashley's clothes to the showers.

And found her stripped naked.

Sitting with her back against the tile wall, she watched the hot water pound her bare legs. The skin was marbled and red. I placed her clothes and the key on a shelf by the mirror, then I walked over to the faucets and twisted them off. I offered her my hand. She pulled herself up with no trace of self-consciousness. As if her nudity was nothing more than a horse without a saddle.

"Sorry." She rubbed the towel over her skin. "I don't want to bug you. But there's nobody else to ask."

"How about the sperm donor?"

She shook her head, then tugged on the pink shirt. But before she pulled on the jeans, she grabbed the soaked pair from the floor and carefully removed a rubber band fastened around the waistband button. She reattached it to the dry jeans, pulled them on, and gave the slipknot a good tug, testing the improvised maternity wear.

She looked at me. "You're probably wondering who's the lucky guy."

"I don't believe in luck."

"Maybe I shouldn't. He wants me to get an abortion."

Condolences, indeed. "What about adoption?"

"That wouldn't help. We're destroying the environment. There are too many people on this earth."

"That's not the baby's fault."

"But why add one more?"

I ground my teeth into what I hoped looked like a polite smile. "Ashley, do you know how many people there are? Total, on the planet?"

"It's a lot." She gathered her wet clothes.

"There are about seven billion people."

"See? Too many."

"And all seven billion can fit inside Rhode Island. They'd still have room to move. Rhode Island. It's a fraction of Washington's size."

"You're lecturing me."

She was right, and I'd just chewed out DeMott for the same reason. "I'm just wondering why you think killing a baby will save the environment."

"First of all, it's not a baby." She twisted her hair, wringing out the water. "It's a fetus, a bunch of tissue."

"Some tissue. It made you puke your guts out."

"You don't understand." She tugged on her shoes. "You're rich, you have a family. I need a job."

I didn't have a reply, because the wicked bind of undercover was that I wasn't rich, I didn't have a family, and there was another plank in my eye. I'd used this very same point with DeMott—without my job, what would I live on?

I watched her lay the towel on the floor, throwing the wet clothes on it.

"I saw your calendar."

She looked up, startled. "You snooped in my room?"

"Only the calendar." And this time it was personal. Not for the FBI. "If you've waited this long, you don't really want an abortion."

She began rolling up the towel.

"Ashley, look at me."

She pushed down on the roll, tightening it like a sleeping bag, then stood up. Her face suddenly drained of color. I grabbed her arm. She was swaying.

"You need a doctor," I said.

"No." She straightened her back. "I don't need anyone's help. My mom had me out here, and we did fine. Thanks to Uncle Sal."

"Sal Gagliardo?" I kept my voice neutral. "He's your uncle?"

"Not my *real* uncle. Not like Eleanor's your aunt. But he and my mom, they had a thing way back when. I was already born. But he sorta adopted me." She picked up her boots, but her eyes had taken on a faraway look. "My mom was a groom out here. Karol Trenner."

"She's retired?"

She looked at the floor. "She died. Skin cancer."

"I'm sorry, Ashley."

When she looked up, there were tears in her eyes. "Everybody thinks Uncle Sal's this tough guy. But when my mom died he changed his barn colors to pink. It was her favorite color. She said you can't feel sad when you look at it."

She was entitled to her opinion. "How long ago did she pass?"

"Six years ago, in October."

I came up with an improbable age. "Then you must have been—"

"For your information," she said, her voice tightening, "I'm legal."

"You don't have other family?"

"I don't need anybody else." She wiped her nose on the rolled towel. "The horses are my family."

I had lectured enough, so I simply nodded, as if that squalid hovel in the barn compensated for a real home, as if high-strung horses and a bellicose mobster provided all that she needed. "Does the baby's father work out here?"

"Stop calling him that. He doesn't want the baby."

Baby. Progress, I decided. No longer just a bunch of tissue. "Don't you think your mom would want you to keep it, like she did with you?"

"Here we go again." She clutched the wet bundle to her chest, soaking the pink shirt. "I'm sick of people bossing me around. Ashley do this, Ashley do that. Nobody ever asks what *I* want."

"What do you want?"

"How should I know!" she cried. "But I can't handle a baby. What about when it starts crying?"

"You can handle a temperamental horse. I'm sure you can deal with a baby."

She lifted the towel. Her sobs made the room feel saturated, too much hot water and hot tears and now her desperate gasps for breath. And in the middle I could smell that cloying scent from her room, as if it had followed me.

"I know you don't feel well," I said, "but at some point, we need to talk about Cuppa Joe. According to Juan, two guys came to the Hot Tin barn and took him."

She didn't move.

"Ashley?"

She lowered the bundle. The color had once again drained from her face. Her lips pursed forward, then pulled back. I thought she was trying to say something, but she pivoted to the shower drain and vomited. I looked away.

A stocky figure stood in the open doorway.

Bill Cooper.

"Ashley!" His voice echoed across the tile. "Get out here."

She stared down at the metal drain.

"You heard me!"

She stood, looking woozy. When she walked to the door, her movements were almost robotic. I picked up the bundled towel.

Cooper grabbed her arm. "In my office. Now."

$\approx$

I followed them back to the barn. Not one word was spoken between them, and Ashley continued to move stiffly, nothing like her usual self. When we reached Cooper's office, he slammed the door in my face.

I stood outside, listening. He yelled, cursed, then told her it was all her fault. She should have forced Cuppa Joe into the trailer. Ashley gave no reply. Only more sobbing.

I made my way to the other end of the barn, still carrying her towel. The atmosphere felt oddly subdued. There was none of the usual bantering among the Hispanic grooms, and even the pony riders, hired for their easy demeanor, seemed anxious, jumpy. The backstretch had been invaded; a horse was taken; and the atmosphere reminded me of a small town struck by violent crime: everyone was on edge.

It didn't bode well for gathering more information.

I keyed open Ashley's pink door and locked it behind me. The room still reeked with its septic odor, but Eleanor was right. The cot smelled of bleach. I threw the towel and wet clothes into the corner, then pulled out my cell phone. Desperate times called for desperate measures.

Jack Stephanson picked up on the first ring.

"I need a quick favor," I said.

"No."

"Pardon?"

"You gave your phone to a civilian, Harmon."

I stared at the horse photos taped to the back of Ashley's door. A full magazine page was about Seabiscuit, with a picture of the horse roaring to the finish. I tried to line up the right words to explain why somebody had my phone, but a bolt of panic shot through my system. I checked my watch. DeMott. He had an airplane to catch.

"Jack, I don't have a lot of time to argue right now."

"No kidding. Do you hear that?"

"What?"

"That flushing sound. It's your career, swirling down the toilet."

"One of the racehorses was just kidnapped," I said. "They even left a note, threatening to kill it. The horse belongs to Sal Gagliardo."

That shut him up.

There was a long silence.

"Gagliardo," he said, "the Mob guy?"

"Yes."

Another satisfying silence followed. I turned in a circle, gazing around Ashley's room and waiting for Jack to get the whole picture. More horse pictures were taped to the wall above the milk crates holding her clothes. Creatures of surreal beauty, graceful and frightening all at once. But there were other photos, and they were more disturbing. A horse missing its right eye. Another with its ear gone, a deep depression carved into its head. Damaged horses. Taped below their pictures were more bumper stickers about animal rights. *Fur Is Murder*, read one.

"That doesn't fit," Jack said. "Just like that tube gizmo, it doesn't fit."

"Because?"

"The Mob is supposed to take other people's horses. You know, cut off the head and stick it in the guy's bed. Why would they steal their own horse? Unless it's for insurance money."

"He probably had a huge policy on that horse." I stared at Ashley's collection of weird talismans. They were placed on the milk crates. Small stones. Wine bottle, empty. "Insurance fraud isn't a bad guess. But they left a note. It's still kidnapping."

"It's a horse."

"Okay, then grand larceny."

"One horse."

"Will you at least run a license plate for me?"

"Maybe."

I wanted to chew him out, but the ice under my feet was thin. "A white trailer was seen taking the horse. The license plate isn't a complete read, but see what comes back on William, Eagle, Apple, Kite."

He said the letters back to me. "W-E-A-K?"

"Right."

"You don't think it's a sign?"

"Everything's a joke with you?"

"No, I'm seriously upset about the civilian with your phone. Especially when you're working undercover. I almost hung up and started a GPS search. Thought the Mob had you bound and gagged."

There was no point defending myself. Jack was right. It was careless. And while I waited for him to pile on the guilt, I read Ashley's bumper stickers. *Eating Eggs Is Murder*. I was tempted to post a rebuttal—*But abortion is a "choice"?*

"He's your fiancé."

"Pardon?"

"Enough with the Southern manners. Level with me, Harmon."

The next sticker read, *If You Wouldn't Eat a Cat, Why Would You Eat a Cow?*

"I need two background checks," I said. "One is for a male, first name Gordon, last name Donaldson. He drives a tractor down here. Father has same name, senior."

Jack didn't reply.

"The second background check is for a female. Last name Trenner, first name Ashley. See if there's any documented connection with Salvatore Gagliardo. Her mother apparently had an affair with him."

"Why is your fiancé here?"

"Find Gagliardo's tax return. See if he claims Ashley Trenner as a dependent. She claims he adopted her."

The next silence wasn't like the others. It was disquieting. Painful.

"Is that it?" he said.

"For now."

He hung up and the phone gave that dull dead sound. But I held it to my ear, reading the last bumper sticker.

It said, *Tofu Never Screams.*

Chapter Thirty-Seven

I slipped past Cooper's door. The shouting continued.

"If they kill that horse, his blood's on your hands!"

The sobbing continued as well. I checked my watch and hurried for the grandstands.

The Sunday crowd was thick, somewhat inebriated, and oblivious to the kidnapped horse. For now. But tomorrow, or the next day, after some reporter saw the police log, the news would spread about Eleanor's reward and the false leads would come like flies to honey. Running up the grandstand steps, I gave my watch another glance. Cutting it close. But the Ghost had enough speed that we would just make it. Swing by Eleanor's house, pick up DeMott's bag, and get him to the airport.

But when I stepped inside the private dining room, I didn't see DeMott.

Or Eleanor.

The maître d' stood at the podium. He was a fastidious bald man who always wore white slacks and an emerald-green blazer. He glanced up from a map where the room's tables were represented in circles and rectangles.

"Hello," I said. "I was looking for my aunt, Eleanor?"

"She just left," he said. "Something about a plane to catch and time being the longest distance between two places. A young man with her—"

≈

Anyone following the Ghost down Interstate 5 ate Italian dust. I pulled into Eleanor's porte cochere in record time and took the front steps by twos.

I found her sprawled on a fainting couch in the wood-paneled den. She held a bag of frozen peas to her forehead and bellowed even louder than normal.

"Three snorts of brandy!" She raised her chin. "When monster meets monster, one's got to go."

I didn't care who said it in what play. "Is he ready?"

"Ready?" She sat up. The bag of peas slumped into her lap. "DeMott—remember?"

"Young lady, I'm not that drunk."

"Fine. Where is he?"

"Where? He took a cab."

I stood rooted, staring as her expression changed. The proud chin lowered.

"Oh dear," she said softly. "I assumed you two had discussed . . . that you couldn't drive . . . I wasn't going to interfere—oh, courage, courage—"

I was out the door before she finished the line.

≈

The Ghost flew through the airport's parking garage, the tires squealing like bad Italian opera. I pulled into the first open spot and sprinted through the garage and across the sky bridge into the terminal. The crowd at the Delta check-in counter was so thick I had to move sideways, searching for that seersucker jacket and wavy brown hair. After several minutes, I realized his "baggage" was Madame. Otherwise it was just his carry-on duffel. I ran to the display that showed departures.

Delta to Atlanta, leaving in thirty-three minutes.

Still time.

The line for security check-in snaked back and forth. Hundreds of passengers. I walked along the outside of the ropes while people trudged forward with boarding passes and driver's licenses and faces looking somewhere between hopeless and condemned. When I came to the end of one line, I turned and walked down the other. It must have looked suspicious, because a rotund man in a rumpled TSA uniform headed straight for me. His eyes looked like he hadn't slept in six years.

"Line starts back there." He pointed.

"I'm looking for somebody."

"Boarding pass?" He opened his hand. "License?"

"I just need to say good-bye."

"Yeah, whatever." He snapped his fingers. "Boarding pass, license."

"There!" DeMott stood on this side of the X-ray machines. He was removing his shoes, placing them in the plastic bin. "I just need two minutes."

"And I just need your boarding pass."

"I don't have one."

His eyes darkened even further. "What?"

"I'm not flying." DeMott was folding the seersucker jacket, placing it in the bin. "Please, before he goes through the X-ray."

The agent walked away.

If I had my FBI credentials, I could flash them at that sick excuse for a public servant. But right now the bad bureaucrat was my only hope. I followed him down the line to where he was harassing a guy whose studded jeans didn't cover his underwear.

"Excuse me," I said. "It's really important."

The TSA agent took the guy's driver's license and ran a small penlight over it, searching for falsification.

"Please," I said, feeling ill with groveling. "He's my fiancé."

"Trouble already, huh?"

I glanced back. DeMott had walked through the arches and now stood at the conveyor belt.

"DeMott!" I yelled.

The faces swiveled toward me.

"DEMOTT!"

The TSA guy moved in front of me. "Hey, knock it off."

But my dignity was already on the floor. So I tried again, louder. "DEMOTT!"

"Do it again," the agent said, "I'll have you detained."

I didn't doubt it. Taking me into custody would make this guy's day. He could convince himself his job actually mattered. And OPR would salivate hearing about my problem.

I watched DeMott shrug into the jacket.

"That's more like it." The TSA guy moved down the line.

DeMott picked up his leather bag.

I whispered, "Turn around."

He walked toward the gates, walking away.

"Please."

Suddenly he stopped. He was patting down his pockets, as if he'd forgotten something.

"Please, DeMott. Turn around."

But he never did.

≈

For a long while I sat in the Ghost, contemplating my options. Things looked so bad that I even considered calling Weyanoke. Leaving a message. Saying what? That I yelled his name across the airport, embarrassing myself, hoping we could at least say good-bye? A message like that would only add fuel to his sister MacKenna's claim that I wasn't worthy of a Fielding marriage. I didn't belong among the First Families of Virginia. But I couldn't send an e-mail either, because DeMott's job managing the estate meant he never had to touch a computer. The postal letter would take days, and between now and then he would think I'd totally forgotten about him.

My only option was to call later tonight, when he got home. Then hope no other Fielding picked up the phone.

But as I drove the Ghost down the parking garage's spiral ramp, my phone started playing "Camptown Races." My heart was doo-dahing with sudden hope as I fumbled for my purse. I decided that TSA troll had some rare attack of conscience. He must've told DeMott some girl was hollering for him. DeMott found a pay phone and—

"Hello?"

"Great lead on the trailer. Got a pen?"

I couldn't speak.

"Harmon?"

"I'm here."

"Is it safe to talk?"

"Yes."

"It took me over an hour working the IDW."

Investigative Data Warehouse. A digital garage of law enforcement data, the IDW held everything from threat assessments and
suspicious contacts to full investigative cases. The data could also
search relationally, connecting cases and suspects by certain words or
even objects. Type in "horse trailer" and it would cough up everything.

"You all right?" he asked.

Somewhere in the back of my mind I knew it wasn't wise to discuss this in the car, which might have a listening device somewhere
on the undercarriage. But I felt too weak to get out of the car, almost
defeated, and I managed to convince myself nobody could understand a one-sided phone conversation. Pulling over to the side of the
toll booths, I opened the glove box. My pen and notebook were still
in there. I flipped past the pages that had DeMott's handwriting. *You
couldn't pick Fielding?*

I felt something kick my heart. "Go ahead."

"I plugged in the letters from the plate but too many vague hits
came back. Since you said it wasn't a full read, I played with some
combinations. Add A, test. Then B, so on. Not that I need a thank-
you, but I got a double hit on S."

I closed my eyes, trying to breathe. The ache inside my chest
seemed unbearable. "A lot of work."

"Yeah. Take down this name. Arnold Corke. Registered owner of
a white horse trailer with a license plate containing all those letters.
He's also got a criminal record."

"For what?"

"Civil disobedience."

"That's quite a leap to kidnapping."

"I don't think Corke stole the horse. He lives on Bainbridge
Island with a bunch of foster kids. *Teenage* foster kids. The ones so

bad nobody else will take them. There's a long record of complaints and police reports involving his kids."

"For . . . ?"

"Loitering, vandalism. Petty theft. Stolen cars. Rape—"

"What?"

"Three years ago. Corke used to bring boys and girls to the farm. After the rape charge, he switched to boys only. Not that it helped. One of them held up a local Bank of America."

"Could he be the same kid?"

"Rob a bank, why not steal a horse? Yeah. But that kid's incarcerated. He's in, uh, Western State Hospital."

"Is that another one of your jokes?"

"He's nowhere near your mom, I checked. They put him in the criminal psych ward."

"What about Corke's civil disobedience?"

"He was protesting the Vietnam War."

"How old is he?"

"He sent a nasty letter to Spiro Agnew in 1973. The Secret Service showed up. Corke was in ninth grade."

"And the parents probably described him as precocious."

"Right. He got accepted to the University of Washington at sixteen, where he stepped up his protests. Doing sit-ins on pharmaceutical research, oil companies, the usual suspects because they made money. But in terms of priors, Corke's record is so old it's antediluvian." He paused. "Geology term. Are you impressed?"

"If you knew what it meant."

"That's so cold it's *glacial*."

I stared out the window. "What about the trailer?"

"You don't appreciate the geology terms, fine. The trailer's only match is Corke."

"How do I get there?"

"Let the local cops handle it, Harmon. His foster kids probably stole the trailer and—"

"And it doesn't make sense. You said so yourself."

"Sure it does. Delinquents meet all kinds in the juvie jails. Think about it. Somebody offers to pay them to steal the horse, so Sal Gagliardo can file for loss on his insurance."

"Is there an actual bridge?"

"To Bainbridge? No. And it's Sunday, Harmon."

"What's his address?"

"You are . . ." Jack's voice trailed off.

I knew what I was. A very bad fiancée. "Address. Please?"

"I knew you'd do this." He gave me the address, then sighed. "I already checked. The ferry leaves from 52 in an hour."

"Thank you."

"You're welcome," he said. "And may the quartz be with you."

Chapter Thirty-Eight

I swung by the condo to pick up Madame, then drove to Pier 52 in Seattle and bought her a Big Mac at the McDonald's next to the ferry terminal. I parked on the boat's lower level, then carried the dog to the open deck on top, walking all the way to the ferry's aft so she could eat in peace. Behind us the sun was beginning to set behind the Olympics, casting golden light over Seattle's skyline of steel and glass. When the ferry's horn blew, signaling departure, I picked up Madame. She was quivering.

"I know how you feel."

The boat pulled away from the dock and I grabbed the rail, using my left hand because the dog was in my right. The sunlight landed on the ring, igniting the stones. Such a specific ring. More geological than social. And no diamonds because I disliked their frigid white light. DeMott knew me so well. And he knew my crazy mother, and my sister who was so self-absorbed she couldn't bother visiting the asylum. He knew this dog, trembling under my arm. And he loved me.

So why was I feeling so hopeless?

Gazing down at the water, I watched as it churned with the engine thrusters that pulled the ferry from the creosote pilings. A hypnotic froth the color of sea glass, it made me feel like I was back on that cruise ship. Pulling away from land, worrying about DeMott.

I glanced at the engagement ring.

Engagement.

When he gave me the ring in December, engagement meant a promise to marry. Life together, forever. But nine months later the word was rearing its head, whispering the more militant definition.

Engagement, a battle between armed forces. I closed my eyes and gulped the salty air. *Do. Not. Cry.*

When Madame growled, I opened my eyes.

The man standing next to us wore Ray-Ban sunglasses and a Hawaiian shirt—bright orange—that screamed, *Look at me!*

Jack.

"Sorry to bother you." He held up a road map. "I'm trying to find Port Angeles. Do you know the roads?"

I glanced over my shoulder. A pregnant woman chased a pre-schooler across the deck, begging the girl to walk. Two teenagers, a boy and a girl, sat in the metal chairs that were soldered to the deck. And an old man sat across from them, reading a newspaper. His face resembled an unbaked potato. I watched him the longest. His eyes kept drifting from the paper to the teenagers. The girl was leaning into the boy, close, as if the wind off the water was cold.

I whispered, "What are you doing here?"

"You need backup." His voice was low, barely audible. "Or maybe a life raft."

"Excuse me?"

"Harmon, you look like you're going to jump overboard."

Madame growled again. I turned away. The ferry was about a hundred yards from the pier. The increasing distance combined with our angle on the water made the skyscrapers look like they were stepping down the hills, shrinking into the sidewalks.

Jack cleared his throat.

I looked over.

"Triple A said I should cut across the island." He was raising his voice again. "Something about Port Angeles being over there." He slid the Ray-Bans down his nose and brought the map closer, like he was nearsighted. He whispered into the paper, "Where's the fiancé?"

"None of your business."

"You're right," he said loudly. "I better stick to the west side." He tapped his finger on the map. "You ever been to that place called Deception Pass?"

Before I could answer, the map billowed like a sail. Jack lunged for it and bumped my hip. Madame barked. The map blew out of his hands and Jack turned to run after it. The old man looked up from his newspaper, following with his eyes, but the teenagers were making out, oblivious to the world. The small child clapped her hands at the silly-looking man who chased the paper kite.

My hip ached where he hit me. Shifting Madame, I noticed my handbag was open. And something was in there. I glanced across the deck. Everyone was watching Jack make a spectacle of himself. I peered into the purse, then set Madame down on the deck.

"Don't run away."

She stood, legs stiff as tent pegs, unsure of the engine vibrations in the deck.

I reached into the bag. Sig Sauer pistol. Small can of Mace. When I looked up, Jack was grabbing the map from the half-wall where it had plastered itself. He headed back toward the aft, passing the mother and toddler. "I should've just bought a GPS," he said.

When he came up beside me, he was trying to fold the map. Then he handed it to me. "Maybe you can do it."

I saw a small black-and-white photo. It covered one square inch of urban Seattle. I folded the map's outer edges, staring at the mug shot, trying to memorize the man's face. He looked scraggly but handsome, his dark eyes filled with a belligerent expression.

"Arnold Corke," Jack whispered. "The radical years."

I glanced over my shoulder, still folding the map. The mother and child were gone. But the teens were still locked together. The old man gazed at them, half fascinated, half horrified. I reached into my purse, moving aside the gun and Mace. I lifted the Saran Wrap with Gordon's bloody Kleenex, placed it under the map, and handed both to Jack. I wanted to deliver the soil samples to Rosser myself.

"DNA sample. Can you get it to O'Brien?"

He raised his voice. "I see what you mean, yeah, that sounds like a good route to take."

I kept my voice down. "Did you do the background checks?"

"You know," he said loudly, "I haven't had a moment to rest on this vacation." Then his voice dropped, almost hissing. "So the fian-cé's gone?"

I looked away. The wind rippled the water.

"He went home," I said.

"Where he belongs."

"Excuse me?"

"He sounded uptight on the phone."

"Is this gun loaded?"

"He says your name weird."

"It's a Southern accent, genius."

"Not that. It's the way he—"

"You don't deserve to know this," I hissed, "but he went to see my mom at Western State. And she couldn't stop smiling."

There. That shut him up.

He watched Madame trying to walk across the deck. She was pausing between each step, uncertain.

"You got to see her?"

"Yes." Sort of. "But guess who's working down there, on her ward?"

He rubbed the stubble on his chin. "I can explain, if you'll give me a chance."

I couldn't see his eyes, the sunglasses were too dark. There was only my own reflection on the black lenses. And I was frowning. Until my eyes suddenly widened. A bomb detonated inside my heart. The heat traveled up my throat, into my cheeks.

"You . . ." I could barely speak. "You didn't."

"I thought Felicia could help."

It wasn't Aunt Charlotte. She didn't send Felicia down there. How stupid of me. How naive. Incredibly naive.

"Harmon—?"

I hated him with fresh passion. "Why didn't you tell me?"

"Mostly because Felicia's a total frosted flake. I thought she'd back out and then you'd be disappointed." He glanced over his shoulder. The man with the newspaper gaped at the teenagers, whose kissing had escalated to groping. "And for another thing, you're undercover. You're not supposed to know everything."

There wasn't enough air. I turned my face into the wind, hoping it would invade my lungs. "How . . . ?"

"How did I get her the job?" He shrugged. "My sister's a shrink. She knows people."

"People like Dr. Norbert."

"Shrinks are always friends with each other. Because nobody else will hang around them."

The ferry blew its horn. I looked over. We were approaching a gravelly bay. It sloped from a ridge lined with large houses, and I could see a couple strolling down the beach hand in hand. Suddenly yesterday's visit with Freud came back. He kept asking about my mother and Felicia. Curious about their relationship.

"Way to go, Sherlock." I turned back to Jack. "Now I'm in real trouble."

"Why?"

"Because Freud was asking about Felicia. And I pretended not to know her. But he knows the FBI put her in there. Right?"

Jack looked at the folded map in his hands. A shudder went through the deck as the ferry slowed its engines. I patted my leg, calling Madame. She ran, scrabbling over the deck, more than ready to be picked up.

Jack said, "How is she?"

"Who?"

"Your mom."

My emotions seemed to swirl with the wind—confusion and resentment, gratitude and hostility—and when the twister touched down, it hit one inevitable fact. I was stuck. Boxed in from every side. A bad fiancée. With too much work. A mother with mental illness. And Jack.

The ferry blew its horn again. The old man stood and waved the newspaper with disgust at the teens who were still locked in lust. He had a slow, stiff walk, and his skeptical eyes lingered for a moment on Jack's Hawaiian shirt. He gave another wave of disgust with the newspaper, and suddenly another emotion joined the tornado ripping around my heart. His scorn triggered a protective feeling for Jack. And I didn't want it.

Lifting my chin like Eleanor, I spoke to the stranger in the Hawaii shirt.

"I'm just visiting," I said, projecting the words. "And I won't be here long."

I followed the old man to the door. Madame felt warm in my hands. But my ears had filled with the sound of rushing wind.

If Jack replied, I didn't hear.

Chapter Thirty-Nine

I drove off the ferry and followed the road to the top of the bluff. I wouldn't admit it out loud, but I was also scanning the rearview for Jack's black Jeep.

I didn't see him.

Fine. Good riddance. My backup would be the gun, the Mace, and Madame, now standing on my lap as we zipped through the town of Winslow. The town had the look of a charming coastal village, although it also looked like the charm had the price tag of the Hamptons. I took the main drag out of town, heading north. The Ghost literally seemed to float down because the two-lane road rose and dipped over the topography. The Puget Lowlands, the name geologists used for this area, was mostly sedimentary soil that had been deposited into valleys scoured from the rock by glaciers. But deeper into the soil, a no-nonsense fault line cut across the island's southern half. Like a knife-score on a baguette, the fault line sliced all the way across Puget Sound and continued under the land holding up Seattle's enormous sports stadiums. Geological records showed the fault released its pent-up energies about once every three hundred years. Since the last big shift was around 1700, the next quake could come at any moment and it would be a stunning earth shaker, the kind that ratcheted the Richter scale past 7.0. I wasn't looking forward to the destruction, but from a geological perspective it would be something to see.

At Mandus Olson Road, I pulled into a grass driveway that matched the address Jack had given me. A high security fence ran on either side of the gravel with a chain and padlock blocking the drive.

I was trying to figure out my way in when a Jeep stopped across the street. The man behind the wheel wore an orange shirt and consulted a map. But as I got out of the car, he sped away.

Madame looked at me, wagging her tail.

"At least you're not mad at me."

She jumped out of the car and walked down the drive, easily walking under the locked chain. She waited for me to follow, but I could see a cable strung through the chain and connected to several small transmitters screwed into the posts. Electricity. I backed up ten paces and ran, hurdling the chain—and falling down on the other side. Madame trotted over, licking my face.

"I appreciate your concern." I rolled on my side and opened my purse. When I picked up the dog, I also grabbed some Ziploc bags from the kitchen. No more Saran Wrap if I could help it. The driveway's gravel was mostly uniform in color and size, a granite that had been quarried and delivered to the site. I placed several samples in a bag, then dug down to the soil beneath, which was *in situ*. Latin for "in the original place," *in situ* soils testified to an area's natural geology. In this case, sand and silt, the usual by-products of glacial erosion and deposition. I put all of it in my purse.

Fields stretched out on either side of the gravel drive. Overgrown grass draped pieces of scrap metal and junk, including an old school bus. The yellow paint was rusting away and the black lettering on its side—Bainbridge Island School District—was riddled with holes. They looked like bullet holes.

I turned around, glancing back to the main road. No sign of Jack. *Fine. Be that way.*

Madame had already run up ahead. I opened my purse, making sure the Sig and Mace were easy to reach, when suddenly the dog was sprinting toward me. I'd never seen her move so fast. And then I saw why. A pack of dogs was chasing her down the driveway. I kneeled, caught her with one arm, and shifted the purse, grabbing the Mace. My finger was about to hit the red button when a guy appeared, running behind the dogs. I kept the canister poised, ready to fire at the first sign of aggression, but the dogs only sniffed around my shoes.

The kid called out, "Who're you?" He looked about fourteen. Dirty blond hair hanging past his shoulders.

"I'm looking for Arnold Corke."

He stayed back a ways, letting the dogs circle us. "You with the county?"

"No." I lifted Madame. Exhibit A. "I'm not a social worker. Is he around?"

The kid had a metal spade in one hand and pointed it down the driveway, from where he'd come. The dogs took it like an order and ran away. The boy turned and followed them and I followed him, while Madame offered low growls that vibrated her rib cage. At the end of the lane, a half-dozen staked goats were chewing circles in the overgrown grass, and an elongated house sat farther back. I counted four smaller buildings and two barns where chickens waddled across the dirt. When they saw the kid, the hens began flapping their useless wings, squawking. Madame twitched.

"Easy," I told her.

The kid picked up a pail and dug the spade inside, flinging corn kernels on the ground. When I asked about Corke again, he pointed the spade at the house. Now that I wasn't with the county, he didn't seem threatened.

Still carrying Madame, I climbed the porch steps to the house. I could hear a voice thundering behind the front door.

"We have a duty to protect the most vulnerable." A deep voice. Passionate. "I want you to always remember the needy. The imprisoned, the abandoned, the unloved."

I waited for a silence, since it sounded like a sermon. Then knocked on the door.

Arnold Corke's dark hair had thinned since his protest days and his skin had wrinkled. The lines crossed his low forehead and bracketed his wide mouth. But his eyes still held some of that belligerent expression. Until he looked down at Madame. Then his attitude shifted.

"Sorry," he said. "We're full right now. Try the Humane Society."

I shifted the dog to my left hand and offered him my right. "Raleigh David."

He took my hand but it was a weak shake. "Arnold Corke."

"Oh, good," I said. "I was hoping to talk to you."

He glanced over his shoulder. The room stretching out behind him was large and open, and picnic tables ran end to end down the middle. Boys and young men sat on benches. Hands clasped. Waiting to finish some prayer.

Corke turned back to me, whispering, "Is this about the road spikes? I already told the county we'd pay for the damage."

"No, sir. This is about a horse."

He shook his head. "You've come at a bad time. I don't have room for more horses either."

"It's more urgent than that," I said. "Can we talk, in private?"

He glanced back once more. Platters of spaghetti were on the table. But the white dinner plates were bare.

"Harris, finish up for me," he said. "I'll be right back."

When he stepped onto the porch, the dogs came running. But now they wagged their tails. At least, the dogs that had tails. They were a mangy bunch.

"They're friendly," he said, reading my mind. "You can put your dog down."

But Madame only walked to the top step and glared down at the pack, panting below. Her erect posture said she was superior to their ranks.

"I've already forgotten your name."

"Raleigh David."

"Raleigh, as in North Carolina? I hear an accent."

"Virginia, actually."

"Long way from home," he said. "What do you need?"

"This morning a horse at Emerald Meadows—"

He held up his hand. "I just told you." His voice was testy. "We're beyond capacity. When I say we can't take another horse, I mean it."

"Mr. Corke." My frustration was rising. I wanted information, and I wanted it now. "Do you own a white horse trailer, license plate W-E-A-K-S?"

"No."

My mouth opened. But I wasn't prepared for that answer. "You don't?"

"No."

The kid who'd been feeding the chickens was walking toward us, apparently done with his chore. He came up the porch, looked at Corke, then me, and stepped inside. It was too quiet in the large room.

"What is it you want?" Corke asked.

"Is there somewhere more private?"

"I hope you're not a spy for the school district," he said, stepping off the porch.

The mangy dogs had run to the chicken yard, sniffing for kernels, but I picked up Madame again just in case. Corke walked to a rail fence. The wood was dry, splintering. And the grass behind it was overgrown like the rest of the fields.

"Okay," he said. "This is as private as it gets around here. I'm expecting you to be honest with me."

I set Madame down.

"Somebody stole a horse this morning from Emerald Meadows. Kidnapped, actually. They left a note. Threatening to kill it. The trailer seen taking the horse had a license plate registered to you."

"Your horse was stolen?"

"No. It belongs to a man named Salvatore Gagliardo." I watched his lean and lined face, searching for any signs that he recognized the name. His frown deepened, but it was hard to read its meaning. I repeated the name. "Sal Gagliardo owns the horse."

"Okay, whoever. What's this got to do with me?"

"The plate. The trailer. Both registered to you."

"You called the police?"

Smart question. What was I doing here, if I called the police?

"Emerald Meadows called them."

He scrunched his nose, as if smelling something foul. "So the track called the cops, and the cops found the plate through DMW and everybody decided one of my boys stole the horse. Brilliant."

When I didn't reply, he reached over the fence and yanked a handful of grass. The shafts squeaked out of their casings.

"My kids have nobody," he said, "for a lot of different reasons. No parents. Nobody who wants to adopt them. And foster care will only turn them into felons. I'm one guy, trying to fill in the gaps. But who cares."

"So it was your trailer."

"I sold it years ago."

"Who bought it?"

But he was extending his long, thin arms over the fence rail. A thick gray horse plodded through the long grass. Its back looked as bowed as a ditch. Madame watched it approach, giving a low growl.

"No, Madame." I turned back to the man. "Who bought the trailer, Mr. Corke?"

"Call me Arnie." He held out the grass in his hand for the horse. "And this handsome guy here is called Pegasus. He's been with us since the beginning."

The horse's gray coat was thin, vaporous as mist over the hide. Blue cataracts clouded the big dark eyes, and when he drew back his lips to eat the grass, I saw most of his teeth were missing.

"Isn't he handsome?" Corke said.

"I really don't want to ask again. Who bought the trailer?"

"Look." He pointed across the field. More horses ambled toward us, the slow progress sending up a shushing sound from the long grass. Evening light bathed their coats in honeyed hues, but when they were closer it wasn't so romantic. Black welts marred their coats. One jaw sagged as if some essential tendon had been sliced, and a Clydesdale pony held its head turned sideways, to look forward from its one eye.

"These are my other foster kids."

The misshapen herd nibbled at his hands and nuzzled his arms. And more came. So many horses. And in a moment's flash the answer came to me, like a word that suddenly fits a crossword puzzle.

"Equus." I turned to him. " E-K-W-A-S."

His smile grew, deepening the lines around his mouth. "That just occurred to you?"

"Yes."

Juan had seen four letters, which he gave in no particular order. Jack had found the missing letter, S, but our discussion was about Corke, not what the plate spelled.

EKWAS.

Equus. Genus classification for the biological family known as horses. *Equus* was also the name evolutionists ascribed to the first horse.

"My wife's idea," Corke said. "She's a poet. She names animals and vehicles. Sometimes kids. That trailer was our first purchase for this place. So the name fit. It was a cheap trailer, and we hoped that like Equus, it would evolve into a higher life form."

He laughed. But I only nodded out of politeness. Evolution fell into the same category as luck—the delusional belief that random chance operated with some significant point. And somehow it struck me as doubly sad that this man in particular had bundled his faith into something so empty. These wounded animals, the equally injured boys, they were all victims of cruelty or neglect. And Arnold Corke clearly hoped for changed lives. Better lives. But the real problem with boys, and girls, wasn't something evolution could fix, if evolution existed—and there was no scientific proof for it whatsoever. Even the evolutionists admitted that. The fossil record told us horses had always been horses, not fish or birds. As for human beings, our problems weren't so much biological as theological. Spiritual. Because no amount of physical change could alter man's generally wicked heart. Only one person could do that. And He was invisible.

But now I understood Corke's hesitancy.

"Mr. Corke—"

"Arnie."

"Arnie, you give kids and horses second chances. But the guy who owns this horse that was kidnapped? He's a bookie. And he's angry. Get my drift?"

He brushed the Clydesdale's blond bangs from its eye. "Promise you'll give them the benefit of the doubt."

"I promise not to jump to conclusions."

He thought about it. "Some boys opened a breeding farm. They wanted to sell racehorses."

"On their own?"

"Yes."

I thought of the stories Eleanor had told me about her and Harry's time with horses. "Breeding requires money."

"That's why I sold them that trailer for twenty bucks." He sighed. "Paul Handler's one of the brightest boys we've ever had. Gifted. Got a college scholarship but dropped out of premed to start his Dark Horse Ranch."

"And Handler has the trailer?"

"I really don't know. We don't keep in touch. I don't believe in breeding horses." He nodded at the pack standing at the fence. "Not when we have horses like this."

"But you helped them."

"They wanted to work. To make a life for themselves. That's a huge step for these kids." He gave a sad smile. "And yet they still don't know how to change a title with DMV."

It wouldn't be that hard for the FBI to track him down. But Corke's cooperation would tell me whose side he was on. "Where's Handler's ranch?"

He said nothing for several moments. The horses nibbled at the grass and Madame crept under the fence, lifting her snout, catching their scents.

"I'll give you his address," he said finally. "But only if you promise not to call the police. And if you promise to talk to him yourself."

Chapter Forty

The night wind blowing across Puget Sound forced everyone inside the ferry. Except me and Madame, who ate a ham sandwich I purchased from the boat's vending machine. I doled out the food so she wouldn't choke it down all at once, and watched the city grow closer. The lights reflecting on the water shimmered in fugues of color.

Jack never appeared.

And twenty minutes later, we were back in the Ghost. I was heading south on the Alaskan Way when I realized another Mariner's game was in town. And it was just letting out. Traffic cops kept us idling at First Avenue, and for seven minutes I watched fans stream from Safeco Field, some of them heading into the Pyramid Alehouse across the street. The stoplight changed several times, but another five minutes passed, and I started to imagine what would happen if "the big one" struck this instant, cracking open this street so the earth could swallow us whole. Without probability models, Madame grew bored and curled up for a nap on the passenger seat. I reached into my purse.

Jack answered my call on the third ring.

"It must've gone okay," he said. "You're not bleeding."

I wanted to know where he'd been, but refused to let him hear me asking. "Corke says he doesn't own the trailer."

"Of course he said that."

"It seems credible."

"Why?"

"He claims the trailer was sold to a kid who used to live there."

I spelled the name Paul Handler. "Corke helped them start a horse-breeding business. Some farm near Yakima."

The Volvo in front of me was creeping forward, the brake lights flashing on and off, as if the driver were anxious to plow through the pedestrians. I felt complete empathy.

"So let me guess," Jack said, "you want a background check on this Handler guy. Now."

"I'll be driving to Yakima tomorrow."

"Harmon, do you really think that's wise?"

"Not really."

"Has anyone ever compared you to a Rubik's Cube?"

"I'll be leaving at 6:00 a.m."

He hung up.

Over an hour later, when I pulled into the parking lot at Thea's Landing, I had the disturbing sensation of having traveled from Point A to Point B with no memory of anything in between. An autopilot trip. Full of preoccupied thoughts. Ideas that roamed and ricocheted and circled back again. But the worst thought was the most incriminating: I called Jack—for the diversion, a light skirmish to avoid the real battle—instead of DeMott.

I wrapped Madame in my jean jacket and raced upstairs before anyone could see us. I filled her water bowl, changed into shorts and a T-shirt, and laced up my running shoes. My fingers were shaking. I kept the dog under a windbreaker, bolted down the stairwell, and burst outside.

We ran along the water, the air tasting of sea salt and wet steel. The red cranes in Tacoma's port loomed over us like claws, ready to pluck us from the street. We ran straight up the hill to the North End neighborhood, full speed, thighs burning, breath like sandpaper in my lungs. Madame took the steep hill like a thoroughbred mutt: all heart. From the top of the hill, the world below seemed to be all lights. Harbor lights. The golden windows in the houses. A white lava of cars driving on the interstate, flowing with a sound like steady wind.

We jogged through the neighborhood until we reached the big Victorian with the porte cochere. An amber light leaked through the curtains of a bedroom window upstairs. Standing on the front lawn, I panted and debated and checked my watch. But when I decided to walk to the door, the bedroom light suddenly went out. I stared at it for several minutes, hoping it would come on again. Until my mind started asking what, exactly, was I going to do? Tell Eleanor all my problems? I was her employee. Cry? And she wasn't my real aunt.

We turned and ran down the hill.

It was past 9:00 p.m. when I carried Madame into the lobby. Sweat beaded at the nape of my neck, rolling down my spine, taking some stress with it. The lobby was empty and I decided there was time to grab Raleigh David's mail. But as I turned toward the boxes, I remembered it was Sunday and I'd picked up the mail yesterday. I was walking away when I realized something was peeking from the metal slot. I turned around. It was a white corner sticking out. Envelope. But none of the other boxes had one. *Uh-oh.*

Management. Notifying me about the building's pet policy.

"We're busted," I told the concealed dog.

I keyed open the box and yanked out the white envelope. My first name was written on the front. Only my first name. And my condo number. In fountain pen ink.

I wanted to rip it open right there. But Madame was squirming. I sprinted upstairs, refilled her water bowl, poured myself a Coca-Cola, and carried it out to the balcony. With the envelope. I sat in the deck chair for several moments. My fingers were shaking again. And a couple was arguing on the patio below. Something about a softball game and car keys that weren't where they should've been. I closed my eyes and offered a convoluted prayer that reminded me, again, how little I deserved grace.

I tore open the envelope.

Dear Raleigh,

Please excuse any illegible words. I'm writing in the backseat of a taxi. And please don't be upset that I left this way. Yes, your car is very fast, but with security checks these days it seemed prudent to leave earlier than you wanted.

Downstairs, the man said something. He said it slowly. Too slowly. I picked up my drink and took a gulp.

Wait. You're always demanding the truth. So let me start over. I left early because I resented having to wait for you in the dining room. I was angry that I didn't meet your Aunt Charlotte. And when Eleanor came into the dining room, I was fuming because you and I spent almost no time together. Unfortunately, my attitude affected Eleanor. She drank too much brandy and began reciting lines about "mendacity." This was one of the worst days of my life.

I could hear the woman downstairs. Her voice was rising. The man said she was overreacting. She told him he always said that.

Want to know what was the best day of my life? When you agreed to marry me. I knew you still had doubts, but that was okay. I knew you would conquer them. But the distance between us is not helping. I'm constantly wondering how you are, where you are, what you're doing—

"So get a cell phone," I said. Out loud.
Down below, the man stopped talking. I held my breath, waiting. After a long moment they began whispering. Heated words. Sibilant whispers.

—and I couldn't wait to see you. Only now it's worse. You look great. Tired, but great. And it's not those clothes, though they're nice. You look . . . alive.
    Do you know what I do every morning? Wake up and think about you. But I'm depressed by breakfast because you're not there. I fill the day with things to do so that I don't think about you. And then I go to bed, telling myself I made it through one more day.
    You know my family. It's full of "perfect" marriages. For appearances. Remember, Raleigh, we said we would break that pattern. Be like your parents, in love. Truly in love. Forever.

I miss you. I love you. I want you to be my wife.

And right now you're at a racetrack searching for a horse that belongs to a guy with a busted shovel for a face. It's your job. I understand. Really, I do.

But you want the truth. So here it is:

You look so alive because you're working around the clock. That's you. Without that kind of challenge, you're not happy.

Oh, wait—the driver says it's five minutes to the airport. I'm going to hurry, bear with me.

I picked up my drink. But the soda wouldn't go down my throat. I held the carbonated fizz in my mouth, letting the bubbles pop on my tongue, tapping against the roof of my mouth. Downstairs a door slammed. The woman yelled—inside the condo now—but the man was still on the patio. He was speaking slowly again. Reminding her about neighbors.

Next week, God willing, I'll be an uncle. But what I really want is to be a husband. And a dad. Now. Not next year. Or five years from now. Or whenever you decide to settle down.

So here's the truth again: you'll be the one who got away.

But it might be worse than that. Much worse, for me. You'll be the one who *wanted* to get away.

I see the planes, we're here, I have to go, forgive this hasty sign-off. I am scribbling now, but perhaps it's best. I love you, Raleigh. So very much. But consider yourself free. No strings anymore.

Your friend forever, and with love always,

DeMott

P.S. I don't have time to drop off this note. The driver has promised to deliver it to the address Eleanor gave me. I am tipping him heavily, so I am hopeful he will follow through. I have to believe that, because I can't write this again. Ever.

P.P.S. Knowing you, you'll send back the ring. But don't. Keep it. Please? That way I can be sure you'll never forget me.

The man was pounding on the door. I heard it open, and then their fight moved inside.

The sky beyond the balcony held Orion, stalking the black depths, searching for enemies to slash. I tried to take a breath and when I couldn't, I forced myself to name the stars. Jupiter. Summer Triangle. Dippers. Something had crystallized inside my lungs, suffocating me. I closed my eyes and tried to imagine myself nine years old again, standing outside with my dad, counting stars. He would be telling me stories and I snuggled against him, keeping warm through the tales of Copernicus and Hailey and Galileo fighting the church.

Memories came back, so clearly they opened my eyes.

"House arrest," my dad was saying. It was a cold winter night in Richmond. We had hot chocolate in thermoses. "Galileo said the Earth was not the center of the universe. The sun was the center. And he was right. But for saying that, the Church put him under house arrest. For the rest of his life."

I remembered thinking, *Not possible. This is just a story.*

"Raleigh, I want you to know this."

"I got it, Dad. The sun is the center of the universe."

"But the other part. About Galileo. How he refused to deny the truth."

"The moral is, never give up."

But my dad shook his head. He surprised me. Always.

"At some point, life will seem difficult to you. Really difficult. That's life—Raleigh, look at me."

"I'm looking."

"When those hard times come, I want you to remember how Galileo found the truth."

"With a telescope."

He laughed. "Yes, that was part of it."

But he pointed to the sky. Black velvet. White lights.

"Those stars are there, every day, waiting in the blue sky. We just can't see them. This is what I want you to remember. The stars shine bright when it gets dark enough. The invisible becomes visible." He paused, watching me. "I don't expect you to understand this. But someday, I hope you'll remember."

The weight of his words pressed into me now, and something splashed on my hand. Hot, wet. Madame walked out to the porch and stared at me. I scooped her into my arms, her body warm from our run. I wanted to bury my face in her fur, but I forced myself to look up.

The stars were bright pinpricks of light. Diamond dust, cast over a black sea. But they were changing now, streaking, each one stretching into a silver sword. A white cross. They looked like those stars in the night sky of medieval paintings, all the stellar depictions of night in Bethlehem. The way artists painted stars in Galileo's time. For symbolism, I always thought.

But maybe those painters had seen those actual stars, there in the night sky. Like this.

Because that's how the stars looked now, seen through tears.

Chapter Forty-One

Before dawn, eyes puffy from tears and insomnia, I drove over Snoqualmie Pass with a dog and a thermos of coffee. An hour later we had dropped down to the other side of the mountains, where a rising sun burnished the bare hills to raw gold and the air shifted from evergreen scents to sage. Best of all, no black Cadillac was following me.

And no black Jeep.

Last night, while I was literally trying to run away from my problems, Jack had left a message on my cell phone. The preliminary background search of Paul Handler said the former foster kid was now twenty-nine years old, owned thirty-five acres just outside Yakima in a small town named Selah, and his juvie record was sealed. The latter meant Handler had committed a crime before turning eighteen, but under Washington law that record couldn't be opened unless he committed a crime as an adult. And he hadn't.

"No immediate threat," Jack said.

I replayed the message. But I was listening for something other than the facts. Jack's tone sounded as dry and flat as this basalt plain the Ghost was now flying over. His closing comment was a clipped, "Have a safe trip."

Have a safe trip?

No sarcasm. No jokes. Basically he was saying, *Have a nice life.*

Which was pretty much what DeMott told me in his letter.

There was plenty of time to think about how Freud would diagnose my reaction to all this. Motoring east with caffeine and the canine, I decided the little doctor would tell me that I was in denial.

Throwing myself into work after a broken engagement. And sadly, Freud would be right, because by the time I reached the town of Selah, it really did seem like my problems were on the other side of the mountains.

I looked over at Madame. Snoozing on the passenger seat. She opened one eye.

"Denial works," I told her.

She went back to sleep.

I used my cell phone's GPS to find the dirt road that wound back and forth alongside the Yakima River. The road leading to Handler's property. But waterfront property in desert climates always went for a premium price, and I wondered how a former foster kid like Handler could afford this spread. A vineyard came up on my left side, laid parallel to the road, where the sun cast hazy rainbows in the morning's irrigation spray. After that I saw a field of horses, running powerfully across the desert land. One was black. I slowed down, taking a good look. In addition to a white blaze, it was much smaller than Cuppa Joe.

I passed an entrance sign for Dark Horse Ranch, and just past that I saw three yurts staked at the base of a short rounded hill. The middle yurt's flaps were rolled up and a handful of guys milled around an outdoor stove, holding mugs and plates. I climbed out of the Ghost. The air smelled of coffee and potatoes.

"You're staying," I told Madame, rolling down the car windows.

She glanced out the window at the yurts, then placed her paw on the gearshift. Preparing for some getaway.

"You are an amusing animal."

I walked toward the tents. The soil was so dry my Dolce & Gabbanas were kicking up clouds of dust. A ranch house sat in the distance. And two large horse barns on either side of a horse arena. Quite a spread.

A stocky man stepped out of the middle yurt, moving toward me quickly, almost urgently. As if he wanted to reach me before I reached the tent. Arnold Corke had called ahead, I could feel it. But I wondered if he would play dumb.

"Help you with something?" he asked.

Dumb, I decided.

"I'm looking for Paul Handler."

"I'm Paul."

His brown hair was long and his short beard was blond, the ends twisted into a short tail hanging off his chin. His mouth was thin, almost sardonic, but his eyelashes were lush and dark. I decided the light-colored beard was a bleach job. An affectation. Like the small metallic arrows that pierced his brows, also thick and dark like the eyelashes. Jack's background check said this guy was only two years younger than me. But his appearance, combined with Raleigh David's, made me feel middle-aged.

"I'm Raleigh David." I extended my hand. His fingers were rough, callused. "Arnie probably called you."

For the next moment, he seemed to weigh the gain-loss of truth versus lies. I could tell, because I was doing the same thing.

"Yeah," he said finally. "Arnie did call me. What can I say? I messed up. I should've changed the title on that trailer."

"So you do own the trailer, license plate E-K-W-A-S?" The words were out of my mouth before I could stop them. They sounded more like Raleigh Harmon, FBI agent. I tried to recover. "I'm just wanting to make sure I didn't drive all the way out here for nothing."

"Yeah, that's my trailer." He shrugged. "I don't see what the big deal is."

"Arnie didn't explain?"

"Something about a horse stolen from Emerald Meadows. With my trailer. But I just laughed. That's not even possible."

"We have an eyewitness."

"They're lying."

"Can you prove it?"

His thin mouth pulled back, a tight smile. Challenging. "You want to see the trailer for yourself?"

I was trying to play it cool, but he was so much cooler it was throwing me off balance. Yes, I expected Corke to call him. Yes, I expected him to play dumb at first. But I didn't expect him to be this forthright.

I followed him past the yurts. The figures inside were indistinct, shaded from the sun. Moving like shadows. I sensed a hush as Handler passed, and when we came to the short hill behind the tents, I saw three rows of trailers. Six were narrow singles, two were doubles, and three were quads—two stalls in front, two in back. And one red school bus. Its dust-covered side advertised "The Pony Express." Handler saw me staring at it.

"We do pony rides," he said. "Birthday parties. For kids."

"You breed horses for pony rides?"

He laughed and once more caught me off guard. Too relaxed. Not the least bit nervous.

"Arnie would only sell me that trailer if I agreed to take in old nags." He shrugged. "No big deal. They're perfect for kiddie rides. And it pays for their keep."

He moved through the trailers, stopping at a faded white single. "Here you go."

One wheel rested on its rim, flat. I got a bad feeling and kneeled by the license plate, wiping away the dirt from the metal.

EKWAS.

Handler was unlatching the back doors. The hinges screeched, dry and rusted. "Maybe you'd put a horse in this thing, but I wouldn't."

The trailer floor was orange, at least where the floor still existed. Most of it had rusted away, leaving behind a lacework of crispy oxidized metal. The grass was growing through the holes.

He closed the squeaking doors. "See what I'm saying. My trailer didn't take your horse."

"It's not my horse."

"Then why're you looking for it?"

"It was taken from my aunt's barn. The guy who owns it isn't the understanding type."

"Who owns it?"

"Salvatore Gagliardo." I raised my hand against the bright sun, reading his expression. "You know him."

He nodded. "Abbondanza."

"Right."

"I sold his trainer some horses awhile back." He wiped his hands on his jeans, removing the dirt picked up from the trailer's handles. "Which horse is gone?"

"Cuppa Joe."

He froze. Now I saw worry in his eyes. No more Mr. Cool.

"That's impossible," he said.

"They also left a note. They plan to kill him after forty-eight hours."

"But—" He squinted, frowning, thinking. "But I sold that horse to them. Last summer. The bigmouthed Wop, he came out here himself."

"Jimmy Bello?"

He nodded. But the frown remained. It angled the piercings in his brows, like arrows pointing at his eyes.

"I drove Cuppa Joe over the Pass myself. What a nightmare. He almost jackknifed us, kicking and bucking. I was ready to open the trailer and let him run off. But I got paid good money for him."

I glanced at the old white trailer. Under the tires, the blades of grass were long and unbroken. I kneeled down again, making one last-ditch effort. I rubbed my fingers over the lug nuts holding the plate to the trailer. But the soil was thick, undisturbed.

"You think I have that horse," he said.

I looked up. He had a disarming ability to switch attitudes in an instant. Now he looked vulnerable. I wondered if his conscience had a volume knob.

"I don't know," I said.

"Do I look suicidal to you? I'd need a death wish to steal a horse from that barn. And I didn't even like Cuppa Joe. When he left, I threw a party."

"And you've heard nothing about this, aside from Arnie's call?"

"Look around." He swung his arm in a half circle, taking in the fields. "If you see that horse, take him. Please."

I stood up slowly, trying to gauge my thoughts. Juan could've misread the plate. But what were the chances on the other end? That Handler sold Cuppa Joe to Abbondanza, and now the trailer traced back to him. I didn't like those odds. And I didn't believe in coincidences.

But the foster kid was already doing his own calculations.

"Why was Cuppa Joe in your barn?" he asked.

"The track shut down Abbondanza. Bello was using snake venom."

"What a creep," he said, with feeling. "That stuff can give a horse a heart attack. But I still don't see why you were keeping Cuppa Joe. For him." He said it like I was an accomplice to the snake venom.

"When the trailers came to take Abbondanza's horses, Cuppa Joe refused to go."

"There's a surprise."

"My aunt's barn had an open stall. Just until he calmed down."

"Who's your aunt?"

"Eleanor Anderson."

"Eleanor?" He raised his eyebrows, the swords leaping. "Living legend Eleanor? She's your aunt? How cool is that."

I nodded, feeling an undeserved swell of pride. And I decided to trade on it. "I could really use some help. Any idea who might've taken Cuppa Joe?"

"Whoever it is, they're crazy. I can guarantee that. Not only is that horse a total brat, the guys running that barn don't fool around."

He started walking away from the trailers and I followed him. But he stopped at the base of the hill, reaching into his back pocket. He took out his wallet and removed a business card.

"If your aunt ever needs horses . . ."

I was about to answer, with a lie, but a woman was running down the hill, behind Handler. She was sledding on her feet, leaving a trail of dust behind her.

"Paul!" she yelled. "Paul!"

He turned around.

"What?" He sounded irritated.

Her face was sweating. The dust clung to her skin. Heavily freckled skin. The dust made the freckles look like more dirt.

"Horse—" She panted. "Horse stuck. Kids. Again."

Handler took off, running up the hill. The girl turned to me. Her freckles were so numerous it was difficult to read her features. The color of old pennies, the dots covered her eyelids and her lips and her ears, even extending into her hairline. Red hair. Long but matted, hanging heavily behind her shoulders.

The word came to me like a thunderbolt: *dreadlocks.*

"Hi," I said.

She took off without a word.

Handler was already halfway up the hill. He had a powerful stride, pure muscular determination. But the girl didn't follow him. She ran toward the yurts. I watched the thick ropes of hair swinging across her back, and Juan's words echoed in my mind. Dreadlocks. Dirty. *Muy* dirty.

I waited until Handler had cleared the hilltop. Then I walked back through the trailers. Three of them had been moved recently, judging by the flattened blades of grass around their wheels. One was black with Dark Horse Ranch written prominently on its side. The second was red, a double, also bearing the ranch's name. But a third trailer was white. A single. Unfortunately, the back end was positioned in a way that it faced the yurts. When I looked over there, people were running from the tents.

I unbuckled the leather belt that had Calvin Klein's initials and used the metal post to pry some soil from the front tire treads. I deposited the sample into a Ziploc bag, then stole another glance at the yurts. The girl with the dreadlocks was coming back. And now a bald guy was with her.

I closed my purse, looped the belt back into my slacks, and was stepping from the trailers when they appeared.

"What're you doing?" Freckles demanded.

"Sorry." I continued to work the buckle. "It was a long drive."

The bald guy kept his head at a weird angle. Maybe to show off the dragon tattoo that circled his neck. Like an iridescent sideburn, the reptile's tail slithered up the side of his face.

"Answer the question," he said. "What were you doing?"

"You really need me to explain?" I smiled.

"She was snooping around the trailers," Freckles said.

"Paul said I could look around."

"Paul's not here," Snake said. "And now you're leaving."

They walked six paces behind me, all the way back to the Ghost. Madame stood with her paws on the window frame, nose lifted, like Washington crossing the Delaware.

"How could you leave that dog in the car?" Freckles said. "In this heat?"

She threw her arm toward the sun. A small green tattoo marked the inside of her forearm. *Elf*, it said. Nickname, I decided. For the elf Santa would've fired.

I tried to smile. "Thank you for thinking of my dog."

"Somebody has to."

Snake lowered his voice. "Easy, Bo."

Madame hopped over to the passenger side, giving me a look that said, *It's about time.*

I turned the key and gazed at the side mirror. The yurts were empty. And my two escorts were running past them.

Chapter Forty-Two

I drove slowly down the road and found a crowd gathered by the river. Handler was in the water with several men. And a horse. Another horse was being led away by its bridle. It was a deep brown horse, almost black. But its legs were gray.

Muddy gray.

I pulled to the side of the road. On the hillside above the river, a group of young boys watched the scene below. They were dark-skinned, with hair so black and shiny it reflected the sun in white patches. One of the boys was pointing at the Ghost, holding something in his hand. An elliptical object, long with tail wings.

I got out, carrying Madame in my arms to the edge of the road. The water turned west, a slow hairpin turn that had deposited enough sand and debris to form a bar. Water pooled behind it. Which was where Handler was with the horse.

"Shovels!" he yelled.

He stood on a plank, and the people on the riverbank slid more boards across the shallow pond to deliver the shovels. A blond girl walked down the boards last, carrying a bridle made of rope. The horse in the water was rocking itself forward and back, muscles flexing under its chestnut coat.

The men dug around the horse's front legs. The gray sediment they flung away was a transitional soil, geologically speaking. Mostly clay. The grains ranging from fine silt to sand. But the wooden planks and the catatonic horse told me something else. The clay had the grip of quicksand. Step in it, as the horse had, and it wouldn't let go. The girl moved to the side, petting the animal's neck as its ears twitched too fast. Agitated. The men gathered on a plank under the horse's chest.

"On three!" Handler called.

They pressed their shoulders into the animal's chest. The front legs came out stiff as plaster casts. The hooves clopped onto the board, and the horse immediately leaned forward, trying to yank out its back legs.

"Hold 'er still!" Handler rushed down the board.

The girl shifted to the front, taking the long head in her hands so that the animal looked directly into her eyes. The men dug out the back legs. When all four hooves were on the boards, the girl walked the animal to the riverbank. The crowd left with them, toward the hill, and the yurts beyond that. Several men collected the boards, stacking them on the riverbank, but Handler was running up the hill again. He headed for the boys who were watching.

The boys scattered.

"I told you kids!" He stopped, watching them run. "No water—no *chúush*! You're gonna kill my horses."

The boy holding the object in his hand looked back.

Hander pointed at him, his finger covered with gray mud. "I'll call the elders!"

The boy started to kick something on the ground. Again and again. It didn't move, but the dry stones scattered. And Handler came running for him. The boy turned and raced down the hill where his buddies were waiting by a barbed wire fence. The boy slipped through the wire like a cat burglar.

Handler watched them go. When he turned toward the river, he saw me watching from the road. He hesitated, then walked down the hill, crossed the bank, and climbed up to the road.

"What happened?" I asked.

"Water rocket." He tilted his head toward his shoulder, using his T-shirt to wipe his forehead. "New toy for the local Indian kids. They come pinch my irrigation line so the pressure builds up. Then fire the rocket off it. Thing launches like Cape Canaveral. But if it scares the horses, they panic, run into the water. I lost one last month. Legs snapped like twigs."

"The horses can't get out of the water?"

He shook his head and looked down at his hands. Most of the clay had already dried on his skin, like thin plaster. But several wet chunks clung to his fingernails. He looked up. "I hope you find Cuppa Joe."

"Thanks, I appreciate your help." I moved Madame to my left side and extended my right hand.

He looked at it, then lifted both hands. To show me how dirty they were.

I smiled. "A little dirt won't hurt me."

He shook. I could feel the fine, gritty sediment on his skin. A small moist piece, clinging to the outside of his palm.

"Good luck," he said.

I nodded, as if I agreed. "Thanks."

I walked across the road to the Ghost, tossed Madame through the window, and used my left hand to open the door. When I glanced back, Handler was heading for the yurts.

Still using my left hand, I opened my purse, removed a Ziploc bag, and pulled it over my right hand, shaking my fingers, brushing my palm.

It wasn't much.

But enough, maybe.

Chapter Forty-Three

The smell of cows on fire led me down Yakima's main drag, taking me straight to Miner's Restaurant. I needed to think, and I needed cheeseburgers—one plain, one loaded. Fries, a chocolate shake, and ice water for the dog. I sat at a picnic table outside in the shade, said grace, divided the food between us, and pulled out my notebook.

I wrote: *Juan misread the plate.*

I considered this theory while eating the cheeseburger. It was possible. Perhaps even probable. After all, Juan had recalled the license plate's letters out of order. And he missed a letter. Or did he?

Next: *Juan lied.*

This theory bounced around my brain while Madame licked clean the burger's paper wrapper. And it was bolstered by Juan's fake social security number. Which, I recalled, traced to Yakima. Specifically, a dead Native American woman. And now the license plate was found on the same farm where Cuppa Joe was raised, just outside Yakima.

I dipped a fry in mayonnaise, then scrawled, *Paul Handler*.

I had two opinions about Handler. Either he had nothing to do with Cuppa Joe's disappearance, or he had everything to do with it. He was strong, determined, and ambitious. He'd turned a tragic childhood into a productive life. Admirable, no doubt about it. But I'd met enough foster care kids during my years of law enforcement to know they often survived through manipulation and deception. The brightest ones sometimes were high-functioning sociopaths. I couldn't decide whether Handler was telling the truth about Cuppa

Joe, or whether all that goodwill was an attempt to blow smoke across his own trail. He did show me the EKWAS trailer. And there was no way Cuppa Joe ever rode in that thing. But Handler's first instinct this morning was to pretend he didn't know why I was there. Why do that, if he was innocent?

My internal radar was screaming as I divided the fries with Madame.

I wrote: *Dreadlocks.*

I didn't believe in luck. But probability was an authentic mathematical theory. And the probability models that lined up inside my mind were jumping up and down, begging for attention. The connection between the Dark Horse Ranch and Abbondanza was suspicious enough. But what were the chances that Cuppa Joe was kidnapped by guys with dreadlocks, and Handler's farm just happened to be populated by a hairy brood? I thought about the redheaded girl, how she wanted me gone. Something was definitely tarnished there, something hard and dark with . . . greed?

I picked up my milk shake. The warm desert air had melted it to a perfect consistency, about three degrees under soft-serve ice cream. It sluiced through the straw as I wrote one final word.

Mud.

Those juvenile delinquents had done me a big favor. Without their mischief, I never would've noticed that cloying gray mud down by the river. It looked so familiar, too familiar. Like the stuff Cooper was using. Although forensics-by-appearances seemed criminally simple, geology operated with it. Minerals had highly specific hues. And similar environments, that thing known as provenance.

I looked down at Madame. "Time to go see the mad scientist."

She wagged her tail.

Chapter Forty-Four

We were bulleting across the basalt plateau for Spokane when my purse started doo-dahing "Camptown Races." Madame continued to snooze in the passenger seat, but as I fumbled for the phone, my heart began making little bleating pulses. That small hope. That remaining spark of light that said maybe, just maybe, DeMott was calling me.

Wrong.

"Harmon, where are you?" Jack said.

I tried to control my voice. "Heading to Spokane. I need to see the forensic geologist. And I need you to dig deeper on Paul Handler. I just saw the trailer with the plate. It hasn't gone anywhere in years."

"You're sure?"

"Positive. It would disintegrate at the first bump in the road. But there's another wrinkle. Handler sold the kidnapped horse to Sal Gagliardo."

"What?"

"I'm not done. The description of the kidnappers fits Handler's ranch hands. That's why I need more information on this guy. Check for any paper trail. Social services. Tax returns, whatever you can find."

But there was only silence on the other end. I gazed down the Ghost's bonnet. The white paint glowed under the blazing sun. "Hello?"

"You need to come in."

"Fine, I'll do the research myself. Just take care of the guards at the front desk."

"No."

"Jack, I don't have any ID to get upstairs."

"I understand. It's not me. It's management. They want you to come in."

An exit blew past. Then a yellow farmhouse, surrounded by fields of wheat.

"Harmon?"

"Come in. For good?"

He didn't say anything.

"So OPR made its ruling?"

"I don't know," he said. "McLeod came by my desk and asked how the case was going. I told him about the kidnapped horse, how you were tracking it down. He said, 'That's too bad.' I thought he meant the horse. But then he said, 'Tell her she has to come in.' When I asked why, McLeod said it was beyond his apprehension."

The malaprop was closer to a Freudian slip. Worried, apprehensive. My stomach tightened into a knot.

"When?" The tone of my voice triggered something in Madame. She lifted her head. "When do I have to come in?"

"Since you're heading in the wrong direction, I'll hold them off until tomorrow. Does eleven o'clock work for you?"

No. It didn't work for me.

But I lied. Again.

"I'll be there."

≈

I walked into the crime lab just before 2:00 p.m. and found Peter Rosser standing on a tripod ladder, leaning toward the exposed I-beam that ran across the ceiling. He was unknotting a nylon noose.

He glanced down at me. "Don't tell me you want to use it."

"When's your last day?" I asked.

"Tomorrow." He tossed me the rope. "Put it in that box on my desk, would ya?"

The box contained several sample nooses, all made from different materials. I rummaged through my purse and removed the soil samples, including the one inside Eleanor's lipstick case. "Any chance you could look at these by tonight?"

"Let's make a deal." He grinned. "I'll take care of it if you come work in my new lab."

"I'm flattered, really, but—"

"But it's like riding a unicycle. You never forget how to do this stuff." He came down the ladder with a black composite rope. It looked like a twisted garden snake. He threw it to me. "In the box with the others, if you don't mind."

I laid the noose inside the box. "Where are the Petri dishes?"

"I knew you couldn't resist." He pointed across the room. "Third drawer down. On the left."

I placed the shallow glass dishes on the counter and marked each with a Sharpie, noting the soils in order of importance—or imperative. I needed to know some things right away, in light of my meeting tomorrow with the SAC. The top two were the soil from Handler's palm and the caked mud inside Eleanor's lipstick case, from Ashley's room. I added several drops of distilled water to Handler's palm dust, because there was so little to sample, and carried the wet clay over to the Scanning Electron Microscope.

"Who's taking your place?" I asked.

"Nobody can take my place."

"Who's got the job?"

"Nice guy." Rosser carried the ladder to a far wall. It displayed posters that described igneous minerals in terms of chemistry, texture, and foliation. "But the man doesn't possess my superior sense of urgency. If you know what I mean."

I touched the SEM's carbon plug to the sediment, coating it, then placed it inside the machine. The SEM made its usual whining noises, but now it sounded like it was crying over the loss of its resident cowboy.

He called out, "What do you know about pyroclastics?"

I hit the switch on the computer monitor. An old monitor, the bulky kind that needed to warm up. Pyroclastics were rocks and minerals formed by explosive igneous action. Volcanoes, mostly.

"*Pyro* is Greek for 'fire.'" I had an arcane knowledge of Greek and Latin. "*Clastic* means 'broken in bits.'"

"I was talking ash, pumice, obsidian." He removed the igneous poster, rolling it up. "What about ash?"

"Highly abrasive, somewhat corrosive, and conducts electricity when wet and won't dissolve in water."

The monitor screen kicked up a colored bar code. Ready to cooperate with the SEM.

"And the gas?"

"Shreds the magma, shatters the rock, fuels the flow." I tapped the computer's mouse, feeling an odd tingle in my fingertips. This moment, this threshold to new knowledge, had more adrenaline than the races at Emerald Meadows. Those races ended. These only launched more.

"Name one famous pyroclastic ash flow."

I watched the screen. Silica appeared first, in high concentrations. "Peter, if this is about the job, I don't want it."

"Pompeii."

"Preschoolers can name Pompeii."

"What about Pelée?"

"Killed thirty thousand people."

"What year?"

I leaned into the screen. Aluminum had overtaken silica. "Pelée blew in nineteen hundred and one."

"Nineteen-oh-two," he corrected. "Gallop ahead seventy-eight years, what do you get?"

Seventy-eight plus two was . . . "Mount St. Helens." I clicked Print with the mouse. "Why do you want to know about St. Helens?"

"I was curious whether a Southern gal such as yourself knows anything about Northwest geology."

I looked up. He had removed the posters and now stood at the counter, looking at my soil samples in the Petri dishes.

"Some of that was raked off a barn floor," I said, "if you're thinking about tasting it."

All the barn detritus also meant the test would take time. The samples had to be cleaned first. And I didn't have time for that.

I pulled the colored bar graph from the printer. Handler's clay had extremely high concentrations of three elements: aluminum and silica and selenium. The SEM also detected the same trace radioactive elements. Identical. Not luck. Not even probability.

Rosser walked over. "What do you got?"

"Provenance on that gray clay."

He grinned. "Puts a spur under your saddle, don't it?"

Chapter Forty-Five

On my way back from Spokane, I only made it halfway. Taking the exit for downtown Ellensburg, I parked the Ghost on West Third. The afternoon temperature was in the high 80s, and when I carried Madame into the Old Mill, nobody batted eye, not even when I placed her in the shopping cart.

I bought Milk-Bones for her fast-food breath, then picked out a pair of black gardening gloves for me. A set of pruning shears, one spade, and a compact but powerful flashlight. In the clothing department, I found black running shorts and a black T-shirt with gray lettering that said *Rodeo Girl*. Keds, in black, were going for $9.99. The checkout clerk threw in a baseball cap that advertised the store. It was black too.

Down the road, I got a room at the Thunderbird Motel. When I asked for a midnight wakeup call, the clerk looked at me funny. I parked the Ghost directly outside my first-floor room and changed into the shorts, T-shirt, and cheap tennies. Madame and I ran to the campus of Central Washington University where the leafy elms drooped in the late August heat. I made eight laps around the college track while Madame rested under the bleachers in the shade. And I prayed for protection. Both for tonight and for tomorrow morning when I would be sitting in the SAC's office.

Back at the motel, I called for an extra-large pizza and jumped into the shower. I washed the Rodeo Girl T-shirt in the sink with a bar of soap and laid it over the air-conditioning unit, hoping it would dry by midnight. When the pizza arrived, Madame and I sat on the double bed. She wagged her tail through my extended grace, where I added another request: wisdom. Tomorrow at 11:00 a.m. Wisdom.

We ate pizza topped with everything but the kitchen sink and watched old cable crime shows. I explained to Madame that none of it resembled real life. But the joke was on me when an actor walked onscreen wearing a seersucker blazer. His Southern accent was soft. I watched his every move. A calm actor. Nothing superfluous. Sensible and kind.

When my cell phone started doo-dahing, I knew it wasn't him. That stuff only happened on television.

"Where are you?" Jack asked.

I gazed around the room. Pizza, shared with a dog. Bad crime TV. Staring at an actor like a jilted teenager.

"Nowhere," I said. "I'm nowhere."

"I can always ping that phone's GPS."

"Go ahead. It'll come up nowhere."

"What were you doing at the crime lab?"

I gave him the background again on the selenium and trace radioactive elements, the mud poultices that were actually poisoning the horses. "That mud comes from Handler's land. Eleanor's trainer, Bill Cooper, brings it in."

"You're sure?"

"Sure enough. And Cooper has refused to tell anyone where the mud comes from." The facts were lining up like dominoes. But I couldn't find the first tile, the original that set the others falling. "Anything on the background checks?"

"I haven't had a chance."

"What if I told you I found the same clay in the room of Sal Gag's groom? On shoes way too big for her?"

"I'd want you to explain it for me," he said.

"All roads keep leading back to Handler and his Dark Horse Ranch. All that's missing is why. If the suits haul me in tomorrow, we might never know."

"You must have some theories," Jack said.

The TV show had ended. I was trying to catch the credits, to find the name of the actor who resembled DeMott. But I missed it. And the next show was some reality TV spectacle. Emaciated women with pneumatic breasts and too much makeup yelling at each other. They were probably supposed to be beautiful, but they reminded me of crazy men in raincoats, flashing their privates—exhibitionists without conscience or shame. Madame rolled over on her back.

"I can come up with a bunch of theories. Handler knows that soil's poisonous, and he's getting paid to sabotage a barn that competes with Abbondanza. But why would he steal their horse? The horse he sold to Sal Gag. See what I mean?"

He said nothing. I clicked through the channels, pausing on a cooking show with some large cleavers and angry chefs.

"Harmon?"

I kept clicking. What TV needed was more shows with real guns. And people who knew how to fire them. "I'm here."

"Can I make a suggestion?"

"Just one."

"You only need one," he said. "Don't do anything impulsive."

I glanced at the black shirt hanging over the air conditioner. "What do you mean by 'impulsive'?"

"Sudden, rash. The stuff Raleigh Harmon does when she's backed into a corner. You want evidence, but—"

"But nothing. OPR will have me sitting at a desk for five years if I can't prove anything."

"There's an open desk by me."

"Ever wonder why?"

"Once. But then I realized the problem."

"Really."

"Yes. Most people can't handle being that close to somebody this awesome."

"I hear Freud is taking patients."

"Listen to me, Harmon. Don't do anything that'll get you in more trouble."

I stared at the shirt. "I just need to check one thing."

"Harmon . . ."

"The kidnapper's note said forty-eight hours. That was about thirty hours ago. So instead of lecturing me, Jack, how about running a deeper check on Handler? Or Ashley Trenner?"

The phone crackled with what sounded like a sigh.

"One last thing," he said. "And if you repeat it during the meeting, I'll deny it. But don't ever change. No matter what they say."

He hung up, and I stared at the TV screen for several minutes. But my eyes were blind to the images, and when I clicked it off, Madame rolled over again, groaning softly. Satiated with pizza. I turned out the light and pulled the covers up close.

My wake-up call was in three hours.

Chapter Forty-Six

We pulled out of the Thunderbird Motel twenty minutes past midnight. The sky held a bright half-moon and a symphony of shimmering stars. I drove south on Interstate 82 and drank coffee while Madame continued sleeping. When the Ghost floated into the small town of Selah, Madame woke up and nudged her nose under my right elbow, climbing into my lap.

I followed the same curving road beside the Yakima River. But this time I turned on Clover Road. A gravel lane, it ran alongside the river opposite Handler's property. When I cut my headlights, the moon flashed on the river, silver as liquid mercury. The car bumped over thirsty tree roots under a stand of elms. When I got out, Madame jumped out too, sniffing the ground and leaving her mark on the gnarled tree roots.

I pulled my hair into a ponytail and tugged on the black baseball cap. My cell phone was on silent ring, but I clicked to the camera feature, then clipped it to the black running shorts. The spade's concave blade fit against the small of my back. I pulled on the gardening gloves and picked up the pruning shears and flashlight. Madame looked like a gray fox in the moonlight. Her ears were pricked for threats.

"Psst." I clicked the flashlight.

She looked at me.

I pointed at the open car door. "Get in."

She jumped over the tree roots and disappeared into the dark.

"I'm serious," I hissed. "Get over here."

Each time I found her she darted away. I tried to keep the flashlight down, sweeping the beam back and forth, trying to track her.

The hair on my neck was prickling. I imagined every threat, from rattlesnakes to night-hunting rednecks. Walking back to the car, I stood by the open door. From the dog's perspective, she had a point. Long drives, hot weather. Confined to a car and a motel room. Now the air had finally cooled, and I was making her stay in the car.

I shut the long white door.

The dog trotted out of the trees.

"Fine." I pointed the flashlight. Her black eyes were shining with victory. "Don't run off again. I mean it."

I hid the car key under the bumper and then we jogged down the gravel road. She stayed six inches off my left ankle and I hoped we looked legit: a woman and her dog taking an early-morning run. Very early. But so what. I faced forward and listened to the river murmuring beside us. When we reached the barbed wire fence that the juvenile delinquents had slipped through, I paused, pretending to stretch out my legs. The pooled river water was as gray as the mud on the sandbar. I kneeled by the fence post, waiting. Madame was close enough to touch but kept circling, sniffing the ground. There was a bold green scent like eucalyptus in the air, and the barbed wire's knots reminded me of Handler's piercings. Spikes that served a similar purpose: Keep out. No trespassing. The former foster kid didn't want anyone coming through the window to his soul.

I pulled her close. Even with cotton gloves I could feel her fur raised stiff between her shoulders.

"Good girl." I set her down on the other side of the barbed wire. "Stay."

I managed to work my arms and torso through the middle space, but one of the spikes grabbed the back of my shirt. I reached behind, tugging. The cotton ripped.

"Rats."

I jogged to Handler's property. Madame stayed in front of me. In a half crouch I dragged the flashlight's handle across the ground. Each time I hit something solid, I clicked on the light on. Mostly I found clumps of desert grass and sage. But at the base of the hill I found a dark spot. Wet. I pulled out the spade and dug through the gritty soil, feeling the cool, buried earth. The irrigation tube wasn't difficult to reach. It looked like a fat snake under the flashlight.

Madame leaned over the hole I made, panting.

"Almost done." I laid the spade against the small of my back, then opened the pruning shears. The jaws bit the tube but the first squeeze didn't cut the plastic. It was durable, strong enough to withstand the temperature fluctuations of the desert. I crimped down again, using both hands, and felt the upper side pop. Water leaked out. I snipped through the bottom half, then opened the jaws again and bit down three inches away from the first cut. Madame growled. I looked up.

The horse looked ethereal, lustrous in the moonlight. It walked around the base of the hill, followed by two more horses. I could hear their hooves striking the rocks. Like the sound of pool balls clicking against each other. Madame gave another growl.

"Hang on." I squeezed the shears. "I'm almost done."

The shears bit through the line's top half. I squeezed again. And looked up. The world was painted with chiaroscuro light. All quartz-colored shadows and charcoal lines, the ashen hues of the horse in front. Madame took one step forward. The sheers bit the tube. I grabbed the section from the hole, stuffing it into my waist band. Then I lunged for the dog.

But she was gone. Running.

"No!"

I raced after her, but she was running at top speed. She went after the horses like a sheepdog, barking and nipping.

"Madame—no!"

The two horses in back ripped past the fence and ran around the base of the hill, disappearing. But the third horse tried to outmaneuver Madame. Changing direction, darting, twisting. But the small black dog refused to give up.

"Stop!"

I tripped, fell. Got up. They were running too fast, the ground vibrating with the heavy hooves. When the horse changed directions, its tail crested like a breaking wave. But it was headed toward the hill and I stopped, pleading silently. *Run up the hill. Please.* But Madame cut off that path, sending the horse galloping to the left. Down. To the water. Madame on its heels.

"No—"

I ran for the river.

"No—no!"

The horse splashed into the pond. Madame stood on the bank, giving one final bark. Victory.

But the next sound chilled my spine. Wet, slurping. The horse, caught in the clay.

I yanked off my cell phone and clicked off the camera. "Don't move, Madame."

The horse was rocking back and forth. I dialed 911 and started talking as soon as the operator answered.

"Dark Horse Ranch. It's an emergency."

"All right, ma'am, calm down. Are you alone?"

"I need help. The river, Yakima River, right off—" I struggled to remember the name. "Clover Road."

Her voice was too calm. "Is there anyone nearby who could be of some assistance?"

"Lady, this is an emergency!" I grabbed a board from the stack on the bank and dragged it toward the horse. I threw it down. The horse's flanks quivered.

"I'll need a little more information." Her voice was placid. "Tell me exactly what's going on."

"There's a horse in danger."

"A horse."

"It's not a joke. It's an emergency. Please send help to the Dark Horse Ranch, across from Clover Road."

She asked for more details. I gave a strangled cry, then cut off the call. A cheap shot, but the horse's head was bouncing up and down. It was snorting, trying to move. And every effort only cemented its legs deeper into the soil.

"Okay," I whispered. "It's okay. Hold on, hold on."

I laid the boards over the water. They wobbled under my feet. I could see the horse's eyes. Too large, bulging, flashing white in the moonlight. I wanted to run for the car, fly the Ghost down the road, escape over the mountains. Toss the tube to the crime lab and pretend this part of the night never happened. But I knew—I knew. If I left, this horse would snap its legs. And die.

I took the spade from the small of my back. The water was over the horse's ankles and it was making a keening sound. Like bagpipes. I tried to remember what Handler had done. The soil was heavy as lead and every spadeful landed on the bank with a sodden plop, wet as death's rattle. Hopelessly, I leaned against the horse's chest, watching the thick vein bulge beside its knee. Pulsing with fear and adrenaline. I wrapped my hands around the right ankle. The water cold, seeping through my cotton gloves. I pulled. And prayed. Leaning into the horse, trying to get it to shift its weight. Suddenly I heard a suctioning sound. Words tumbled from my mouth. Thanking, pleading, begging.

I rushed for the left ankle, but I could see the problem. The horse was leaning on this one leg. I stabbed the spade into the clay, throwing the soil. I heard a high-pitched wail. But it wasn't the horse.

In the distance two cones of light bounced through the dark. Chrome glinted in the moonlight. The sound of the engines grew more distinct. ATVs.

I glanced at the riverbank.

Madame was facing them, her tail stiff. I worked the last of the soil from around the left leg, threw the spade on the board, and yanked up on the ankle. The horse didn't budge. I threw my weight into its shoulder, hard. Enough to throw the animal off balance. When I grabbed the ankle, it lifted and I guided it onto the board.

But now the horse leaned forward, like the horse this morning. Trying to yank out its back legs. And I could hear their voices. Close. Yelling.

I placed my hand on the horse. "Please don't move. Please wait for them."

The eyes were black. Obsidian marbles. And I could see dots of white light. The headlights, coming near. I wanted to bolt. But I moved slowly across the board, hoping not to spook the animal.

I jumped for the riverbank.

"Madame, run!"

We were at the barbed wire fence in under a minute. Scooping up the dog, wanting to smack her rear end, I tossed her on the other side and scrambled through the wires. I glanced back, once. The machines had stopped on the bank, headlights aimed at the horse.

We sprinted down the road. I'd lost the flashlight and when we reached the trees, I was tripping over the roots.

"You're in trouble," I panted at Madame. "Big, big trouble."

My heart was pounding so hard it hurt. I flung my gloves into the trees, grabbed the key I'd hidden under the bumper, and pulled the tubing from my waistband. Inside the car, I keyed open the glove box, threw the tube inside, and locked the panel.

The car growled forward in first, bumping over the roots. I didn't turn on my headlights.

I didn't need to.

Coming through the trees, the blue lights flashed like strobes. Swirling. Cutting through the darkness.

Police lights.

"No more funny business," I told the dog. "You hear me?"

Chapter Forty-Seven

I remained hopeful even as the police cruiser came bumping down the road. Even as the officer stepped out of his vehicle with his right hand on the butt of his revolver. Even as he shined a Maglite beam directly through the windshield into my eyes. Even as Madame crawled down to the floor, suspecting trouble.

I still hoped for a getaway.

Rolling down my window, I offered him Raleigh David's driver's license before he had to ask. He pointed the Maglite at my fake identity.

"I called 911," I confessed. "I was walking my dog, we've been driving all day, helping a friend move to Spokane, and then I saw the horse."

He shifted the light, shining the beam on Madame. She cowered on the floor.

"You called?"

"Yes, sir. On my cell phone. I was so worried. But it looks like you got here in time. I'm so relieved."

He handed me back the license and lifted the beam, raking it through the trees. The light was powerful enough to catch bits of the ATVs across the river. "Yeah, they got it covered. Thanks for calling."

"No problem, Officer." I smiled, slid the gearshift into first, and was releasing the clutch just as another set of lights came toward us. The beams seemed more elevated than normal. A truck. And it stopped on a diagonal, blocking my way down the narrow road. The driver's door opened. Paul Handler stepped out. He called to the officer. By name. And when he walked past the Ghost, he didn't bother acknowledging me.

I looked over at Madame. "We are toast."

The two men stood behind the Ghost, talking. I grabbed my cell phone, keeping it in my lap as I dialed Jack's number. In the side mirror I saw Handler pointing at the Ghost. Jack's voice mail picked up. The officer began walking toward my car.

"Jack," I said. "I need some help. Serious help."

≈

I was measuring the women's holding pen in the Selah Police Department at twenty minutes before 4:00 a.m. My method consisted of walking from one concrete wall to the other, then subtracting the number of steps needed to bypass two Hispanic women who sat in the middle of the floor, buried under a saffron-colored blanket. They seemed to want to sleep, blocking the overhead lights with the blanket. The lights burned with a sickly green fluorescence that made the blanket look blue in places. The women refused to lean their backs against the wall, and I decided they knew more about holding cells than FBI agents did.

Pacing back to the bars, I once again arrived at the sum of eight feet by eight and a half feet. Not big enough to escape the reek of ammonia that rose from the open commode attached to the back wall. The odor made my eyes water, and for some reason made me think of my mother. Maybe because the asylum smelled of disinfectant. Maybe because I felt helpless. Alone. And maybe because my current discomfort was just a fraction of her agony. I leaned against the bars. Blinking.

Several minutes later the night officer walked down the hall. Officer Brent Joiner. He was driving that cruiser that caught me by the river. He had a scuffing stride in his black cop shoes. It left charcoal hash marks on the beige vinyl, while his large head swiveled from side to side on its short neck. Like a medieval Mace attached to a short chain. There was much about Officer Joiner that seemed medieval, beginning with the patch sewn onto the shoulder of his blue uniform: the Selah Police Department's symbol was a Viking wielding a broadsword.

"Where's my dog?" I said.

Officer Joiner cast his head toward the yellow mound of blanket. "Yo. Loopy and Doopy. Wake up."

One woman pushed her head out. Large dark eyes squinted at the light. Her companion's head rested on her shoulder, mouth parted sleepily. Front teeth chipped.

"*Que?*" she asked.

Joiner swung his big head toward me. "You gonna tell me what you were doing down by the river?"

The woman waited. But Joiner seemed content to ignore her, now that he'd woken her up. She gave a soft sigh and tugged the blanket back over her head.

"Where's my dog?" I repeated.

"The mutt's tied up in my office, until the pound opens."

"The pound?"

"No license." He smiled.

"It's attached to her collar."

"For Virginia. Your driver's license is Washington. So the dog's illegal."

"You're locking me up over a dog license?"

"Paul Handler says you were at his place yesterday morning."

"That's right."

"You didn't tell me that part."

"I hardly know you."

The head swung. "What is that, some kinda joke?"

No. This was no joke. It was reality, unspooling like some fatalistic retelling of a medieval fable. I had stumbled into the rural fiefdom run by a direct descendant of the Sheriff of Nottingham.

He said, "You tell me what you were doing at Handler's place, and maybe I'll just ticket you for the dog."

I pretended to consider his offer. "It's no big deal. Mr. Handler and I spoke about racehorses—my aunt owns a barn, at Emerald Downs, the racetrack? After leaving Handler's place, I drove to Spokane. For business." I wasn't about to let this guy in on my undercover status. For one thing, he was clearly tight with Handler. "I was driving back from Spokane, and the dog was restless. The river looked nice when I had passed it earlier in the day. So I stopped there." The story was close enough to the truth that I almost didn't count the omissions that were so numerous they created a black hole. "By the way, when do I get to make my phone call?"

"We'll get to the phone call."

He whipped his head, glaring down the hall. A woman walked toward us wearing a white shirt with another Viking patch. The cord to her headset dragged alongside her. Some modern strand of Rapunzel's hair.

She handed Joiner a plastic bag. "Those nice boys at the ranch just brought this in, they did. And Ortiz called. She's on her way over."

Joiner's head swung toward the blanket. "Yo! Mexes. Your ride's coming. *Federales.*"

The dispatcher pointed to the bag. "They said they found it on Paul Handler's property. They said somebody cut up his irrigation line."

"Lynette," he said slowly. "Who's answering the phone?"

She left without another word. He waited until she reached the end of the hall, then peeled back the bag.

My pruning shears were covered with sand.

"What're these?" he asked.

I shrugged. "Looks like gardening tools."

"You've never seen 'em before?"

The bitter bile rising in the back of my throat tasted of omission mixed with commission. I swallowed all the *oughts* and *shoulds* and pleaded *forgive me.*

"When I was out there this morning, I saw some kids fooling around. Handler said they play with his irrigation line. That's how the horses get stuck in the mud."

"Those kids wouldn't destroy it."

"Pardon?"

His head was swinging. "I know those punks. That irrigation line's their favorite toy. No way they'd cut it up." He pointed a thick finger at the blanket. "How many you smuggle out?"

"Excuse me?"

"To pay for that sweet car?"

I shook my head, flabbergasted.

"You don't want to give me a straight answer? Fine." He raised his voice, directing it at the blanket. "Yo, Loopy."

The same woman looked out.

"This *chiquita*," Joiner said, "you know her? I want the truth. *Verdad*. Then I'll let you go."

She shifted her eyes, looking at me for a moment. Her expression seemed both desperate and resigned, a woman so tired and worn out she was past rational thought. Her dark eyes seemed to weigh the offer. She opened her mouth, about to say something, but another expression crossed her face, wrinkling her forehead. Then her face went slack, like some last flicker was snuffed out.

"Me no know," she said.

"Liar." Joiner held up the bag, shaking it. At me. "I'll find out what's going on here. Believe me."

I believed him. And I thought of my gloves, flung into the trees. The pieces of my shirt on the barbed wire. My DNA on the steel prickles. My flashlight. By the morning light, it would all be found.

"You can't keep me here," I said, "without charges. And I still have a phone call left."

"You know what your mistake was?"

I waited.

"Handler said you showed up at his place all fancy-schmancy. But you came back at night practically in camo. Just happened to drive down that road, nowhere near the highway. And you just happened to see the horse in the river, when somebody cuts his water line. I know what's going on."

"Do you?"

"Yeah. Drugs. That's how you paid for the car. Somebody on that ranch. What, they messed up a deal and you're getting even?"

I didn't reply.

The female desk attendant reappeared at the end of the hall. She cupped her hands around her mouth. "Ortiz!"

Joiner pivoted and spread his black shoes into a wide stance, drawing his shoulders back. He glared at the woman walking toward us. Small enough to be called petite, she wore plain dark slacks and a blazer. She walked purposefully, so straight and even that her black curls didn't bounce. The hair framed cheekbones prominent as Pueblo plateaus, and when she glanced at me, quickly, her eyes were like two pieces of the night sky, each lit by one white star.

"Or-tease." Joiner reached down and adjusted himself. "How're they hangin'?"

"Better than yours."

"Except I have the equipment."

"No, what you have are fantasies." She smiled with joyful disdain. Her teeth were large and white and balanced the strong upper half of her face. She nodded in my direction without looking at me. "I'm taking that one."

"What?" Joiner said.

"Open the door."

"Why her?"

"None of your business."

The big head swung toward me. "What's the FBI want with you?"

I tried to look scared, which wasn't that hard. If Ortiz was an agent, I was in trouble. Big trouble.

"FBI?" I said. "I don't want to go with the FBI."

Joiner crossed his arms, smug that I'd seen his side of things. "I know about the drugs," he said. "I'm onto this case."

"Read the statutes, dummy. She was on Indian land. That's federal jurisdiction."

"But"—he pointed at the yellow blanket—"immigration. That's federal." His voice was rising. "Those two Mexes have been here all night."

The slur didn't have any visible effect on Ortiz. Until she spoke.

"Open the door, before I make you sorry you came to work tonight."

His head hammered at the air. "Something's going on." He keyed open the cell door. "And I'm gonna find out what."

Ortiz ordered me to turn around and place my hands behind my back. The woman under the blanket lifted a corner to watch. Her eyes filled with more unspeakable expressions. I thought I saw sympathy. But mostly I saw gratitude, that she wasn't the one getting hauled away. Ortiz slapped cuffs on my wrists, squeezing them tight.

"My dog," I said. "I'm not leaving without my dog."

"Joiner, did she have a dog?"

He slammed the cell door shut behind us. "It doesn't have a license."

"Fine. I'll add it to the list. Bring it to my car."

Chapter Forty-Eight

Special Agent Ortiz led me out of the police station. I saw early morning light drawing an outline over the mountains in the distance, like a glowing white pen. The agent stood five-foot-four in sensible shoes, but her grip on my arm felt like somebody twice her size. She was pressing her thumb into the tender spot above my elbow, making sure the pain radiated down to my wrist, where the cuffs cinched tight enough to make my fingers feel numb.

A maroon Chevy Blazer was parked in the loading zone. She opened the back door and leaned into me. Whispering.

"Brace yourself. Yakima's only so big."

She yanked my arm back just as some primal instinct clicked inside my head. I dropped my right shoulder. Too late. Her tight fist connected with my solar plexus, doubling me over. I gasped, staring at the ground, and felt my stomach convulsing.

"Cute dog," she said.

I turned my head, still struggling to breathe, and saw Madame running from the station's front door. A blue rope was tied around her neck. Joiner held the other end, jerking it. But the dog pressed forward anyway. Choking. Just like me.

Ortiz shoved me into the Suburban's backseat. I leaned my forehead against the cage wire that separated the front seat. My esophagus was opening and closing like a baby bird begging for food.

Ortiz put Madame in the back, then jumped into the driver's seat. She turned the key.

Joiner stood at her open window. "What about those Mexes in the cell?"

"Let me guess. You caught them cleaning motel rooms."

"No papers is no papers!"

"Call INS."

Immigration.

"But you said I should always call you first."

"*Next* time. Don't you listen? I said call me next time. This is this time."

She burned rubber out of the parking lot. I heard Madame's claws scrabbling. I turned my head. The rope was still around her neck. It reminded me of the nooses Rosser packed up in the state lab. But all I could do was stare out the side window, watching dawn orchestrate ochers and pinks and diaphanous blues. By all appearances, a day of promise. Only I knew better.

"How did you find me?" I asked.

She sat close to the steering wheel, probably so she could get her short legs to the gas pedal. "Agent Stephanson."

I nodded.

"And you're lucky that guy back there didn't shoot you."

I wasn't about to get into my philosophy of luck right now. Not with this woman.

"Joiner's trigger happy?"

"Joiner's problems go way beyond that. I meant those freaks on the Handler ranch. That's where he picked you up. Right?" Her dark eyes stared into the rearview mirror.

I nodded. "But I didn't see any weapons out there."

"Wake up and smell the enchilada." She pulled a hard right turn.

I leaned against the door, listening to Madame slide across the plastic floor mat. "Our background check on Handler didn't show any violent priors."

She lifted her dark eyes again. "I've been watching them for two years. Ever heard of Elf?"

I remembered the tattoo on the dreadlocked woman. Elf. "Yes, I met her."

"*What?*" Ortiz pulled herself up, hands on the steering wheel like she was going to rip it off the dash. "You what?"

"Elf. The redhead. I saw her tattoo."

"And I'm the one stuck in the sticks," she muttered. "Hey, big shot, ELF is an acronym. Equine Liberation Front."

I closed my mouth.

"Haven't you heard of them?"

I shook my head.

"Think PETA on steroids. They're totally nuts. ELF bombed a research building a couple years ago. University of Washington. Killed a grad student. The lab tested mechanical devices on animals—equipment that would be used for amputees. But these nuts don't care about people. Only animals. They later fire-bombed a pharmaceutical lab in Oregon. It was using equine placenta for a potential cancer drug."

She stepped on the gas. Madame's claws sounded like scuttling crabs.

When it seemed safe to speak, I said, "Why would they be on Handler's ranch? He's breeding racehorses."

"Because racing goes against the animal rights philosophy?" Her eyes seemed to glitter in the rearview mirror. "It's a cover. I'm convinced. They want us to look the other way."

The residual spasms in my solar plexus said Special Agent Ortiz didn't look the other way for anyone, or anything. I tried to be grateful that she'd hauled me away from Joiner. But it wasn't that simple. She was small, but built for war. She met my gaze in the mirror.

"If you'd called me," she said, "I could have told you all this."

"I'm working undercover at Emerald Downs racetrack."

"That's why you were at Handler's?"

"A horse was kidnapped."

She took the exit for central Yakima, speeding through the city. It looked flat and empty at this hour. A lone man walked down a sidewalk, leaning as though fighting a strong wind, although the litter in the gutter lay motionless.

"It doesn't fit with animal rights," I said. "They left a note. They're going to kill the horse in forty-eight hours." I couldn't see my watch but pressed my face into the cage, trying to read the dashboard's digital clock. "That was about forty hours ago."

"What did the note say exactly?"

"'Forty-eight hours, then we start killing.'"

She turned into a parking lot next to a square white building. Two cars were in the lot, both the standard-issue sedans typical of law enforcement. Ortiz drove the SUV. Which meant she probably managed the Yakima field office's equipment, or she had some rural specialty. Migrant workers, immigration. That would explain why Joiner thought she was coming for the other women in the cell. She tapped in a code on the remote clipped to her visor. The building's garage door rose. She parked by the elevator.

"Do I need to brace myself again?"

Her grin was too large for her face. "That was for your benefit. Not mine."

She grabbed something off the front seat and hopped out. When she opened my door, I saw a briefcase in her hand. She grabbed my elbow, flung me from the car, and smiled.

"I wouldn't want to ruin your cover," she whispered.

Madame barked. Stuck inside the vehicle. Ortiz let her out, then used my elbow to steer me to the elevator. Madame followed, her tail hard and straight, like a billy club. Ortiz glanced at the dog.

"She's cute, but she's mean," she said.

We never see our mirrors, I decided.

On the second floor, she led us down a bare hallway to an unmarked door with a security pad. Ortiz typed in the code and pushed the door open with her foot. Madame walked in first, scoping the space. The field office's interrogation room. Metal table bolted to the floor. Cheap chairs on either side. Acoustic tiles on the ceiling, with the smoked-glass dome protruding. The somewhat concealed camera.

Ortiz unlocked my cuffs, and despite the numb fingers, I managed to slip the rope off Madame's neck. She thanked me with a wag, then lay at my feet under the table, eyes on Ortiz. The agent didn't sit. She kept a military at-ease posture, hands clasped behind her back. There was a certain percentage of agents who came to the

Bureau through the armed services, and I was certain she was among them. And something else. Like every kid who'd been told they'd never amount to anything, Special Agent Ortiz was proving her worth, constantly, bitterly, making sure that accusation was wrong.

"Two and a half years ago," she said, snapping open the briefcase, "a guy smashed a truck into a pet store. One of the big chain stores. The alarm went off. But he didn't want the money. He ran through the store opening cages. Dogs, cats, parrots, gerbils. He released them all. Except the fish." She removed manila folders from the briefcase. "By the time Yakima PD showed up, he was gone. The truck was in the front window, and with all those animals running around, their first priority was to round them up. Snakes, he released snakes. They never found the guy."

She opened the top folder.

"They ran prints on the truck and the animal cages, but came up empty. They called us because the expensive breeds added up to grand larceny. I ran the prints through our database and got a match." She tapped the folder. Her nails were short and straight, no polish. "Same prints left behind at the UW bombing. ELF."

"But you didn't tell the local PD."

"Trust a guy like Joiner? He wears a uniform because he wants power, not because he cares about right and wrong. No, I called the Seattle office. They connected me to the Portland office because our guys down there had just picked up a woman who broke into the zoo. Tried to set the animals free. She coughed up six names."

"Just like that."

"Revenge." Ortiz gave a big smile. "Her boyfriend dumped her." She picked up the photograph. "Here's the guy. Thor."

The image was grainy. "What kind of name is Thor?"

"Nickname. Nobody uses real names in ELF. They live like squatters and only work for cash. No records."

I squinted at the photo. Like most images lifted from video surveillance, it was mostly smudges. But I could see glasses. Dreadlocks. A beard. And a pole-thin body that, with all that hair, made him look like a mop wearing granny glasses. "Not my idea of a ladies' man."

"I told you, they're nuts."

"What happened to the source in Portland?"

Ortiz sneered. "Her parents lawyered her up. She got off with community service. But before she stopped talking, she said Thor built the bombs. He's some kind of mechanical genius, majored in engineering at UW. But without a real name or even his age, we couldn't get school records."

Ortiz handed me another photograph. "The girl in Portland. Brain of a beetle."

Her dark hair was tucked messily behind large ears. Her blue eyes were dull and sloped down at the outer corners in an expression of perpetual melancholy. The lost soul.

I handed the photo back to her. She adjusted her posture, rolling her shoulders. Army, I decided.

"And somehow you tied Thor to Handler's ranch?" I asked.

"Not 'somehow.' I went to a lot of trouble."

I nodded. Certain of it. "How did you do it?"

She gave her first indication of melting. "I ran that picture from the security camera in the Yakima *Herald-Press*. It said there was a five-hundred-dollar reward for information leading to his arrest. Two days later a hay distributor called me. Claimed he saw this same guy working at a place called the Dark Horse Ranch."

"He identified him from that photo?"

"He was positive. But when I ran the usual six-man lineup, our so-called witness got squishy. Basically he saw a white kid with glasses and dreadlocks. No judge is giving me a search warrant based on that." She almost sighed, but I doubted she knew how. "So I've been watching that place. Waiting. I know they're there."

There were more grainy shots of Thor. Blurs, mostly, as he raced to the cages.

"Do you mind?" I touched a second folder, underneath.

She shook her head.

Case notes from Portland. I glanced over them, flipping through the pages. There was a scanned copy of a color photo. Not as grainy as the surveillance images. I saw young people standing in a field.

Some kind of picnic. Posing for the camera like a team photo. I felt some sympathy for the "squishy" witness. All those dreadlocks made them difficult to distinguish. But one girl had short hair. The ends were uneven, like she'd hacked it off with a pair of kindergarten scissors. Coppery hair. Her thick arm dangled around a friend's shoulders. Face covered with freckles. I lifted the photo, reading the data sheet stapled to it. Sketchy information. *Sally Jamison?* was one guess for the short-haired girl. Beneath that, other guesses. *Univ. of Wash.? Social work?* I flipped the photo back over, staring at her face. I followed her arm. To the wrist.

"I saw her at Handler's ranch."

"Really?" Ortiz sounded almost happy.

"Just about positive."

She straightened. "Oh. I get it. You think a positive ID's going to make up for what happened tonight."

I felt a temptation half spawned by sleep deprivation. I wanted to tap my thigh and sic Madame on her. But Ortiz would probably shoot the dog. Or me.

"Actually," I said slowly, "that never crossed my mind. It was this mark on her wrist." I tapped the photo. The mark was just a dark smudge in the picture but in the same spot. "I saw it. It said *Elf.* But she's got dreadlocks now."

Ortiz snatched the photo from my hand. "Five-seven?"

"Around there."

"Her nickname is Rain. Rainy?"

I shook my head.

"Rainbow?"

"Wait," I said. "I heard a guy call her Bo. Short for Rainbow?"

Ortiz had picked up a data sheet, searching for more information. I glanced at my watch. My eyes were dry and struggling to focus.

"I know this is important," I said. "But I've also got to find that horse. Forty-eight hours is almost gone."

Ortiz shook her head. "You still don't get it."

"Get what?"

"Animal rights."

"I got it."

"No, you don't," she said.

I was so wrung out, so tired, that my mind was on time delay. I could feel a thought pressing forward through the fog. But it was taking too long. And Ortiz wasn't the patient type.

"The horse is fine," she said. "Wherever he is. They won't hurt him. People. That's what you need to worry about. People. Because ELF actually likes killing people."

Chapter Forty-Nine

Ortiz drove us to the police impound lot where I picked up the Ghost.

I filled the gas tank and bought coffee for myself and a breakfast sandwich for Madame. The dry russet land passed in a blur, and when we climbed Snoqualmie Pass, the wind was swirling among the white-capped peaks, sliding into the car, whistling like a real ghost. My eyes kept shifting to the glove box.

The small door was still locked. But the three-inch tube inside pointed at me like an accusing finger. It was evidence, yes. But of what? Maybe Handler's tie to the race fixing. Maybe an act of terrorism against the track. But definitely evidence of how far I'd drifted, despite all my vows to tell the truth, the whole truth, and nothing but the truth. *So help me, God.*

I lied to my mother. Aunt Charlotte. My fiancé. The cops. The shrink. My case agent. The only person I hadn't lied to was Eleanor, a professional actress. Trained for deception.

I was braking the Ghost down the steep western side of the pass when the doo-dahs rang from my purse. Madame raised her head on the second round. She was using my purse as a pillow. We waited for voice mail to pick up the call. Twenty minutes later I pulled into North Bend and parked outside Twede's Café.

Jack's message was deceptively simple: "We're meeting in the SAC's office. Wear your armor."

I looked over at Madame. She quirked her head, wondering.

"Me too," I said.

≈

The wind had whipped Puget Sound into an angry cauldron, bubbling at the bottom of James Street. I turned right on Second Avenue, then took another right on Spring Street and hung a left midway up the hill, pulling into the short bay at the FBI's parking garage. My phone rang again. Jack, following my cell phone via the GPS. Making sure I showed up. I didn't even bother looking at the caller ID.

"Quit worrying," I said. "I'm downstairs."

"Good. Because I want out of this place."

I pulled the phone from my ear. *Harborview Hospital* was on the caller ID. "Sorry," I said, "you have the wrong number."

"Nice try, Raleigh. I know it's you."

It took me two seconds. "Felicia?"

"Yeah, Felicia. Who needs a ride."

My mother's favorite orderly. The woman Jack hired to work at Western State. But I felt a moment of utter confusion. No sleep, too much stress. And Felicia, flying in from left field. All I could think of was, "How did you get this number?"

"Jack. Now come get me. I'm sick of hospitals."

The Ghost faced the hinged metal door, the bland entrance that offered no clues to who occupied the building or what went on inside. I squinted my eyes, trying to focus. Something about Felicia's voice. The problem. "Felicia, what are you doing at Harborview?"

"Those crazy people made me sick."

"Who—?"

"Not your mom," she added. "She's fine. Well, you know, she's—"

"I know."

"But Harborview says I have to leave. Now. And I lost my apartment, just so you know. I need a place to live."

Her tone implied that this entire mess was somebody else's fault. In particular, mine. Felicia's apartment was part of her drug rehab program, a halfway house rental.

"What happened with the apartment, Felicia?"

"Oh, they're having a cow because the rent's late."

"How late?"

"Just three months."

"Just?"

"I can't exactly pay it now. I don't have a job."

I closed my eyes. Dry, burning. "You quit."

"Hey, if you think that job's so great, you go work with those crazies."

"Nice."

"Not your mom. I'm talking about the guys eating paint so their pee glows. And you need to come get me. Now."

I looked to my right. Two women were coming down the steep sidewalk, hands splayed on their thighs to keep the wind from lifting their skirts. They walked around my front bumper, glaring at me through the windshield. Madame replied with a growl.

"Felicia, now is not a good time. I'm heading into a meeting—"

"And I'm, what, on vacation? Raleigh, the hospital's kicking me out. Where am I supposed to go?"

"Ask Jack. You want to blame somebody, he's your man."

"I'm not speaking to him."

I hadn't slept in more than twenty-four hours. It felt like sand was embedded under my eyelids. And now Felicia's whine needled into my ear. My sigh had no restraint. "What happened?"

"I told him this was all his fault. You know what he said? He said I should ask the doctors if they knew how to do a personality transplant."

"I'd like to help you, Felicia, but I'm swamped. Isn't there anyone else you can call?"

"Like Booker?"

Booker Landrow. Her drug-dealer boyfriend. Ex-boyfriend. Jack put him behind bars, but with overcrowding and leniency, he was probably out again. I gazed out the driver's side window. The electronic card slot inches away waited for my FBI identification. Which was upstairs. In a folder. Waiting for the meeting to begin.

"Felicia, I'm sure there's somebody you can call."

"Here we go again. All nicey-nice when you need something from me, but when I ask for one small favor, suddenly everyone's too busy. You know what? I'm heading straight for a pipe. At least it makes me feel better."

She hung up. And I growled, actually growled. Madame quirked her head at me.

"There are no words," I said.

Felicia Kunkel would get an extra boost from smoking cocaine *and* blaming the relapse on me. Or Jack. I dialed his number.

"I'm downstairs," I said. "Get them to open the door."

"Don't hang up."

I stayed on the line. Moments later, the metal door rattled up. I pulled forward. Jack came back on the line.

I said, "Felicia just called."

"No need to thank me," he said.

I hung up on him and parked in a visitor's slot by the guard shack. For one split second, I considered taking Madame with me. My security blanket. For the little girl inside of me who felt like she was being sent to the headmaster's office. I keyed open the glove box, took out the tube, and picked up my bag. Madame was watching me.

"I probably won't be long."

≈

The elevator opened on the top floor and I walked over to the SAC's receptionist. There was a salad on her desk. Probably told to stick close for the next hour.

"Special Agent Raleigh Harmon," I said. "I have an appointment."

She was pressing buttons before the words were out of my mouth. She knew. The boss had told her to stay for lunch. "Have a seat," she said. "They'll be right with you."

I did the same thing as last time. Standing at the floor-to-ceiling windows, I gazed out at the cliff-jumping visibility and the pedestrians who looked insignificant from this distance.

"Agent Harmon."

Breathe.

"You can go in now."

There were too many faces inside the big office that had the best view. The SAC remained behind his desk and McLeod stood to his right, leaning against the credenza again. But the guy who left before our last meeting was sitting opposite the SAC. Taking notes. And now Jack was here too, perched on the windowsill to the SAC's left. He was the only person who didn't look at me. He stared down at the floor, as if something interesting was happening on the fine blue carpet.

"Raleigh," the SAC said.

The only open chair was next to the note-taker. The padded seat reminded me of my lie-detector test. I placed my hands in my lap, wondering about sensors. The note-taker turned to look at me. I smiled, the official smile, but this guy was an expert at the game. His dispassionate expression masked everything. Except his eyes. The eyes belonged to somebody dismayed by people refusing to behave like numbers. I looked away, blinking, and felt the scratching pain that almost extinguished fear. Almost. But anxiety always blew on itself, coaxing embers into full blazes. My pulse kicked in my wrist.

"I wasn't planning on meeting this soon," the SAC said. "But OPR delivered its report to me yesterday. I called Allen to find out the status of your UCA—"

McLeod jumped in. "I just went with what Jack told me."

If Jack was supposed to leap into the discussion, he ignored his cue. He continued to watch the carpet. Sunlight streamed through the window behind him, outlining his head and broad shoulders. The way dawn looked this morning, the light tracing the ridges. That seemed like a long time ago.

"Jack and I agreed," McLeod finally said, realizing his agent wasn't going to speak. "We both thought you should go look for the horse. Nothing else, it would break up the mahogany."

Jack lifted his head, looking directly at me. The green in his eyes was like some rare earth mineral, from a deep mine in a remote location.

There was another silence, so I opened my mouth, ready to explain the situation with Cuppa Joe.

But the SAC cut me off.

"And then we got a call from Yakima first thing this morning."

Jack looked over at him. "We?"

Ever so slightly, the SAC gave a conciliatory nod. "Agent Ana Ortiz claimed there was a problem with one of our agents. A rather significant problem."

Jack was looking at the floor again. But everyone else was staring at me. Waiting. The note-taker—who had yet to be introduced—held his pen poised. I glanced at McLeod. The red suspenders looked tighter than normal, the white shirt sticking to his skin. I looked at the SAC. But there was nothing.

Because I had nothing.

Except the truth.

Placing my forearms on the chair, I suddenly wished the furniture had polygraph sensors. Then they'd know it was the truth. I laid it out. All of it, beginning with the EKWAS license plate, my visit to Bainbridge Island, and the trip to Selah to interview Paul Handler. How the trailer hadn't been moved in ages. Sensing piqued curiosities, I plunged into the forensic geology. Poisonous clay. Radioactive elements leaving a literal trail of evidence from Handler's ranch to the racetrack. "These particular minerals are so specific they're as good as fingerprints." I reached into my bag, removed the tubing, and placed it on the SAC's desk. The jagged plastic ends were covered with dirt. It looked crude, almost vulgar, against the pristine wood.

"An irrigation tube similar to this, if not identical, was hidden under the starting gate at Emerald Meadows. It was used to blow something into the air, just as the gate opened. A horse belonging to Eleanor Anderson died. If this tubing matches the pieces in the state crime lab, that would give us two significant connections to Handler's ranch. I'm certain there's enough for a search warrant. Paul Handler would shift from a person of interest to a suspect. There's also another aspect, with his ranch hands. They're part of an animal rights group. Agent Ortiz probably mentioned that part."

The ensuing silence seemed like a good sign. At first. But it went on too long. Holding my breath, feeling a pulse tap at my temple, I decided they needed more information.

"Ortiz has been watching Handler's place for several—"

The SAC held up his hand. His fingers were long, like the startling length of Byzantine icons, pointing to the Almighty. The difference was the SAC's eyes weren't mournful. Or even vaguely spiritual. The man had the pellucid gaze of the decision maker, the person who conquered the upper rungs of the federal ladder and whose memory of that climb didn't involve feeling sympathy for anybody, including himself.

"Let me jump in here," he said, as though permission were necessary. "According to Agent Ortiz, you trespassed on Indian land, destroyed another man's private property, and almost killed one of his horses. Then you forced a colleague into a compromising position with local law enforcement. Finally, Ortiz claims you have jeopardized her own case."

I hated her all over again.

"Raleigh," he said, "it sounds to me that you're conveniently glossing over those actions."

"No, sir, I'm not glossing over anything." I glanced at Jack. The light shifted slightly behind his head. One nod. Encouraging me. "My actions were my own, I understand that. And I accept full responsibility. But right now our first priority should be life and death. The people who kidnapped that horse left a note. It said *the killing* would begin in forty-eight hours." I looked at my watch. "That was forty-seven and a half hours ago. Agent Ortiz herself pointed out that the note doesn't mean the horse. These people are animal rights fanatics. They don't kill horses. They kill people."

"What . . . people?" McLeod said.

"Anybody who gets in their way."

The SAC's face twitched. "Quite a large demographic, wouldn't you say?"

"Yes, sir. But I can narrow it down. People at the racetrack. Agent Ortiz believes some of Handler's workers are responsible for a bombing at the University of Washington. The medical lab?"

The SAC didn't move.

"The same group that bombed the pharmaceutical company in Oregon," I said. "Thoroughbred racing, in their eyes, is just as bad as medical research on animals. Sir, if you'll call the state lab, they can confirm what we're dealing with. The mechanism under the starting gate required considerable planning. We're not dealing with novices."

I waited, feeling spent. There was no reaction. But it was different than the previous quiet. Now it seemed that nobody wanted to look dumb, uninformed, below his pay grade.

"Sir, with all due respect, we didn't have enough for a search warrant. Now we do. That's why I went to Handler's property. And time is running out."

I glanced at McLeod. He was running a hand over his jaw, back and forth. I knew that gesture. Wracking indecision. McLeod wanting to follow his instincts, but was concerned that it meant deviating from standard FBI procedures. From management protocol. And it meant he heard me. Slowly, I turned to the man on my right, the note-taker. OPR. He met my stare with another blank expression. Ice on my burning heart. I turned to the SAC. He was looking at McLeod, and I didn't like his expression. *What did you expect her to say?*

Jack said, "Don't forget the barn fire."

"What barn fire?" the SAC asked.

"Somebody lit a fire in one of the stables and locked Raleigh inside. With a panicked horse. She almost died."

The SAC looked at McLeod, who replied weakly, "It's in my notes."

Jack turned toward the SAC. "You need it spelled out? Here it is. We thought this UCA was about race fixing. But Raleigh's hard work has revealed there's more. Much more. She could've quit after the fire—" He looked at Allen. "It was suggested she quit. But the threat on her life only made her more determined. Now she's presenting something solid. Bigger than race fixing. With what she's uncovered, we might finally nail the perps responsible for bombing the medical lab."

The SAC shook his head. "Jack, I appreciate your loyalty. But you're missing the point."

"Am I? Your point is she overstepped the boundaries. Again. Okay. Rap her knuckles. Again. Dock her pay. Again. Go ahead. Those are the rules. She just told you she understands. But she's also describing an immediate threat. To the public." He looked at each man, stopping finally at the note-taker. "Is anybody listening?"

The note-taker only scribbled faster, struggling to keep up, as the SAC lifted a paperweight from his desk. Amethyst. The size of a fist. I remembered seeing it last year, when this same man offered me a full commendation for good work. With merit pay. Like the dawn this morning, it seemed so long ago. So far back, it might never have happened.

He opened a green folder. Inside a large jaw-clamp held the stack of paper. My official record. The start in the lab that shifted to Quantico after my dad's murder. A new agent who immediately put up a fight, refusing to ride the newbie circuit, moving from city to city until the Bureau said stop. I was staying in Richmond; my mother needed me. And then all that head-butting with my Richmond supervisor, and her disciplinary transfer, and the cherry on top: OPR's fresh verdict about the cruise ship.

And that wasn't even the last entry.

The barn fire would go in there—discharging a weapon under-cover. Driving with a civilian in my car without Bureau permission. Giving that same civilian my cell phone. While undercover. And then last night's events, so easily delineated by the SAC. Trespassing, destruction of private property, animal endangerment.

Breathe.

"Raleigh, what you're offering us is more speculation." The SAC was turning the pages in the file, surveying my life. "An expensive horse was stolen. That's theft. A note threatened some kind of action but it's vague. Did they demand a ransom?"

"They want the races to end. That's their demand."

"You didn't answer my question. Is the track's security working out the necessary steps with law enforcement?"

"Depends on what you mean by 'necessary.'"

He looked at McLeod, head of Violent Crimes. "Have you heard from the track regarding any kind of kidnapping?"

McLeod shook his head. The SAC turned to me. *There, you see.*

"Sir, with all due respect, the track's security doesn't know most of this. Agent Ortiz has been documenting the Equine Liberation Front and—"

"So you see," the SAC continued, "it's difficult to put credence in your theory. It conveniently shifts attention from your own actions, from the way you've handled yourself." He glanced at the man taking notes. "OPR has ruled on the cruise ship matter. And in light of these recent developments, it's clear to me that their conclusions are correct. You have done some stellar work for the Bureau in the past. But you stretch the rules too often. You seem to think you have the freedom to make any choice whatsoever in the field. Agent Ortiz's phone call completely confirms OPR's decision. You are immediately relieved of this undercover assignment." He looked at the note-taker. "Also beginning immediately, I am asking OPR to launch a new investigation . . ."

He kept talking but all I heard was the semblance of order. Alphabetical order, I decided. A for Agent and B for Bad and C for Correction and D—Don't expect my support ever again. My mind kept filling in the words for the sequence of letters. E for Effective immediately or Entirely worthless, but when he said the "probation," my mind went blank. The next phrase was "severe cut in pay grade." I looked at Jack. His eyes were too green, still. I glanced out the window and saw the waves. They seemed to roll between the glass walls of the skyscrapers, rising and splashing and rising again as the SAC began talking about fidelity. But now the word struck me as out of alphabetical order with the FBI's other initials. Bravery and integrity. McLeod was rubbing across his jaw again, conflicted, and when I turned to the note-taker, I realized who these men were.

Pragmatists.

Managers. The practical people who ran things. And ran people. From their perspective, hunches probably seemed like witchcraft. Even hunches based on knowledge.

The SAC was discussing with McLeod my docked pay, but my next thoughts came unbeckoned. I saw those nights with my dad. He told me about the days to come. Hard times. And he told me to choose the truth.

Despite all my good intentions, I had somehow chosen wrong.

When the SAC's planar voice came to an end, I saw him replace the papers. He laid the green folder on the pristine desk and set the paperweight on top. Holding it down.

"Raleigh," he said, "is there anything you'd like to say?"

I waited, making sure the note-taker was caught up.

"Yes, sir. You once told me judgment calls would determine my career."

The SAC shifted his gaze. Perhaps combing back through his own words. Searching for implications. Wondering if this was a trap.

"Yes," he said finally. "I have said that."

"You also told me some of the best agents push the limits."

He did not acknowledge those words, not with the pen from OPR scratching paper. But he said it last year, right before he gave me the merit pay.

"I realize the FBI doesn't encourage that," I said. "But there are times, in the field, when the line isn't clear. Completely clear. And yet something has to be done. I've always chosen action. That's how I work. But I'm going to make another judgment call now. For once the line seems really clear." I stood up. "You'll have my letter of resignation by tomorrow."

McLeod jumped. "Raleigh, nobody's asking you to quit."

"I know that, sir."

"So give it a year," McLeod said. "You can petition to return to active duty. Twelve months desk duty. Then the whole thing will be neither hide nor there."

But the malaprop wasn't believable for another reason. Too much leaden paperwork had accumulated in my file. My assignments would now be void of judgment calls. Background checks on federal judges and Senate assistants. Reading tax returns for the white-collar division. Calling to confirm phone numbers. I looked at Jack. The light behind him had once again turned him into a bright outline. But I could feel his eyes. I could feel their color.

I placed the cell phone on the SAC's desk, right beside the plastic tube.

"I would turn in my gun, but it was confiscated by the fire inspector." I looked at the OPR guy, wondering if he would run out of ink. "I didn't mean to lose my gun. Believe it or not. It started with a misunderstanding." I turned back to the SAC. "I'll make sure the gun is returned to the Bureau immediately."

I extended my right hand. But the SAC hesitated. I might be the type of woman to walk out of here and hire an attorney, alleging there was unfair treatment because I was born with two X chromosomes. But vengeance wasn't mine. And standing there, holding out my hand, I felt the worry slipping off my shoulders. An almost dizzying feeling.

"Thank you," I said.

"What are you thanking me for?" He still hadn't taken my hand.

But I was thankful for everything. For what rolled off my shoulders and for what tumbled away. For the yoke that was tender. For the dark where the stars shine bright. For the moment I would see those stars. Eventually. My dad had told me so. And I promised never to forget.

"I just wanted to say thank you. That's all."

He shook my hand. Quickly. Like somebody checking an item off a long list of detestable tasks.

And then I turned and walked out the door.

Chapter Fifty

I waited for the parking garage guard to raise the door to Spring Street. One hand on the gearshift, I could feel something inside, pushing down, an imperative to get out before somebody from that meeting ran down here and tried to stop me. McLeod. Jack.

I zipped out before the door was fully up and gunned the engine up Spring Street. Madame sat on the passenger seat, watching me.

"I'm fine," I told her.

I turned right on Ninth and wondered how the dog and I would get around town when Eleanor took back her car. I couldn't buy a vehicle; there was no money. And I couldn't rent one, not with Raleigh David's license. I zipped through the narrow roads of Capitol Hill until we reached the city's trauma hospital. Even on a sunny day, the building looked like a battle-weary field hospital. I parked in the loading zone and found Felicia eating a candy bar in the lobby, holding a backpack in her lap. She didn't say much until we got to the car.

"Oh, I love this dog!" she exclaimed. They met last year, when she and my mom became friends. But she was more excited about the car. And then suspicious. "I thought you weren't rich."

"Felicia, are you positive you lost your apartment?"

She swiveled forward in the passenger seat. Madame had climbed into the back, where she looked at me with more than her usual amount of skepticism.

"Somebody's already moved in. I told you they were like this."

Yes, she told me. When I drove her to rehab last year. She said Christians couldn't be trusted. Felicia's alternative to the free room and board offered by a gospel mission was to stay on the sidewalk with the florid-faced bums. And now the same litany of complaints fell from her mouth.

"Do one thing wrong, and you find out quick what those people are really like."

"Wrong." I pulled away from the curb, feeling angry and frustrated. I had enough problems right now without Felicia. "They're holding you accountable. And you don't like it."

She closed her mouth. I turned left on Ninth Street and glanced in the rearview, ignoring Madame's doubtful gaze. I decided the final nail in this day would be seeing that black Cadillac. I started circling the tight city blocks, navigating through residential streets, making sure it wasn't with us. And suddenly I realized Felicia had stopped talking. At the light on James Street, I looked over.

Her brown hair was straight and brittle, the skin greasy and marred by red zits. But more disturbing was the heavy meniscus of water hovering on her lower eyelid, preparing to fall.

"Felicia, I'm sorr—"

The tears fell. And the light turned green. I slid the gear into first, but what I felt was the shift inside my own heart. My selfish heart.

"It'll be okay," I said lamely.

"You . . . don't . . . know." She wiped at her eyes. "I'm back where I started. Look!" She shoved up the sleeve of her sweatshirt, brandishing her bare arm. The skin was covered with an angry rash. "I get clean, go to work, and I still look like I'm doing crack!"

I had to admit, she didn't look good. Her face was enflamed. And the red sores were back. Like crack sores.

I softened my voice. "What happened at Western State?"

"Those people are totally crazy." She wiped her eyes again. "I was trying to be nice. You know? Especially since I've been messed up too. But the guy eating paint was the last straw. He wanted his pee to glow."

I had stopped at the light at Fifth and James, facing the water. But the view was marred by the smell in the car. Felicia. Sour, bitter, unbathed. "What was he doing?"

"It started out with him telling the other patients he wanted to

check for bugs. You know, like listening stuff? And they're all so paranoid they thought it was a good idea. So he took all the clocks off the
wall and scraped off the paint. Then he ate it."

I thought about it. "Glow-in-the-dark paint?"

"How'd you know?"

Radium, that's how. Radium-laced paint was used in glow-in-
the-dark clocks during the 1940s and '50s. But the mineral released
alpha and gamma rays, sometimes enough to set off Geiger counters.
The clocks were still out there, but no longer manufactured. "How
many clocks?"

"Nine. You should have seen what happened. Nobody knew
what time it was. And that guy was in the bathroom with the lights
off. Raleigh, his pee was neon. They hauled him to the infirmary.
And I got sent to Harborview, all for being nice to him."

"But you're all right?"

"They say. I had to stay in a room by myself for twenty-four
hours. And I still don't feel so good."

My heart flicked a beat. "What about my mom?"

"She's fine." Felicia sighed, like I'd lost track of her point. "My
next kids will probably have two heads."

All I could think was, *Next kids?* She had three already. In foster
care. But now wasn't the time to bring that up. For one thing my
head was throbbing from lack of sleep and food, from quitting the
job that had been my life for almost ten years. And I still had to get
Felicia someplace where she wouldn't pick up a pipe. And get the car
back to Eleanor. And find out whether Aunt Charlotte would let me
move in with Madame when she had those infernal cats ruling her
house . . . and still Cuppa Joe. Gone. And killing ready to begin.

When I came up Spring Street again, I parked one block up from
the FBI building, on the left-hand side of the road.

"Wait here," I told both Felicia and Madame. "Don't move."

"I'm hungry," Felicia said.

Grumbling under my breath, I jogged across the street. The
Seattle Public Library looked nothing like a library. Somebody had
paid far too much money to make it look like a deformed iceberg.

But the abstract spectacle still included the mundane, such as pay phones. And he picked up on the first ring.

"They'll take you back in a heartbeat," Jack said.

"That's not why I'm calling. Felicia's in my car. Come get her. We're across the street."

"She's not talking to me."

"Jack, I've got bigger problems than you two."

"I'll be there in a minute."

"Thirty seconds." I slammed down the phone and stomped back to the car. Madame had moved into the driver's seat, desperate to get away, and Felicia was picking at a sore on her arm.

She said, "You can forget it. I'm not dealing with Jack."

I remained on the sidewalk, the Ghost on my left, facing uphill on the one-way road. I kept one hand through the open window, reassuring Madame. And trying to talk to God. Here I had forsaken lying, and my reward was Felicia Kunkel. And waiting for Jack. Sixteen minutes passed before he walked out of the FBI building. And then I had to see every woman on the sidewalk rubbernecking at him.

He walked up beside the car and leaned into the open window. Madame growled at him.

"Felicia." He put one hand on the roof of the car, drumming his fingers. The veins rose on the back of his hand. But his voice was tender. "Felicia, look at me."

I glanced down. She was staring straight ahead.

He straightened. "I tried. But she's a piece of work."

"She's your piece of work."

"Harmon, I was trying to help, both you and her. And your mom."

"Drop the guilt, Jack. Felicia already tried it." I dropped my voice. "She lost her apartment. The options now are a homeless shelter, where we both know she'll hit the pipe, or you can pony up money for a hotel room."

"Me? Take her to your place."

"Pardon?"

"That condo's got two bedrooms."

"And I'll have to be out of there tomorrow. Since the assignment is over." I leaned down again. Looking at Felicia's rigid profile, I felt a long-suppressed scream begging to get out.

"What about your aunt?" Jack said. "Your real aunt."

I was still staring at Felicia's profile, but only because I didn't want to acknowledge Jack's idea. Aunt Charlotte. Felicia. Why didn't I think of that? Probably because I was wondering about myself. Where I would live. My selfish heart again.

"Say what you want about Felicia," he said, "but she's no thief."

She yelled, "I heard that!"

I stood up. It might work. But for some reason I didn't want to say that. The wind tunneling up the hill gusted with scents of pine and musk. His skin.

"One more thing." He held out a cell phone. "I had the whiz kids fix it so for the next week your calls will get forwarded to this number. That's the best they could do, since you're leaving." He paused. "Unless you come back."

He held out the cell phone. But I didn't take it.

"Harmon, you need a phone. Especially if you're going to do what I think you're going to do."

"What?"

"Try to find that stupid horse. And I know you don't have another cell phone because you just called me from the pay phone at the library. Yes, I traced it." He smiled. "And by the way, that guy left a message on your old phone."

One split second. But it felt longer. *DeMott.* "Who called?"

"Somebody named Rosser."

I nodded. But saw an odd look on Jack's face, like he was hurt. I flipped open the phone. An older model. Something lying around the whiz kids' lab. The FBI wouldn't miss it. I stared at the LCD screen that displayed my name. My real name. *Raleigh Harmon.*

"Thank you."

"No problem," he said. "You can keep the Sig Sauer."

"It doesn't belong to the Bureau?"

He shook his head. "Hope you find the horse."

I waited, expecting a wisecrack. And maybe he was waiting too, so I could point out how this whole situation with Felicia was entirely his fault. But the silence stretched out. The city noise fell between us. A bus wheezed up Spring Street. People chattered past us. The sunlight turned his eyes blue-green. Caribbean waters. Warm. And life teemed below the surface.

"Hell-llo? Is anybody listening?" Felicia whined. "I said I'm hungry!"

Chapter Fifty-One

Back in Richmond, my aunt's house would barely make the historical record. But on the West Coast, her three-bedroom craftsman was considered old. I pulled into the narrow driveway designed for a Model T and opened my door. Ready to get this over with. But Felicia stayed in her seat. She clutched a Styrofoam carton of take-out teriyaki, purchased by Jack. Clutching it because I said if one drop touched the seat she would go straight to the homeless shelter.

Not only did she not spill a drop, she gave me hope.

"I kinda abandoned your mom, didn't I?"

This was the part of Felicia that kept me hoping. The part my mother never forgot. Derelict, damaged, so self-absorbed she put herself before her children, Felicia's heart was also capable of making sudden changes, like a baseball that looked like it was headed for foul territory, only to swerve inside the white line at the last possible moment.

"Felicia, I think you were trying to help."

"I should've tried harder."

And with that, she got out. Slung the backpack over her shoulder. Headed for the house. As though nothing of importance had just been spoken.

Madame followed her up the front steps to the porch, but since I didn't see Aunt Charlotte's decrepit Volvo in the driveway, I walked over to where the key was hidden under a fake granite boulder. I knelt down, feeling fear and relief and guilt. But mostly fatigue. I was so very tired, and I was prying my fingers under the rock when the front door creaked open.

I stood up.

"I remember you," the voice said. "I read your aura."

Oh, dear God. No. No, no, no.

"Felicity, right?"

"Felicia."

I felt a flash of rage. I repented—and things were only getting worse. It felt like God was piling on the frustration. Felicia wasn't enough. Here was the woman who had yanked the plug on my life, sending my mother swirling down the drain. The woman who opened her big mouth on the cruise to Alaska and told my mom I was an FBI agent.

Claire the Clairvoyant.

"Raleigh!" She had a voice as tuneless as a dented trombone. "I thought you were on some secret mission."

"Some secret," I muttered.

"Charlotte wanted me to check on the cats. Their auras have been a little off. She's been busy at the store."

My aunt's store, Seattle Stones, was flypaper for goofy New Agers. People like Claire, who right now was trying to restrain the cats with her stubby legs. The cats were probably desperate to get away before Claire read their auras again. I looked around for Madame. She had stepped off the porch and stood on the small front lawn. I turned back to Claire. My headache was getting worse.

"Tell Aunt Charlotte I'll call her soon. And Felicia needs a place to stay." I looked back at the dog. My heart sank. "Felicia, can you watch Madame for me?"

"Really?" she said.

"Feed her whatever you're eating. Make sure she gets walked. Don't give her chocolate."

Claire narrowed her eyes. "Where are you going?"

"None of your business," I said.

"You're doing something secret again, aren't you?"

I opened my mouth, savoring my chance to speak the truth and tell her that for a clairvoyant she was the densest person on the planet. But a horn suddenly blasted from my purse. I actually jumped. The cell phone. Muzak. It wasn't "Camptown Races." But it was just as annoying. I pawed through the bag. Jack's idea of a good joke. Old-fogy tune. Retirement music on the cell phone.

"That's Tijuana Brass." Claire started imitating the horns. A natural affinity. "Whaa-whaa-whaa-whaa."

I headed for the car and Madame followed.

"No, girl." I could barely speak, sending her away again. "You have to stay."

I turned my back, like the coward that I was, and looked at the caller ID. *Emerald Meadows*. I flipped open the phone.

"Hello?"

"Where are you!"

Eleanor.

I bent down and gave Madame a kiss, then pointed to the house. Eleanor, meanwhile, was informing me that I was heartless, that I had no idea what it was like for an old lady to worry, and how dare I do that to her, and did I know how abandoned she felt? I watched Madame walk slowly up the stairs, her tail down, as Eleanor described her attempts to reach me at the condo because she couldn't remember my cell phone number. When I climbed into the Ghost, driving down the street, turning on Pike and feeling like my eyes were on fire, she began quoting something about getting old. I pulled over to the curb and waited until she took a breath.

"I quit."

"That's just grand," she said. "Giving up, right when I need you. Here I thought you were made of tougher stuff."

"The FBI has relieved me of the undercover assignment."

That closed her mouth.

So I continued. "I decided to quit. Effective immediately. Raleigh David is gone. And I'm no longer an FBI agent."

"They fired you?"

"No, I wasn't worth firing. Which is different from being worth keeping. Didn't you once tell me most people's lives are trails of debris?"

"Mrs. Venable, she said that."

"She was half right." The other half—the half that mattered—was what we did with the debris.

"And you're going to leave me," she cried, "with all this mendacity?"

"I'm sorry. But it's your car. Your condo. Your checkbook."

"I hate apologies. Especially for the truth. Who said that?"

"You did."

"Never mind. Will you work for me, on the same terms?"

I took a long, deep breath. The relief washing over me was greater than what I'd felt in the SAC's office. Because this wave was grace.

"Raleigh?"

"Yes, ma'am. I'm here. And I'll work for you."

"Good. What do we do now?"

"Call Mr. Yuck."

"What a ghastly beginning."

"Call him and tell him the truth. About me."

"Must I?" She sighed. "This charade has brought me so much delight."

"And tell him I'm on my way. I need to talk to him. It's a matter of life and death."

"Raleigh," she said, "everything is a matter of life and death."

Chapter Fifty-Two

M r. Yuck's security staff was woven discreetly throughout the backstretch, with half of them disguised as guys who picked up litter. I only noticed them because as I passed they lifted radios to signal my progress toward the chief's office.

When I reached the grandstands, the final man was planted beside a steel door. A video camera hung above it, like a vulture.

"Where is he?" I asked.

He pointed at the door with his radio's rubber antenna. The moment I touched the knob, the lock buzzed. Behind it was a concrete-lined hallway that descended into the ground by about five degrees. The air felt chilly, dank, and another camera waited over the next door. Again, the lock buzzed when I touched the door handle.

Charles Babbitt, aka Mr. Yuck, was pacing a windowless room that was not much larger than my cell at the Selah Police Department. It felt like a bunker furnished with one desk and no chairs. And no windows, though it had plenty of views. Dozens of flat-screen monitors blinked with images of the track. Entrances. Bleachers. Guard stations. The Quarterchute. And eight views of the dirt oval, dividing the mile loop from starting gate to finish line.

"I knew you were lying," he said.

In the dim light of his hovel, his olive clothing looked more gray than green. His paddle hands reminded me of a mole. And the ghoulish complexion suddenly made sense.

"You must see a lot of lying," I said.

"That's all I see. And you're not particularly good at it."

"Thank you."

I meant it. But he wrinkled his nose and turned back to the monitors.

"Eleanor explained that I'm no longer with the FBI?"

The paddle hands took hold of each other. "She claims you're working for her."

I nodded. "Do you still have the note?"

"I turned it over to the police."

"But you kept a copy."

The nose wrinkled again. So I began describing my trip to Yakima, tracking the license plate and the trailer to Paul Handler's property. I even told him about the problems caused by me taking—okay, *stealing*—the tubing, and how the horse got stuck. His eerie hazel eyes remained on the monitors while I spoke. The horses walked in a line toward the winner's circle, single file. It was the last race of the day. And I held nothing back. Because all I had was the truth.

"The note talked about 'killing,'" I said, "but they don't mean the horse."

"Of course not."

"You knew?"

He gave me his dolorous smile. "The same way I knew you weren't Eleanor's niece. Nobody steals a horse from Sal Gagliardo and kills it. Not unless they want to die, and that's too much effort for suicide." He bent forward, peering at the view of the Quarterchute entrance. A black-haired man stood in the sun, smoking a cigarette. He gazed amiably at the backstretch. "The note was another bad lie."

A jockey strolled past the smoker. His helmet was tucked under one elbow. Mr. Yuck leaned in closer, his lashless eyes widening on the image.

"Have you heard of ELF?" I asked. "Equine Liberation Front?"

The jockey spoke to the black-haired man, who offered him his cigarettes. But instead of taking one cigarette, the jockey walked away with the entire pack. A sound rose in Mr. Yuck's throat, a vibrating bug sound, like cicadas in the South. He watched the black-haired man step back inside the café. Only then did he turn to me.

"ELF losers picketed the track's opening last year. But they left. Moving on to bother someone else."

"Maybe. But SunTzu is dead, and I think they made a mistake. They intended to hurt the jockeys." It was difficult to tell if he was listening because the bulging eyes were fixed on a teller unlocking a safe. As she placed the money inside the bin, his blunt nose nearly touched the screen.

"We're past the forty-eight-hour mark," I said. "ELF has been known to plant bombs."

"And I have extra security stationed at every entrance. And elsewhere."

"It's somebody on the inside. There's no other way they could have buried that tube. And you know that." Ashley was my first suspect. But she had an alibi. When Cuppa Joe was taken, she was vomiting in the shower. That didn't completely eliminate her from my suspicions, but I also couldn't imagine her doing anything to hurt a horse. "I'm not sure who it is, but somebody's helping them."

"The problem is the barns. Privacy!" His rotund body seethed. "Owners and their privacy."

"I can look around the barns."

He turned, evaluating me with those tunneling eyes. "If you're so sure we're in danger, why isn't the FBI here?"

My turn to stare at the monitors. "The FBI isn't prepared to take action at this point." A familiar figure crossed the screen. Pale hair. Long. "But I think the FBI is making a mistake."

Ashley Trenner stepped into the women's showers, disappearing from view.

"And what is it you expect from me?" he asked.

"The truth."

His smile was even stranger.

"I know, I lied to you. And everyone else. But I promise to level with you from this point forward. And I'd appreciate it if you did the same. We can start with you telling me what information you have."

He turned, watching a boozy crowd that milled around the beer garden. The grandstands were thinning. A hot dog vendor counted bills. But the flickering views gave me vertigo. I wanted to close my eyes. And sleep. And wake up to find none of this had ever happened.

But Mr. Yuck continued to watch the images, unblinking.

"You can leave now," he said.

"What about my offer?"

"It's under advisement," he said.

Chapter Fifty-Three

In the parking lot, I stumbled for the Ghost, rolled down both windows, and closed my eyes. Within seconds, I was gone, gone, gone, dreaming of DeMott and my mother and the SAC who somehow melded with Dr. Freud and told me I had many problems. I woke up with a gasp. But even after realizing it was only a dream, another bolt of panic hit me. My firearm. If that didn't get back to the Bureau, the suits would come after me.

I turned the key and roared toward Black Diamond Road.

Walter Wertzer was standing alone in the fire station's lunch room, waiting by the microwave and blowing his nose. When he turned toward me, I couldn't tell if he had allergies or a cold, but the red bulbous nose combined with the sprouting gray hair and broomy gray mustache made him look like an ash heap with one coal burning in the middle.

I said, "My name is not Raleigh David."

The microwave dinged, as if awarding points for the correct answer. Wertzer tore open the door, sloshing the contents of a bowl. I smelled salt and gummy starch, that heavy scent of my grade-school cafeteria. Chicken noodle soup. He carried the bowl to a small table. I followed him. But I didn't sit down.

"I was working undercover for the FBI," I said. "Now I'm not."

"You were playing games with me the whole time?"

"I was doing my job. I regret that it meant lying to you."

He threw a plastic spoon into the soup. It floated, which seemed to make him even madder. "Do you have any idea how much money I spent on that polygraph? It might surprise you, Miss David, but I've got a budget."

"Harmon."

"What?"

"My name is Raleigh Harmon." I opened my purse and tore a page from my notebook. I wrote down the ten digits. "Call this number. Ask for Allen McLeod. Head of the Violent Crimes unit. You can send him the gun. It doesn't belong to me. Not anymore."

I offered him the note. He picked up the spoon instead, chuckling coldly.

"Nice try. You're a liar. Whoever you are."

"You're right. I'm a liar."

The spoon stopped in midair. His mouth waited. But his bloodshot eyes had the narrow focus of the physically ill, when even the simplest functions required too much concentration. One eye was watering. He closed it, then slurped the noodles off the spoon.

"I have another confession," I said. "I manipulated that lie detector test."

The spoon hesitated again.

"I ate a lot of salt. Enough sodium to juice my blood pressure. I made sure my heart pounded on the supposedly factual questions. And I knew what Deception Indicated meant."

I had his full attention now.

"It's not an excuse, but I was trying to protect my undercover identity. I wanted to keep my job, and I didn't know what you planned to do with the information. But I didn't set that fire. And if you want to re-administer the test, I'll take it."

"You already wrecked my budget."

"Ask me. Now. Anything. I promise to answer truthfully."

He picked up the pepper, shaking it over the greasy surface. I waited, figuring he was trying to load his best shot. A question that would surprise me, catch me off guard.

"What about the smoke detectors?" he asked.

"Pardon?"

"I knew you couldn't answer straight."

"What smoke detectors?"

He tried to chuckle and ended up coughing. It was a cold, I

decided. Not allergies. A summer cold. The kind that ignited the worst self-pity. Winter's misery always had company, but summer colds were singular sufferings in a world that was sunny and warm and completely unfair. He pressed a finger against the bushy mustache. With a hernia, every sneeze probably felt like a knife.

I tried again. "What smoke detectors?"

He started eating. His bitterness filled the air, heavy as the salty broth. But it didn't work on me. Not now. Not after what I'd just been through. With Ortiz. With the FBI. Jack. Felicia. Claire. I stared at him until every noodle was gone. And when he finally looked at me, his bloodshot eyes seemed annoyed. And just a little bit sad.

"You really don't know," he said, "do you?"

Chapter Fifty-Four

In his sterile office, a long table had been added. It was covered with a mountain of white plastic disks. Smoke detectors.

I did a rough count and stopped before one hundred.

"When the track refurbished the barns," Wertzer sniffed, "they put in new smoke detectors."

The plastic covers were loose, hanging on their hinges. Wertzer picked one up. I could see the inside mechanisms. Every smoke detector had three parts: a printed circuit board, an electronic horn that resembled a small bicycle bell, and a brass cylinder.

"May I?" I held out my hand.

He handed me the detector. I touched the brass cylinder.

"That's the ionization chamber," he said.

"I know."

The cynicism was back. "You know?"

"When the smoke gets inside the cylinder, it knocks an electron off the oxygen and nitrogen atoms in the air, ionizing them. The negative electron gets attracted to a plate that has a positive charge, and the positive atom heads for the plate with the negative voltage." I touched the bell. "Then this goes off."

He stared at me.

"I worked as a forensic geologist. For the FBI. Before I was an agent. Which I'm not anymore."

He rolled his eyes. "I wish I could run another polygraph."

"And this time I'd pass it."

He gave a weary nod, as if to say this last story was so preposterous it was probably true.

I picked up another plastic disk, checking it.

"We dusted them for prints," he said. "They were clean."

"All of them?"

He nodded and sniffed.

An idea was ticking at the back of my tired mind. Nobody would wipe down a bunch of smoke detectors unless . . . The batteries. Nine-volt batteries. There were hundreds of nine-volts powering that tube under the starting gate. I lifted the plastic cover.

"Oh rats," I muttered.

"What's the matter?" he asked.

I opened another disk. And another. All the nine-volt batteries were snapped into their cap buckles. The red and black wires snaked to the circuit board.

"Were any batteries missing?" I asked, just in case.

"Not that I saw."

"And why was the track getting rid of these?"

"They were too sensitive."

I looked at him. "I was in that barn fire. Sensitive smoke detectors are a good thing."

"Sure. For smoke. But that heavy stink in those barns? It tripped up the really good detectors. They can't tell the difference between smoke, hay, dust. All of it interrupts the electrical current. One horse with bad gas could set off the whole barn."

I looked down at the disk in my hand. The only thing that looked different from a standard smoke detector was the ionization chamber. It was dented, only that didn't seem like something done by the manufacturer. I picked up another disk. Its chamber was dented too, and scraped at the bottom. Pried open.

"By the way," he said, "I found all of these piled up near your aunt's barn."

"Really," I said. *Dogged.* The man refused to give up. He was still testing my story. "She's not my aunt. And again, for the record, I had nothing to do with lighting that fire."

He sighed and blew his nose.

I lifted the chamber's metal cap, and suddenly that tickling idea ran down my spine. The upper ionizing plate was undamaged, but the lower plate caught my attention. It was wobbling, wrenched off its base. Although batteries provided voltage, most detectors' ionization chambers were run by a different power source. Alpha particles. When I was in the FBI lab, the smoke detectors often wound up in mineralogy for forensics. Radioactive minerals provided the alpha particles. And most manufacturers used Americum 241. A thin layer was deposited on a piece of foil that was encased inside the metal shield to prevent any radiation leakage. One detector usually contained one microcurie of radiation, which the brass casing could easily block. The danger came when the ionization chamber was breached or disturbed.

When airborne, Americum 241 was deadly.

I yanked off the lower plate.

"Hey!" Wertzer said. "What are you doing?"

"It's gone."

"What?"

"The alpha emitter." I pointed to where the foil should be. "The ionizing strip. It's gone."

"So?"

I picked up another detector. "Are all the bottom plates loose?"

He grabbed one, checking for himself.

"You handled these?" I asked.

"Why?"

Because I was looking at his watering eyes. The red nose. The way he leaned against the table, as though standing required too much effort. His "cold" could be a sign of a weakened immune system. "Who else touched these?"

"Two guys from the station. They helped me load the truck."

"Where are they?"

He hesitated. "Out. Sick."

I placed the disk on the table and backed away. "All three of you need to get to the hospital. Have them test you for radiation exposure. And call a HazMat team. Get these to the state lab." I looked around for something to wipe my hands on. "Tell the doctors you were exposed to Americum 241. The half-life isn't short."

"How long?"

Plutonium and radon were more well known, but Americum 241 had a half-life that was lodged in my memory because of its clean arithmetic. Roughly double its name. "Five hundred years," I said.

Wertzer stared at me for a long moment. Then he said, "I almost wish you were lying again."

Chapter Fifty-Five

I washed my hands three times at the fire station, then climbed into the Ghost and headed straight back to the track. My mind raced over new speculations. About Handler and the tubing mechanism. Smoke detectors and Cuppa Joe—how did the kidnappers get that bellicose horse into the trailer? Ashley's "morning sickness" provided an alibi, but that didn't mean she wasn't involved somehow. But with so little sleep, my mind struggled to focus, and I forgot one detail. Coming down the Valley Highway, I glanced in the rearview mirror.

The black Cadillac was three cars back.

I stepped on the gas and threaded two lanes of traffic. But he stayed close, all the way to the track. I downshifted, ready to make a U-turn and catch him, but he was already pulling his own about-face, speeding away. I wanted to chase him down, but right now he wasn't my biggest problem.

I parked the car in the private lot and jogged across the backstretch to Mr. Yuck's bunker. His guard offered me a blank look.

"It's urgent," I said.

He murmured into the radio. But the reply was loud.

"I'm busy. Tell her to come back later."

"There might not be a later," I said. "Tell him. Now."

≈

The human mole was still pacing the television screens. But with the day's races over, he seemed even more restless. The remaining public moved aimlessly about the track. A couple strolling by the white rail. Old men walking through the grandstands. Picking up discarded betting tickets. Casting them away again. Their freedom seemed to set Mr. Yuck on edge. He kept his eyes on them as I spoke.

"The fire inspector showed me the smoke detectors."

"Not this nonsense again." His small hand paddled the air, dismissing my words. "I told him, if he's got a problem with garbage, take it up with somebody who cares."

"They were used to build a bomb. A dirty bomb."

He turned. "Bomb?"

"The radioactive source is missing from all those trashed smoke detectors."

The pudgy fingers tickled the air, beckoning me to continue.

"Every detector has an alpha emitter inside, but somebody removed them. In the hundreds, it's an effective weapon. Not to mention the fallout."

"Nuclear fallout?"

"And public relations. Who would want to come here if a nuke went off?"

His eyes slid toward the screens.

"Right," I said. "Why risk their lives, when they can wager on their computers. Or an off-track betting parlor. One dirty bomb would be a death blow to the track's business."

I saw a strange light in his bulging eyes. And he was smiling. I had just described a nightmare scenario, but the dour smile pushed into his fleshy face. This horror was the stuff he dreamed about.

"Ready to tell me what you have?" I asked.

"Whatever you need," he said.

≈

From Yuck's bunker, I hurried across the backstretch, heading for that corrugated steel building where Gordon had been toking his joint. Two days ago, I realized. That didn't seem possible. Forty-eight hours? And then another thought flitted through my mind. The day DeMott was here. And another idea, crueler: Why didn't I call DeMott and tell him about my resignation?

Because DeMott would say, *"Come home. Now."*

Opposites attracted in magnets and ionization chambers. Electrons and protons. The particles could be trusted to find their missing halves. But in love, I wondered. Our differences were so extreme. He wanted Weyanoke, that life under a protective bubble. But this is what I wanted—unvarnished moments, stripped of all pretense. Alive. Fully alive.

When I reached the maintenance building, no music was playing. And this time I stepped inside the front door. The hangar-like space smelled of diesel and grease, and a metallic hammering sound was coming from the other side. Following the bangs, I found a middle-aged man standing beside an enormous tractor. He held a long wrench, and the machine's side hood was propped open, resting on a bifold hinge. The man's eyes were hooded, bagged with dark circles.

"Excuse me," I said. "I'm looking for Gordon Donaldson."

"Junior or senior."

"Senior."

"That's me."

I held out my hand. "Raleigh Harmon. I'm with Hot Tin."

He moved the wrench to his left hand and shook. A cold and dry grip, but strong.

"I need to ask you a few questions," I said. "Your maintenance crew removed some old smoke detectors from the barns. In the early spring?"

He frowned. And looked even more tired. "Smoke detectors?"

"Yes. Your crew took them out of the barns. Then put in new ones."

Mr. Yuck explained it this way: The track paid top price for the best smoke detectors, and then the owners complained about the false alarms scaring the animals. They demanded replacements. The maintenance crew took care of it. But Emerald Meadows kept two maintenance crews. One for the five-month racing season, and a year-round crew that was much smaller. Gordon Donaldson was in charge of both teams.

Gordon was also responsible for grooming the track.

I tried to smile politely. "You remember? The smoke detectors that were too sensitive?"

He tapped the wrench on the tractor. "Sonny, you know about this?"

A muffled reply came from under the machine, and Gordon Junior slid out. The pothead lay on a rolling board, his face streaked with thick brown grease.

His father said, "You know about this?"

"The office told us to replace 'em. That's what we did. End of story."

He slid back under the tractor.

Senior glanced at me. "There you go."

I deployed another smile. "But aren't you in charge of maintenance?"

"I am."

Junior called out from under the machine, "You weren't here that day. You were driving Mom to Fred Hutch."

His father glanced at me, preparing to explain. But the pain in his eyes made me interrupt.

"I heard about your wife's medical condition." Her blood, Junior told me. Doctors didn't know what was wrong. "I'm sorry."

He puckered his lips, as if holding something inside from getting out. "So what's the problem? The smoke detectors don't work?"

"Oh, they work fine. But the problem old ones were never thrown out."

He glanced down. "Junior!"

Junior slid out, looking even more irritated. "What?"

"What'd you do with the detectors?" Senior looked at me as another question came to him. "Wait. Why's it matter, that they weren't thrown out?"

"Right now I'd rather not say."

He hesitated but seemed to accept the answer. Not submissively. But as a man with pouched eyes and a dying wife and a callow son. "Answer her," he said.

"You might've noticed," Junior said. "We're busy. I just never got around to throwing them out."

"Seems odd," I said.

Junior refused to meet my eyes.

"More than a hundred detectors would take up a lot of space." I glanced around the maintenance garage, then down at Junior on his board. "Unless you had plans for them."

Junior looked at his father. Then quickly looked away.

"Well?" the older man said.

"I told you, I just didn't get around to it. Like I said."

"The arson inspector just collected them." I turned to the father. "Each one is missing an important component."

Senior straightened and placed one boot on the sliding board. He gave it a quick shove, but Junior caught himself before going under the tractor again.

"What d'you got to say?"

Junior scowled. "I dunno."

But his father seemed to detect something. That parental radar, picking up a sound. "You know something."

"I'm telling you, I don't know."

Senior looked at me. His frown said he wasn't buying it. But he seemed too tired to fight.

I looked at Junior. "You must see so many things, standing at the back door."

He gave me a scowl. Caught but not fessing up.

"Who tampered with them, Gordon?"

"I've got too much work right here. Why would I walk all the way over there?"

"Over where?"

He looked at me like I was stupid. "Where I dumped 'em."

"Which was . . . ?"

"The medical clinic."

"What?" His father jumped in ahead of me. "What'd you do that for?"

"I threw a tarp over 'em."

His father looked incredulous. "This is what you're doing when I'm not here?"

Junior flicked a glance toward me, full of hate. His dad had a different work ethic. And I'd riled it up.

"I was following orders."

"Junior." He lifted the wrench. "If you get me fired . . ."

"Excuse me." I wanted to get in my question before the beating started. "Who told you to put them there?"

Junior clammed up again.

I wanted to grab the wrench, start the pounding myself.

"She asked you a question!"

"Brent."

"Brent?" Senior blinked. "Brent who?"

"You know," Junior said. "The vet's assistant?"

≈

I ran down the backstretch, holding the phone to my ear.

"Personnel file on Brent Roth," I told Mr. Yuck.

"Who?"

Another one, I thought.

"Vet's assistant," I said. "He had the maintenance crew leave the detectors behind the medical clinic. Told them he would make sure they were disposed of properly. For the environment."

A cloudy silence fell over the phone, and I was still waiting for him to speak when I walked into the Quarterchute. Birdie was gone. The grill was closed. But the old guys still crowded around the gingham tables. Nobody wanting to get home. Probably empty apartments and cable television and maybe a cat. Then again, given my home life, who was I to judge?

"Hello?" I said into the phone.

Mr. Yuck had hung up.

My second call was speed dialed, because Jack had programmed his number into the system. Using the number 1, of course.

"So you're still alive," he said.

"The fire inspector's sending in my Glock. Let McLeod know."

"Harmon, if I'd known Ortiz was that kind of person—"

"You haven't met her?"

"No."

"Next time, remember the Alamo."

"Raleigh—"

I stopped. Not just because he'd used my first name. It was his tone.

"If I'd known Ortiz was like that, I would've driven to Selah myself and gotten you out of jail."

"So you owe me a favor."

"Ashley Trenner, right. I got her background check."

"Go ahead."

"She's one of Corke's kids. The guy on Bainbridge? He used to take in girls too. But there was a rape. I mentioned that, didn't I?"

"Yes. She's not—"

"No, not the victim. But she was seventeen when it happened. The state allows legal emancipation at that age. She left, and she's been on Sal Gagliardo's payroll ever since. And you were right. He claimed her as a dependent on his taxes. When she was at Corke's place."

Uncle Sal.

I turned to look at the old guys, huddled behind me. The Polish Prince was holding court. His story made the bald heads nod. Toothpicks waggled between dentures.

"Thanks," I said.

"But . . ."

"How did you know?"

"I know you, Harmon."

"I need another background check."

Jack was silent. I didn't expect anything else. My request was over the line, since I was no longer with the FBI. But I plowed forward.

"Brent Roth. Male, midtwenties. Works here as an assistant veterinarian. Everything and anything. If you can find it."

"You ask for a favor," he said, "and then doubt my skills?"

"I don't doubt your skills," I said. "I doubt that this guy left any trail."

Chapter Fifty-Six

The vet's heap-on-wheels wasn't parked outside the medical clinic. And the main door was locked. I pressed the buzzer three times, then cupped my hands over the sidelight window. It was dark inside.

I walked down the side of the building, over an apron of rounded pea gravel. By the back door, two galvanized tin boxes waited, marked for laboratory pickups. Both boxes were locked. Farther down the back side, I saw two blue tarps. Under the first, I found an assortment of mechanical parts—pulley, chains, plastic rings. Replacement parts, it looked like, for the ceiling contraption that carried SunTzu to the exam table. I felt nauseous, remembering that morning. That strange, wet morning. It came back with vivid details. Ashley's sodden hair and loving words, murmured into the horse's ear. And Brent. I thought about his arrival at the track. The vet radioed him. Searching. He was late coming, and then he ignored the jockey lying broken on the ground. But something tingled on the back of my neck. Brent's priority—and only concern—was the horse. Not the human being.

I lifted the second tarp.

There were three oil drums, just like the one Junior used to hide his joint. Each was marked with spray paint—*Paper, Glass, Plastic*. The paper recycling didn't look that different from the mess blanketing the vet's van and office, and the drum marked *Glass* held brown and green bottles with their labels dutifully removed. But the third drum, labeled *Plastic*, was almost empty. A half-dozen empty Gatorade bottles sat on the bottom. The clear plastic milky with age.

I turned a slow circle. Junior was insisting Brent wanted the smoke detectors disposed of properly. In recycling bins. If some Gatorade bottles later covered a bunch of plastic disks, who would have noticed? Not the vet, who left himself Post-it notes to remember his own glasses. And blue tarp had covered the drums, protection from the rain. Sixty yards to my right, the barns sat perpendicular to the medical clinic. But only the backs were visible. I couldn't see any stables. Only one thing was certain. My first impression of Wertzer was dead-on. That guy was a bloodhound, an investigator who scoured a place for the smallest fire hazards. I imagined him finding this oil drum full of paper, sitting directly under a wooden building. Then discovering smoke detectors. He never would have imagined they were kept to make a dirty bomb.

But I might have missed it too. I couldn't understand why, after I renounced lying, God would send Felicia Kunkel. All her whining and complaining seemed like punishment.

But I was wrong.

There was no such thing as luck. And there were no coincidences. And all things worked together for good . . .

Including Felicia's sores.

Chapter Fifty-Seven

The vet's fire-hazard-on-wheels was abandoned between two hot walkers. The back hatch door was lifted like a sail, and the sweating horses were eyeing it like it might bite them.

I followed a Hansel-and-Gretel-like trail of torn bottle wrappers and plastic caps into the next barn. At the far end of the gallery, I saw Claire Manchester. She stood with her muscular arms crossed over her thin chest, and with her hollow cheekbones she reminded me of a pirate's flag. Skull and crossbones. The impression grew stronger when she opened her mouth.

"Back off," she said. "He's not done with my horses."

"I was looking for Brent."

"So am I. I'm going to kill him."

"Pardon?"

"I scratched two races today. All because the boy wonder never showed up. We're going through Lasix like water."

The old vet lumbered from a stall. He held empty syringes in one liver-spotted hand. But he kept his other hand out, against the wall. Like Eleanor, he struggled to walk over the uneven sawdust floor. And when he saw me, his face sagged.

"You too?" he said.

"I can wait."

"You've got no choice." He pulled a piece of paper from the chest pocket of his plaid shirt, squinting at the scribbled words. "I've got four more barns ahead of you."

"And you're not done here," Claire said. "Olive Lamp needs Banamine for that colic. *If* it's even colic."

He sighed. "You want a blood test?"

"Blood test!" Her hands flew out, landing on her bony hips. Elbows akimbo. "Enough with the blood tests. They're all negative, but I still have to pay the bill. No wonder that zit-faced assistant went into hiding."

The vet nodded. He nodded like a man habituated to a nagging wife. She kept after him as he walked down the gallery and didn't stop until he had turned into another stall. Then she spun toward me, continuing the diatribe.

"I'm going broke." She raised her voice, calling to the vet. "The vet bills alone are bankrupting me!"

When the vet came out of the stall, his walk picked up a sudden quick cadence. I followed him down the gallery, fleeing Claire's fury, but he didn't seem to notice me. He was patting his shirt, his pants. He climbed into his van, and the busted shocks dropped four inches. Then he started patting again, the same places he patted before. I climbed into the passenger seat, onto the newspapers. He looked over at me. He seemed distracted.

"What's the matter?" I asked.

"Can't find my glasses," he said.

I pointed.

He reached up, patting his head. "Oh. Thanks."

"No problem. Where's Brent?"

He turned the key and chunked the gearshift into reverse, turning around in his seat to look out the rear hatch, which was still up. As he passed the hot walker, the horses rattled their heads, shaking the leashes.

I tried again. "Is Brent around?"

"Two days left in the season and he calls in sick. I told him this would happen."

"What kind of sick?"

"Stomach bug. That kid pushes himself too hard." He shoved the gear into drive. "I told him to take a break. Did he listen? Now I've got to take his rounds."

The wind rushed through our open windows and blew out the

back. With one hand on the wheel, the vet tried to read the slip of paper.

"Have you ever looked into those recycling bins behind the medical clinic?"

"Just what I need." He racked the gearshift and got out. The shocks sprung up.

"Pardon?"

"Just what I need." He walked to the back. "Another woman telling me what I'm doing wrong. Okay, it's a mess. Who cares? Find somebody else to pick on. I'm an old man."

He grabbed the rope handle and yanked. The drawer squeaked out.

"I'm not concerned about the mess," I said. "I want to know why Brent stored the smoke detectors back there."

He rummaged through the white boxes, tearing them open and throwing the litter over his shoulder. "What?"

"Smoke detectors. Taken out of the barns. After the renovation."

"Yeah, scared the horses. So what?"

"Brent kept them."

He hesitated. Then returned the bottles inside the boxes, marked Rx. Time was moving away from me, I could feel it. Forty-eight hours were gone. And the track only had forty-eight hours left in the season. I started with the missing Americum 241, because he was a doctor. Every doctor understood nuclear radiation. And I kept talking while he removed the small glass vials. But he didn't seem to be listening.

"Have you ever seen someone with radiation poisoning?" I asked. "It starts out looking like acne. Then it gets worse. The sores get bigger. They start weeping."

He waved the scrap of paper as if swatting a fly. "I don't have time for this."

He shoved the drawer closed and started for the next barn.

I called out to his back, "You were right about the Glock."

He stopped.

"My name is Raleigh Harmon."

He turned around.

"I came here to work undercover for the FBI. Eleanor thought there was some race fixing. But that wasn't it. And I'm no longer working for the FBI. I quit."

He looked down at the notes in his hand, walked back to the van, and yanked open a different drawer. This time he lifted his chin to read through his bifocals. Despite every molecule inside me screaming for action, I waited. Some people couldn't be pushed. I stood listening to the breeze coming down the backstretch. It smelled of horse and hay and manure. I could hear the newspapers, rustling like sighs inside the van. And suddenly they told me what was wrong. This van. That office. He took comfort in a certain amount of messiness. The man made nests. He brooded and hunkered down and he didn't like change. For almost fifty years he'd managed to keep his peace among these competitive and restless people. And here I came, full of lies and uncomfortable questions, and he was no dummy. He recognized the Glock for what it was.

"I'm sure you've wondered about him," I said. "Beyond his working too hard."

He continued to read the notes. Or pretend to. "You lied to me."

"I'm sorry. But now I'm telling you the truth. The season might end with a bang. Literally."

"What's that supposed to mean"

"When Americum 241 gets airborne, it's deadly. And I think that contraption under the starting gate was just a trial run."

He reached up suddenly, grabbing the back hatch. I jumped back. He slammed it down. "And you expect me to believe Brent had something to do with that?"

"Think about something. When SunTzu and the jockey went down, where was he? You kept yelling into the radio, telling him to get to the track. He showed up last."

Two grooms walked from the barn. They glanced at the vet, taking us in. They were speaking to each other in Spanish, walking to the hot walkers. The vet watched them unsnap the bridles.

"Did you hire Brent?"

"The girl came to me. She said her friend needed a job."

"What girl?" But I felt a knot in my stomach.

"Ashley. She told me he was a good worker. And cheap." He turned to me, his old Celtic face sagging again. "You know what it's like, trying to find somebody who'll take orders from me?"

"Did he always have that acne?"

The vet looked down at his hands. He stared at the vials, as if he'd already forgotten what they were for. "No," he said. "He looked bad. I told him to take some days off. Go get some sleep."

"Where does he live?"

"Here."

"Where?"

"In the clinic."

"He's living in the clinic?"

"I did the same thing, saving money for vet school. And he was helping me out. He took my night calls."

I remember my visit to the vet's office. Brent came in, looking sickly and tired. But if he lived there . . .

"Doc Madison?" A voice crackled from inside the van. *"Doc? You there?"*

The vet opened the passenger side door and dug through the trash on the floor until he found the radio.

"I'm here," he said. "Who's this?"

"Petey Smith, Barn Two. We're waiting for Brent to come—"

"You ever hear the phrase 'hold your horses'? I'm moving as fast as I can."

Petey Smith started to complain. The vet dropped the radio into the front pocket of his pants. Petey was still talking when he slammed the door and headed for the barn.

I felt like a puppy running after him. "Is Brent in the clinic now?"

"No. His brother picked him up."

"Where's his brother live?"

"How should I know?" He turned left, moving under the eaves. "Somewhere over the pass."

"Yakima?"

The vet stopped.

"Or maybe Selah," I said.

The radio crackled again.

"Doc, hey, Doc!"

The vet pulled the radio from his pocket slowly, but he twisted the volume all the way down.

As if he couldn't bear to hear any more.

Chapter Fifty-Eight

The safest place to make a phone call seemed to be the Quarterchute. Even the old guys had shuffled for home. Two janitors remained, one wiping down the tables while the other swabbed the floor with a mop, moving in rhythm to some Tex-Mex music that lilted from a boom box on the counter.

I walked over to the betting window in the far back and hit speed dial. Jack answered on the first ring.

"Brent Roth," I said. "He's building a dirty bomb."

"Harmon, I still have a job. And I want to keep it."

"The guy called in sick. His *brother* came and got him. Guess where the brother lives? Selah. That's Handler's ranch."

"Who told you that?"

"The veterinarian. And here's something else. The guy's showing signs of radiation sickness. Sores all over his skin. Weird mood swings. Jack, forty-eight hours are gone. And this guy's not playing games."

"Harmon, if zits and mood swings were grounds for arrest, the jails would be full of women with PMS. So if you don't mind—"

I hung up.

For the next three minutes, I paced along the back wall. Then I checked my phone. No call. I kept myself from calling him by staring at the photographs on the wall. Winning barns, from years past. I saw Eleanor and Harry together. A happy middle-aged couple. Then Claire Manchester's barn. And Abbondanza was there too. Most of the photos showed a tiny platinum blond. I leaned in. She was identified as Karen Trenner. And the resemblance to her daughter was striking. When my cell phone rang, I checked my watch. Sixteen minutes. Not bad. But the janitors were looking over, hearing the Tijuana Brass horns. *Whaa-whaa-whaa.*

I flipped open the phone. "Thank you."

"What if I'm calling to say no?"

"You wouldn't."

"Only because you're falling fast."

"Do you have the background check or not?"

"We're back to Arnold Corke."

"What?" I said.

The janitors looked over again. I gave a little wave, tried to smile, and dropped my voice. "How?"

"He's another one of Corke's unhappy campers. Drug addict mother. Brent Roth went into foster care early. By ten, he'd moved to Corke's place. No dummy either. He got a full-ride scholarship to UW. Guess what he studied."

"Jack, spit it out."

"Physics and engineering."

Ideal for bomb-making. "Now do you believe me?" I said.

"Hard to say. This far out on the limb, I can hear it cracking."

"What would convince you?"

"Facts. Like, who's paying the taxes on that trailer?"

"Why that?"

"Harmon, this is the People's Republic of Washington State. If it moves, the state slaps a fee on it. So if Corke still has the title, which is what Handler said, then the bill would come to him every year. Maybe he's helping these guys more than he wants to admit."

"That would take me days to find out."

There was a long silence. The janitors were wiping down the counters, scrubbing the grill. But beyond the picture windows, the backstretch was empty. And the oval waited. For tomorrow. And the last day. The perfect day to set off a bomb.

"Jack, do you want me to beg?"

"No," he said. "I want to keep my job. And you're asking too much. So all I can tell you right now is, good luck. And yeah, I know. You don't believe in luck. But right now, that's all you have."

Chapter Fifty-Nine

I searched for Ashley.

The showers were empty, and when I circled back to the barn, she wasn't in the stables. Cooper's office door was open, so I glanced inside. Ashley wasn't there, but Cooper was sitting at his desk. The bottle of whiskey was open. And his face had a rosy glow. But his smile said his good mood was more than booze. He only smiled like that when his horses won.

But something else caught my attention too. His shirt.

It was definitely the same blue shirt Claire Manchester bought from Tony Not Tony. But the connection was less certain. Was she bribing him to lose? Or were they having some kind of love affair? Cooper. Claire. I shuddered at the thought.

"Have you seen Ashley?" I asked.

"I fired her," he said.

"For what?"

"Not doing her job. I haven't seen her all day."

I turned and headed for the back of the barn, toward the grooms' studios. The horses were kicking the plank walls, but with no perceptible rhythm. Almost catatonic. I rapped on Ashley's pink door. There was no response. I tried the knob.

It was unlocked.

When I stepped inside, closing the door behind me, the room still had that hydrochloric acid odor. But now it was mixed with a false sweetness. Soap. No, I realized. Shampoo. Her strawberry shampoo, the stuff that drove Henry the Ate crazy.

Beside her bed, a half-eaten banana was next to a saltine. I could see her U-shaped dental impression in the chalky fruit. A bath towel was heaped on the floor, and a row of puddles like kettle lakes stretched to the clothing bins. The last time I was here, everything was folded neatly into the milk crates. But now the shirts hung messily, as if yanked out. I stepped over the puddles and stood in front of the crates. Something else seemed different. But I couldn't decide what. The top shelf still held her mementos. The wine bottle. It had been moved to the side. And the green glass was pushed up against some small stones. I read the label again. There was a handwritten date. March of this year. I picked up the bottle. Chardonnay. From the Yakima Valley. I felt a familiar prickle running up the back of my neck. The rocks she'd gathered were fine-grained, igneous. Russet-colored. Dusted with a whitish clay.

They were arranged in lines on the shelf. Vertical lines, and horizontal. Three stones connected by one stone followed by another three stones down. It was . . . a letter.

H.

Next to that, another three stones down. But two were at the top of the line. Two in the middle, two at the bottom.

E.

The third letter was a straight line with a foot: L.

HEL.

Hell?

I turned around, taking in the room. No signs of struggle. But the bite of a banana. Towel dropped. Water puddled on the floor. I could see her long hair, dripping wet. No struggle. But rushed. Hurrying.

I turned around, reading the stones again. Over and over. I realized what was wrong.

She ran out of stones.

The word she wanted to spell was HELP.

Chapter Sixty

Feeling almost blind with fatigue, I managed to drive to the condo. I set my alarm for one hour and when it beeped, I woke up feeling like my nap lasted thirty seconds. I stumbled into the shower, dressed, and drove to the convenience store.

The Indian family was eating dinner behind the checkout counter. I asked Raj for a cheeseburger and fries. To go.

"Let's do the salt," said the girl with the pigtails.

"Let's do sugar," I said. "Pour eight packets into a large coffee cup."

She went to work and fifteen minutes later, I was heading east, sipping coffee sweet enough to be served as tea below the Mason-Dixon line. Every other thought, I had to remind myself why the FBI couldn't help with Ashley. She hadn't been missing twenty-four hours—the minimum length of time necessary for someone to be declared officially missing—and nobody was going to take those abbreviated stones seriously.

Not even Jack.

When I reached the Dark Horse Ranch, a late sunset was making the dust in the air look like glitter. When I drove past the yurts, a fire blazed in a pit. The dreadlocked youth sat around the flames like bohemian cavemen, and they watched the Ghost pass. I didn't stop by the trailers and continued to the end of the gravel drive. The house had the plain and efficient lines of Depression-era farmhouses. No porch, no patio. It was shelter built for eating and sleeping and working, day after day after day. When I got out of the car, my fatigue made me feel as stripped down as this simple country home.

All I had was the truth.

And time was still running out.

Through the screen door I could see Paul Handler. He wore shorts and a T-shirt, and when he saw me, his eyebrows lifted. The sword piercings gave a metallic salute.

"I came to apologize."

He stayed behind the screen door, not opening it.

"And I'll pay for the damage to your irrigation line. And the horse, if it's needed."

He pushed open the screen door.

The front room was sparsely furnished. In one corner, a small television sat on top of a dresser. The screen was black. And a long couch was covered with batiked tapestries, its one end beside a doorway that looked like it led to a kitchen. The bare wood floor seemed to slope, but that might've been my fatigue talking. Standing there, I could still feel the road moving under the car.

"Are you alone?" I asked.

He nodded. "Everybody's over at the fire. Why?"

"You didn't steal Cuppa Joe."

He almost laughed. But he was still too angry. "You drove all the way out here to tell me that?"

"Because I finally realized why you wouldn't do it. You're too successful. This ranch is doing well. So well you can afford to hire all those kids from Corke's place."

As if hearing the name, a dog wandered into the room from the kitchen. He was an old golden retriever and his fur had turned white. Handler watched him walking ponderously toward us.

"He drilled it into you kids, didn't he?" I said. "Take care of the helpless. Broken kids, broken animals." I could still hear Corke's words, standing on his porch as he admonished the boys to watch over the most vulnerable. "He said you were one of his brightest. But I'm willing to bet you're also the most realistic. Not idealistic. Like Brent Roth."

The dog reached Handler, then crumpled to the floor. It let out a sigh that turned into a groan.

"I haven't seen Brent in years," he said.

"That's convenient. He's missing."

"I said years."

"Could it be eighteen months? That's about how long he's been working at Emerald Meadows."

Handler's mouth parted before he could catch it.

"Surprising, isn't it?" I said. "A guy like that goes to work at a race-track. Where they keep horses locked up and hopped up. Working them like machines. Brent's living there too. Great way to hide. Stay anonymous. You know who got him the job? Ashley. Did you teach him vet skills or did Corke?"

He gave a quick whistle. The dog struggled to its feet. It plodded behind Handler, following him into the kitchen. I opened my handbag and placed my right hand on Jack's gun, then walked into the kitchen.

"You came at a bad time." He opened the oven door.

It was a white stove and it didn't match the refrigerator, which was black. Bachelor choices. But nothing compared with the floor. Brown indoor-outdoor carpeting, covered with dog hair.

"I was just about to have dinner." He tossed two potatoes on the oven's rack. "Why don't you come back another time?"

"Ashley's missing too."

He turned.

"Right. And she's pregnant. She said the baby's father wants her to get an abortion. Because the planet's already overpopulated. Humans are bad for the environment. Sound like anybody you know?"

When the floorboards creaked, Handler hadn't taken a step. The dog was lying still on the floor by its water bowl. I stared at Handler. The next sound was unmistakable.

Retching. Followed by a moan. A soft moan. Female.

"You're alone, huh?"

Handler licked his lips. He blinked. A toiled flushed. I placed my right index finger alongside the gun's trigger and listened to the water cascading through the pipes inside the thin walls. Loud as a waterfall. The floor creaked again.

I began backing out of the room.

He said, "You don't understand."

I moved into the front room. To my left, stairs rose to the second floor. And a narrow hallway led to the rest of the first floor. I stood at the bottom of the stairs, listening. The toilet was refilling somewhere down the hallway. I kept my back to the wall and followed the sound to the bathroom. The door was open. I did a quick head-check. It was empty. And run-down like the rest of the house. I saw a claw-footed tub converted into a shower with a curving metal rod affixed to the ceiling. A shirt hung over the rod, drying.

It was pink. Bright pink.

Gun raised, I continued down the hall, glancing forward and back. I could hear the dog lapping water in the kitchen. The next door down was closed. The cast-iron knob felt cold in my sweating palm. I twisted it quickly, throwing open the door and jumping back.

Nothing.

I moved to the door frame. The room was dark. The light from the hallway showed a bed against the far wall. She sat up. Her blond hair swung forward.

"Ashley," I whispered. "It's me, Raleigh."

She pulled the sheet to her chest. I moved into the room, back to the wall. The stench was ten times worse. Acrid and cloying. Vomit, but with something greasy, like human decay. I stole glances at her and scoped the room. Low bureau. Closet door, closed. Her blond hair. Listless. When I was certain we were alone, I looked at her again. Her face was puffy but the body was thin. And something was wrong with her head. Her hair. She was bald in places.

"I'm so sorry."

Her mouth trembled.

"I thought you were somebody else."

I closed the door. I felt a wave of vertigo. When I looked up, Handler was standing at the end of the hallway. The old dog stumbled to his side.

"I could've told you," he said. "She's got cancer. She's dying. Are you satisfied?"

I nodded.

"Good," he said. "Now get out before I call the cops. Again."

Chapter Sixty-One

Sitting in the car, I wondered about my sanity.

I kept looking back at the farmhouse. How could I have been so wrong? The pink shirt. The retching. But that woman, gasping like a dying breath. I closed my eyes, trying to get rid of the image, and somewhere far away I heard horns. Brass. Ringing inside my purse.

I flipped open the phone and stared at the caller ID.

"Never mind," I said. "You're too late."

"That's impossible," Jack said. "I have perfect timing."

The sun had slipped behind the western hills. A half-moon was rising in the gloaming light, its ivory edges hazy. In these last fractional moments of day, under the heathery blanket of dusk, everything looked fragile. Perishable. The barns, the horses, the fences.

"You're late and I was wrong."

"Well, you're definitely wrong," he said. "But I'm not late."

I tucked the phone between my ear and my shoulder and shoved the gear into first. The driveway was rutty. The Ghost resented the gulleys.

"Thanks for rubbing it in," I said. "Just what I needed."

"Harmon, what you need is another check on those trailers. There's more than one plate."

One foot slammed into the clutch. The other hit the brake. "What did you say?"

"Turns out there are two EKWAS plates. One belongs to Corke. But the other one belongs to Handler. It has an Oregon title and registration."

"How did you find out?"

"Remember what I said about taxes? Well, Communist Oregon is worse than the People's Republic of Washington. And since I have an actual job"—he cleared his throat, significantly—"I decided to run one big general IRS check on Handler. He's delinquent on taxes in Oregon and has been accruing fines. But the fines on a horse trailer are small, so they haven't come after him. Yet."

"Oregon?" I stared out the windshield. The purple light in the sky was turning black. "What was he doing in Oregon?"

"From his paper trail, it looks like Handler had a horse farm around Eugene. Right after he left Corke's place. But he lost the property two years later. Foreclosure. He came back to Washington and next thing you know, he's the owner of that parcel of land outside Yakima. And if you were still working here, you could find out how he paid for it."

I glanced up into the rearview mirror. The farmhouse windows threw columns of light on the dark ground.

"But," Jack said, "as a final favor I decided to check. Final, Harmon. Did you hear that?"

"Yes."

"His cosigner on the mortgage is a company called Abbondanza."

A white noise was ringing in my ears. And my second wind shifted into third. Farther down the driveway, by the ranch's entrance, I could see a faint outline of the yurts, illuminated by the flickering orange light in the fire pit. People were moving around the fire. Dancing, it seemed. They looked like Kokopelli figures.

"Harmon."

"Yes."

"Where are you?"

"At Handler's."

"That's what I thought. I'm calling Ortiz."

"Jack, I'm already her—"

He hung up.

I drove onto the grass and hid the Ghost behind the trailers at the base of the hill. I got out, shoved the gun into the waistband of my jeans, at the small of my back, and would've donated an ovary for a Maglite. All I had was the half-moon and my cell phone's LCD screen. In the night air, the sound of the dry grass cracking under my tennis shoes sounded as loud as twigs snapping. I leaned down, searching for any trailer that even vaguely matched Juan's description. I finally found a white single and rubbed my fingers over the license plate, trying to read the embossed metal like Braille. I lifted the phone, squinting.

EKWAS. Oregon.

It was parked all the way in back, with its hitch pointed toward the open field. The moon shining on my back stretched my shadow over the white doors. I grabbed the handle, then remembered how the other EKWAS trailer squeaked when Handler opened it. Just in case, I turned it by centimeters. The moon made the paint look silver. And when the door opened, I could see her eyes.

Her terrified eyes. Like the woman in the bedroom.

But Ashley Trenner had another reason to be scared. A dull swath of duct tape covered her mouth. Her wrists were bound together, and something was tied to her body. My eyes were still adjusting, but suddenly I could see them. Bricks. Taped bricks. And there was enough light for me to see the black irrigation line. It snaked around her like an asp.

The bomb.

Ashley shook her head.

"You're going to be okay," I said.

She tried to talk. But the tape blocked her words.

"Don't worry. I've got—"

The pain came suddenly. Stabbing between my shoulder blades. I looked at Ashley. Her eyes were too large. Scared.

"Get in," he said.

I didn't move. He stabbed again.

I picked up my right knee, as if to step into the trailer. But I kicked back, like a donkey. My foot connected. Hard enough that air *oomphed* from his lungs. I dropped my cell phone and reached for the gun. But as I spun around, something hit my wrist. The gun fell. I dropped to my knees.

The girl named Bo held a burning torch. "Get her gun!" she yelled.

I was slapping my hands on the stiff grass, searching. I felt something hard, grabbed it. My cell phone. I swept my hand over the ground. Desperate for the gun. But suddenly I couldn't breathe and my teeth had clacked together. I felt myself lifted off the ground, landing on my back.

I looked up at the night sky. The torch. And a moment later, my gun.

The tattooed bald guy aimed the barrel at my face.

"Now we understand each other," he said. "Get in the trailer."

My abdomen ached. I rolled over slowly, trying to breathe. I was on my knees when I looked up again. Brent Roth stood behind him.

Worse, I could see the weapon in Brent's hand. A stick. He got me with a stick.

"We found the smoke detectors," I said. "And we know what's missing."

Bo lifted the torch. Her freckles were like soot, smeared on her skin. She glared at Brent.

"How does she know?"

"She doesn't," he said.

I stood, moving by inches. The trailer's back edge pressed into my calves. One step backward and I was gone.

"The FBI's on its way," I said.

"What?!" The Skull shook the gun.

"She's bluffing." Bo turned to Brent. "Isn't she?"

He stared at me. The nice assistant vet was gone. I felt a stab of shame, looking at him. *How did I miss this?* His skin was waxen. The cold, dead look in his eyes.

"No," he said. "She's not bluffing."

"But you just said—"

"I changed my mind!" He snarled. "She wouldn't be here unless she knew. And the Feds will bust us for the labs."

Bo waved the torch, cursing. And the Skull was shaking; I could tell because the Sig's barrel was moving around too fast. But Brent seemed calm. Preternaturally still. The pocked skin was slick with perspiration. And I could smell his odor. That was the stench in Ashley's room. The poison, leaking from his body.

"Give up now," I said, "it'll be a lot easier. For all of you."

He looked over my shoulder. Squinting to find Ashley.

"She didn't tell me," I said. "And you need to get to a hospital. Right away. You're very sick. You're dying."

"Nice try." He smiled, coldly. "I'm a doctor."

"You're not even a vet. You're a physics dropout."

The Skull's mouth fell open. "They're onto us, Thor!"

Thor?

I looked at Brent. *Thor?* I tried to recall Ortiz's surveillance photos. That mop with glasses. Running through the pet store. The hair was short now. And the next thing hit like a thunderbolt. Why he squinted so much. No glasses. It was Thor. Right in front of me. Ortiz would kill me.

If they didn't do it first.

And they were arguing which to do—kill me, then kill Ashley. Or kill Ashley, then kill me. And what about getting to the track? Maybe, Bo said, they could hook me and Ashley to the bomb. Get rid of us both at the same time. I was listening to them but was also having one of my out-of-body experiences, when my mind went somewhere to think, floating up above the fear and panic, and in that moment I saw something move behind them. It crept. Sneaking up. I glanced at Bo. Her eyes were wild, the torch swinging back and forth, and when it swung back again, I could see it clearly.

And then I heard it. Unmistakable.

The racking shotgun.

"Youse three," he said. "Add your faces to the dirt."

They looked at me. But I didn't understand either. His gruff voice was foreign. Russian?

"Ey-yay-yay. Faces, I tell you. To the dirt. Or I will appreciate to shoot you very much."

Hard on the consonants, mangling English. I combed through the words, translating. He said "youse three." I took a chance.

Reaching out, I snatched my gun from Skull. Bo held the torch, and the light showed her face. It looked fisted with anger. Furious.

"I'm sure you can count," I said. "It's two guns, one torch, you lose."

Thor was moving to his knees. He folded down like a stick man, breaking in pieces. The Skull went down too, face to the ground as the man had asked. Only Bo hesitated.

"Hands on the back of your head," I said. "Rainbow."

When she went down, there was nothing between me and the man with the shotgun. I lifted the torch, wondering if he planned to shoot me after he killed them. Steal the bomb? Right now, anything seemed possible. And nothing made sense. There were shiny circles on his clothing. Buttons, I realized. On a dark suit. It made him look stumpy. He was short, his hair oiled and forced back from his square Slavic forehead. Left hand forward on the shotgun, he steadied the long barrel, keeping it pointed at the three people on the ground. But in the flickering torchlight I saw a flash of metal. Gold. On his finger. A ring. A gold ring on his pinkie.

Just like the one shining through the Cadillac's windshield.

My shadow. In the flesh. Sal Gag. He must have figured out where Ashley was.

The stubby man lifted his eyes to me.

"Toots," he said. "You got cell phone?"

I nodded. His accent broke each word. Every syllable a full stop.

"You make call. Police? Say, We got bad guys."

I wanted to make a call, all right, but I needed to find my phone. Keeping one eye on the man, I lifted the torch and searched the grass. Then I shoved the torch's staked bottom into the dry ground until it stood upright. Each shove dimmed the flame. And I refused to let go of the Sig. I flipped open the phone, ready to press "1," but I never got to make the call.

A siren screamed behind me. I turned. Red lights flashed against the night sky, and they were followed by blue lights. And white headlights that sliced through the dark like swords. I glanced at the Russian.

He was gone.

I leaned forward. Blinded by the lights, I thought. My eyes weren't adjusting.

But he wasn't there.

I could hear cars skidding on the gravel. Doors slamming. I held the Sig pointed at the people on the ground, who had followed the man's orders and put their faces to the dirt. And when Ana Ortiz came around the side of the trailer, she was her own beam of light. Headlamp strapped to her forehead, she held an MP-3, poised and ready. The semiautomatic rifle was compact and lethal. Like the agent.

I raised my hands. "It's me."

"Who are they?"

"Meet Thor."

She smiled. The big teeth glowed in the dark.

"Rainbow's here too. I don't know the other guy."

"I do," Ortiz said. "Name's Snake."

More car doors were slamming. Headlights bounced over the grass. I saw flashlight beams raking across the trailers. Four officers came up behind Ortiz. Each one was twice her size and each one accepted her barking orders. Cuff the three people on the ground, round up the rest of the ranch hands.

Slowly, very slowly, I slid the Sig into the small of my back. The cops had cuffed Bo, Thor, Snake. I took five steps forward. The grass was broken, the blades snapped in half. I looked out, into the dark. The field stretched thirty yards, then disappeared around the hillside.

"What's wrong?" Ortiz said.

I turned around.

"We need an ambulance." I pointed to the open trailer.

Ashley was still there, waiting.

Scared out of her mind.

"You'd better call a bomb squad too," I said.

Chapter Sixty-Two

The next day, Dr. Norbert greeted me in his office. He wore his unguent smile, and it told me that nobody from the Bureau had remembered to call the shrink. Let him know it was now Game Over. An understandable oversight. I'd kept Jack busy. And last night's events buried him in paperwork.

"Raleigh, you look tired." Freud settled into his comfortable chair. "Is something bothering you?"

"Something's always bothering me. That's how I'm built."

"I suspect that's true. Please, have a seat."

"No thanks. I just stopped by to let you know I quit."

He looked at me for a moment. "You quit . . . our sessions?"

I shook my head.

"The undercover assignment?"

"Nope."

"Your job." Not a question. A statement. Shocked.

"Effective immediately. I would've called you, but I had some loose ends to tie up."

"This is deeply troubling."

"Not really."

Dr. Norbert frowned. "Sudden decisions aren't healthy for someone like you. You see the world as either-or. You're not dealing with—"

"But I feel better."

"That will pass."

Maybe. But sometimes reality was either-or. Lies or truth. Hell or heaven. Life or death.

"Please, Raleigh, I would like you to sit down." The doctor adjusted his posture, ready to make all things relative again. "If you insist on quitting your job, the least I can do is help you gain some closure."

"I have closure."

It came last night. When Ortiz showed up bossing grown men twice her size. Closure came when Ortiz gave me her pocketknife to cut the duct tape around Ashley's wrists. And her ankles. And when I gently removed the tape from her mouth. The tape was wet with tears. I felt closure when Ortiz stomped away with the officers, taking the three suspects into custody, and I led Ashley out of the trailer. She was trembling. And people were yelling, far away, over by the yurts. I walked Ashley in the other direction, toward the field where the stranger disappeared. In the distance two horses stood watching. Moonlight and shadow. That eerie sixth sense of animals.

"Brent's the father?" I asked.

She wiped her eyes. Nodding.

"How long have you two known each other?" I asked.

It was a trick question. And unfair, perhaps, right then. But I needed to know if she was honest. Truth, or more lies.

"I met him after my mom died." She wrapped her arms around herself, hugging her own body. "I got sent to foster care. But at least the place had horses." She gazed at the animals watching us. She lowered her voice, as if she didn't want them to hear. "Brent was in the same place as me. I always had such a crush on him. He was so good with horses. But he never looked twice at me. Then a couple years ago I came out here to see some old friends. Brent was here working on the ranch. For Paul." She looked at me. "You must know Paul."

I nodded.

"And then Brent asked me if I could get him a job at Emerald Meadows. I was so happy. The horses needed him. Doc Madison's burned out. Everybody knows it."

"When did the romance start?"

She looked at me. New tears hovered. "He would sneak into my room. In the barn? It was fun." She looked away. "I was always careful. You know, with birth control. My mom drilled it into me before she died."

"But you forgot."

She shook her head. The long blond hair looked white in the moonlight. "I actually decided I didn't really like him. He was different from what I thought. Mean. Really mean. So finally I told him, I don't want to see you anymore. Not like, you know . . ." Her voice trailed off into the dark.

I didn't want to hear the rest.

"He showed up at my room, acting weird. I thought he was drunk. But now I don't know. He raped me. And then I found out I was pregnant." She clutched her sides. "He said, Get an abortion. That's what Fauna always did."

"Who's Fauna?"

"His girlfriend, she lives here. But she's really sick. Cancer. Brent told me the baby was evil. And I was evil for keeping it." Her hands shifted to her stomach. "Yesterday he came into my room and said I had to choose. Get rid of the baby, or something bad would happen to Cuppa Joe." Her voice trembled. "He was crazy. Scary crazy. I said I needed some time to think about it. I went to the showers, and then you came and said Cuppa Joe was gone."

"Ashley, I don't want to scare you. But he's got something called radiation poisoning. It affects the brain. People can get paranoid."

"That's it, that's what he was. Paranoid. I asked him, after SunTzu died, what happened. He told me he couldn't talk. He said the police were watching him." She waited for me to say something. Her face was as pale as the moon. "He said you were a cop."

"He set that fire, in Solo's stable?"

She was quiet.

"Ashley."

"It didn't seem possible. But after SunTzu was . . ."

"Gone."

She nodded. "I started remembering stuff. Things he said."

"Such as?"

"After that fire. I got our horses out. And I saw them dragging you away. I ran back. There was Solo. Her leg. *Broken.* Brent came to put her down. But he was cold about it. I said something, and he just stared at me. Then he said, 'Sacrifices have to be made.' I thought he was threatening me, about the baby. But after SunTzu . . . that's when I started to realize. He'd changed. Totally changed."

Not totally, I thought. Brent Roth was a killer. Of people. The radiation poisoning only extended his deadly intent. Suddenly one sick horse could be 'sacrificed' to the greater cause. The same way he sacrificed people's lives for animals. All for the greater good. But now I realized something else. Why the horses at Emerald Downs were getting sick. Cooper's mud laced with selenium and trace radioactive minerals wasn't good. But the real problem was the contaminated man administering shots. Petting noses. His sweating hands palpitating their abdomens—transferring Americum 241 straight into their systems. Horses were sensitive creatures. High-strung thoroughbreds even more so.

"Brent's job was to take care of the winning horses?" I asked.

"Well, yeah." She shrugged. "Doc Madison, being the vet, he's got the big stuff. Torn ligaments. Surgery. The winners are pretty healthy. Brent could do most of what they needed."

It might have looked like race fixing. But it wasn't.

I glanced back at the trailers, past the yurts. Another red light was swirling down the driveway. The ambulance. I led her back toward the commotion. She didn't resist. She followed orders. That was Ashley. The obedient girl. Compliant. Always thinking of the horses. And Thor had played her like a broken pony.

"What about Uncle Sal?" I asked.

"What about him?"

"What's his relationship to Paul Handler?"

"Same as with all of us. He helps him."

"Helps him how?"

She shrugged. "I don't know, whatever he needs. That's the thing nobody understands. Uncle Sal's a big softy. He likes helping people. Paul's sort of like that too. Most of the time. He tries to help people."

"People like Brent?"

"Well, not really. They always kinda hated each other."

We were beside the trailer. The doors were still open and the shadows from the moonlight fell inside. The tubing still looked like a snake.

"I think Brent really wanted to hurt Paul," she said. "He didn't like him breeding racehorses. I should have thought about that when he asked me to get him a job. Because it was all fake. He just wanted to hurt people. Especially Paul. That's why he kidnapped Cuppa Joe."

"Do you know what happened to the horse?"

"Yes." She sighed, relieved. "I saw him. They hid me in the back barn. Paul never goes in there. But I saw Cuppa Joe."

When we walked up to the ambulance, Ortiz was still barking commands. I saw hunched shoulders in three different cruisers. Bo's dreadlocks looked matted under the dome light. I held Ashley's elbow and explained as much as I could to the ambulance guys. Radiation. Pregnancy. Specialist needed. They looked baffled. I wrote down my phone number and told them to give it to the doctor. I was expecting a call sometime today.

"Raleigh," said Dr. Norbert, "your sudden decision is dangerous. I don't think you understand what I mean by closure."

But I did understand. Our visits had revealed his handiwork. Dr. Norbert specialized in pulling things apart, then patching them up with the crude repair work of psychology alone. But I needed healing. Spiritual. Supernatural. The closure that came with the knowledge that despite my wicked heart, it was finished. And I was loved.

"Thanks for the offer," I said. "What I really need is to see my mother. Her dog's in the car."

The glasses glinted.

"Please," I said. "For her?"

≈

The recreation room on Ward Three was a cavernous space. At one end, a middle-aged woman played at a craft table. But all the other patients were on the other side, filling three couches that faced a large television. On the screen a couple was dancing a rumba. The woman

wore a red-sequined dress, sparkling like polished rubies. My mother
sat on the first couch. Enraptured by the dance. I held Madame in
my arms, waiting.

"Nadine," said the nurse.

She rose automatically, like somebody answering a ringing
telephone. She wore blue slippers. They were soiled around the
edges and slid over the floor with a hushing sound, some sad whisper of separation. My throat squeezed closed, so tightly it seemed
to strangle me from the inside. Madame's tail thumped against my
side. It hurt from last night's kick. But not as much as the ache in
my heart.

My mother looked up. Her startle reflex was delayed, thick, far
away. "Raleigh?"

The gray stripe in her hair looked even wider. And her porcelain skin seemed like crepe, dehydrated. Medicated. But under the
glassy gaze, I saw her. There. Deep down inside. The real Nadine
Shaw Harmon. The woman who went to Pentecostal tent revivals
wearing toreador pants and stiletto heels. Who sang off-key hymns
and shook her hand and made music with her bangled wrists, ever
thankful. She was there. Deep inside. The woman who loved me.

I lifted Madame. The words had to be pushed out. "She misses
you."

She opened her arms, holding the dog like an infant. The glassy
eyes returned to me. She tilted her head.

"Are you . . . all right?"

My throat was completely closed. No words would come out. I
glanced behind her, to the television. Another woman was dancing
now. Only she was sashaying in reverse. Her gold lamé dress flying
the wrong way around her legs. Somebody was rewinding the tape
but the couch sitters watched, thrilled, as if backward was just as
good as forward. Why not, I decided. Some things did run backward
and forward. Even names.

Roth. Spelled backward: *Thor.*

My mother pet the dog and shifted so she could see the backward
dance. When it ended, a commercial came on. Some pharmaceutical

ad. But the talking man didn't hold the patients' attention. One by one they stood and wandered over. An assortment of sorrow and psychological distance and childlike wonderment. They formed a line to pet Madame, as if waiting for their meds, and my mother introduced them formally. Using the dog's entire name. Madame Chiang Kai-Shek. Years ago she had plucked that name from thin air. Not really understanding its implications, but liking the sound of it. Regal, imperious, fitting the dog. Words meant things to my mother. She was wired for words.

And she was wired for the truth.

Madame politely accepted the ham-handed patting. But I felt another swirl of emotions. Sadness, because we were here. Acceptance, because this was life, raw and real. And joy, simple joy. She looked happy, showing off her dog. And if Dr. Norbert were a trustworthy shrink—if he were really interested in closure—I would've told him about another emotion.

Jealousy. I envied the dog in her arms, soaking up her love.

When the dancing came on again, the patients filed back to the couches. They sat dutifully, facing forward, hands on knees, like children told to behave in church. I looked around the room again. The woman at the craft table was gluing pink glitter to her cheeks. Like blush.

My mother watched the television.

"Mom?"

She turned.

"Can I talk to you for a minute?"

She looked back at the television. I felt my heart crack open and some kind of honey began pouring out, pure and honest. It took me a moment to realize what it was.

Relief.

Amid all these swirling emotions, I felt relief.

Finally. I could tell her the truth.

"Mom, I don't work for the FBI."

She looked at me. "You don't?"

"No."

She turned toward the television again. A panel of judges was giving numerical scores.

"Would you like to see my room?" she said.

⁓

It was a single room. With her own bathroom. I felt a long sigh release inside me. Strange what I'd worried about. This one practical matter in the middle of a disaster felt like a victory: she didn't have to share her bathroom.

"Raleigh, you look tired. Are you sleeping?"

I nodded. Then stopped.

That wasn't true.

"I'm having trouble sleeping."

"They'll give you something. They have lots of things here."

She placed Madame on the bed. A twin-sized bed. The white sheets were so thin the mattress's gray ticking showed through. The dog walked a tight circle on the beige blanket, circling and circling before lying down.

I walked over to the window. Iron bars were soldered to the brick windowsills. The glass was old, like the rest of the building, and a century of gravity had tugged at the quartz molecules, making the view look slightly wavy. Down below a green apron of lawn led to a gray fieldstone wall that once was enough to keep the insane on campus. Now cars zipped down Steilacoom Boulevard, rushing past the Gothic buildings. Across the street, a baseball game was being played in the park. Beyond that the exhibition halls waited, empty. And from this height I could also see over the tall hedges that guarded the anonymous graveyard. That sad place where Jack and I had our debriefings.

I leaned forward, nose to the glass.

He was there. Jack.

"Charlotte came by yesterday," she said. "I got a blue stone."

I turned around. She began working the object from under the mattress. Lapis lazuli. A beautiful piece of contraband. I was sure my aunt ascribed some psychic power to it. But I wasn't worried. My crazy mother had found a pen. On the wall behind her bed she had drawn a large cross. Like the private bath, it felt like another victory. But victory over everything, including death.

"Such a pretty blue." She looked at the stone. "Pretty pretty pretty. Blue."

I waited. But she was showing the stone to Madame.

I glanced out the window. A car was pulling up behind the hedges. It parked next to Jack's black Jeep. Cadillac. Black. Tinted windows. The driver got out. He wore a dark suit and he gesticulated with his hands. Too far away for me to see, but I sensed his gold pinkie ring.

"I worry about Charlotte," she said.

I turned around. "Really? Why?"

"She seems so . . ."

Several moments passed. Whatever word she wanted, it had escaped her.

I looked out the window. Jack clapped the man's shoulder. Handed him something. Friendly. Buddies.

"Lonely," she said. "Like you."

The dog jumped off the bed. She started exploring the bare vinyl floor, pausing and sniffing. My mom got up and walked behind her. The dog wagged its tail. I wondered when I would tell my mother about DeMott. Whether I could ever explain why. She wanted me to marry him. But I wanted what she had with my dad. Not some imitation of it. No matter how good it all looked.

I opened my mouth, hoping to say something about my loneliness—*It's not so bad, I've learned to live with it*—when suddenly those brass horns exploded in the Coach bag. I hurried, ripping the top open, pawing for the phone, hoping to shut it off before it disturbed her. If it hadn't already.

"That song!" She drew in a breath. But she smiled. The way she used to. "That song, your father. He used to play that song. We danced in the den. Do you remember?"

I didn't. But I didn't shut off the phone. Not when one good memory was coming back.

"Dad liked this song?"

She put her hands on either side of her face and closed her eyes. She was . . . blushing?

"Your father, he always sang the words to me." And then it came. The off-key voice. The sudden tabernacle of abandon. *"This guy,"* she sang. *"This guy, he's in love with you, oh, he's in love . . ."*

I turned, staring out the window.

The black Cadillac was driving away.

But Jack.

Jack was still there.

Chapter Sixty-Three

And he was there when visiting hours were over.

I drove across Steilacoom Boulevard, around the baseball field, and down the narrow path to the cemetery. I parked behind the hedges. He wore running clothes again. But not all black this time. Green shorts. White T-shirt.

I got out of the car. Madame ran ahead, ready for fresh air.

He looked at me. "I heard you met my brother-in-law."

"That's who was following me, in the Cadillac?"

"You knew?"

"He's a bad tail. Really bad."

"I'm not surprised." He shrugged. "He's from Estonia. Never really learned how to drive. Funny thing is, he runs a limo service. I thought he could use some work."

"You paid him to follow me?"

He looked at Madame. She was tiptoeing around the sunken graves.

"Jack, answer me."

"Harmon."

"What?"

"Do you remember that day when you walked into the Seattle office?"

It was almost a year ago. I was shipped out by my Richmond supervisor. And when I walked into the Seattle Violent Crimes unit, I realized the full extent of her punishment. I was the only female agent. And Jack's hazing began immediately.

"I've tried to forget that day."

"You came out of the elevator. I looked up from my desk. You walked through the bullpen to your cubicle, tossed your stuff on the empty desk, then looked around the room like you wanted to shoot somebody. I thought, 'That's her. That's the girl I've been waiting for.'"

"To torture."

"Absolutely," he said. "I needed to know what you were made of."

"Yeah. Thanks."

"I found out it's steel. Harmon, you're made of steel. But it's only a shell. A steel shell. Because your heart is way too tender."

I looked at the dog. She was sniffing a sunken grave, and I wondered why my throat was closing again.

"When did you first notice his car?"

"Right away."

"Good girl." He grinned. "But he came in real handy last night, didn't he?"

Last night I didn't see him. Exhausted, sleep deprived. My mind was filled with theories and night was falling.

"What are you, Jack, a stalker?"

"I promise, he's not following you anymore. You can go do whatever it is you're going to do." He paused. "You are going to do something, aren't you?"

"Yes."

"Okay, good. For a while there I was worried you didn't have a job."

Madame tiptoed to the rail fence, as if thoroughly creeped out by the graveyard. She trotted to the hedge, sniffing the leaves.

"No ring?" he said.

I looked down at my hand. On the other side of the hedge a baseball bat cracked. It was that solid *plink* when aluminum struck the ball. The crowd cheered.

I didn't say anything.

"Well," he said, "I better start running before it gets dark."

I could feel my throat. It was trying to open again. But this time the words didn't need to be pushed. They were slipping out, rolling over my tongue before I could stop them. Three words. Three words that I never thought would come from my mouth. But I looked into his eyes, those green eyes, and the wind carried his good pine scent to me.

And I said, "Can I come?"

Acknowledgments

As far as I know, Dr. Norbert doesn't haunt Western State Hospital. Like all the characters in the Raleigh Harmon series, "Freud" sprang from my imagination.

But real people help me with these books. Here are the generous and gracious:

First up is somebody I've never met. John Popp. He works at United Airlines lost-and-found in O'Hare Airport, and he discovered a tiny Moleskine jam-packed with notes. Because of Mr. Popp's diligence, I didn't have to write a completely different book—*after* a nervous breakdown. Also, I'd like to thank you readers for all the notes, tweets, and words of encouragement. I am so deeply grateful: thank you.

As pretty and nice as her name, Kris Flowers coordinates public information for Western State Hospital. She gave of her time and knowledge. As with the book's characters, all scenes are grown from my fertile imagination, not direct observation. Mental illness is a serious and devastating problem. But without a sense of humor, we cannot help anyone, especially the most damaged among us.

A terrific tribe of scientists and law enforcement personnel answer my questions (perhaps they're insane). From that point forward, all mistakes are mine. Special Agent Jamie Barrett gave insights into domestic terrorism and animal rights' activism. The blond bombshell Marti Holman, a former cop now retired from the Department of Defense, answered my undercover questions. And once again, Bill Schneck with the Washington State Crime Lab in Spokane, Washington, and FBI Special Agent (retired) / forensic geologist Bruce Hall took time to deal with my dumb-as-a-rock mineralogy questions.

If you ever want to meet real-life characters, hang around a race track. Foremost, Stewart H. Flax. Former jockey, current gentleman extraordinaire, Stewart selflessly shared his time and knowledge—while undergoing dialysis treatment. Yet nary a complaint slipped his smiling lips. Additionally, Sally Steiner and Dr. Michael G. Mason of Emerald Downs put up with me morning after morning. Horsewoman Sage Hollins offered a "worm's eye view" of a groom's life, while novelist Catherine Madeira taught me to appreciate the mystery, sensitivity, and personality of horses. Karen Trenner donated generously to Jubilee REACH, a wonderful organization helping disadvantaged families and children, which won her the right to name a character in this book. Karen chose her daughter Ashley. Though I've never met her, my instincts told me the "real" Ashley was beautiful and kind-hearted, just like my imaginary friend.

Every mom confronts a ceaseless war of daily skirmishes. Hallelujah! But providence sent in steady reinforcements. On this book I am indebted to my editors Amanda Bostic of Thomas Nelson and novelist Traci DePree. Also, the Crazy Carpool—Susan McBride, Courtney Emmanuels, Lorie Wise, and Ann Fullington—which forgave me when I forgot the kids who were standing in the Seattle rain. Susan Madeira faithfully and fearlessly holds down the fort at Heritage Homeschool Co-op. And when the spiritual war really cranks up, God always dispatches sisters. The Fall City Sisters from Mars Hill Church prayed (and fed me) through some heart-wrenching trials—Anna Blaney, Michelle Johnson, Stacie Rose, Mary Weber, Susie Woodard—love you gals! And hugs to my kinda cousin Kris Robbs and the other lovely PEO sisters. Debbi Goddeau, my Mount Holyoke sister, listens, advises and laughs. The supply convoy is run by her mother, Saint Joan, who dispatches armadas of Italian cookies right on deadline. And each year, I tip my dented homeschool helmet to the teaching inspirations of Sara Loudon and Christine Proctor—gifted at sparking curiosity in young minds, seamlessly instilling intellectual discipline.

My heart is captured by family, from oldest to youngest: ninety-seven-year-old Dr. Bob Simpson still cracking wise and telling me to *do* something with my life, to seven-year-old Serena Labello, a young girl growing into a great beauty.

I cannot imagine life without my witty and wacky and wonder-filled sons. The Dynamic Duo of Daniel and Nico. Every day with you guys feels like a dream come true. And I'm blessed to live with a real-life hero: the Hunk of Italy. My husband, Joe, commands the ground war, leads our family forward, and keeps cool under strafing enemy fire.

Honey, you're the best.

It would be redundant to say that again.

But certain facts bear repeating:

Honey, you're the best.

Soli Deo Gloria

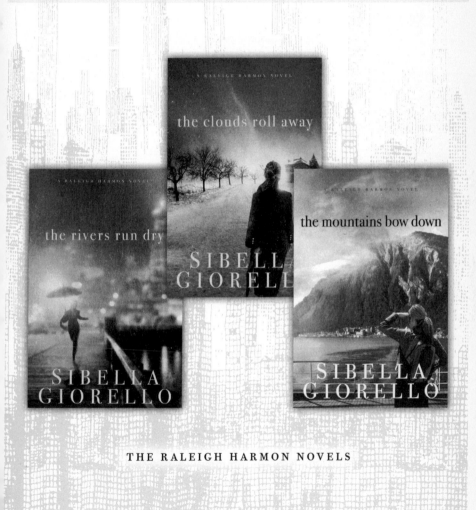

About the Author

Sibella Giorello began writing as a features reporter for newspapers and magazines. Her stories won numerous awards, including two nominations for the Pulitzer Prize. She won a Christy award for her debut novel, *Stones Cry Out*. She lives in Washington state with her husband and family.